# BUT NOT
# FOR ME

Bronzeville Books, LLC
269 S. Beverly Drive, #202
Beverly Hills, CA 90212
www.bronzevillebooks.com

Library of Congress Control Number: 2024932029

ISBN 978-1-952427-60-2 (hardcover)
ISBN 978-1-952427-61-9 (paperback)
ISBN 978-1-952427-62-6 (ebook)

First Edition

Cover Painting: Jim Gleeson
Book Design: Reggie Pulliam

# BUT NOT FOR ME

## ALLISON A. DAVIS

BRONZEVILLE™
— BOOKS —

*To Leola King, Queen of the Fillmore, and all the men and women who breathed life into the Harlem of the West*

They're writing songs of love, but not for me
A lucky star's above, but not for me
With love to lead the way
I found more clouds of gray
Than any Russian play could guarantee

Songwriters: George Gershwin / Ira Gershwin
*But Not for Me* lyrics © Warner/Chappell Music, Inc.

Enjoy all of the songs mentioned in this book
with this playlist from Spotify:

# TABLE OF CONTENTS

# CHAPTER 1

"Urban renewal is Negro removal," said Walter, wiping his spotless bar. Kay tilted her glass. The whiskey's roughness hit her throat. "Something happen, Walter?"

"They don't mean for us to have anything."

Kay finished the whiskey and glanced around the club. Her stomach ached.

"They're evicting us from our apartment at the end of the month, so developers can build fancy stores and apartments for rich white folks," he said. "We have to move."

"You've lived there a long time." Her lawyer mind went to facts.

"Ten years," said Walter.

"Are they paying you anything to move out?"

Walter shined an already shiny glass. "Not a dime."

She pushed her glass towards Walter. "That's not right. I don't understand it."

He poured her two fingers of whiskey. "Understand this. Redevelopment's coming through here like the angel of death. Just a matter of time."

"I'm so sorry." The specter of redevelopment razing one Victorian after another was an unwanted guest on this Friday night.

Walter's angst felt like a storm coming on, and a knot of anger formed in her gut. She left it to fester as the music started up. Her foot tapped rhythm on the bar stool rung.

The saxophone's solo caressed Kay. The horn player, a dark, handsome man in a tailored blue suit, performed flawlessly. Kay wondered how she'd look on his arm and what her mother would say, and reached for her whiskey. She tapped her glass to the beat of the piano playing under the standup bass. The gentle brush brush of the drums curled around her like the cigarette smoke swirling above the tables. She knew the tune, "You and The Night and the Music," written by Arthur Schwartz. They played it with a slower beat in C minor, very West Coast cool. Her hand formed the chord on the bar. She wanted to play.

A few couples danced and Kay envied their comfort. Others sat at candlelit tables covered in white linens. The clatter of dishware and murmuring voices bubbled under the music. The crowd applauded the sax player's solo.

Ladies who worked in shops during the day, or scrubbed houses for others, now wore hats, gloves, and tight-waisted dresses. Men, who labored at the shipyards or in construction, dressed in sharp wool suits and ties. A stylish woman in a white hat held a cigarette and leaned into a lighter held by a good-looking man in a fedora. Here, the drudgery of day fell away into the elegance of night.

Until Walter reminded her of what happens on the other side of the club door.

Kay's eyes drank in what she wanted to see and avoided what was outside the door. Sunset murals adorned the walls, gorgeous Art Deco mirrors reflected the elegant dining room, chandeliers dripped cut glass, sparkling even when dimmed. Mahogany furniture upholstered in red velvet on lush carpet matched the luxurious drapes held by tiebacks with festoons and cascades.

She relished the food smells, perfumes, even the cigarettes, breathing in that life. Kay nodded at Percy Henderson, Blue Moon's bass player and band leader.

Across the room, Leitisha Boone, Blue Moon's owner, directed waiters, suggested a wine, seated a regular at his favorite table, complimented a jacket, and straightened silverware. Looking like she walked right out of a Lillian Bassman photograph, she wore a red satin dress and pointed matching shoes. Kay felt frumpy in her plaid skirt and brown jacket. She hung her jacket on the back of the bar stool.

Miss Leitisha came up to her smelling of Chanel and kissed her on the cheek. "How are you sweetheart?" Creamy brown skin, hair perfectly coifed, Leitisha was the only woman club owner in the Fillmore.

Kay admired Leitisha, a fearless businesswoman, a role most women shied away from and men disparaged. Her level of service and business acumen made her one of the wealthiest women in San Francisco.

The two women touched cheeks.

"You gonna play some tonight, Sugar?"

"Oh, you think those boys will let me up on stage?"

"If they're not too afraid," said Leitisha. "They get nervous, seeing you come in, knowing they gotta play better."

The front door banged open like a shot. "Nobody move!"

Both women jerked up and turned towards the door.

Four uniformed policemen stood in the doorway. One with some girth appeared in charge and pointed upstairs. A young, skinny cop ran up although the only rooms upstairs were restrooms.

"What's the problem officer?" Leitisha stood tall.

"We got a tip gambling was going on here. We're searching your bar. Stay where you are." He pointed. "Maguire, you and Tilden check back there." The two cops turned towards the kitchen.

The music stopped. Voices rose from the dining room. As soon as the cops' attention was elsewhere, folks crept out.

Leitisha spoke calmly. "There's no gambling going on here, sir."

"We're going to make sure." He grabbed a bottle of champagne, flicked it against the wall, spraying glass and liquid on the carpet, all the while keeping eye contact with Leitisha. She did not flinch.

The cop strode into the dining room and tipped over a table causing four people seated there, three colored and one white, to jump up to avoid spilled wine and food as it fell onto the red carpet. "You shouldn't be in here," the cop said, glaring at the white woman.

Two of the waiters quickly snuffed fire from the candles, watching the cop before they started to clear the debris.

Kay slid off her bar seat, slowly put on her jacket, and secured her purse on her arm. The cop had targeted that white woman in the dining room. An exit through the kitchen led to the alley but two cops were back there, and a crash and frightened squeals said "no." Safer to follow the other customers out the front.

Kay held her breath and maneuvered behind the cop in the dining room, keeping an eye on him and the front door.

She hoped there wasn't a fifth cop outside taking note of who left.

Percy glanced in her direction. He walked the saxophone and bass behind Walter, who opened a closet on the side of the bar.

Kay had heard about "raids" from the newspapers, targeting burlesque clubs and sex joints. But the Blue Moon? She reached the front door, backed out, not wanting to be seen, questioned or, God help her, arrested. Leitisha gave her a cold eye across the room as she pulled the door shut behind her.

Kay hurried past the cop cars behind the crowd that had formed from the neighborhood. She crossed the street, halting on the corner. She couldn't go home, not until the cops left and she saw that the Blue Moon was okay. The cops meant to be frightening. Why had they targeted the club?

She stood in the shadows, waiting for them to leave. The people on the sidewalk, customers, other bar patrons or owners, talked in low tones. "Here they go, cops rousting for no good reason." No one spoke directly to her. Finally, the two police cars drove away. Kay made her way back to the Blue Moon.

She draped her jacket on the back of the bar stool and hooked her purse underneath. Walter brought drinks to the few patrons remaining, picking up empties on his way back.

Kay followed Leitisha's voice to the kitchen. A bag of flour had been cut open and strewn about. Dishes and bottles were broken, scattered on the floor. Kay bent to help, feeling sick.

"Now don't do that, you'll get flour and red wine all over your clothes." Leitisha pushed her away from the mess. "Go on out there and play some music while we get this cleaned up."

Leitisha's red dress was dusted with flour.

"I want to help."

Leitisha's eyebrows went up. "After they're gone you want to help."

"I wouldn't be useful if I got arrested." Kay wiped her hands on a towel. "Did they arrest anyone?"

"Not this time, just made a big mess. Sending me a message, I guess. Now go on. We won't be able to do any more dinner service, and all those folks up and left without paying once the ruckus started. We might as well sell a few drinks with the music."

Cook mopped the floor while Sylvia and Tildy wiped down the rest of the kitchen. Kay went back out to the bar to find Percy, the band leader.

"Leitisha asked that we get some music going, and I'm itching to play. So sorry about this raid."

"The sign of things to come." Percy sipped his wine and stared straight ahead. "At least you have somewhere to go." He nodded outside.

Did he blame her for leaving?

Percy drained his glass and set it down hard. "Fillmore's all we got. They don't let us live anywhere else. Even Duke Ellington ain't welcome at no downtown hotels and stays up here in the Fillmore. Now they saying we're living in trash, that these are slums. This look like a slum to you?" His gaze traveled the elegant room. "They know we don't got no gambling in here. Come on, let's play."

The sax player came up to the bar. "Walter, let me have a beer?"

"Byron, you ready to play with Miss Kay?" Percy asked over his shoulder.

"Oh, yeah." The sax player's smile was wide. "Pleased to meet cha."

Kay again assessed his physical qualities, vast in his perfectly tailored suit.

"Sure you can, baby." Byron tipped his hat and headed upstairs towards the restrooms.

"I like your new sax player," Kay said to Percy.

Percy nodded at her. "He's okay to play with on stage, but not off."

She smiled at his protectiveness.

When they got instruments out and were ready to play, Kay let the sax player help her up onto the stage, noted the feel of his hands, working hands, money earning hands.

She nodded at tall, handsome Randy Weston, the band's regular piano player, sitting at a front table with a beautiful woman in a white sequined dress and gloves. The dining room had been picked up, and a few patrons remained for drinks.

"Ok, then, Missy, you call it, what're we playing?"

She wanted to lift their mood, and her own. "How about a little Gershwin, Mr. Henderson?" She teased them with a sad love ballad, knowing that this band played popular bop and blues. She caught the sax player rolling his eyes. She played a few notes to get his attention.

"Gershwin, ok. How you playing it?" Percy role-played with her.

"Like this," and Kay started in on "But Not for Me" arranged like the recent Miles Davis recording, pure bop. "You guys with me?" she called out over the tune, knowing she'd fooled them.

They laughed, and even Byron, the sax player, got it. "We're right with you, Miss, don't worry." And they played all over that melody and then some. Magic exploded in her head. Her fingers hit the keys on their own, in and out of the melody. She ended her solo to enthusiastic clapping and liked the sax player's warm smile.

After the set, she nursed another drink while the band played a blues tune. She loved this nighttime world, dark, close, and beautiful. Here, nothing mattered except the music. She swayed in her chair; her foot kept the beat.

Tires screeched against the curb as a cream-colored Cadillac DeVille pulled up in front of the Blue Moon. Marvin Wright, a well-known Fillmore businessman and Miss Leitisha's landlord, staggered from the sharp car towards the Blue Moon. He jerked open the door, holding it for a young girl in a tight skirt, processed hair, and hot pink lipstick.

"Champagne, Walter!"

"Can this night get any worse? What's he up to?" Leitisha said to no one in particular.

Kay decided to stay for one more drink to see what happened.

# CHAPTER 2

"Here I was hoping the evening would wind down and Saul would come by. Not get raided, and not this." Leitisha watched Wright like a hunting cat.

"Miss Leitisha, we need champagne." Wright indicated a come here, nearly knocking over a tall palm. Walter scrambled out from behind the bar and steered Wright to a corner of the dining room. The few patrons left turned to gawk. The band played an up-tempo swinging blues.

Leitisha blocked his view of the room. "You hush up Marvin Wright. You're not the only customer in my club."

"Don't look too popular tonight," Wright said, peering around the dining room.

Kay watched them from her seat, hearing them over the music.

"Marvin, I want to see some ID for your lady friend." Miss Leitisha gestured around her club. "I just had the cops in here rousting me, and I know those redevelopment folks are aching to bust me for underage drinking."

"Why do you talk to me like that?" Wright situated the girl on his lap. "Have some respect. I got more real estate, including your real estate, than any man in the Fillmore." He tossed a $20 bill on the table. "Now you bring me that champagne." He squeezed the young girl, who giggled, her eyes unfocused. Walter went to get the champagne.

The girl draped herself around Wright. Kay turned so she wouldn't stare. Maybe the girl was sixteen?

"I'm dead serious, Marvin Wright."

Walter stopped short, champagne and bucket stand in hand.

"Ah, go on, Leitisha, she's old enough. Now, why don't you sit down here," Wright patted the chair next to him, "and have some of this champagne with us? Speaking of redevelopment, I want to talk some business with you."

Walter brought some glasses and set them on the table. He stood to the side to open the champagne. Wright snuggled with the girl.

Leitisha sat down and leaned across the table. "What business do you want to talk about at this late hour and you in your cups? I think you should get yourself home."

Kay pretended to watch the music, still eavesdropping, her whiskey glass nearly empty.

"Look here, Leitisha, these cops are rousting you because you shouldn't be running this business. Men came to see me last week, to demand that I sell my real estate for 'development.' That includes this building." Wright surveyed the club. "I have a better idea. I won't sell to them. Instead, you sell Blue Moon to me. Let me help you run it. Woman shouldn't be doing this all by herself."

Men didn't like that a woman ran a business. Kay heard it whispered around when she went to other clubs in the Fillmore.

"My last act on earth would be to sell you my club."

"Women don't have a head for business. Isn't that right, sweetie?" Wright squeezed the young girl.

"My business runs fine—you get your rent in full and on time."

"Don't get all high in your seat. Women should be pleasing a man, not working late into the night in a club."

"This is one of the finest lounges in all of Fillmore, in all of San Francisco. No riff raff in here." Miss Leitisha eyed the young woman in Marvin Wright's lap, "It is perfectly respectable for me and any other woman who wants to come here. You ask Wesley down the street at the Texas Playhouse if he can say the same thing."

Miss Leitisha leaned right in Marvin Wright's face. "Just because you got all this real estate, that don't make you a businessman. You buying up stuff like toys. You got to know the customers, know your entertainers, know what to order, how to feed them, how to watch the liquor so's nobody steals it from you. And that you can't serve underage girls in your club."

Marvin Wright reached for the champagne and the young girl slipped to the adjacent chair. "You be careful Leitisha. Those developers are around offering a lot of money for the property. I can make a deal with them, and then they'll shut you down, you won't get nothing. Nothing for this," he waved his arm around the club. He handed a glass to the young girl.

"The new California Department of Alcoholic Beverage Control is itching to fine me and here you are tempting them with this girl." Leitisha dropped her voice. "She's not going to get me shut down. Walter, tell him, he has to leave."

"You heard her, Mr. Wright, you have to go."

"And make sure he pays for the champagne."

"What? We didn't even get to drink it."

Kay couldn't break away. Her hackles were up.

"You can think about that next time you bring an underage girl in here to drink with you. Good night, Marvin."

"I ain't going. We're gonna sit here and drink this champagne."

Miss Leitisha took the arm of the young woman. "I'm sorry honey, I'm not getting shut down because of you. If you're drinking, you have to leave." The girl squealed. Leitisha walked the unwilling young woman to the door.

"You'll be sorry," Wright called to Leitisha. He left holding onto the young girl, the champagne bottle in his other hand. "If this is the way you treat important customers, you be closed soon."

"You keep acting like a common thug, you soon be dead." Leitisha shouted at him from the open door. The sax player wailed a loud solo.

Wright and the girl climbed into his Cadillac DeVille. Kay noticed the black-and-white parked across the street. What now? They raid the place and then they stake it out? She watched the cops follow Wright as he drove away. Her hackles were on fire now.

# CHAPTER 3

AUGUST 2, 1958 · SATURDAY MORNING, 2 A.M.

Thursday Zimpel stood his collar up against the foggy wind of the San Francisco summer night. The two bullet holes in the back of the man's head stuck in his mind's eye. He stared into the alley, the cream-colored Cadillac starkly lit. Police officers stood guard outside the circle of light.

"So, Flanagan, tell me again in detail what happened here," Zimpel said to a young uniformed cop.

"Well, Inspector, we took the radio call, and me and Crawford here," he pointed to his partner. "Like I said, we showed up and . . ."

"Do we know who made the call?" Zimpel asked.

"No, sure don't. They called the station through the operator and hung up." The young cop shook his head.

"Did you ask them?" Zimpel nodded towards the small crowd gathered on the apartment house stoop, lit by a bare bulb. Women in robes and curlers. Men in wifebeaters, porch light shining on their shoulders. Lanky boys with eyes that said nothing.

"Well, it was only those folks," Flanagan nodded at the crowd. "They wouldn't tell us nothin."

Zimpel knew Flanagan hadn't asked. "You need to do the work, Flanagan."

Flanagan stared at him.

Zimpel gestured at the scene. "What did you find when you got here?"

"Just what you see here, the nigger in his big Cadillac there with his head

. . ." The young cop caught a look from Zimpel and started over.

"We found him dead and called it in. Didn't let no one near him."

Zimpel studied the Cadillac. It was a new DeVille, big teeth in front and fins in the back—a beauty. A rich man's car. "What else did you see?"

"That's it." The officer gestured with his hands out, wide-eyed.

Zimpel sighed. This kid would never make it off the street. "Think back. How did you find the Cadillac?"

"Right here, hasn't moved."

"Any of the doors open?"

"Huh? Oh yeah. The passenger door was open."

"Was the light on inside?"

The cop understood now. "Yeah, yeah, the light was on in the car, and the light went out when we shut the door."

"I know it's natural to shut an open door but next time don't touch the scene, at all. Get it?" This wasn't Flanagan's last mistake.

Zimpel walked over to the Cadillac and peered inside the passenger window. He shook out his handkerchief and carefully opened up the passenger door. Any prints on the handle were likely smeared when the cops closed the door.

The smell of blood hit him first, metallic and pungent. His eyes focused on the dashboard. Pristine leather except for the splattered blood and brains. He combed the scene with attention to anything out of place. Nothing on the floor in the back seat except a champagne bottle—he left it for someone else to bag, assumed they'd only find the victim's prints. He ran his hand and handkerchief under the front seat and came up with a yellow gum wrapper. Juicy Fruit. He held it to his nose. It still held the scent of the gum. He placed the wrapper in a small manila envelope. He then leaned in and put his nose close to the back of the passenger seat, perfume, a bit cloying, roses maybe? The gum wrapper and fragrance did not belong to the victim. They belonged to someone else. Someone who had recently been in the Cadillac.

"Hey, Crawford said that this guy's a big shot. I mean look at that car.

What's he doing with that kinda car?" Flanagan glanced at Zimpel. "We saw him thrown out of one of those bars, you know, in the Fillmore. The one run by the colored lady and she was the one that done it. She yelled at him she was going to kill him." He wanted to be helpful.

Zimpel shook out a cigarette, flipped open his Zippo, lit his cigarette and snapped it shut, sliding it into his pocket. He took a long drag, staring at the officer.

"Her name is Miss Leitisha Boone, and she's an owner of a nice restaurant and jazz club called the Blue Moon." Zimpel reflected that there might be trouble for Leitisha if Marvin Wright had been at her bar right before he was murdered.

Flanagan stepped back. "Yeah, whatever you say, Zimpel. They told us to watch the club, so we were, and we saw them argue. Hey Crawford, tell him."

"Who told you to watch the club?"

"I saw that lady toss out the big colored man. She threatened to kill him because he said he was going to shut her down." Crawford ignored Zimpel's question and nodded at the corpse. "Doesn't take a big person to put two bullet holes in someone's head. Those Negroes kill each other sure as not." Zimpel heard some murmuring in the crowd beyond the lights and tape, glanced around to see if there would be trouble.

"Who told you to watch her club?" Zimpel grabbed Flanagan's arm.

"We got orders. Maybe you need some orders, too." Flanagan pulled away.

"Who, Crawford?" Zimpel got in the cop's face. Crawford stared him down, so he knew the orders came from high up.

"Maybe if you stuck with your own kind more, folks would talk to you, too." Crawford straightened his uniform.

Zimpel read the eyes of the crowd, none of whom were talking to them. He'd learn who gave the order after writing these guys up for messing with the scene. "Get statements from these folks standing around to see what they know." He pointed his finger at Flanagan's chest, "Be respectful. You are not going to get any information by treating people badly."

Zimpel scanned the crowd and buildings around them. On a porch with a view to the alley, a large woman in a pink robe with curlers in her hair stared at the scene. Her husband, his arm around her, leaned into her ear. The woman nodded back at him, her curlers bobbing as they went inside. Zimpel would have given a week's pay to know what they said.

Two slugs in the back of his head made it a professional hit. The Chicago Outfit had shown up in San Francisco, mingling with the Italians already involved in the LCN. Zimpel preferred the Italian "La Cosa Nostra" or LCN rather than "mafia." The West Coast was a different animal than New York.

Maybe Wright crossed them. Marvin Wright owned many properties in the Fillmore besides the Blue Moon. With redevelopment moving in on the Fillmore, maybe someone wanted Wright out of the way, save them some dough. Or the unions who would reap jobs from the redevelopment projects were looking to streamline the process. Or someone was mad at him for some other reason. He'd have to figure it out.

Crawford's statement about Miss Leitisha's threatening Wright made a good motive for murder. The City and Redevelopment Agency would look for a fall guy to blame it on, someone who might stand in their way.

He dragged on the cigarette, watching the containment of the scene. Because he hung out in the Fillmore jazz clubs where most of the patrons were Negro, he was the closest thing they had to a community cop. When Wright's murder came in, it became his case. Some of his colleagues didn't trust him because of it, like those beat cops. Didn't change how he worked cases though.

He joined the Army like most of his generation and, after the War, he settled in San Francisco. When shipbuilding companies recruited labor from southern states for the war effort, thousands of Negroes moved to San Francisco, which meant banks started redlining, and deeds and leases restricted non-whites to Chinatown and the Fillmore.

This de facto segregation made getting trust and witnesses difficult. He was an outsider, and with so few Negro cops, and no Negro homicide inspectors, he did his best.

Zimpel observed the photographers documenting the scene. Others preserved what evidence there was around the victim and in the car, including bagging the champagne bottle. The beat cops asked questions without much interest or effort. He scanned windows overhead knowing someone saw something.

His lieutenant arrived, got out of the car, and spoke briefly with Crawford and Flanagan. Zimpel took a last drag on his cigarette and tossed it.

"I heard that the lady that owns the club gave him some beef tonight before he left." He jerked his thumb towards the DeVille.

Zimpel shook his head. "You the one who told these yuks to keep an eye on the club?"

"What are you insinuating Zimpel?"

"If you have an ax to grind here, I got a problem with that." Zimpel patted his pockets for a cigarette. Was his lieutenant motivated by money, wanting redevelopment to progress faster? The higher up, the more susceptible to politics.

"You too close to this to handle it?"

Zimpel eyed him. "Too close" because he knew the real facts and not the made-up ones.

"This was a professional hit, two bullets in the back of the head." The medical examiner was removing the body. "He was her landlord, and they did business together."

"Not mutually exclusive—maybe her business needed him gone. You don't know, do you?"

"I do know. She's got a viable business—had no reason to throw it all away with this."

The lieutenant raised his eyebrows. "You talk to her or we'll pick her up and talk to her."

Zimpel lit a cigarette. "I'll talk to her." They wanted an easy out with this murder. Leitisha needed to watch her back.

"Hey doc."

The lanky medical examiner peered over his glasses at Zimpel.

"Look for lipstick . . . everywhere?"

The medical examiner nodded.

Someone was with the victim when he was shot. She was either dead somewhere else, about to be dead, or she got away. He was hoping she got away. If so, he had a witness. He looked out into the fog. Now he just had to find her.

# CHAPTER 4

## AUGUST 2, 1958 · SATURDAY

Kay cinched her robe and pushed open the blue wool curtains. She watched the paper boy going door to door, the gray light anticipating sunrise. She set up the percolator, Hills Brothers. On a good day you could smell the coffee roasting; the plant was near the Bay Bridge.

She loved this little apartment and her independence—having her kitchen and living room the way she wanted. After law school, hard enough with all the guff she got for being a woman, she had searched several months for a job as a lawyer, and not as a secretary or paralegal. She talked one of the smaller firms into hiring her, and it gave her a space to be her own.

Her parents gave her a few pieces of used furniture for her apartment: a twin bed that belonged to her grandmother, an old kitchen table and a couple of chairs, and her childhood piano, a spinet upright. Good enough to practice on and loud enough to cause her neighbor to pound on the wall from time to time.

"You're the only one who plays it," her mother had said.

She got out her coffee cup, scooped cream off the top of the milk bottle into a bowl and stuck a piece of bread under the broiler.

Her kitchen had a small ice box and a gas range. She was close enough to the streetcar for work and the Fillmore. Like last night, after playing at the Blue Moon, she was home quickly and slept hard.

She tuned the radio to KCBS 740 AM for news while she waited for the coffee to finish. She worked today, as she did most Saturdays, to keep up with the other associates, all male, and her boss, Frank Bianco.

"Good morning, we bring you this latest News Bulletin: Marvin Wright, prominent Negro businessman, was murdered on Third Street last night. The real estate mogul was found shot in his Cadillac."

She turned up the radio. ". . . getting dangerous in that part of town, like the Fillmore . . ."

Last night, Marvin Wright didn't seem like a man about to die. She pulled her robe around her tighter. This was awful. Someone shot Marvin Wright? She knew someone who was murdered? A murder connected to the Blue Moon? Maybe crime is increasing like they say. She needed to think through what this meant. Her morning took a different turn.

She turned off the coffee and the broiler, put the cream into the ice box, and got dressed. She wanted to walk, to think, to digest this news before she went into the office.

The elevator came. "Good morning, Miss Schiffner."

Louis made it a point to learn all the tenants' names. Having an elevator man and a doorman made Kay's parents feel better about her renting an apartment. The doorman, Mr. Jeff, was visiting his mother for the week. Mr. Louis worked a little extra, so someone was around early and late.

"Good morning, Mr. Louis, how are you today?"

"I'm fine, thank you, Miss Schiffner. You up bright and early."

She watched him manipulate the controls.

"Yes, well, yes." Pulling on her gloves, she gave him a smile. "Have a nice day."

"You have a nice day, too, Miss."

She headed to Caffé Trieste, a fairly new North Beach coffeehouse filled with beatniks and artists, with a short streetcar ride into North Beach. The Caffé's creative atmosphere drew her. It was a noisy place to get quiet inside her head.

"Espresso please," she said to the young man with a goatee and a panel hat. Self-conscious in her suit, she glanced about for a place to sit and found a table in the corner. She unpinned her hair and shook it down to fit in better. She removed a small notebook from her handbag. It held her calendar and notes about work, about music, songs she wanted to learn, and music ideas of her own. The coffee was deliciously bitter.

She wrote down Marvin Wright's name and underlined it. He was the Blue Moon's landlord. She then wrote "landlord" underneath.

Kay recalled the last time she had spoken to Marvin Wright, before seeing him last night.

Sometime in June 1958 Leitisha had organized Fillmore businesses to protest against the Redevelopment Agency and the onerous terms it was forcing on their foreclosures. Hard enough for her to run her business as a woman. Her credibility and stature to protest wasn't strong. She needed allies. Miss Leitisha convinced Kay that, being a lawyer, she had sway with Marvin Wright, enough to ask him to take a visible role in their efforts.

Kay, reluctant to jeopardize her career by participating, still wanted to hear Marvin Wright's opinion of what was happening, so she agreed to speak with him.

Wright's office was above Jimbo's Bop City, a building he owned. Kay knocked on the door, which was ajar. "Mr. Wright, I'm . . ."

"Kay Schiffner, the lawyer piano player. Come in." He stood as she entered the room. "We met at the Blue Moon."

"Yes, you have a good memory. Thank you. Leitisha wanted me to come by to see if we discuss how to push back against redevelopment."

He laughed, not in a mean way. "Right to the point. I like it. Please, have a seat." He gestured to a small couch across from his desk. He sat in the client chair. "Leitisha sent you up here thinking you can change my mind about their protest." He shook his head. "They won't listen to a Negro protest. These folks are all focused on the money."

Kay pushed back. "You're a prominent landholder, you pay taxes, surely they would listen to you. Redevelopment could give a coalition of community leaders like yourself a say in the proceedings, and at the least, fair compensation."

"We ought to have a say," said the big man, "But you're white, and you don't understand just how invisible, or worse, we are. I had done my share of 'sayings.'" He laughed again. "They ain't listening to any of us. Like I said, there's too much money involved here."

"They can't just displace . . ." She stood, not able to sit still.

"They can when they are out for the almighty dollar. It's not even about race anymore, its poor folks. People who don't have power."

"You're powerful. You own half the Fillmore." She raised her voice, wanting to be understood.

"And with a stroke of the pen and a vote of the spineless board of supervisors, I lose it all to eminent domain—you understand that, being a lawyer and all—and gain a certificate to trade for property that will never come." He paused, got up, looked out the window, put his hands in his pockets and turned back to Kay. "It's an illusion of power. Hard enough to own property—that is the key in this country, to own property." He turned back to the window. "Fighting them head on won't get you anywhere—got to figure out an angle, some way to leverage it." He tilted his head at her and narrowed his eyes.

"You joining that protest?" he asked her. "You could be effective. A white lady lawyer would get their attention."

"I," she hesitated. "I'm only helping in the background. My law firm wouldn't be happy seeing me adverse to the developers."

"Then you see my point."

# CHAPTER 5

She omitted that last point when she described her meeting with Marvin Wright to Miss Leitisha. Not taking Wright's refusal lightly, Leitisha then asked her to come to the hearing, to speak for them. "We need you. You're a lawyer."

"The board of supervisors isn't going to be persuaded by what I have to say, I'm not part of the community, hard enough for a woman lawyer to get treated like a lawyer. And, I'm not an expert in property or eminent domain law." Truth was, she didn't want to be exposed supporting this cause and hurt her chances of progressing at the law firm.

"Nonsense," said Miss Leitisha.

Leitisha's coalition didn't have a chance going up against Redevelopment without political power and a good eminent domain lawyer. While he refused to protest directly, Wright's own greed protected the Blue Moon as long as he held out on selling.

Even so, his heirs may not have the same choices. Kay stared at her notebook. She wanted to maintain the status quo. Change was inevitable. She needed to find her place in the change, to try and make it better, and not just for her.

A conversation in the coffeehouse drew her attention. Three scruffy-looking men and one lone woman, likely still up from the night before, cigarettes in their hands or in overflowing ashtrays, coffee mugs full, sat around a table full of paper and litter. The men spoke as if they were the only ones there, waving their arms, picking up notebooks and reading aloud to one another, a storm of creative energy.

The lone woman ignored the men and wrote furiously in a notebook, her long black hair hanging on either side of her face like curtains. She wore a black turtleneck, black stretch pants, and short black boots that zipped.

Kay felt the confines of her pencil skirt, the garter that squeezed at her waist and thighs, and the itch of wanting to create pinching her brain. I'm more like them.

Her office felt as awkward as her tight skirt, though she was grateful to have her own office after a year, with a file cabinet, a desk, a telephone, and a window towards the bulky elevated freeway. Part of Redevelopment's first project, the Embarcadero Freeway, hid the bay beyond, having displaced the old produce and meat markets along the Bay piers. Kay hated that freeway and the so-called "progress" it stood for.

Mr. Bianco's secretary, Irma, dressed in her typical tight dress and high heels, came by the minute Kay arrived at her desk. "Frank wants to see you in his office. Said as soon as you came in." Irma glanced at her watch, then walked back down the hall, her high heels clacking. The meaning was obvious. Kay was late, even on a Saturday.

"Frank?" She held a pad of paper and stood in his doorway; his brow furrowed over a document.

"Kay, ah, there you are," Frank said.

She put a slight smile on her face. Act conciliatory. Get out of here unscathed.

"We need to get the Madison contract out asap. Where are you on it?

"It'll be on your desk within the hour."

"It should have been here when I got in this morning." His eyes went back to the document on his desk.

Her blood pressure spiked. Work stress, the thrill and the curse, demanding top performance. Every day brought a new test to prove herself.

"Frank, are we doing any redevelopment work?" Maybe she could combine her wanting to help Leitisha with her law firm work.

"What?" He glanced at her over his glasses, then back to the document on his desk. "Not at the moment. I would love to, lots of money there. Why?"

"I'm doing real estate transactions. Redevelopment doesn't seem that different."

"If you don't have enough work to do, I have more for you. And it's different work from what you're doing. I'm sure you have no idea."

She heard, "You're being stupid" in the tone of his voice. Still, she pushed one more question. "Maybe I could learn about that work by dropping by the redevelopment hearings this week?"

He gave her a sharp eye. "If no one is paying us, we're not going." He put the document down and looked over his glasses at her again. "Just get the Madison contract finished and bring it to me."

As she turned to leave, he wasn't quite finished. "I need you focused on your work, not asking questions around where you don't belong." She stood in the door, waiting for him to finish with her. "I get the clients, you do the work. I need you to be a billing machine."

He laughed yet he was dead serious. "Like working on the McCann transaction this afternoon, please? We need to get documents to the client by Monday morning. He was reticent about using a woman, and I talked him into it. Don't let me down."

He always ended by reminding her she owed him, that she should be grateful for what he gave her. Kay nearly curtsied, both obliged and chafed at his tone. She was a good lawyer.

"Sure, I will, I'll get it done." She didn't have any choice.

# CHAPTER 6

## AUGUST 2, 1958 · SATURDAY EVENING

Kay stayed past 6 p.m. to draft the contracts Frank needed for Monday, and one more she anticipated he would ask for. Why did she even bother with an apartment? She should set up a cot right there in her office.

Even after a long workday and playing last night, Kay felt the pull of the Blue Moon. The irritation of her skirt and the office was an itch to get dressed up and play. Her hands were hot. She stretched her fingers.

She prepared for the evening as if playing music was her vocation, and not an afterthought. After soaking in a bath, she gingerly set her toes into stockings, and, carefully keeping the seam straight, hooked them into the garters. She slipped a party dress over her head and inspected herself in the hall mirror. The black pattern on the polished cotton looked chic. She cinched the belt, slipped into black pumps, grabbed gloves, and picked out a hat. She clipped on white pearl semi-circle earrings, checking her effect in the mirror, willing herself to feel as gay as she appeared.

Kay slowly pulled bobby pins out of her hair, then loosened her curls into waves. Everyone dressed up for the Blue Moon and she wanted to belong. She had the blues bad.

She heard "Love Me Tender" blasting from the neighbor's slightly ajar door as she waited for the elevator.

Rolled up in her handbag, the music to a new song for her, "Every Day I Have the Blues." She climbed aboard the streetcar, its clattering, bell ringing, and pull of the brake setting up a rhythm in her head. She hummed a tune and stretched her hands. Restaurant windows illuminated the night. Streetlights cast shadows on people walking to and from the clubs and restaurants.

When Kay arrived, Miss Leitisha sat at the end of the bar drinking coffee, her account books in front of her. Unusual for her not to be directing the girls in the kitchen, or steering the waiters in the dining room.

"Miss Leitisha, how are you? Are you ok?" Kay asked. Walter put a drink in front of her.

"Don't you look all dolled up. You meeting someone tonight?" Leitisha gave her a wink.

"I worked all day, want a drink, and need to play. And I'm concerned. I heard about Marvin Wright's murder." Kay put a couple dollars on the bar, tipping her glass to Walter.

"I appreciate your concern. It was a terrible thing, and shocking for sure." Leitisha shook her head.

"What does that mean for the Blue Moon?"

"His family will take over being the landlord. They have other worries besides me. Now go play tonight, and we'll all take our mind off of this." Leitisha's focus went back to her account books.

Kay's stomach clenched. Maybe she should eat something.

"You need a good lawyer, Miss Leitisha, to fight redevelopment."

"You a lawyer, you help me." Her bright eyes burned into Kay.

"I don't know eminent domain law—you need someone skilled in that practice. And being a woman, very few judges would listen to me."

"It don't matter what kind of lawyer you are, it's all politics. You'll do as well as any of them." She waved her hand and turned to Walter to discuss some inventory purchases.

Saul, Leitisha's boyfriend, was a lawyer, where was he? She went back to her drink feeling dismissed. She'd figure out someone to represent Leitisha and the club.

The band dove hard into a blues set.

Kay stood from the bar and slipped into the kitchen. She sat at the worn oak table pushed against the back wall.

"Can I get you a bite Kay?" Sylvia smiled at her. The service was reflex. Sylvia managed Leitisha's kitchen.

"Thanks, Sylvia, maybe a biscuit?" Kay wanted something easy on her stomach.

Sylvia brought over a basket, warm, and some butter.

Kay buttered the biscuit, remembering nights when this table was pulled out for the occasional staff dinners after the last patron had gone home. Most nights, people were happy to put on their coats against the fog, go home to their families, and sleep. But once in a while, maybe for a birthday, the staff would sit around this table and eat well.

Tonight, the kitchen bustled with Saturday evening orders, the air pungent from frying, sautéing, chopping of crisp salads, marinated shrimp circling cocktail sauce, boiled greens. A woman with large arms, her name might be Marjorie but everyone called her Cook, did all the meat cooking. Tildy, the kitchen apprentice, methodically chopped vegetables. Leitisha was a perfectionist and chose every steak, crab, and bean that came in to ensure cooking at its finest. And one of her sources was Henry.

Henry came in from the back, carrying a sack of sweet potatoes, a large bag of carrots and a box of broccoli. He owned a farm in Salinas and delivered fresh produce to the restaurant. He was here late tonight.

Tall and ebony black with muscles that sat comfortably on his large frame, he was ageless, maybe 40 Kay guessed. His smile was minimal and confident.

Henry stood behind Sylvia without touching her. She stirred and tasted without turning. He leaned over, barely touching her shoulders, his eyes closed, breathing her in. Sylvia leaned back into him then, as if they were melting into one another. She turned and he kissed her quickly on the cheek, their eyes met, and then he went to get the rest of the vegetables. Love thick and delicious like a good roux.

Chicken sizzled on the stove and sweet iced tea sweated in pitchers. The magical smells moving through the kitchen and the impeccable organization lifted Kay's mood. She'd see if the band would let her cut in. It wasn't her regular night.

The band had switched to West Coast cool. The trumpet player, Lester, had recently played at the Black Hawk down the street with Gerry Mulligan. "That boy's got some Black in him, plays that baritone sax with soul."

"Don't let Miss Leitisha know you was down at the Black Hawk."

"Ah, it was a late gig, and it was cool man, the Eye-talian guy, he's ok."

Percy gave Lester a side look, not believing it.

"Hey, don't forget Dave Brubeck," said Kay.

Lester laughed. "You, too, Miss Kay. You gots some soul in you, too, maybe enough for Johnny Otis. Come on up and play a number with us." The invitation made her shine inside.

Kay stood at the piano making eye contact with the band members. Maybe it was the biscuits or her pert dress, or maybe it was Lester's inclusive comment, she got up there to play. Her hands touched the keys, like wind on still water, rippling sound.

"You hear about that little Filipina gal? She won the talent show at the Ellis. Otis named her 'Sugar Pie' and got her all fixed up."

"I heard that girl before, she can sing blues man."

"Rumor was her cousin showed up in Otis' hotel room before that, a 14-year-old girl, and started singing at him. She got the gig, so DeSanto decided she would try."

Otis was a major bandleader at the time, and ran a talent show out of the Ellis Theatre. Kay had heard about the girl, named Etta James, and the street talk was that she sang like crazy.

"I'll ask him to hire me next." Kay said, not meaning it. She rarely ventured from the Blue Moon, feeling safe and anonymous there.

"Y'all gonna gossip or play?" With that, they launched into "Walking Shoes," a Gerry Mulligan tune, which picked up the pace considerably. She liked the version he recorded with Chet Baker in 1952.

As they played, Thursday Zimpel walked into the Blue Moon, nodded at Walter and set his hat on the bar. A rainstorm was moving in with lines of gun metal gray clouds carried by a cold wind. When he told people back home he lived in California, they thought surfing, not chilly San Francisco.

Walter held up a beer glass. Zimpel shook his head. "Gimme a Coca-Cola, Walter. I need to talk with Miss Leitisha. Is she in the kitchen?"

"Yes sir, she is."

# CHAPTER 7

A few patrons glanced at the white man in the trench coat and dark brown hat. All the regulars knew who he was. A white cop who patronizes a Fillmore club gets known pretty quickly.

As the band finished the number, Leitisha saw Zimpel at the bar. "You gonna stir up more trouble for me?"

Zimpel sighed. "I'm here to prevent trouble."

"You hear we had a raid last night? Killed half my dinner crowd."

"Maybe use a different metaphor?"

"What?"

"Marvin Wright was murdered late last night, out on Third Street."

"I know, I heard." She handed him a copy of the Chronicle sitting on the bar. On the front page, there was a photo of the Cadillac with the passenger door open.

Those cops had let some press person photograph the scene before he had it photographed. He needed to get those photos. And mention this in his report.

"And besides, Tildy lives in the Bay View, and the neighbors were all talking about it this morning."

Zimpel made a note to ask Tildy what was said. "I am in charge of the murder investigation. There was some talk about how you threw him out of the Blue Moon last night."

"Like most folks, he act right most of the time, 'cept when he's drunk.

Not anything different." She took a tray with a check and cash on it, looked it over and handed it back to Edward, one of the waiters. "I threw him out of here more times than last night, but I didn't kill him."

"I'm not saying you did. I'm telling you what I heard."

She pointed at his drink. "Maybe you need a beer, and not that soda pop."

"Humor me, Leitisha, I don't want someone knowing more than I do if I'm investigating this." Zimpel started over. "Marvin Wright was in here last night?"

"Yes."

"And he was with a girl?"

"Yes, that's why I threw his ass out. He came in here drunk with an underage girl. I don't need that headache with those new ABC bureaucrats itching to fine me or shut me down."

Zimpel's assumption was correct. "What did she look like?"

"She looked like a floozy, short skirt, processed hair, face full of makeup with bright pink lips." She eyed him. "Why?"

Zimpel noted the "bright pink lips." "Maybe she was a witness. Would you recognize her?"

Miss Leitisha waved her hand at him.

"Did you serve him champagne?"

"He demanded it and then didn't pay for it. He put $20 bill on the table and then took it back and walked out with the champagne."

"Are you sure he took it back? His wallet was empty when we found him."

"Well, I didn't grab his wallet before he left. Maybe he gave it to Walter. I don't know."

"Was it a Moet?"

She gestured towards the bar. "Ask Walter. I was more concerned about not getting busted for having an underage girl in here drinking."

"So what's this about a raid?" He had heard her say she got raided.

Leitisha's eyebrows up. "You didn't know."

He shook his head. They were really going around him.

"Four cops, two cars. Said they heard there was gambling. Just a ruse."

"Gambling? Here? Yeah, I'm sorry." He knew that some cops did fake drug raids. This was new.

She gestured towards the dining room. "They made a fuss at the white folks here and broke some bottles of champagne and wine. Dumped food in the kitchen. Childish stuff. For what?"

"No one was arrested?" he asked.

"That wasn't the point," she said.

She was right. He was really mad now. They weren't wasting any time trying to pressure her. He needed to work this case, or they were going to work her.

"You might get busted for worse than an ABC violation, maybe for this murder, if I don't figure it out."

"Me? Now that's silly, I didn't mind the man, except when he's drunk here with an underage girl. You think I killed him?"

"Yeah, that's swell, Leitisha, how well do you know me?" Zimpel tapped his pockets for his cigarettes.

"Pretty damn well I would say." She gazed out over her dining room. Folks coming and going, eating and listening, tables being cleared and set, with the music playing over it all. "So I can't see what evidence anyone would have that would connect me to that. I don't own a gun."

He clicked open his Zippo and lit his cigarette. "Understand ABC's enforcement is gentle compared to the pressure to find this prominent man's killer."

"'Prominent? They don't care about a successful Negro businessman—they just want his land, that's what they're after. Including this." She swept the room with her arm.

"Well, I care who killed him, and I want to find whoever did it." If only to protect her.

"Thursday Zimpel, I believe you do, and I appreciate your concern. Unless there is something I can do right now, I have a business to run."

Zimpel's protective instincts itched. "Will you at least talk with Saul?" He hoped her white Jewish lawyer boyfriend could insulate her from the pressure he was seeing.

"I told Saul about Marvin being killed, worried about the lease, and he said don't pay them any mind. He said not to worry, so I won't."

Zimpel worried. At least she had done that. "Ok, I'll find out what's going on. Please keep a low profile especially with Redevelopment until this blows over?"

"I got a good eye out, believe me. They haven't gotten me yet. This is the Fillmore and it belongs to us. They want to take this away with their so called 'redevelopment' they are going to have to pay me, and pay me good, for it."

Leitisha touched Kay's shoulder and motioned for Walter to get Kay a drink. "There's another hearing Monday starting at 1 p.m. We're going to be there for the coalition. Be good if you showed up, so you know, we have mixed company." She winked at Kay.

Kay felt the hope and ask in her voice. After Marvin Wright being murdered, she wanted to help Leitisha in a tangible way. Being part of the crowd there would give her support.

Frank would be heated with her if he found out she was there, stepping outside the lines he'd drawn. But he didn't need to know.

"Maybe I can break away during my lunch hour."

"Folks see you standing with me, knowing you work with Bianco, give me credibility."

Leitisha didn't intend for her to remain in the background. "I can't publicly endorse you, Leitisha, understand that. I'll get in trouble at my job."

"It'll be ok," said Leitisha. "We'll see you tomorrow."

Kay wasn't sure it would be ok, but now she was committed to coming. That solid feeling she had while playing on stage yielded to a slow roil. "I'll try," said Kay. She'd do her best to remain invisible. Leitisha had already left to greet a regular. Kay decided to catch the streetcar, her blues returning. Zimpel noticed Kay's reluctance and knew this town voiced vicious backlash if you stepped outside the lines drawn to keep the races separate. The police conducted regular raids, like last night in the Fillmore, to discourage interracial dating. He did his best to keep them out of the Blue Moon but was a target himself, and obviously not able to protect even his close friends. Maybe it was time for a beer. He motioned to Walter.

Percy came over and leaned on the bar, nodding at Zimpel. "Heard Lena Horne was in town, staying at the Booker T. Maybe she'll play in the lounge tonight."

"The Bronze Venus," said Walter.

"Yeah, she's amazing. What's going to happen if they tear down that hotel? Won't be any place for colored folk to stay when the white folk want us to entertain them."

Zimpel took a swig of the beer, cold and perfect. Marvin Wright also owned The Booker T. Washington Hotel, popular and necessary for traveling musicians who weren't welcome in the downtown hotels. Billie Holiday, Count Basie, Duke Ellington, doesn't matter how famous, if you were Black, that's where you stayed.

Zimpel got up and walked over to where Leitisha was standing at the door. "Haven't seen Saul around here lately?" Zimpel didn't like the absence of the lawyer when Leitisha was vulnerable.

"Waiting me out, thinks I won't be a businesswoman for much longer, thinks it's too much for me."

"He doesn't know you as well as he thinks he does, if he's waiting on that."

"Yes, you're right. I'm a business owner first. Be that way until the day I die."

Zimpel had a bad feeling as the band played "They Can't Take That Away From Me."

# CHAPTER 8

## AUGUST 4, 1958 · MONDAY MORNING

Zimpel finished a cup of coffee and took the elevator to the ME's office. Marvin Wright's autopsy was this Monday morning. Zimpel had never seen so many brass animated. His lieutenant called him yesterday, on a Sunday, told him there was lots of heat on this homicide especially from the Redevelopment Agency to the mayor to the police chief and down to him, as it was holding up property transfers.

"Let's not let a bunch of red tape hold up progress," he was told. Since when had a murder investigation been red tape? He was glad the lieutenant prioritized the autopsy but was wary of this pressure on his investigation.

The Medical Examiner's office was stuck in the back of 750 Kearny Street with few windows and no frills. The porcelain tables looked like something that belonged in a men's public restroom. Dr. Levin joked they were embalming tables and had been there for years. "Someone must have gotten a deal on them some time ago and they just stayed."

Zimpel pushed opened the door to the examining room and the smell hit him. The odor of decay didn't make him nauseous anymore, but he never got used to the Pine-Sol smell that hung in the air around it. He reached for a cigarette. Dr. Levin's tall, thin frame was already bent over the large body of Marvin Wright.

Dr. Levin didn't look up when Zimpel walked in. "Autopsy's not really necessary. No mystery how he died," said Dr. Levin, making a "Y" incision crossing in front of the throat and then down the torso. He peeled back the flesh and pointed with the scalpel. "He had an enlarged heart, and I suspect he had high blood pressure, man built like him." Levin cut out the heart organ and put it on a scale. "Hey, Jackie," Levin called.

A young man in a white coat with red hair burst through swinging doors to the autopsy room, out of breath. "Dr. Levin?"

"Help me with this exam," Levin nodded at a clipboard, which the young man went to pick up, dropped and then picked up again, self-conscious. The young man did not look at the body.

"What's the matter, Jackie?"

"Never been this close to a Negro." He glanced quickly at the body, and then back at his clipboard.

"Black, white, Chinaman, all the same laying on the slab. We deal with the dead, however they come to us. Remember that." Levin sighed. To Zimpel, he said, "New. Always having to break in someone new."

Levin turned back to Jackie. "Write this down." Levin then methodically went through each organ, cutting it out, weighing it, and calling out the weight, notes, and the young man dutifully wrote it down. Zimpel grunted and stayed to the side smoking his cigarette. Every so often, Levin would tell the kid to take a photograph, then write down notes for the photograph.

Levin turned to Zimpel, a bloody scalpel still in his hand, "I already did your external exam."

Zimpel's eyebrows went up. "And?"

"As you know, two small caliber bullet holes in the back of the head, close. No muzzle print, but burns, so within inches, no exit wound." Levin sliced the scalp and peeled it back, then turned on the skill saw. The noise curled Zimpel's hands into fists. He had dropped his cigarette on the floor and no doubt would hear from Levin for his sloppiness.

"Like a big plate of tomato aspic," Levin pulled out the back of the brain.

Another food ruined for him by the ME.

Levin placed the organ in a tray, took his scalpel and peeled out first one bullet, with a ting, and then the other. He reached for one with his gloved hand.

"Here's your bullets. Small caliber, .22 maybe, just enough to do the job."

"Professional," said Zimpel. "That's good doc, I'll take those when you're done and hopefully we can find the gun." Zimpel glanced up again, reaching for another cigarette. "And?"

Levin turned to him, "Your 'trace' evidence?"

Zimpel nodded. Levin got a smirk on his face.

"As you implied, there was a lipstick smear at the base of his penis. Boy got a rubdown before he went." Levin pointed to his notes. "We were able to get a faint sample. Not a high-end lipstick—like something you would find at Woolworth's." Levin had washed his hands.

"Hey, Jackie, get him sewn back up, and do a careful job, we can't be sloppy, and then put him in the Frigidaire when you're done." The young man stared at him with wide eyes.

Levin nodded to the door, "Let's go to my office."

His office was a tiny cubbyhole piled with periodicals, books, and framed certificates. A dirty coffee cup sat on the corner of a crowded desk. Levin pulled out a pipe, thumbed in tobacco and carefully lit it. The sweet smell filled the room.

"I can maybe get you enough to try and match a color. If you bring me a sample."

Zimpel's eyebrows went up. "Helpful."

"It's a bright—some call it 'hot'—pink color." Dr. Levin continued. "And someone helped themselves to what was in his wallet."

"Yeah, we noticed that at the scene."

"Man like that, with champagne in the backseat, doesn't go out without cash."

"Hoping that there are fingerprints on the wallet." Who took the money? The murderer, the girl, or his cops?

"I wouldn't count on it but they're looking."

Zimpel put his cigarette out. "Why'd you do this doc?"

"What? Become an ME?" He laughed. "Same reason you became a cop and then a homicide inspector, I suspect. To get the bad guy. To solve the mystery. Only I do it with science." Levin tapped his pipe out. "Well, got one more to do this afternoon. I'll get you the report within a day or two."

Zimpel nodded, and grimaced. He left the ME's office and then left the building, glad to hit fresh air. The smell would stay with him all day.

# CHAPTER 9

Kay talked herself into going to the redevelopment hearing. No one would know she was there; she'd show up for Leitisha then leave. She marked up one draft contract and gave it to the secretarial pool to type and get to Frank. Then she drafted a second document, along with the exhibits, and left it with Frank's secretary, hoping the two contracts kept him occupied so he didn't come looking for her. Under the guise of getting lunch, she jumped on a streetcar to the Civic Center.

Kay surveyed the large City Hall room with high ceilings and echoing voices. A microphone was set up for public comment with a stenographer and clerk to the side, and a sheriff's deputy ready to keep order if need be.

Cigarette smoke hovered like the fog this city was known for. On a dais at the front, the supervisors presided over the hearing, rustling papers and speaking to their aides as they listened and asked questions, the last word between the neighborhoods and developers. While the crowd was mostly men, one supervisor was a woman: Mrs. Clarissa McMahon, a lawyer. It was possible for a woman to work as a lawyer and win an election. Kay watched her interact, wanting that kind of power.

Herman Weiner, at the microphone, spoke on behalf of the Redevelopment Agency. He talked about their "great work" of "clearing the slums" and economic rejuvenation. Kay's experience in the Fillmore contrasted with his descriptions of "rat infested" slums and urban "blight."

While Kay scanned the crowd for Leitisha and her group, she overheard two men talking about Marvin Wright and turned her back to them to listen. Surrounded in thick cigar smoke, they kept their voices low. "They are calling this a civil rights problem, with the likes of Marvin Wright speaking for them." His voice squeaked with worry.

"We have the law on our side. Let Wright take his complaints to Congress." The other man took a puff on his cigar and exhaled into the air. "But he can't do that now, can he?" Both men laughed.

Kay felt invisible, all the power in that room.

A Negro man in a gray suit walked to the microphone to give a public comment. Kay didn't know him and wondered if he was part of Leitisha's coalition.

"What is Redevelopment going to do for the 1,350 households and 358 businesses that would be displaced by this plan?" He raised his voice to get over the din, and feedback came through the speakers. "The planned housing for the area would only accommodate half of the residents. You are tearing down a vibrant and flourishing neighborhood and closing established businesses."

Weiner spoke over him. "These buildings are falling down, restaurants can't pass inspection." He grabbed the podium with both hands, "Children live in rat invested flats." He spoke of the Fillmore as if it were garbage to be cleared.

The man tried to speak again. "Your facts, sir, are simply wrong, and are a product of racism and . . ."

Weiner waved his hand. "Your time is up." The sheriff's deputy stood up staring at the man, who put on his hat and picked up his briefcase. There was no posted time limit. "There is no discrimination," Weiner said. "We are treating everyone exactly the same, as the plan will level the entire area clean and build it back up."

Kay noted the "everyone" he referred to as being treated the same were the residents of the Fillmore. Folks started clapping and others booed. Kay glanced towards the boos and saw members of the neighborhood coalition, and headed toward them. Leitisha, dressed impeccably, clutched her purse in one hand, her notes in the other.

"Leitisha, do you know that man who just spoke?"

"No, but I will. You'll do better."

Kay's gut constricted. "Leitisha, I'm not making a statement."

Leitisha held up a hand, and focused on Weiner's continued comments.

"Redevelopment is good for San Francisco business, so I know you can all get behind it. We are going to beautify this City and make you proud to live in it."

"We won't be able to live in it," said Leitisha. "They don't want us here."

Kay touched Leitisha's shoulder in the noise to tell her she wasn't speaking when she heard someone behind her.

"Hello Kay, what are you doing here?"

Oh no, someone recognized her. Her stomach dropped. Murray Stalton worked in a firm that frequently teamed up with Bianco.

"Oh, here for work. What are you doing?" She hid her worry with a smile.

Murray frowned. "Working with the unions." He pressed her. "So who are you working with?"

Kay nodded towards the well-dressed man now quietly speaking to one of the Supervisors. "Who's that guy?" He was one of the two men she had overheard earlier.

"Oh," Murray did like to show off. "That's Brad Mullin, Mid-City Development, one of the project leaders on the A-1 Area." Murray lowered his voice. "Now that guy is powerful." Murray smelled of cigarettes and coffee.

"That guy," said Kay pointing, "is one of the private redevelopers?"

"Shh, don't point. He has a big role with the Redevelopment Agency coordinating several projects, and big money." He paused. "Bianco better be on the right side of this."

Kay stepped back. "Just curious."

Murray's eyes went from her, to Leitisha, and back to the group before he walked away.

Leitisha's face was tight, her head shaking at Weiner's comments and the crowd's apparent agreement with him. Kay glanced at her watch; she was already late getting back.

The clerk announced the public microphone was open for comments again. Miss Leitisha walked up to the microphone. "My lawyer wants to make a statement that redevelopment is uneconomical and bad for the Fillmore residents, and you can't tear down people's homes and businesses and not compensate them." She looked pointedly at Kay.

No. No. Kay whispered, "I am not prepared to speak, can't do this off the cuff. I have to get back to work." Leitisha's face dropped.

If Frank knew she was here speaking against the developers, she'd lose her job. Holy Mother, this can't be happening.

"Sure you can, just go on." Leitisha pushed her towards the microphone and then stepped back. All eyes in the room focused on her.

Every molecule of her body screeching tires of stress, Kay cleared her throat and spoke into the microphone.

"The Fillmore Neighborhood Coalition will not make any substantive comments at this meeting. However, it reserves its rights, and intends to submit a written statement from the Coalition to be part of this record to address the issues listed, including Fifth Amendment taking issues. Thank you." There were murmurs around the crowd.

"Please state your name for the record."

"For the record, I don't represent the Coalition. Please refer to its written submission." Kay was not going to put her name on the record.

"You said you wanted to help us," Leitisha said, in a loud whisper.

"I do want to help. I can't be the lawyer for the Coalition, stand up in public. I have conflicts, I...that's why I said you would submit a statement. We will get someone to do it on behalf of the Coalition."

"That won't do nothin'. They won't read it. We need to speak out so people hear us, and see someone pushing back. We have to tell them, and loudly." Leitisha's jaw was grinding.

Sitting on the streetcar, exhausted, facing all those people, having to back down. Working and pretending all day, only letting go at night weighed on her. Fighting social pressure to work as a lawyer drained her. She was sweating and chilled at the same time. She felt lightheaded on her empty stomach. And now she had alienated her friend who might lose her club. It broke her heart to think about it.

# CHAPTER 10

Zimpel stood outside Marvin Wright's home. He wasn't bringing news of the death. The newspapers had done that; he hoped someone from the department had come before now. He took a breath and walked up to the door.

"Mrs. Wright?"

"Yes, may I help you?" Behind her was a picture of Jesus over a table full of flowers. She appeared church strong, but he sensed a vulnerability about her. Her eyes were red, although her makeup was perfect.

He introduced himself and showed her his shield. "Do you mind if I ask you a few questions?"

She carefully read the identification, then turned her back on Zimpel, leaving the door open. "Had cops here asking me all kinds of questions. Like how did my husband afford that Cadillac. Not about who might have murdered him."

Zimpel stood very still, knowing that she must have suffered through questions that reflected the same prejudice as the beat cops had exhibited at the site. "I'm sorry."

The wife shrugged and turned around. "You might as well come in." She spoke with defiance tinged with fear.

"I'm sorry for your loss, Mrs. Wright." Zimpel removed his hat and stood in the doorway.

"Thank you."

"I'm an inspector. It's my job to find who killed your husband."

"And those other fellows?"

"I'm sorry if they were rude."

"I'm sorry, too. But I can't do much about that now can I?"

"Was your husband getting pressured to sell his property?" He only knew to just keep doing the work.

She gestured towards the sofa. "Please have a seat, Inspector Zimpel."

She had noticed his name, remembered it, and used his title. He sat down.

The sofa was white leather and spotless.

"What do you know about my husband, Inspector?"

Thursday thought about the young girl with Wright the night he died. "Your husband owned a lot of real estate in the Fillmore. With the Redevelopment Agency wanting to take over that neighborhood, seems to me he might be a target."

She nodded. "There was a barrage of calls, and when he wouldn't sell for the pittance they wanted, they resorted to ugliness."

"What kind of ugliness?"

"The usual kind, Inspector Zimpel. When they assume that you're too stupid to see the money they're flashing at you. The money meant nothing without the neighborhood, without a place to live. They redline us. Where else are we going to buy a house?"

"I understand. I have seen it happen already, renters first, then the businesses. Do you have anything in writing, or remember any names of the people that pressured him?"

She paused a moment and then got up and went into the next room. Thursday heard her searching through papers.

"Here's one letter that he received. I remember it being sent here to the house instead of to his office." She pulled it from the envelope and handed it to him. "It's not nice."

Thursday read the letter. It was a threat, set up like a business offer.

"He received more correspondence like this at his office?"

"More than likely. He was mad they sent it to the house." She glanced at him. "You know what they're doing, don't you?"

"I know. And I suspect that they perceived your husband was in the way."

She nodded to herself. "Any prominence and they move against you if you're a Negro." She stood. "Ok, Inspector, let's see what you can do. I'll get you a key to his office. Maybe you'll find something there."

"You didn't share this with the other officers?"

She moved her shoulders slightly. "They didn't ask about any of this. They would have ignored it or worse, thrown it away."

Someone wanted Wright's property faster than he wanted to sell it. Maybe there were more threats, in writing. The hit was too good, too clean. Too business-like.

She handed him the keys fixed to a leather fob with Wright's initials. "The first key is the door, the second key is the drawer in the desk. That's where you might find something useful."

Wright's office was above Jimbo's. On his way over, he stopped at the Blue Moon. He shook his head at Walter and went straight to the kitchen.

"Sylvia, may I speak with Tildy for a couple minutes?"

Tildy glanced at Zimpel, but kept peeling potatoes at the sink.

"I heard you might know something about Mr. Wright's murder?"

"Oh, no, I don't know anything." She continued to work.

Zimpel exercised patience. He could feel the fear even in folks who knew him. "Maybe you heard something?"

"Some folks," she paused and glanced again at Zimpel then back to her peeling, "might have seen something that night but didn't trust going to the police." She stopped, holding a potato. "They got no reason to believe anyone would listen to them, and then maybe they'd get picked on. Or worse."

Zimpel asked, "What's the best way to figure out who might talk to me?"

"Maybe go to the church near Revere Street and talk to people there, or there was usually a pickup basketball game going on, something like that."

She told him where they played. "You get sitting with folks, and they might feel it's ok to tell you things." This time she caught Zimpel's eye, and he felt her fear, but also some strength to change what she could.

After he searched Wright's office, he'd figure out when to head over there and who to talk to. Needle in a haystack time.

He spent a couple hours going through Wright's desk, a box of papers, an elaborate calendar, seemed the man kept track of everything he did. Thursday carefully went through a stack of correspondence in a drawer on the left, and bingo. Here was the cache he was looking for. Entreaties from developers, pushing for a deal. Some not so polite. At least three different big companies. He decided to take the letters. Maybe some unrequited love here pushed someone to expedite the process.

# CHAPTER 11

## AUGUST 5, 1958 · TUESDAY MORNING

Kay got into the office extra early, hoping to make up for her long lunch the day before. She had just poured a cup of coffee and sat down to work when she heard the click of heels from the hallway.

Irma stood in her doorway. "Mr. Bianco would like to see you as soon as convenient." The last word dripped from her mouth.

"I'll be right down." She grabbed a pad of paper and drafts of the recent documents.

"Kay?" The sharp edge of his voice warned her. "Long lunch yesterday?" Frank's hair was askew.

"Just ran some errands." Damn Irma for keeping track.

"Where is the other agreement for the McCann deal? We need the shareholder agreement."

"I put it on your desk Saturday." Her eyes moved over the desk. "Here." She handed him the document.

"Put it in my In-Box," he pointed, "not on my desk. You need to be more conscientious. You know what a risk I took hiring you."

The same stick he always held over her head.

He shook some papers at her. More was coming.

"I got a call a little while ago, someone asking me why we were at the redevelopment hearings yesterday." He stared at her. "Was that your errand?"

He knew. Murray must have called, that look he gave her at the hearing.

Now she had to take the consequences.

Her intentions and actions had no meaning but what others made of them. Leitisha was mad and Frank was mad, and she only wanted to work hard for each of them.

"I just stopped in to listen."

"You weren't listening at the microphone." He ran his hand through his hair that stayed standing. "You don't seem to understand how precarious your position is. Clients see you associating with . . . those people."

Those people. "I was put on the spot. I didn't go to speak." Stay calm, be the reasonable one. "I was only there for a minute."

"A minute is all it would take for us to lose a client—if someone recognized you, and apparently someone did—I can't afford this, and you certainly can't." He paused, holding up one of the documents. "I'm disappointed. You need to keep your head in the game."

"Well, I didn't know she was going to invite me to the microphone. I had to say something."

"I can't believe you didn't see how they would use you," Frank said.

She hadn't expected Leitisha to do that to her, so he was right there. "They are trying to save their businesses, their neighborhood."

Frank shook his head. "You have to see reality. Those aren't real businesses and that's no way to live. We need to tear out those slums, reduce crime, and modernize our city, like we did at the waterfront. Picture it. A modern boulevard, national department stores, and high-rise business towers. What we need to transform the heart of our town." He gestured widely with his arms.

It wasn't a slum, she had never seen any crime there, and she hated that "modern" ugly freeway that now spanned the waterfront. She didn't correct him.

He stood, handing her some documents. "And in any case if you want a family, you better not wait too long."

"You think I'm here to find a husband?"

"Well, at some point, it's too late." He raised his eyebrows.

In her head, Kay said, "I didn't go to law school to get a husband. I went to law school to be independent and not have to get a husband. I came here to have a career."

Instead she said, "Frank, let me know about the shareholder contract, and I'll get the rest of the documents ready for closing." She turned to leave.

"That's my girl, keep that work flowing."

Frank shouted to her back, "I'm going to the baseball game today. Now that's a sign of the times, having a professional baseball team in San Francisco. You can't hold back progress."

# CHAPTER 12

Distracted, Kay nearly bumped into Brian Giamatti in the hallway. "Oh, excuse me, Brian." How did she get hired here when everyone else was a first- or second-generation Italian man?

"How are you?" His eyes searched her face. Not a passing hello.

"Busy." Something was up. "Working on closing documents for the McCann deal the rest of the week."

"Do you have a minute?"

Kay was wary. Some of the male associates resented her. They felt she was taking a man's job, who needed it to support his family. Others assumed she was looking for a husband and didn't take her seriously. She didn't know which attitude he'd have.

"I overheard you," he looked apologetic, "talking to Frank."

"About the McCann deal?" He eavesdropped on her conversation with Frank?

"About redevelopment."

"What about it?"

Giamatti glanced up and down the hall and lowered his voice. "Look, this is none of my business, but if you want them to get help, call Michael Zorn."

Kay nodded toward the coffee room, not wanting Irma to overhear. "I don't mean to be ungrateful, but why are you helping me?" she asked him once the door was closed.

He was a hard worker, they all were, and dressed well, but otherwise she didn't know much about Giamatti.

"My dad, he's a reporter for the Chronicle."

"I didn't know that."

He glanced at his watch. It was a Rolex. The male associates made more money than she did. "Anyway, there's stuff going on, and if you're going to get mixed up in it . . ."

"I can't get mixed up in it if you were listening. I'll get fired."

"Well, then, refer him to your friends in the Fillmore."

They both glanced over to the door.

"How do you know I have friends in the Fillmore?"

"The guys, they said they heard that you go down and play piano."

The guys talked about her? The notion made her cringe. "I do, but I gather they don't approve."

"Ah, they don't know anything." His eyes softened. She noticed they were brown.

"So, you get a cut of the referral or something?" Why would he refer someone?

"No, I just know from my dad that Zorn's the guy. He's one of the few attorneys in San Francisco who knows about eminent domain and isn't in the pocket of Redevelopment." Brian paused. "He's a trust fund baby, so bribes mean nothing."

"What bribes?" She hadn't considered bribes.

"My dad's finding some graft, and is getting pressure not to report."

Her mind went back to the men exchanging documents during the hearing. "Who's pressuring him?"

"Sort of everyone." His voice became quieter. "The editor is avoiding the story, Dad's had threatening letters, and someone's been calling and hanging up. Be careful if you start asking questions."

"Is that why we're whispering?"

"And the fact that it's not good for our jobs, as you found out." He reached out and touched her arm, sliding his hand from her elbow to her hand. "You need someone to watch out for you."

She stepped out of his reach. This was his intention.

"Hey, you don't have to be like that." He touched her again. "You're smart, and pretty. Maybe go out sometime?"

His question was impossible. "I'm not sure it's a great idea to date people you work with."

"Sure it is." He gave her a big smile. "You won't be here forever."

She smiled but wanted to spit for getting taken into his confidence only to have him play the dating card. "Thanks for the information." And for letting me know what your price was.

That whole interaction was odd, his overhearing her, his fear, which was real, and then his clear motivation for getting her ear. She'd have to avoid him now.

He had suggested hiring a lawyer not open to bribes. Bribes.

At least he gave her concrete advice, assuming it was true. She wanted to get Leitisha a good lawyer and get back in her good graces.

She started in on the next contract. Frank said she was there to get a husband. The associates were trying to date her. She looked at the clock. She had a dinner at her parents' house tonight for her brother's birthday. She loved her family, but it was going to be more of the same pressure.

She walked into her parents' house without knocking and was met with the smell of her father's pipe and her mother's meatloaf. She hadn't yet hung up her coat or said hello when her father spoke to her from behind his newspaper. "Says here you were at some redevelopment hearing for the colored woman that owns that club."

She got in the newspaper? Frank will be very unforgiving.

"I had only gone to listen." She hated apologizing for getting trapped.

"Are you representing that woman? I can't see your law firm…" The tone of his voice told her he hoped that she wasn't.

"Well, good evening to you, Daddy. Nice to see you. So glad I came to dinner."

"Now, you don't need to get sarcastic. I'm looking out for your interests, since it seems you're not doing such a good job of it."

Kay counted to three and shook her head. "She's not my client, she's my friend and wanted me to act for her coalition and I explained I had a conflict. She's hiring another lawyer." As she said that, she decided to call the lawyer Giamatti had mentioned.

"What you're doing with a 'friend' like her, and her coalition, can't be a good place for a young woman. You see what they say, these are slums and full of crime and who knows what." He snapped the paper for emphasis, still holding it front of his face.

She pictured the sax player. "You mean for a young, white woman. It is very respectable, you should come down. Everyone there is dressed up. Like going to church."

"Well, yes, that's exactly what I mean. That's a nice club for colored people with their music, but it's not a good place for you to hang out." Now her father had the paper folded down, and he met her eyes over the fold.

She stood her ground, but her stomach tightened. "I'm a musician, and I play jazz. Look at Marian McPartlin."

"Who?" He had flipped the paper back and was reading again. He had made his point, and engagement was over.

"Never mind." Kay followed her nose to the kitchen where her mother was throwing butter into steamy potatoes and mashing them with the electric hand mixer, trying to keep the cord out of the bowl.

"Here, let me help," said Kay taking the mixer from her.

"Thanks honey." Her mother leaned over to kiss her on the cheek. There was a chocolate cake on the sideboard, her brother's favorite.

A meatloaf rested on the stove, bacon strips across the top, cooling. Her mother carefully loosened it from the pan and slid it onto a platter, then set it on the table.

"Kevin, come down here and wash your hands, then get the milk out of the Frigidaire." She turned back to the stove, "and Kay, please put napkins on and the salt and pepper." Kay pulled the salt and pepper shakers out of the cupboard and folded paper napkins at each place.

"Dear, we're nearly ready, will you come and cut the meatloaf?" Her mother called out to her dad, and then put the rest of the meal on the table.

Her father sliced the meatloaf into thick slices. Before they ate, her mother held her hands in prayer and said grace.

"You know, you went to law school, you were supposed to find a husband. It was the perfect place; you weren't supposed to be a lawyer." Her mother passed the meatloaf, then the mashed potatoes and carrots and peas.

"I like being a lawyer and I'm good at it." What might her mother have done if she'd had a career?

"Of course. You are smart. But what are you going to do about a family?"

"I have a family. I have all of you." Kay smiled but didn't feel it.

"Pass the mashed potatoes, Kevin, and eat some vegetables."

Kevin wrinkled his nose at the peas and carrots, and passed them back to his sister.

"And your father is right. You need to stop going down to that club. It's not a place where you'll find anyone suitable to date, much less marry."

Kevin snorted under his breath and took another spoonful of mashed potatoes. Kay kicked him under the table. She wished the milk was whiskey.

"I want to play music. No, not just music, I want to play jazz. And the only place I can do that is in the Fillmore."

The dinner tableau stopped, silence draping them like heavy curtains as her parents stared at her, not saying anything. Kay swallowed. Her brother continued to eat.

"I don't want you to be disappointed in me, and I don't go that often," she filled silence by backtracking.

"Oh, honey," her mother said. "We aren't disappointed in you at all, we want the best for you. I don't want you to wake up one day and realize that you should have had a family." She was half joking, but half not.

Time to take this in another direction. "Kevin, what did you get for your birthday?"

His eyes lit up. "A 45 record player!"

She smiled, handing him her gift, three 45s, two Elvis and a Miles Davis she'd snuck in. He was crazy for Elvis.

What a turbulent time they lived in. Her father had avoided the worst parts of the recession and Joe McCarthy had thankfully died the year before, ceasing to haunt people with false conspiracies and lies. But this tearing down of the Fillmore in the name of urban renewal was troubling. Kay surveyed the dinner table. Normal life goes on, even when the world is unsettled and in turmoil.

# CHAPTER 13

Kay wanted Leitisha to hire a real eminent domain lawyer. Someone who could be a champion for her. She'd go in after work, suggest this Zorn guy, and make peace with her.

Before Kay reached the bar, she felt it. Leitisha caught her from across the room, then glanced away, talking to a customer. Randy Weston was on the piano and Walter glanced up but didn't set out her drink.

Kay shivered, wrapped her arms around herself. She wanted a whiskey. "Walter?"

She followed Walter's gaze to Leitisha, who took her time coming over to the bar, stopping to chat, or laugh with patrons at the tables, gesture to one of the waiters to bring something, patting someone on the shoulder. Her smile dropped when she got to Kay.

"Is something wrong?" Everything was wrong.

"Is something wrong." Leitisha said. "You embarrass me in front of our entire coalition and in front of the Board of Supervisors. You don't even try to defend us. Why did you even speak into that microphone?"

Kay's heart beat hard, her stomach roiled. Leitisha set her up, and now she was blaming her that she was unprepared. Leitisha was saying it was her fault. "But I wasn't prepared, you didn't tell me . . ."

"What did you think?"

"But I told you, I am unable to speak publicly on behalf of the coalition, I have a conflict."

"Then maybe you need to think about that conflict. Maybe you need to think about why you come here week after week, play music and have a grand old time, but we're here fighting for our lives."

She had assured Father Michael in confession she maintained her balance. But it wasn't ever equal, her two lives. Her job came first because of the money. She needed the money to be independent. Without it she wouldn't be able to come to the Blue Moon and play music. Being on her own was everything; not having to be taken care of by anyone else was her freedom.

"Leitisha, I think the world of you and this club, and what you've done. And . . .," Kay's eyes touched on Walter, the musicians.

"I don't know what you do during the day, but this is our work, this is what we do, who we are, and where we live. And it doesn't matter how hard we build it up, those white men, they come and take whatever they want." Leitisha's arms were taut, her jaw set.

"That's what I wanted to talk to you about. To hire a lawyer who knows eminent domain."

Edward, one of the waiters, brought Leitisha a check. She read it, saw who it was from, and nodded, her body relaxed now. "Yeah, you can put it on his tab. He's slow, but he's good for it."

Leitisha turned back to Kay. "I'm not hiring any more lawyers, they take my money and do no good." She shrugged. "Like you."

Kay wondered what she cost Leitisha.

"Not sure you should be playing music here, when you got so many other places you can go. We can't go anywhere but the Fillmore. We can't stay anywhere else. And now we can't even live here."

Kay nodded. First work, and now this. It made her sick.

"Before you play here again, you need to think about all that, and think about what you want to do. We don't need you here using us up without helping us out."

# CHAPTER 14
## AUGUST 7, 1958 · THURSDAY

"Bless me father for I have sinned . . ."

"Go on."

Father Malone's black cassock and profile blurred through the confessional's opaque screen. He always recognized her voice, making her self-conscious. Confessions were heard on Thursdays.

"Father, I've come to confession because I'm burdened. I may have endangered my job, and upset my parents."

Father Michael Malone, as her priest, was aware of her double life and forbidden to speak of it outside the confessional. His Irish accent made him sound less judgmental. Her own grandfather had come from County Cork in Ireland, but she didn't remember him.

"I lied to my parents," she paused "several times this month, and to my boss."

Father Malone sighed audibly.

"And I was a bad person."

"Deceit 'tis a bad sin, because it leads to other harms. But a bad person? The sin doesn't make the person bad." He paused, "Is this about your going to ta' jazz clubs again?"

"Yes Father." She squirmed on her knees.

"Ya half one life you live during the day, and another at night. Ya been saying you can balance them, but you're not always in control. Your work will be too much, or your friends at the Club see you being careful about your other half, and tire of your halfhearted friendship."

He was right. It irked her. She was unfairly blamed by Leitisha for not being effective at the hearing. She never thought of it as halfhearted. Maybe he had something there.

"Why don't ya take your family's advice, and settle down—you've a good education, find a nice husband . . ."

And sometimes the wisdom was lacking. "Father Malone, no disrespect, but why did you become a priest?" Kay understood religious fervor. She didn't understand how a man, like Michael Malone, handsome, smart, could never have sex his entire life? She couldn't ask him that of course. But didn't that make him crazy? Her mind drifted to the Black sax player and she quickly pulled it back. Not in church.

"'Twas a calling, a calling from God," the priest said. Good thing he was unable to read her mind.

"Well, it's the same with my music. It's my gift from God and it would be a sin to waste it."

The priest responded quickly. "But it's not safe for you."

"Just because Negroes live in the Fillmore doesn't make it unsafe. It is completely safe. I love it there. I have friends, you should come."

He paused. "Not a complete stranger to the Fillmore as I've come down to ta' churches there. And the people are quite nice."

"You should minister to everyone." She'd get him to come down, get another person on their side. "You really should come hear me play."

"You're right. Let me know next time you play, I'll come."

"Deal." If he came and approved, maybe her parents would come. If her priest and her parents thought it was all right, and didn't believe the Fillmore was a slum, and needed to be torn down, others would agree. If Leitisha ever let her play again. "Is that my penance?"

"That, and 10 Hail Mary's, one Our Father and ask ta good Lord to forgive you for continuing ta deceive your parents and your boss. You should sit down and talk with them seriously about your life. They have their wisdom to impart and it can't hurt ya to listen to it. Lying to others, you're also lying to yourself, and it cheats you. Work on being honest, startin' wid yourself.

Bless you and go in peace, in the name of ta' Fader, ta' Son and Holy Ghost."

As she knelt at the communion rail in the beautiful old church, light floating through the stained glass saying her prayers, she should be thinking about her parents and her job and God's forgiveness. But it was Leitisha's forgiveness that was on her mind, to let her back on that stage.

# CHAPTER 15

AUGUST 8, 1958 · FRIDAY AFTERNOON

Anxiety rose as heartburn when Walter saw the small, white man with a black briefcase open the door to the Blue Moon. Dressed in a suit and a tie tied too tight, he had to be some government type, not a customer. Walter went back into the kitchen, where Miss Leitisha was reviewing preparations for dinner. Leitisha was demonstrating to Tildy how to fold napkins.

Walter cleared his throat and stood still. "What do you want Walter?" asked Leitisha not turning from her folding and pointed, staring at Tildy, who looked like she was going to cry.

"Miss Leitisha, a gentleman just came in . . ."

"Yes, yes, get on with it."

"A white gentleman," he said slowly.

"We serve Black and white, Indian or Chinese, doesn't matter in here Walter. Go serve him up a drink."

"Miss Leitisha, I think he's some sort of inspector, I have a bad feeling about him."

"Nonsense, Walter. In any case, we haven't done anything wrong, all of our permits are in order, there's no cockroaches, no nothing. We're ship shape here."

Leitisha stirred and tasted the gravy ("more pepper and cook that up, tastes like paste"). Walter stood another minute and went back to the bar.

While he was gone, two more white men, one short with a pencil mustache and the other with some heft, came in with a boy. Three white men and a boy in the club this early, none of them were customers that would come here for a drink. Walter did not want these white men in his bar.

"Hey, what do have to do to get a drink around here?" The mustached man's head swiveled around. He sat awkwardly at the table, trying to look nonchalant. He put his cigarettes on the table.

"Very sorry sir," said Walter, putting bar napkins out. "What'll y'have?"

The man turned around and looked at his companions. "We'll have two beers," he said pointing at the tap, "and a Coca Cola."

Walter drew the beers slowly, his stomach in a knot. He poured the cola into a glass with a little ice. He shook off memories from Arkansas, and finished topping off the beers. He took the man's money, gave him change. No tip. A bad sign right there.

Walter turned back to setting up for the busy evening, keeping an eye on the men. He saw one of the men push a beer in front of the kid. Walter set the glass and towel down, and began to walk over to ask for identification. The young man was clearly too young.

Before he got there, the white man with the briefcase got up, laid a citation on the bar already filled out and announced, "This bar is closed until further notice. You have violated the ABC laws and we are pulling your liquor license."

Walter's heart sank. "Sir, sir," he stammered.

The old fear appeared again, unbidden. He had a new book bag for school, and white kids surrounded him. He knew they were going to take it. Fighting them could get him killed. He had that same feeling now.

"You have served someone who is clearly underage, which violates the terms of your ABC license and it is being revoked immediately." The little man stared at Walter like he was a bug.

Walter knew better than to argue with a white man. "You'll have to speak to the owner, Sir, please wait a minute." Walter went to the kitchen in a hurry. "Miss Leitisha, please come."

"Walter, what is it? We are getting dinner."

"He yanked your liquor license for serving . . ."

"What did you do?"

"Nothing, I did nothing. I served a man at the bar. He then . . ."

"Never mind." Leitisha wiped her hands and marched into the bar area.

"I'm Leitisha Boone, the owner. What is the . . ."

"Lady, your establishment is now closed." The man was standing in the door. "You were serving an underage person, and your license has now been suspended."

"Sir, please tell me your name."

He squinted a moment and then spoke. "My name is Richard Doermann, and I'm an agent for the California Alcohol Control Board, and I have suspended your license to serve liquor." The man was barely taller than Leitisha. He straightened his hat.

"Excuse me, who did we serve?"

The two men and the young man had left. Walter was beside himself. "They were sitting right there, the man with the mustache ordered a beer for himself and the other man, not for the kid, they ordered a cola for the kid. I would have asked him for identification."

"I beg to differ. You served . . ."

Walter was not used to raising his voice, especially to a white man, but this was too much. "Sir, you are mistaken."

"Boy, I am not mistaken."

Walter stiffened. The word "boy" brought fear and a flood of bad memories. This was 1958 not 1938 but Walter felt himself getting smaller.

"You dare to accuse my bartender of serving someone underage and they ain't even here? This is nothing short of harassment." Miss Leitisha did not harbor past fears, or if she did, she fought through them. "I will have my lawyer contact your office."

"Lady, you are closed. No getting it back. This is the end."

"First of all, I get due process, and this isn't it." Miss Leitisha followed the man out. "Just because we don't have a liquor license doesn't mean we closed. I got food and I got music. You been paid to do this, I know it."

Her words stabbed at his back as he hurried out the door. "Well, you're not going to win, you're not."

"Miss Leitisha . . ." Walter said.

Finally, she took a deep breath, smoothed her already perfect hair, straightened her dress and followed Walter back into the club. In a calm voice, she turned to him.

"What happened here?"

Walter grabbed his dish towel. "That was the man, the white man I told you about in the kitchen." He grabbed a glass to polish. "I knew it was going to get bad ever since that redevelopment project came in 1956, it was bad and getting worse." He told her what happened with the two men, with the young man.

She shook her head. "This was a set up. They is after me." She smiled. "That's good."

Walter gave her a look. "How?"

"Means we are getting to them. We are strong." She turned to Walter and gave him a hug. "We'll get through this, don't you worry."

"Are you gonna call Miss Kay?" They needed some help fighting these white folks.

"No I'm not. She's not the only lawyer and she doesn't want to get involved. We'll take care of this."

Walter said, "I'll go make a sign, so people will know." He appreciated Miss Leitisha's strength, but he still felt bad. They'd spent a lot of time rolling that rock uphill and he felt that it was coming back down, and fast.

# CHAPTER 16

## AUGUST 8, 1958

Zimpel turned off the baseball game and surveyed the neighborhood. He was alone as usual.

The lieutenant made it clear to him. "Zimpel, you spend all that time in the Fillmore hanging out with colored folks. The other inspectors don't want to hang out in those neighborhoods and don't believe they can get information that way. So you're on your own."

So be it.

These neighborhoods, like Butchertown, thrived with local information and news in the barber shops or small groceries where one might get a tall boy or some milk, maybe on credit.

His eyes grazed over the site where Wright had been murdered. All that was left was some remnants of the tape where they had roped off the scene. Zimpel scanned the porches, windows and streets around the murder scene to understand the vantage points. Someone saw what went down, but who?

He remembered seeing lights on the porch of the apartment building next to the scene, people milling about. Someone had seen something.

Zimpel heard yelling, the sound of a ball bouncing and walked around the corner. As Tildy had described, there was a pickup game being played hard on a half court behind a cyclone fence. He watched for a minute.

Five tall guys, four in baggy shorts, one in long sweats, all with short hair, sneakers, playing three on two, laughing, giving each other jibes. One of the two taunting, "We can take you three, we that good."

Zimpel stood outside the fence and watched. They glanced in his direction, letting him know they saw him, but kept playing, and kept up the talk among themselves. "You drink too much last night, Tyrone? You movin' awful slow."

"What you say." The man called Tyrone did a neat layup. "See you do that bro. Fo' sure, we gonna beat you both."

"Not bad for playin' in the heat," said a third man, making a pointed look at Zimpel.

"Mm, hmm." The man in the long sweats nodded, and glanced at Zimpel as he passed the ball. Zimpel nodded at him and kept watching, now standing at the entrance to the playground.

The ball came in his direction and Zimpel grabbed it. All action stopped on the playground, five pairs of eyes staring at him. Nothing but the wind moved for a few seconds, sweat glistening on the foreheads of the young men. It registered who Zimpel likely was, a white man in their playground, their neighborhood on a Friday. Had to be a cop.

Zimpel tossed the ball back hard to the man in the long sweats and took off his jacket, dropping it out of the way. "I know you're playing fine two on three, but I think I need to even it up." He stepped out into the court. The men continued to stare at him, unbelieving.

"You playing?" said the young man named Tyrone. "You gonna keep up with us, white man?"

"Nah," said Zimpel, noticing they slipped their language a little, code-switching. "You gonna show me how's it done, right? Come on."

Reluctant at first, they started throwing the ball around. The sweat, the banter, Zimpel's leather shoes and their teasing melded into a hard played game, filled with the sound of the ball hitting the rim, laughter, breathing, scuffing and the bouncing ball.

"Oh, lookatchoo, the heat's getting hot."

They laughed at their joke. After sinking a final basket, Zimpel leaned over breathing hard, his hands on his knees.

"We take your breath away old man?"

"Oh yeah, you're not sweating, right?" Their language changed again, talking directly to him. He straightened up, went to get his jacket, and then turned back to them. "You already know I'm a cop."

They all looked at each other and then at him. The tallest guy with the long sweats, Willie but they called him "string bean" or just Bean, nodded. "Yeah, we knew. Old white guys rarely come down here for pickup b-ball."

"Maybe I should do it more, do me good." His breathing was finally beginning to even out. "I'm an inspector with SFPD."

"Oooh, an inspector," said Tyrone.

"Dry up." Willie shot him a glance. "You here because that swanky man, Mr. Wright, got knocked off the other night?"

Zimpel nodded.

"They really care if a nigga got killed in his own 'hood?" It was the youngest of them, with lighter skin, a little shorter than the rest, but the fastest of them on the playground. They called him Shrimp, which didn't seem fair.

"I care." Zimpel shrugged. His shirt was damp and stuck to him. "It's my case, and I want to close it. Someone must have seen something. I was here that night. There were lights on all around. Folks watching from the porch." Zimpel turned his head particularly in the direction of the apartment house.

The young men looked at each other. Tyrone bounced the ball in front of him.

"I gotta get home. My opinion, colored man that rich—the man not going to stand for it, gotta take him down." He shrugged. "Later."

They said goodbye, and the others started to leave. Willie stayed put.

"I didn't see anything, but I heard some things."

"Hearing things can be helpful." Zimpel bent to tie his shoe, moving slowly, happy to stand there all day to get some gem.

"I heard that he was with a quiff with a classy chassis, and she got away."

"Anybody know who she is?" Zimpel's theory involving the lipstick and the chewing gum was solid, especially since she was also seen in the Blue

Moon. "She from here?" From Leitisha's description, she had to be local.

Willie shook his head. "Might."

"Anyone see her run away?"

Willie shrugged.

"Maybe someone you heard it from might know."

"Might." Willie stood there.

"I'm willing to listen, they want to talk to me." Zimpel handed him a business card and Willie checked it out, then put it in his pocket.

"I guess you do, Inspector Zimpel," said Willie. He smiled and put his hand out, and Zimpel shook it firmly.

"Come by anytime inspector, but get rid of the shoes. The slipping and sliding isn't helping your game." He nodded, and then walked down the hill.

Zimpel pursed his lips and tilted his head. He was a kid during the depression, lived in a neighborhood in New Orleans where no one had much money. They lived near a large Negro family. Zimpel played basketball with Andrew, a boy his age, out in their driveway. They didn't go to the same school, couldn't even get a soda at the same hamburger joint. Different worlds overlapping over a basketball, sweat, and adolescent boy stuff. Zimpel learned about life over those pick-up games.

Exercise and information. Been a good day. He needed to find out who the girl with Wright was. And what else they saw. Maybe Willie will convince his source to come and talk to him, now that he trusted him.

He needed a beer.

Zimpel pulled his car up near the Blue Moon. As he approached, he saw a handwritten sign on the window: "No liquor served until further notice." What was that about? Leitisha wasn't one for temperance.

# CHAPTER 17

The bar was empty, and only a few people sat at tables, eating. The bandstand was empty. It was early, but this was Friday afternoon, and the musicians should be warming up the happy hour crowd.

Walter carried boxes from the kitchen and set them behind the bar.

Zimpel asked, "What happened?"

"Miss Leitisha got set up by some squirrel at the ABC." Walter shook his head. He rarely said a bad word about anyone.

"When?"

"Earlier today. I saw him come in, and I knew."

Zimpel felt for a cigarette. "Was it a set up?"

"Oh yeah," said Walter. "Clear as day. I watched them do it, but it was like I was invisible. No one's going to listen to me."

"Please tell me everything." Zimpel sat at the bar. Walter handed him a cola, and then told him.

When Walter was done, Zimpel walked back to the kitchen. Leitisha sat at her desk in the corner. With Zimpel at her back, she said, "What do you want, Thursday Zimpel?"

"They are coming after you." He was alarmed for her. This was too much attention. The cops watching the bar and now this?

"I know. I see it. I called Saul. We'll let the lawyers handle it."

Zimpel worried that Saul wouldn't feel the urgency. "It can't stick—it was clearly a set up. Did you ask Kay?"

"She don't want to help me keep the place from redevelopment, she won't want to help with this." The venom surprised Zimpel. She turned to him. "She came in Wednesday night thinking I'd hire another lawyer. I told her to go home and think about how badly she wants to play here."

"You weren't fair, admit it. You conned her into coming to the hearing and then put her on the spot."

"I don't need you telling me what I'm doing Inspector Zimpel. Are you through? Because I have some work to do." She turned back to her desk.

Leitisha held a grudge but this one might hurt her. She needed someone to help her get her license back. He'd ask some questions himself. The agent had the citation filled out in advance, Walter said. And came in on a Friday before the weekend, to do the most damage. Smelled like a set up. Maybe the "squirrel" would be in his office.

The appointees of the newly formed Department of Alcoholic Beverage Control with its constitutional mandate were full of themselves and their power.

Walter had given him the citation, and Zimpel copied down the inspector's name and the names of the witnesses.

He found the guy's office door with "ABC" in big letters and the man's name, Richard Doermann, in smaller gold letters. There was no receptionist. Maybe it was all too new.

As he went to knock on the door, a young man in a suit exited the office, his hat down low, and brushed by him. The guy looked vaguely familiar and he filed the face away to think about later.

The slight man that Walter described sat at a desk in this tiny office, barely room for the desk, file cabinet and guest chair. His desk was immaculately ordered, papers neatly stacked, pencils sharpened upright in a glass container, desk blotter cleared.

"Can I help you?" The man squeezed his eyes when he blinked.

This neatnik would only be impressed with power bigger than his. Zimpel took out his police identification and shoved it under the little man's nose. "Inspector Zimpel."

"What's this about?"

"I'm doing an investigation. I heard you shut down the Blue Moon this afternoon."

"My job is to strictly enforce the laws of the Department of Alcohol Beverage Control, including and most especially underage drinking. I am in law enforcement, same as you."

Zimpel felt no kin to this man. "I have a witness that says you set up the Club, that the kid was never served any liquor. That your shills fed it to him. The shills whose names were on your form before you even entered the restaurant." Zimpel leaned over the agent's desk, making himself big like a predator.

"All I know is that an underage person was drinking in that establishment. And your witness is biased, and a Negro besides. No one will take his word over mine."

"I will." Zimpel kept leaning over the desk while the man, his hands on the desk, backed away.

"It will make no difference. We will have a hearing, the license will be permanently revoked, and that club will close."

"And redevelopment will take possession, cheap like. So, who's paying you off? Was that who just left your office? Giving you the payoff?" Big money was greasing the wheels of redevelopment, and no one was going to speak out about it. He would have to.

"I resent that statement officer."

"Inspector. I'm a homicide inspector." Zimpel meant to be menacing.

The little guy's eyes widened. "I take my job seriously and underage drinking is exactly the kind of violation we need to police if our new department is to maintain credibility."

"Yeah, you do your police job and I'll do mine. Graft is a pretty serious crime, Mr. Doermann, and I got my eye on you. This revocation is BS, and I suggest politely now, that you drop it." Zimpel didn't wait for an answer. He would talk with Saul and make sure there was someone good at the hearing. He pulled the door sharply behind him.

He really needed a drink now.

# CHAPTER 18

Zimpel stood at the corner of Post and Fillmore, holding a sack with a six-pack of beer. The low sun emitted a beautiful yellow light. He was pissed off about the ABC agent, and pissed he couldn't drink at the Blue Moon. He was going to stand there and drink this six-pack until he decided to do something about it.

Obvious that the ABC agent contrived it all. The witnesses had lied, and most likely for some dough. Maybe the witnesses were his way to the truth.

An older man stepped along the sidewalk, his suit pressed and fitted, his hat low over his rheumy eyes, which shifted from a Victorian house with the front wall torn off to Zimpel's bag.

"Looks like it's missing its front teeth, like me." The older man smiled showing his gaps.

The noise of demolition accented his statement. A stairway poised in midair, like a ballerina, hung from a crane. White laborers piled scrap wood and debris onto a long-bed truck with round, front-end fenders. Dust and scraps flew like small fireworks.

Zimpel handed the man a beer from his bag after opening it with a church key from his pocket. The man tipped the beer to him.

"Zimpel, what you doing out here drinking on the street?" A tall, thin man, carrying a barber's white coat over his arm walked over to the two men and shook hands with both men.

"Fenton, you know this man?"

"You need a haircut, Zimpel."

"I'll come by later on. I got something to do." Zimpel ran his hand through his hair. It was getting shaggy.

Fenton laughed. "I cut his hair. This here is a San Francisco police inspector."

The older man's eyes grew wide as he considered Zimpel and the beer in his hand.

"Want a beer, Fenton?"

"Sure, long as y'all looking at the scenery, I'll join you."

Zimpel pulled another beer out of his bag, opened it, and handed it to Fenton.

Zimpel turned to the old man, "Thursday Zimpel. Yeah, it's a shame to tear down all this history, displace all these businesses."

"You're right Mr. Zimpel. Raymond Greer." The older man shook Zimpel's offered hand.

Zimpel didn't correct his title.

Fenton took a swig of the beer and looked at the label. "It's more than a shame, it's the end of the road. I worked in this neighborhood for 17 years and now they tell me, 'Here's a piece of paper, now get out.' What about my goodwill? What about the cost of moving my barber chairs? Nothing." Fenton took another swig of beer. "And where am I gonna go?"

Zimpel turned to Fenton. "You, too?"

"Yeah, big commercial value here on these properties. Have to get rid of us, we in the way."

A large Black woman in a purple dress with a matching hat and gloves approached them. Aubergine. She gave all three of the men a disdainful look.

"Here I am coming from Church, and you men are out here drinking on the Sabbath." She pursed her lips.

Fenton didn't blink. "How you doing Miss Corrine." He gestured towards Zimpel. "Do you know Inspector Zimpel?"

"Sabbath? Saturday afternoon?" asked Zimpel.

"For Seventh Day Adventists," she said nodding. She scrutinized him.

"Are you this police officer?" She showed Zimpel his card.

"Yes, that's me." The card he'd given the basketball player. His police work created this coincidence.

She nodded. Zimpel waited.

"You were playing basketball with my son and his friends earlier today."

Fenton and Mr. Greer gave Zimpel a wide-eyed look.

Zimpel nodded. He was grateful his efforts came through. It was worth the time.

"My name is Corrine Wilson," she held out her gloved hand.

He took her hand and shook it, a light touch. She took a deep breath and looked at the sidewalk, then back up at him. He relaxed his shoulders and resisted offering her a beer. She made it pretty clear she didn't approve of them drinking on the street.

"May I speak with you for a minute?"

Zimpel nodded at the other two gentlemen, who tipped their beers and smiled at him.

After they had walked further towards the corner, she lowered her voice and held her handbag with both her gloved hands.

"You spoke with my son, Willie?"

"Yes, he nearly wore me out." Zimpel smiled.

She smiled back. "I didn't want to talk about it, it scared me."

"I understand."

She nodded. "Willie said you were serious about getting whoever murdered poor Mr. Wright. So if he believes you, so do I." Corrine Wilson shook her head. "They don't much care about the truth."

"I do." He knew she was right and didn't want to give her any bullshit, but he gave her his truth.

That gave her courage. "I wanted to tell someone, but I didn't want to get into any trouble, not with the law and not with the man who had the gun." She gave Zimpel a searching look. "When Willie said you had come by looking for someone to talk about what they saw, well, I took it as God answering my prayers."

"Yes, ma'am." Certainly answering his. Zimpel was grateful either way.

"And here we are, it's God's will that I should find you today."

"Yes, ma'am."

"We . . ." she hesitated again. "We live in the apartment building on Third Street, where, where Mr. Wright was found, you know, in his Cadillac."

The couple on the porch, the woman in rollers, the concerned husband. He calculated how far it was, recalled one streetlight.

"We keeping watch out for the neighborhood," she added. "And we saw that Cadillac pull up with its lights off and park. I don't know what he was doing or that it was Mr. Wright then." She paused again, taking a breath.

"And then, after a few minutes or so, we saw another car, a long black limousine." She slowly pronounced LI-MOO-ZINE and made a gesture showing that it was long, her handbag now in the crook of her elbow.

"You don't see those too often in our neighborhood," she nodded at him. "So me and Bill, that's my husband," she stopped as a couple walked by and waited until they had strolled out of hearing. "We watched. We saw a man get out of that limousine . . ." She shut her eyes and made a sign of the cross and said "Blessed Jesus" under her breath.

"I appreciate this. Go on," Zimpel said gently. "What did you see next?"

"I saw a man get out of that limousine, walk over to the Cadillac. A girl ran away, I heard her heels a-clickin'." Corrine made a face.

"Then we heard it, the gun, two times. Sounded like a firecracker. Would have thought it was except we saw the man." She shook her head. "That scared me. I hid then, didn't want nobody looking up and seeing my face staring out at them, no sir." She glanced left, then right.

"Did you see anything distinguishing about the man? Was it a white man that shot him?" Zimpel asked.

"Oh yeah, he was white. All you saw was the color of his face. Too far away to see much else."

"Mustache? Facial hair?"

She shook her head. "Not that I saw from there."

"How was he dressed?" Zimpel resisted taking notes but wanted to ask the questions now. He didn't know if he'd get another chance. She was nervous.

She glanced again before she spoke. "Had on a long black coat, gloves and a nice black fee-dor-a." She touched her head.

"He got out of the passenger side?"

"Yessir. On the right side of the limo, near the Cadillac."

"Then what happened?"

"He got back into that limousine and took off. That's when we, we was the ones that called. There's a telephone in the hallway, we called from that. We didn't want nobody to know it was us." She was nodding at him now, swaying a little, holding her purse so that it banged on her knees. "I am scared of that limousine."

"It's ok. They won't know." At least for now they won't know. "Did you get a look at the girl?"

She shook her head. "It was dark out, I mostly heard her," Corrine touched her own halo of straightened hair. "Too far and too dark out to see her face."

He pointed at the diner on the corner. "Mrs. Wilson, can I buy you a cup of coffee?"

"That's very kind." She smiled. "I need to get home, takes a while on the streetcar."

"Thank you." said Zimpel. "This is really helpful."

God bless you, Officer Zimpel."

Zimpel watched her walk towards the streetcar. He needed to play a few more pick-up games. And, find a white man in a limousine who wanted Marvin Wright dead and let a young Black prostitute run away.

# CHAPTER 19

Fenton and Mr. Greer had left while he was talking to Corrine.

The two witnesses listed in the ABC citation had the same address, a rooming house on Bush Street. Zimpel opened another beer. The account from Corrine Wilson cheered him. He was getting somewhere He was going to have some fun with the ABC guy.

The underage witness wasn't listed on the citation. A way for the lawyers to attack it but he'd leave that to them. He headed for the witnesses' address.

As he entered the rooming house, the top half of a Dutch door with a countertop was open into one of the studio apartments. A sign posted said "Rent Due Every Monday. $7.00." Zimpel poked his head in. A strong smell of sauerkraut and Pine-Sol, and the sound of canned laughter.

A large woman with her hair in a bun and jowls like a basset hound sat in a recliner in front of a television. Zimpel hit the call bell sitting on the counter and she glanced up at him, pausing for the split second it took her to realize he wasn't going to be a customer.

"What d'ya want?" Her motion to stand was intricate. Both hands on the side of the chair, which thumped forward, leaning heavily into her knees and then thrusting herself up with stiff arms, and finally, pulling down on her dress in the back.

He read her the names from the citation. "Do they live here?"

She stood at the counter in the doorway. He saw her hesitate for a second, but she didn't take him on. "Yeah, they are tenants but they ain't so great, you know. They in trouble?"

"Let me ask you something," Zimpel said, putting a $5 bill on the counter. "Anybody come by here asking for someone to help them out, or to see these guys even though they didn't know them?" He was fishing here, but the beer was making it amusing.

The woman closed her fist around the bill. "A little guy in a suit wanted to know if a couple of guys wanted to make some dough. I always want my tenants to earn money, so's they can pay me, and I found a couple of them. Why?" She narrowed her eyes at him. He saw broken veins in her cheeks.

A little guy in a suit sounded like his ABC agent. Zimpel showed his ID. "They were helping out the tax department, and they were witnesses so I wanted to talk with them."

"I'd call up but there's only a phone for the hall. Can I give you the room number?"

"Sure, that'd be swell." He smiled at her so she'd know she was cooperating with the police, something she probably didn't do that often.

"Room 235, second floor, end of the hall on your right."

Zimpel walked up the stairs and found the door. He stood for a moment outside, hearing voices but not what was being said. He knocked on the door.

"Go away."

"Open up. I'm a friend of Mr. Doermann." Zimpel heard "shit" and scraping of a chair. He hoped they didn't go out the fire escape. "I need to talk to you about your witness statements," he said. The door opened a crack. He held up his ID.

"Huh? An Inspector? We didn't kill nobody." A white guy with a pencil mustache and a face that had seen some action held the door open a few inches.

Zimpel smiled. "Because you guys helped out Mr. Doermann, an ABC agent right? I have some questions."

"Uh, yeah, oh yeah. We helped him." Like they were good citizens. The one with the mustache opened the door wider. "He said he was closing down places that allowed underage drinking." He turned back to the second man, black-haired with silver streaks, a creviced face, who was probably strong once but now hunched over a bit, smoking a cigarette. There were beer bottles on the table. They both laughed.

"You guys been in the joint?" They stopped laughing.

"It's ok to tell me 'cause I can find out anyway." Zimpel stood relaxed.

"Whatchoo wanna know for?"

The guy with the mustache must be the brains because he did all the talking.

"You know what perjury is?" The two men stared at him big-eyed. "It's a felony. You do time if you get convicted of perjury. Especially if you've already done time." Mustache-man went for a cigarette.

Zimpel pulled out his notes from the witness statement. He waived the paper in front of them. "You signed your witness statements under penalty of perjury, right?" He put the paper back into his pocket.

They stared at him. Mustache's cigarette smoke made him squint, and then turn away.

"How much did you get paid to do this?" Zimpel kept at them.

The guy sitting at the table slammed his chair forward and mustache gave him a look that hushed him up.

"Look, your landlady already told me that Mr. Doermann came looking for you to do a job for him."

"But it was legit, legit he said. He showed us his ID. It said ABC, big as day."

"Yeah. And what did this guy look like?"

Mustache's eyes went wide. "Like a skinny little preacher in a black suit. He seemed all official and . . ."

"And his name was Doermann, right?"

The two men nodded. The man at the table still didn't speak.

"How much did he pay you to go order a beer at the Blue Moon?"

"$25 bucks each. Paid our room for the month and then some."

Someone besides the ABC was paying big money to these low-lifes. "So he told you to set up this club right?"

"No, that's not right, not what the guy said. And the guy," Mustache man now looked to his friend. "Mr. Doermann . . ." The strong, silent man nodded, "said it was all on the up and up."

"Except that he got you to lie, right? You ordered those two beers and handed one to the kid."

Zimpel's last beer was wearing off. These guys were scum. "Who was the kid?"

The guy shrugged his shoulders. "Mr. Doermann brung him. Said put the beer in front of him after you order it, and then we left." He gave big eyes to Zimpel. "We don' wanna go back in the joint. We was just trying to pay our rent."

"Don't leave town, as they say."

Zimpel worked his way back downtown to the ABC office. If the guy is busting people for money, he might still be there. He walked right into the pipsqueak's office, where he was dictating a letter to a cute girl. He had a secretary after all. ABC guy was working hard into the night.

"So you're hiring ex-cons for $25 each to lie for a pretext to close down the Blue Moon? That's how you uphold the Constitution?" Zimpel slung it at him like dung. "These guys were ex-cons and now they're scared—and you should be, too, because perjury and bribery are pretty serious crimes."

Doermann stared at Zimpel. The secretary stood to the side. Zimpel liked having a witness, even it if caused Doermann not to speak.

"And their landlady remembered you, so you can't run them off, and her and so on. I got you." He paused to let it sink it. "If there's no hearing or action to be taken against the Blue Moon, then there'd be no reason to tell anyone about the bribes or the perjury, right?"

Zimpel eyed the secretary and the man, then closed the door solidly behind him. It was good to be a cop.

The victory was only temporary. The change coming was beyond his ability to stop it. A tsunami of urban renewal would sweep away life in the Fillmore.

# CHAPTER 20

Kay held a hand out to push open the lavatory door but she slipped. "Oh, shit." Her right leg wobbled. Her hand went to the door jamb to steady herself and she could hear someone behind the door. The bathroom door opened, and a well-dressed woman studied her from head to foot. Kay avoided the stare and went into the lavatory. She saw herself in the mirror, pale, her makeup worn off. She opened her purse to pull out a lipstick and it dropped on the floor, rolling to the side of the toilet. The tile was dingy stained, and the floor hadn't been swept in a week. She picked up the lipstick and put it back in her bag, and went into the stall.

She placed toilet paper on the seat, which kept slipping to the floor.

Screw it, I gotta go. She lifted up her skirt and pulled down her panties and sat heavily. Her stockings were run and ripped, drooping around her ankles. Damn. No wonder that woman gave her the once over.

She struggled to unsnap them from her garter belt, difficult as she had her purse hooked on her elbow, to avoid touching it to the dirty floor. She yanked one off her foot, nearly toppling over. Flats would have been the better choice tonight. And not having so much to drink. Too late for that.

Zimpel opened the Frigidaire and stared at the empty shelves. He should learn to cook. He got in the car and automatically drove to the Blue Moon. He didn't go in.

Instead, he made his way over to 1836 Fillmore, to the Texas Playhouse, where Wesley Johnson, Sr. was the proprietor, and had $3,500 in silver dollars embedded into the bar.

"Hey Wesley, how's it going?" Zimpel greeted the owner as he made his way to the bar.

"All good. Busy or not, better to have a good time than make money."

"Ha, if you say so. You seen William Frazier tonight? Looking for him."

Wesley rubbed his chin a minute. "Zeke, you see Frazier tonight?"

"Ain't a big place, Mr. Zimpel. Look up. He be sitting over there talking to Miss DeSanto."

Frazier sat with his chair tilted back, a whiskey and beer in front of him. Zimpel was tall enough, but Frazier had a full head on him, was strongly built, and wanted to be an inspector. He worked harder than most but being Black, he wasn't eligible for promotion.

"Frazier." Zimpel said it low after walking over from the bar.

"Zimpel. Whatchu doing here? You know Miss De Santo?"

"Nice to meet you." He nodded at her and turned back to Frazier. "Wanted to talk to you about community policing."

Frazier laughed with no light in his eyes. "I appreciate you, Zimpel, but I don't need you feeling sorry for me. It is what it is. They loves Willie Mays in this town but he still can't stay at the Fairmont."

Zimpel glanced from DeSanto to Frazier. "I need information on the Marvin Wright murder."

"Ah, come on. Miss Boone done him, right?" He laughed again.

"Where d'you hear that?"

"Station talk."

Zimpel cursed his lieutenant and those patrol cops.

"She didn't kill anybody."

"Ooh. You got some skin in that game?" Frazier's eyebrows went up.

Zimpel drank his beer.

"They gonna pin it on her anyway, don't matter."

"Not if we solve it. You want to be an inspector. I need your help." Zimpel ignored Frazier's nonchalance or what it covered up. Frazier knew folks and worked at being useful.

"Not the time, Zimpel. I need to pay attention to a pretty lady." He gave DeSanto a wide, toothy grin. "Let's talk tomorrow, when the whiskey isn't talking for me." He drained his glass, still making eye contact with Miss DeSanto.

Zimpel turned to go and stopped when he heard a familiar voice.

"I'm supposed to be a lawyer, to know what to do, but I don't." Kay walked unsteadily up to the bar.

Zimpel noticed her legs were bare when she leaned heavily into the bar. She held her liquor like a man. He'd never seen her wilted like this.

"Kay, lemme give you a ride home."

She swayed slightly and shook her head. "Thursday, hello. Going to go over to Bop City and get in on the late-night jam. I gotta play."

"What are you doing here? Why aren't you at the Blue Moon?"

She shook her head. "Not since I embarrassed myself in front of a microphone, pissed off my boss and Leitisha, too." Her eyes were half shut, one hand on the bar, the other holding her glass of whiskey.

Leitisha's revenge for Kay not doing what she wanted ended up like this. Zimpel didn't see any good outcome from her going over to Jimbo's right now. No stockings, half drunk or worse, they'd give her the eye for sure. Or taking a cab so late at night.

"I'll come watch for a bit, need to go over there anyway," which wasn't true, but she wouldn't agree to let him take him take her otherwise.

"Great, it'll be fun," she said, holding her whiskey, "This tastes good."

Zimpel smiled sadly at her and they clinked glasses.

Frazier came up to the bar. "Your girl's not doing too good." Zimpel hoped she didn't hear.

"Yeah, not my girl, but going to keep an eye on her for a minute anyway." Frazier nodded at Zeke for another drink.

"I might could talk to a few folks. Whatcha looking for?" Frazier said, now serious.

Zimpel glanced at Kay who was still nursing her drink, and followed Frazier back to his table, glad Frazier was game.

"In particular," Zimpel stopped talking, glancing at Miss DeSanto. He didn't want anyone overhearing this.

DeSanto got up and smoothed down her dress. "Have a seat, I need to go powder my nose. Don't go away, honey?"

"Not to worry," said Frazier.

As much as he liked women, Frazier liked the quest, he liked being a cop. Zimpel counted on that and he sat down. "I'm looking for a young quiff—and I don't want anyone else looking for her," Zimpel said in a low voice.

Zeke came out from around the bar and brought him an Anchor Steam.

"You're a good man, Zeke.

"You alright yo'self, but you still gotta pay for it." Zeke laughed.

"Yeah, yeah." Zimpel put money on the tray and Zeke left. Zimpel pulled out his cigarettes, offered one to Frazier who shook his head.

"I'm serious I don't want this getting around. A young—like very young—prostitute was with Wright when he was shot. So she either set him up, or for some reason, they let her live."

"Who's they?" Frazier asked.

"A limo was seen pulling up to Wright's car while he was getting a blow job."

"A limo."

Zimpel saw the lights come on. "Yeah. White man in an overcoat and black Fedora, shoots Wright, gets back in and the limo leaves."

"Who saw this go down?"

Zimpel took another swig of his beer and made eye contact with Frazier.

"You already getting Black folk to talk to you. What do you need me for?" He drained his glass.

"They heard the girl run away. Heard her heels 'a-clickin.'" Zimpel paused, enticing Frazier back to the hunt again.

"We have any details on her?"

Zimpel took out an envelope, and then pulled out a piece of paper with a smear of pink. "She favors this lip color."

Frazier stared at the paper for a minute, then a slow smile lifted his face. "How you knew it was a blow job." It wasn't a question. Zimpel saw they were on the same wavelength.

Frazier rubbed his chin. Zimpel stubbed his cigarette out. Frazier glanced up at him and smiled. "They wanted her dead, she'd be dead. Someone owns her. Has to be it."

"She wasn't paid off?"

"They going to trust her out there with money? That's a weakness. Nah." Frazier sipped his beer. "Means someone controls her. She's not on her own, but part of a crew. They can off her whenever," Frazier nodded. "I might know where. I'll get back to you, but now I need to get back to something else." His lips curved up even more as he spotted Sugar Pie again. "Let's talk tomorrow." He nodded over at Kay, who had put her coat on and was headed for the door. "You got your hands full now."

Zimpel heard him laugh as he grabbed Kay's purse hanging on her chair and followed her out.

# CHAPTER 21

"Come on, Kay, let me take you home." His concern went beyond her bare legs and disheveled look. She stumbled exiting the Texas Playhouse.

"No, no, I'm fine." She stood as if to prove it. "I'm going in. I have to play."

He stepped to the curbside and gave her his arm. He wondered if he should get the car. She leaned heavily on him and her breast grazed his hand. Supporting her, they made it to Jimbo's.

Stubborn. Her most consistent trait. An attractive woman who exuded confidence, both as a working female lawyer and an accomplished jazz player. Not tonight. Something had ahold of her tonight. He wasn't going to leave her alone.

When he came back from the lavatory, Kay's coat draped over a chair in the back and her purse on the seat showed her path to the piano. She was already talking with Frederico to get on stage.

Jimbo's didn't serve beer so he asked Althea for the stash. She found some Anchor Steam for him. He left a dollar, enough for half a six pack, to recognize her thoughtfulness. He'd watch and hope it wasn't a disaster.

Folks were still coming into the crowded room, with the music playing over the murmur of conversation.

A couple of musicians from Duke Ellington's band were causing a buzz, although there was always a buzz going on in Bop City, where new music bubbled out of these late-night jams. Charlie Parker, Max Roach, Miles

Davis, you never knew who was going to be there.

"You know your way around here," said a young man holding a saxophone, nodding at Zimpel getting another Anchor Steam from Althea.

"Yeah." Zimpel realized what the man meant was that even though he was white, he knew how to get a beer in Jimbo's. He drank the beer and balanced on the edge of the chair, careful with the purse.

"She's going to get the cymbal thrown at her tonight," said the young man, describing the drummer's proclivity of tossing a cymbal at a below par musician to get them off the stage.

"I hope not," said Zimpel.

He watched, ready to get her out of there if he had to. Kay drank plenty and performed anyway. Tonight she was more desolate than drunk. Twice she took her hands off the keys, having lost her place.

The young man shrugged. "Some nights you're on, others? This place, it's a classroom, a conservatory, a performance room all at one. You learn behavior, like your friend, she's not going to do too good tonight." He nodded to the side. "John Lewis was playing earlier. He'll probably go back up."

"Ah, Modern Jazz Quartet."

The young man was impressed. "You're hip." He nodded at John Lewis again. "He got them to hold a jazz festival in Monterey, he and Dave Brubeck. We'll see how it goes, got a good line up. Billie Holiday and Gerry Mulligan."

Kay was determined to play, her hands ached to jump, she felt it in her gut.

She tripped pulling out the piano bench. She was swaying on the seas, the room falling. The band gave her maybe ten seconds to sit and broke into "A Train," a relatively new tune that Strayhorn wrote and Ellington played.

She loved Billy Strayhorn but for her life, she mixed up the key the band was playing it in. She glanced up to catch someone's eye, but no one responded.

Kay took a breath and got into the melody. She was sloppy.

Tonight her hands were listening to someone else, and not her brain. When it came her time, she froze and botched her solo. The others came in on top of it. Disconnected. No bond between her and the players.

I can't do this. I can't play anymore.

Frederico shook his head at the end of the number. Zimpel stood up. The drummer threw his cymbal, and it crashed on the floor.

She wanted ten more drinks. This was it, she was washed up. If she wasn't capable of performing at Bop City, she was out of the running. She'd never play Blue Moon again.

She came down from the stage in a graceless state, and made her way over to Zimpel.

"Are you ready to go now?"

"I was awful Thursday; I can't play anymore." Her voice was tired, drawn.

"You can't play tonight, Kay. Come on, the car is close." He carried her purse and jacket.

# CHAPTER 22

When Kay first got the nerve up to play at Jimbo's Bob City, she was ready, sharp, and had that pitted out feeling in her stomach, excited and scared at the same time.

She had started playing piano before she learned to run. The sound fascinated her, and her parents never tired of telling how she'd sat at the family upright piano for hours, making them crazy as she sounded out songs. Her mother got her piano lessons but soon understood that Kay was more Errol Garner than Chopin. Her parents listened to Big Band music and Kay ate it up.

She started hanging around Jimbo's Bop City while she was in law school. Musicians from all over came to jam at Jimbo's after hours. Negros weren't allowed to stay in downtown hotels, or eat in the fancy restaurants, so when they finished playing at the Fairmont or even the Black Hawk, performers like Duke Ellington and Dinah Washington would stay at the Booker T. Washington in the Fillmore, and show up for a late supper and jam session.

No one there questioned her hanging out and listening to the afterhours jam. Sometimes the place got raided by the cops because they didn't like the race mixing, especially if it got romantic. But otherwise, it was all cool. She longed to play.

Everyone who loved to listen to jazz music showed up especially late into the night, after the paying gigs. Folks were sometimes invited to play, or others sat in, but Kay didn't have the courage to get up there. Until she did.

One late night, after several Irish whiskeys, Kay stood between numbers, wiped her damp palms on her skirt, and went up to the band leader, Federico.

"I'm Kay Schiffner, I'd like to play some piano if that's all right?"

"This ain't no piana recital, you know." He did not say it unkindly.

She nodded. "I play bop, I can do cool, and I can play some blues. Whatever you want."

Federico hesitated a minute, gesturing to the men on stage. "Young lady wants to play a number—y'all ok wid dat?" He said it low. Kay was grateful because she didn't want to be called out in front of everyone if they said no.

Kay saw the eye contact between the band members, reading the skepticism on their faces. Only the bass player gave her a sympathetic look. No one said anything. The late hour and alcohol were in her favor.

"You gotcha sheet music?" the horn player asked.

She stepped onto the stage. "I'll be all right if I know what key you want to play it in." She got a little more side eye but ignored them, sat on the bench knowing that the room was staring at her, even in the din and chatter.

"What are we playing?" She was grateful the bass player was at least getting the title of the song out before they started in.

"Straight No Chaser." The drummer called it looking hard at Kay.

She nodded. Monk's 12 bar blues tune. "B flat?"

The horn player shook his head. "Let's play in F."

Testing her. Kay focused, running through the tune in her head, not the easiest start. Drummer counted one, two . . .

Kay played timidly at first, simply hitting the notes, staying out of the way of the musicians, who knew each other's playing. But by the second bridge the music worked its magic and she felt more comfortable. Then, in a moment she would never forget, the horn player nodded at her to take it. As the notes played out from her brain to her hands, she felt the room tune in. She had made it through with decent applause, and felt a shifting inside her. Change was coming. At the end of the number Kay got up and turned to leave.

"Percy Henderson, Miss," said the bass player. "Glad you came by."

"Kay Schiffner." She extended a hand, which disappeared into his large warm hands. She felt musician's callouses on his fingers.

"Nice to meet cha."

"Yes, good to meet you." She liked his kindly eyes.

"You did alright. You want to play some more like that?"

"More than anything. I admit it took me some time to get into it."

"But you did it, right?" His smile had dimples and was infectious. "Why don't you come by the Blue Moon on Friday? We doing some loose sets and we can fit you in a bit, see how it works."

Now all of that was gone. Kay stood at her window in her robe, holding coffee, the morning gray with fog. Her head pounding from the whiskey and the humiliation.

# CHAPTER 23

Staring out at the Embarcadero Freeway, Kay lost focus. Spent yesterday in bed, hung over. Today wasn't much better. She glanced down at the contract that needed to get done today. She'd read the first two pages twice, her mind wandering off.

She hated her office view now that the freeway construction came between her and the waterfront.

She was unwelcome at the Blue Moon and got booted off Jimbo's stage for playing like some tourist rube. Her concentration scattered, she stood and stretched.

She got herself through law school; she should be able to figure this out. She wanted her music life back, existing somewhere between reclaiming Leitisha Boone's good graces and placating Frank Bianco.

When Marvin Wright died, he owned numerous parcels of property in the Fillmore. Maybe if she traced what was happening with his property, she'd learn the fate of the Blue Moon too. Probate was slow to work, giving her time to get some facts together, and then find a good eminent domain lawyer for Leitisha to fight redevelopment.

She'd review the grantor/grantee files first to determine the current ownership status of the property. Housed in the City Assessor's office in City Hall, these were public records used to generate the property taxes for the County of San Francisco.

The office was quiet. She stepped out for a few minutes, hoping no one, especially Bianco, would notice. She rode a streetcar up Market Street, and then walked over to Polk Street to the City Assessor's office. She started by looking up Marvin Wright's name, and then writing down the parcel numbers of the properties and tracing each piece through any transactions. She was sure Wright held some of them through corporations.

One brand new entry seemed odd. She double checked it, and sure enough, one of Wright's properties within the Fillmore, off of Eddy Street, had a new owner: Mid-City Development.

The new owner had exercised eminent domain through the Redevelopment Agency in the last couple of days. That didn't seem right. It meant Redevelopment could foreclose on the Blue Moon without probate if it chose. That made her sick. She took careful notes and went back to the office.

As she came into the reception area, Irma was there, waiting on her. This summoning by Irma was getting irksome.

"Mr. Bianco wants to see you right away." With that she gracefully clicked back down the hallway in her high heels.

Kay was only graceful on the piano. She ducked into her office and grabbed the latest version of the McCann purchase agreement, wondering when her head and body would feel normal.

"Hello Kay." Frank was giving her a fake smile.

"Here's the latest draft of the McCann purchase agreement." She set it on his desk and stood, not being invited to sit.

He took the agreement. "Where you been?"

She hated his tone, as if she was an errant child, and not a lawyer like he was. "I ran an errand. Working every day including Saturday leaves me little time to do some necessities." He didn't keep track of the whereabouts of the male associates.

"You need to understand that I need you here, both mentally and physically. We have critical deadlines coming up."

There were always critical deadlines.

"I need to know I can rely on you."

Here came the lecture again. How he did her such a favor to let her work there.

"There is a wave of economic change taking over the city that you and I can't stop, but we need to get on board because we, as a firm, can profit from it—it's called F-I-R-E."

"What?" Now he wasn't making sense.

He nearly stood, giving her a solemn face.

"Finance, insurance and real estate, F-I-R-E. It's being pushed by Redevelopment and it's backed and supported by the unions, the construction companies building the new stores, boulevards and residences, and by us, their lawyers." He glanced up at her. "Get your head out of whatever it is that's distracting you and get back to real work."

She'd written the name down somewhere. Here it was, Michael Zorn.

She went to give it to the secretarial pool, then decided to do this footwork herself so it didn't get back to Irma. Kay looked up and then called Michael Zorn's office, the trust fund baby, eminent domain lawyer. Who didn't take bribes. He answered his own phone and sounded out of breath.

"I'm really busy, but maybe you can come by at the end of the day?" He gave her the address. "Be sure to ring the doorbell when you come."

Kay worried he sounded too busy to help Leitisha, but didn't have an alternative. She worked diligently until early evening to keep Frank off her back, completing revised agreements for the client meeting to which she was cordially not invited. Her male colleague would present the revisions, as the client might not trust the agreements if he knew a woman wrote them. And if she showed up to the meeting, she'd be mistaken for a secretary anyway.

Zorn's office was way over on Davis Street, among the warehouses, away from the Financial District. She glanced at the address she had written down and up at the building again, which was modest. This was the address, but no sign or "shingle" outside told her a lawyer worked here. If he had so much money, why didn't he at least have a sign out?

She pulled on the doorknob. It rattled but was locked tight. She saw a button to the right and pushed it. She heard a buzzer, the door vibrated under her hand, and clicked. She pushed the door open. It closed heavily behind her. Her eyes adjusted to the dim light of the hallway.

Her handbag was crocked in her elbow, and she had gone out without gloves or a hat because she didn't think this was that kind of meeting. Now she was sure it was not.

# CHAPTER 24

"Hello?" She called out down the hallway.

Music, something classical. No, opera. A man's voice, tenor.

"Sorry, sorry, back here." A man around her same age came up the gray hall. He wore a white button-down shirt but no tie. His hair was shaggy and unstyled. He rubbed his hand over a day's growth on his face and gestured down the hall. "Here, come in, sorry, not very organized. You're Kay Schiffner, right?"

He shifted from one foot to the other, restless as a working bee.

"Mr. Zorn, I . . ." She held out her hand, not sure which way to turn.

"Michael, Michael, please." He shook her hand quickly, then gestured to a gray metal desk and two serviceable if shabby chairs. A Remington typewriter sat on the desk. He turned on a lamp.

She glanced at the file cabinets with drawers too full to close and the overflowing bookshelves. Papers everywhere in disarray. This was the eminent domain expert?

"Please," he said again pulling out the desk chair and clearing off a file for her to sit down.

Kay wasn't sure what to say. "You don't have a secretary?"

Zorn ran his hand through his mop of hair. He had brown hair, brown eyes, skin that looked like it spent time outdoors. "Uh, no. The nature of my work . . ." He sighed and finally went still.

"I take, uh, unpopular positions on issues, in cases. Hence the buzzer."

He gestured. "And I don't need to endanger anyone else, so if I need some kind of work done, I send it out to a service, and then not the same service."

"Is that why you're so nervous?" Kay, her leg crossed over, watched him. He was in danger from his work?

"Yeah," He laughed. "I guess I am. I'm good at what I do, and my opponents don't like that."

"Good." He may be her expert after all. She couldn't save the Blue Moon and Leitisha, but maybe he could. "First, what is that music?"

"It's Caruso, singing some classical opera." He waited a beat. "That's Celeste Aida – it's fairly old. He's wanting to win on the battlefield and with Aida."

"Caruso?" He was listening to opera?

"Yeah, it's an import 45. They're hard to get. Why are you here?"

"I don't know where to start, but everyone keeps sending me to you." So he listened to music while he worked? She liked that idea.

"Start from the beginning." Zorn's nervousness settled down. "How does redevelopment involve you? Do you know how rare it is that you have a job as a lawyer?"

"Of course, I'm aware. That's why I'm here, so I don't lose that rare job. In fact, it was one of my colleagues who mentioned you first." Why did men always remind her that her job was a gift? She earned it.

"What do you mean you might lose it?"

"My boss isn't happy I'm helping someone against Redevelopment and he's really coming down hard on me."

"Who's your boss?"

"Frank Bianco of Bianco and Associates."

"Ah, Frank Bianco, old SF Italian family. I know his brother who has the restaurant in North Beach."

"Small world." He knew folks. She wanted him to take Blue Moon's problems from her. "I need this job for me to pay my rent, stay independent. He's made it impossible to do anything but his work, and definitely not something adverse."

She decided to tell him her real reason. "I play jazz piano, or I used to, at the Blue Moon, a Fillmore Club."

He nodded. "Wow, a working lawyer and a professional piano player. I see your dilemma."

She hadn't told anyone but her priest about both parts of her. "I need to find help for the owner with her fight against redevelopment so I can get back to playing." She didn't like how all this sounded. "Sorry, I'm blurting it out, not really in order."

"It's fine, tell me however it comes."

His attitude gave her confidence. She continued.

"The landlord of the club, Marvin Wright, was murdered," she saw Zorn nod, "and then the ABC set up a fake sting and revoked the liquor license. They are setting up the club to lose value so the eminent domain will be easier."

Zorn leaned towards her. "Marvin Wright owned the property the club is on?"

"Yes," said Kay. He didn't ask about her playing jazz in a black club. He focused on the work. "I need you to help the club owner because I can't. I don't know eminent domain law."

Zorn nodded and got up. Kay watched him go down the hall deeper into the building. A minute later, he yelled, "Do you want some coffee?"

What was he doing now? Her hangover headache sat at the base of her neck.

She followed him down the hall. Zorn stood in a tiny kitchenette with a hot plate, a small ice box, smaller than hers, and stuff everywhere.

"Sorry, sorry, here." Away from the work, his flightiness returned. He handed her a mug of steaming coffee.

"It's a long story." He waved his hand around what was obviously his living space in the back of his office, a cot, disheveled with clothes and bedding. "Come on, let's go back." He had a cup of coffee in his hand, and some papers under his arm. "Do you need milk or sugar? Sorry, should have asked."

"No, the coffee is delicious." She'd never tasted coffee so fragrant and flavorful. The entire room smelled of it.

"I roast the beans myself, dark French roast, until the chocolate and mahogany tones blend under a heavy sheen of bean sweat," he said with enthusiasm, "and then grind them. Good, yeah?" He gave a boyish smile.

The air held the scents he'd described.

A man who roasted his own coffee beans. The Trieste used coffee beans in the espresso, but this was extraordinary. The taste showed the labor of doing it paid off. Kay cleared a corner of the desk and set down her mug.

Zorn unfolded the paper he had carried in. "Here's a map of Redevelopment Area A-1. Now where did you say the club was?"

Kay scrutinized the map. "I'm not sure it's on here." She examined it again. It's outside that area, here, Fillmore near McAllister." Seeing the map made her realize how big this project was. Kay felt sick. A lot of destruction. "This is just A-1?"

"Yeah. A-2 is bigger. So your club is in that area."

The Blue Moon was in the A-2 District but that didn't make her feel better.

"I know about Marvin Wright, but tell me what you know anyway." He pulled out a notebook from the stack of papers, wrote a couple notes and looked up expectantly.

A colleague who wanted to hear what she thought, in her own words. All of this was new. "Wright had turned down working with the neighborhood coalition. Apparently he was negotiating separately. I knew that from talking to him, and then overhearing someone at last week's hearing."

"You were at the hearing?" Zorn asked. "I thought Bianco didn't want you going near redevelopment."

"I went during my lunch and didn't tell anyone. But Leitisha Boone, she's the owner of the club, introduced me as the speaker and it was awkward. I wasn't supposed to be there, and suddenly I was in front of a microphone."

"You didn't know you were going to speak?"

"No. She put me on the spot."

"What did you say?"

"Nothing really. I just said the Coalition would submit a statement in writing and got out of there as soon as I could."

"That was fast thinking, good job."

Everyone else thought it was a disaster. "Leitisha didn't think so. She told me I failed her by not speaking out. She told me I wasn't welcome to play piano at the Blue Moon anymore."

"And you still want to help her."

"Well, yes, I want to help her, she's being pushed out of her business unfairly and without any recourse, or money, frankly. Thing is, I feel guilty. I had a sweet deal there, but no stake in the neighborhood. Every night I went home to my apartment, which is safe from redevelopment."

"Well, that's not your fault, but I see why you would want to help. That's what I do."

"But it got back to Frank that I had been there, and that's how I ended up here. Someone needs to help Leitisha, and it can't be me."

"Doesn't she have her lawyers on this?"

"I am not sure her lawyers can deal with this." Kay had not seen Saul, Leitisha's lawyer-boyfriend, at the Blue Moon lately. "I don't think they want to touch it."

Zorn nodded, thinking, and sipping his coffee.

"So why do you do this work?" She asked him. And live like this? She knew he had money, he could live in a nicer place.

Zorn ran his hand through his hair again. "My father made his sizeable fortune on the backs of nonunion, underpaid labor, then retired. I became a lawyer instead of taking over the business. I am balancing out what he did. Business pilfering from the working class has to stop."

"Redevelopment claims this project will benefit the working class."

Zorn snorted. "That's all bull. First, they are shutting down an entire neighborhood of hard working 'working class' people and businesses, shuttling them to Bayview or Marin City, or wherever they haven't redlined them out." He stood now, moving around again. "The work that is created, all the demolition and then the construction, the unions are making sure only their white guys are doing it, with no benefit to folks from that neighborhood." He spoke to her as if arguing to a jury. "Like putting up a dam and drowning a culture."

Zorn voiced her same fears about the Fillmore.

"Can we stop them from closing the Blue Moon?"

Zorn sat back like a doctor about to give bad news. He shook his head. "Unlikely we can stop this now, with all of its momentum. Too much money, too many players involved. People were asleep at the switch and the folks affected have no representation or power, and it got away from them politically before it even got to me. We can make Redevelopment give decent compensation for the businesses if we sue, and that is what I am aiming at for now."

"If, Miss Boone wants to hire me to represent her, we can add her to the lawsuit we are preparing. The other stuff that's happening to her, like the liquor license? I don't have the time to deal with that." He shifted in his seat and swigged at his coffee. "But I can tell you what to do, and you can do the legwork."

"I can't do any of it. That's why I came to you."

"Yes, that's what you said." He nodded at her. "Miss Boone needs to be ready to push back in every way she can to keep them from stealing her business."

"What does 'every way' mean?"

Zorn shrugged. "Be prepared for anything. Right now, there's not a lot of recourse in the courts, at least not yet. It's a street battle. A developer is using unfair tactics against her to weaken her before they proceed with eminent domain. You need to be vigilant, and push back whenever you can." He drank some of his coffee. "And watch your own back. They're ruthless."

# CHAPTER 25

Zimpel was at his desk reviewing the autopsy report, which had come ridiculously fast. He was pushing his investigation to get ahead of the politics. He thought about his potential witness, the girl, when he turned around. Frazier was standing there in his uniform, ignoring the looks he was getting from the other inspectors. Zimpel nodded at him and the two left together, going outside.

"I can't take that stare down, like I'm supposed to be fetching them coffee," Frazier took off his hat and worked the brim around.

"What d'ya got?" Best way to make Frazier feel better was to treat him like he was an inspector. Leave the other shit alone.

"I did some asking around, like who might be servicing well-to-do Negro businessmen, and I got a name." He laughed. "Someone from my old neighborhood, I know the guy."

"Yeah?"

"Here's the address, but you need to let me go in there. I don't want to agitate him, and have him kill that girl." He handed Zimpel a piece of paper with an address. Looked like lower Potrero Hill.

Zimpel nodded, thinking that he was probably right.

"I'll get an ok for you to go with me and we'll go over when you're ready."

"That's going to be a . . ."

"I'll get it done," said Zimpel. "They're pressuring for a result. They want someone arrested. And like yesterday. It's holding up 'progress.'"

"Poor man's dead, and all they want is his property." Frazier shook his head, then gave a cold smile. "Probably why he's dead."

Zimpel nodded. "Has something to do with it. With all this pressure, I should be able to get help." He needed to keep control, to solve the case before the money and power got impatient.

"Call me? I'll go whenever."

Frazier turned back to do his walking beat.

Zimpel went down the hall and asked if the Lieutenant was in.

The sergeant in charge of the watch desk shook his head. "Brass is out. Lieutenant and the Captain." He shrugged. "Have no idea."

Zimpel wanted to get clearance for Frazier and follow up on the lead. The girl was the key. Delay hurt him.

He went back to his desk. He'd start with limousine companies. He had to keep working.

# CHAPTER 26

Zorn got her motivated. Kay searched for data to use against Redevelopment. First, she painstakingly catalogued each of Marvin Wright's parcels, in between drafting documents for Bianco & Associates transactions, and made a chart. It gave her a way to win back Miss Leitisha's good graces. The information she was collecting and organizing showed at least one property handed directly over to the developers, possibly violating the regulations.

The same bankers and developers kept cropping up. With so much money moving around, she was sure she'd make other connections. She worked late to make up for sneaking away to review city records.

Kay copied her chart for Zorn to get his feedback and hoped that her help would make him more inclined to help Leitisha. When he didn't answer or buzz her in, she scribbled a note and slid the envelope under his door, hoping he would see it among the detritus of his office. "I went over grantor/grantee files, tracing the current status of Marvin Wright's properties. Here's a chart I made from it."

Walking to the bus, Kay resolved to speak to Leitisha tomorrow and show her the chart to convince her that she was on her side, and to persuade her to join Zorn's group of businesses that were suing Redevelopment, the best defense against what was happening.

At home, she practiced diligently on her upright, learning new songs, causing the neighbors to pound on her wall. She had to get back on the keyboards. She wasn't getting much sleep, but that was okay if she played piano again.

## WEDNESDAY MORNING

The receptionist told her she had a call on Line 2, a Michael Zorn.

"Hello?"

"It's Zorn. Thanks for that information you dropped by."

"You're welcome." She rarely received praise for her work. This felt good.

"Won't you get sideways at work?"

"Not if he doesn't know."

"Right. I'll keep that in mind."

She lowered her voice, glancing at her office door. "Wright died only ten days ago, no probate has been completed, and I found that one parcel of his property on Turk Street has been transferred already."

"And the new owner is one of the developers." Zorn paused. "Strange that they got the property right away. It should have gone through the Redevelopment Agency as the owner in eminent domain."

Kay heard papers rustling in the background and pictured his messy desk.

"Yeah, interesting."

"What is?" she said.

"That developer, Mid-City, was one of the companies I was researched as receiving 'funny money.'"

"What do you mean, funny money?" She remembered Brian Giamatti saying something about bribes.

"Untraceable capital coming in, maybe from organized crime. Hard to say. You sure you don't want to work for the good guys? You're doing good work here."

"You mean for little money and behind a buzzer." Silence.

She squeezed her eyes. That was stupid. "Oh, sorry, didn't mean . . . thank you. I'm glad to be useful."

Zorn laughed. "Virtue has its own rewards. Someone has to do it."

"If they transferred one of Wright's properties, they may transfer others including the Blue Moon, without the proper process. After the contrived ABC bust, what's next?"

"Yes, this is all helpful to see. Don't tell your boss, you might be screwing your own clients." He laughed.

"Shhhh. Don't even say that out loud."

"I could really use someone like you to help me out, you know."

She felt the pull to the work, too. "But how do you get paid?" She didn't have a trust fund, how would she pay her rent? This work motivated her like nothing she had done for Bianco.

"I get paid eventually, it works out, that's contingency. Did you talk to Leitisha Boone yet about joining our lawsuit?

"I am going over there tonight after work to talk to her and will report back." She was resolved now.

"We're filing this week. If I add her later, we have to bring a motion and I don't know if it'll be granted."

"Understood." She resolved to convince Leitisha to join the lawsuit.

Kay finished up so she could get out of there and get over to the Blue Moon.

# CHAPTER 27

AUGUST 13, 1958 · WEDNESDAY EARLY AFTERNOON

Walter was setting up the bar—they had finally got their license back—when he heard tires squealing, doors slamming, and three white cops pounding so hard on the door to the restaurant he thought the glass would break.

"We want to see Leitisha Boone, right now." The lead cop was red in the face and yelled through the glass door.

Walter's hands shook as he unlocked the door. The lead cop pushed his way in.

"Please wait here . . ." started Walter.

"We're not waiting!" The lead cop motioned to his men to go into the restaurant. The waiters stood and watched.

Walter's stomach fell. Another raid? "Miss Leitisha, please come quick. There's some police at the door and they are asking for you."

"What now," she said coming out of the kitchen. "First my liquor license and now . . ." She stopped when she saw the cops coming towards her. The two cops took both her arms, like she was going to run away. The lead cop roughly turned her around and put handcuffs on her.

"What are you doing," she said. "Get these off me, what is the meaning . . ."

"Leitisha Boone, you are under arrest for the murder of Marvin Wright. Search the place boys. One cop strode to the kitchen, the other bounded up the stairs toward the lavatories.

"Don't you mess up my place," she called out after the two cops.

"Walter," she turned to her bartender, "call Mr. Saul. We gonna need a good lawyer. Tell him what happened."

"Found it," the young cop said smugly, coming out with a gun sitting in white butcher paper, string hanging off his hand.

"What's that?" Miss Leitisha said.

"What's it look like? A gun. The murder weapon."

A chill sliver pierced Walter. Here's how they do you.

"I don't own no gun."

"Well, we found it in the meat locker, where the snitch said it would be. Said it was hidden in with your meat stores, and sure enough, there it was."

"That gun is not mine." Miss Leitisha's eyes flared fury. "You took that back with you, and planted it yourself, huh, boy, isn't that right."

"Who are you calling boy?" said the lead cop, pulling on her arms so hard Leitisha cried out. Walter went to help her and another cop stood in his way. Walter stood still, right in the cop's face. He was mad. Punching the cop wouldn't help Leitisha. By now the entire kitchen and wait staff surrounded the cops.

"You go home, this place is closed." The lead cop pushed Leitisha through the crowd of employees toward the door.

"Don't you close this place. You know what to do." Miss Leitisha spoke over her shoulder.

"Wait." Tildy, resolute, met the cop's gaze straight on, and she pulled a shawl around Miss Leitisha's shoulders. She secured it through Leitisha's arms, gave her a kiss and backed off.

When they had gone, the silence was thick and cold. Everyone looked at each other in shock.

"They just arrested Miss Leitisha for murder."

"That's what the man said."

"What we gonna do?"

"I'm going to call Mr. Saul, like she said. We going to need a lawyer." Walter decided to call Thursday Zimpel first. Walter was worried about

Miss Leitisha down there with all those hostile white cops.

As Zimpel hung up from his call with Walter, making reassuring comments, he turned and slammed his hand into the wall.

"What the hell, Zimpel."

"Who made the arrest in my homicide case?" He glanced around, but the other inspectors avoided his gaze. Someone knew what went down. "This shit doesn't happen unless the DA authorizes it." He went into the Lieutenant's office.

The Lieutenant looked up. "I know why you're here."

"What the hell? It was my case. I have some leads, and they don't lead to a Black woman club owner."

"They found the murder weapon in her meat locker."

Zimpel slammed the door and nearly took the window out.

"Relax, Zimpel. It's out of your hands. The DA wanted this case cleared, they got a tip, followed up, and there it is. So it's done. Go to your next case."

"Since when do we get cases taken away from us without anybody talking about it?"

"The Chief wanted this cleared. He was getting pressure from City Hall." He paused. "It was holding up redevelopment."

Zimpel closed his eyes tightly, his hands balled into fists. He took a breath, opened his eyes and made eye contact with the Lieutenant.

"This is a ruse. You know it and I know it."

"It's outta our hands now. Lynch has it."

"Well, that doesn't sit well with me. I'll go to the DA if I have to. This is bullshit." He left slamming the door again. Somebody up high was moving the chess pieces around to suit themselves.

First, he needed to see where they were holding Miss Leitisha and make sure she was treated right. And see if Saul was here, getting her a lawyer if he wasn't acting for her himself. Saul didn't do criminal law but he had a lot of pull in this city.

Zimpel walked down the hall to where the interviews would be taking place. He nodded to the cop outside the door and looked in the window. Leitisha was at one end of the table, an untouched cup of coffee in front of her, a black shawl hung from her straight shoulders, and an expression on her face that would freeze the sun out of the sky. He was a homicide inspector and this was his case. He didn't give a damn about anything else right at that moment. He entered without knocking.

There were two homicide inspectors in the room. Ralphie Siever, a senior inspector, and Seamus McGivern, one of Cahill's boys. McGivern gave Zimpel a sharp look. Siever was affable enough, and a little embarrassed.

"Hey Zimpel, we solved your case."

Zimpel nodded at the two inspectors, too pissed off to speak.

Siever continued, trying to be the nice guy. He was an idiot. "Maybe you can get her to talk and admit she killed Marvin Wright, Zimpel. She's spitting fire at us and otherwise isn't saying anything. Says she wants to talk to her lawyer." Siever laughed. "Like colored folks got lawyers."

Miss Leitisha looked at Zimpel but her face gave away nothing. She was smarter and wealthier than both of the cops interviewing her.

"Give me a few minutes with her and let's see what I can do." He wasn't going to give them anything. He had to play this right to get her out of there.

"Sure, Zimpel, happy to take a break." Siever and McGivern got up. Zimpel noted that McGivern didn't say anything, but he'd be on the horn telling all to whoever gave them the order to pick up Leitisha.

When they left the room, Miss Leitisha slumped down in her chair.

Before she said anything, Zimpel warned her. "They can hear what you say. And see you." He nodded at the window and lowered his voice. She sat up straight again.

"This was my case, and they did this without my knowing it, so I'm sorry about this, Miss Leitisha. Looks like somebody targeted you."

"Oh, yes, first with the ABC agent and now this planted gun. I don't own a gun."

"I know. I'll check it out—they haven't said it was the murder weapon."

"Oh, they assume, some stupid colored woman gonna get all worked up over some man, and shoot him, because she wants to show him. If I was like that, I'd never have a successful club. Did someone think to call Saul?"

"Walter said he did. I'm sure between him and Kay, they'll get a lawyer down here for you. In the meantime, I'll keep you safe until we can get you out."

"They said someone told them I did it, and where the gun was. Some snitch. Other cop say they saw me throw him out of my club. Someone is setting me up."

"It looks that way," Zimpel said. He was sure of it.

"So now what?"

"Hang tight, let me see what's going on. I need to play my part."

"I know. I appreciate this. You know I'm innocent."

"Yes, I do, Miss Leitisha, yes I do."

# CHAPTER 28

Someone heard it on the radio. She overheard talk at the office. She read it in the headlines on the way home. Guilt hit her first. Then frustration. She didn't do enough, fast enough, she didn't ask her soon enough, and here she was back in her safe place sitting at the bar at the Blue Moon while Leitisha was in jail.

The whiskey's sting countered her internal distress of Leitisha arrested on a lie, the Fillmore's dying a slow death from greedy redevelopers, and her having to ford a racial divide to play jazz piano. She lifted the glass again. The band was playing Round Midnight, an old Monk tune, and it sounded mournful.

Walter glanced at the door as Zimpel walked into the restaurant. Zimpel nodded at Walter and walked up the stairs to the restroom.

"Thursday, I came by to talk to her about the lawsuit . . ." He was gone and she turned to her whiskey.

"You must be off the clock," Walter said when Zimpel returned. He pushed a chilled glass of beer toward the cop.

"Yeah." Zimpel drank more than half the glass and pushed it back to Walter, who filled it up again.

"They made a decision without even talking to me. Came from the DA and the Chief. I have no idea where the snitch came from, but they believed I am biased, so they didn't tell me."

"What snitch?" She glanced from Walter to Zimpel. They knew things that weren't on the radio.

Walter shrugged and wiped the bar. "They found a gun in here when they arrested her."

"A gun? Leitisha doesn't have a gun here, does she?"

Zimpel drank more beer but this time only took a healthy slug. "The snitch said that she had a gun, so they came in here and found one." He sat on the bar stool, drained the glass and Walter reached for it, filling it again.

"I spoke to her," he said to the unasked question.

"You talked to her? Was she all right? I can't believe she's in jail."

Thursday ignored her. Kay pushed her glass towards Walter.

"Thank you, Walter." He treated her like he always had. She was back here drinking because Leitisha was in jail.

"She's strong, and I made sure folks knew there'd be consequences if anything happened to her. Where the hell is Saul?" Zimpel looked up at Walter.

Kay wondered the same thing. Where was Leitisha's lawyer boyfriend through all of this? The restaurant was slow, only a handful of tables were full. Dishes clanking, everything had an edge to it.

"I called him," said Walter. "After I called you. They said he wasn't in, but they'd get the message to him. That was around 2 o'clock. They come for her right before that, while we was fixing dinner, told us to close but she said no, stay open, so we open."

Zimpel glanced at his watch. "Well after nine now." He drank more beer. "I'm going to go back to the kitchen and look."

Kay met Walter's eyes. "This can't be happening. Something has to turn this around."

"I seen this kind of thing before. This country, they keep shifting Black folks around, using us for their chores, to do their work. But nobody wants us living nearby, staying in their hotels, eating in their restaurants. Moving us on now, that's what this is about."

"It's so unfair."

Walter finally smiled at her, but it wasn't a warm smile. "Life ain't fair,

Sugar, it's just life. I already lost my apartment, now maybe I'll lose my job. I got a kid in private school, at St. Ignatius. You know how hard it is to get a colored kid in St. Ignatius?"

"I'm sorry Walter . . . I didn't realize he was at SI."

"S'ok Miss Kay. Ok to talk about the world the way it is, not the way we want it to be. Yeah, we're Catholic from my wife's people. Somehow, we get him in and pay for the Catholic grade school, and he does so well, they make an exception." The glass Walter was polishing broke in the towel.

Kay jumped. "You ok?"

"Yeah, musta had a crack." He tossed the towel with the glass into the garbage, picked up the shards that fell, and wiped down everything one more time.

"I don't know if it's good for him to be with all those white people in that school. He tries to be like them instead of what he is." Walter shrugged. "Hard to be the first."

Kay felt outside the circle looking in, finding incomprehensible the rules, written or unwritten, that kept non-white people separate from whites and what it felt to be excluded from so much. A turmoil of anger and love churned inside of her, and she didn't know what to do with it, like being hungry and sick at the same time. She leaned towards Walter. "We'll get through this; we can make it right."

He patted her hand. "You a good person, Miss Kay, and if something can be done, I'm sure you gonna do it. But they found that gun, and unless we know who put it there, they do what they always do."

"They can't do this, arrest Leitisha to close down the Blue Moon." Kay's lawyer brain ran through scenarios, down checklists, over each facet of the problem.

Walter continued. "What's happening here is no different than what's happening all over the neighborhood. You don't take the papers and leave when they want, you get arrested, you get evicted, you get a big water bill, or someone vandalizes your house. Redevelopment done arrested all of us." Walter wiped his already sparkling clean bar, his head down, his shoulders hunched.

Zimpel came out from the kitchen. "Walter, do you know the delivery schedules?"

"You ask Miss Sylvia? Most of them deliver to the back usually, and I don't always see them."

"I took a look at the meat locker where they found the package. Folks come and go, she said, but someone is always in the kitchen."

"That's right. I see Henry when he comes, at 2 or 3, after the farmers market but before dinner gets started, and then later, to take Miss Sylvia home. But we get other deliveries all day long—the baker come in the morning and that delivery goes direct to the back door. We get dry goods every so often. The butcher, the fish monger, wine, booze," he waved his hand. "Some I see, some I don't."

"Gun showed up somehow, and we need to figure that out."

"I don't see how, but that's your job not mine," said Walter.

"The gun is the key to get this off her back." Kay said to Zimpel. "Do we know who the snitch is?"

"They are saying it's confidential. They don't want to endanger the witness."

"They won't tell you? Something wrong with that."

She was right. If they kept the identity from him, it must be a lie. He needed to watch who he talked to.

"Why are they hiding whoever it is from you? The cop didn't plant the gun?"

Zimpel was glad to see Kay back at the Blue Moon, and involved.

"Nah. That guy's a jerk, but I don't think so—told Sylvia I'd come by tomorrow to talk to everyone. They're in the middle of dinner and then need to go home. Quite a shock today." He finished another beer. "My hunch is that someone planted the gun, and then, they say through the DA's office, fed the information to the cops."

"People don't wander in and out of Miss Leitisha's kitchen. She's strict and it's kept spotless clean. You don't get that by being casual with deliveries."

Zimpel nodded. "I'll talk to them tomorrow, see what we see." He put some money on the bar. "You wanna take a ride, Kay?"

That was something new, inviting her somewhere. Maybe it was the beer. Or that he was her appointed rescuer, after the other night when she got stupid drunk and failed at Jimbo's. They hadn't discussed it. He might want to date her, but he never asked. Just as well. She had her hands full with her career.

She downed her whiskey. "Where we going?"

"Let's ride by Saul's house. I have a feeling about something. I'll give you a ride home afterward, unless you're playing tonight?"

She shook her head. "Not tonight." Bad enough she was drinking there behind Leitisha's back. The band was laying a blues tune she was trying to place. "Yeah, let's go. Why isn't Saul here, being worried?"

"Exactly. G'nite Walter, see you tomorrow."

Walter looked up at both of them. "You good people, but you naïve. Go with God. You hear anything, let me know."

# CHAPTER 29

AUGUST 13, 1958 • LATE WEDNESDAY NIGHT

Zimpel had no rational basis for his lack of confidence in Saul except his gut. Saul Weismann was a big-time lawyer and Leitisha's boyfriend, who did nice things for her, took her on trips, bought her jewelry and fancy clothes. He hung out in the club, had big dinners in the corner with his business cronies, and loved the music. But Saul frequently commented that he didn't like Leitisha working so hard, and tried to get her to get a manager—a man of course—so she could travel with him on his business trips. But he didn't marry her and she wasn't going to give up her club, so there it was.

"You ok?" They drove over to St. Francis Woods, the tony neighborhood where Saul had a big house.

"I'm fine and the whiskey's fine, if that's what you're asking." She gave him a side glance. "Thank you for the other night. I appreciate you looking out for me." Awkward to mention it, but hardly a secret.

"You're a damn stubborn woman who doesn't much like being looked after, but you needed it on Saturday."

Kay was flattered his image of her remained favorable. Not many men would be so kind. "Yeah, well, right now Leitisha needs looking after and needs an arraignment so she can be bailed out. Don't like the idea of her in jail like that—what they might do to her."

"She's been through a lot in her young life. She knows what's called for in this situation."

He didn't believe what he was telling Kay. Being a Negro in a prison was being lost. "I'm hoping they'll give her bail, sometimes for certain homicides they don't." Zimpel didn't think she'd get bail. He'd have to find a way to shift blame on the person who did this—someone in a black limousine—and quickly.

"Oh please, she's not a criminal, and she owns a business. They would only deny it if she would skip town, and that's not something she would ever do."

Zimpel knew the same rules didn't apply to Leitisha. Kay hadn't been exposed to the other side of Negro life. She saw the good side, not the ugly one. They wanted her badly for this. Badly enough to set it up, freeze him out, and not let him complete his investigation.

They pulled up to Saul's house and the lights were on.

"He's home," Zimpel pulled over to the curb. A figure stood in the window. Good. He didn't want to have to wake him up, but he would have.

Zimpel and Kay went up to the door and rang the bell. The grounds were manicured and orderly. The door opened to plush white carpet. Saul was a short man with a full head of white hair, and older, still strong, with a healthy tan.

"Inspector Zimpel and Kay. Given the hour, I take it this isn't a social visit."

"Yes, sir," said Zimpel. "We've been attempting to reach you. Someone at your office told Walter Jenkins that you were out of town."

"Walter must be mistaken because here I am." Saul gave them a big smile.

Zimpel wondered why Saul was dodging Walter.

"Please come in. Let me get you a drink. I'm sorry, do you mind taking your shoes off? Hard to keep a white carpet clean."

"Saul, Leitisha is spending the night in jail. I don't want a drink. We need to act."

"Now Kay, no need to get excited, showing up late on a work night. You're lucky I'm up. If you called my office, you'd know we hired a criminal attorney; he's very good."

"We did call your office and got put off. I don't understand how you can even talk about sleeping when Leitisha's in jail."

Zimpel didn't want to go inside in his socks and have a drink with Saul. He wanted to know if Saul was going to help Leitisha. He crossed his arms and leaned on the door jam. Kay was likely to take a swipe at Saul if he kept telling her to calm down.

"I don't know why you couldn't reach me. It should all work out."

"What should work out? Is there an arraignment? Have you arranged for a bond? This is political more than criminal. You know that, right? They already tried to take her liquor license and now this."

"You need to calm down. These things take time."

Her voice went low and cold. "You need to stop telling me to calm down and talk to me, lawyer to lawyer. Or did you forget that I'm at Bianco and Associates and actually do know what I'm asking about?"

Zimpel felt anger come off her like heat.

"Yes. I know that you are a lawyer. I'm sorry, I didn't mean to imply that you were being unprofessional."

That's exactly what his patronizing tone meant to convey.

"And I don't mean to be rude and direct," which Kay didn't mean either. "Who exactly is working for her?"

"I have recommended Joel Edelman, do you know him?"

Zimpel stayed quiet. Keeping it within the tribe. Saul was dodging Kay's questions.

"Yes, I know Joel. He's a leader in the Bar Association. Good. I'll call him. Now, when is Leitisha getting out?"

"Now, you don't need to call him, he's very busy. He'll get her out but it may not be right away."

Kay took an audible breath. Saul's patronizing was costing her. "Yeah, we're all busy, but I'm not too busy to help Leitisha."

"Don't you think I know what's happening here?" Finally Kay had pushed Saul to react.

"I'm not sure. You don't seem concerned."

"That's rude of you to say. If that's what you wanted to discuss, it's under control, and it's late." He went to shut the door.

Kay stuck her hand on the door and pushed back. "It's not true, what they say about Leitisha, none of it. What are you hiding?"

Kay stayed focused. Zimpel was enjoying this exchange at Saul's expense.

"I don't like your implications." Saul, uncomfortable in the doorway in his stocking feet, his hand on the door. Kay did not let up.

"Did you know this? Leitisha had formed a coalition, and Marvin Wright knew about it and helped her. He was simply drunk that night. Now I'm worried they will take her business while she's in jail."

"Well, I knew that they were cordial, but there were certain things of which we didn't speak. This redevelopment, she was over the top with it."

"She's not over the top considering they are decimating the neighborhood and stealing her business." Kay made a wide gesture.

"Now is not the time to discuss that. If you'll call the office . . . ."

Zimpel finally bounced off the wall. He stood tall over Weismann. "Now that we know she has a lawyer, I'll tell the cops to lay off her until her lawyer gets there. They've been wanting her to confess." Zimpel paused, waiting for Weismann to jump in. Had he done anything since she was arrested? "I told her not to talk to them."

"Confess? You've got to be kidding." Kay's fury was physical, her clenched hands, her tight shoulders, her eyes. "Idiots. You're all idiots if you can't get her out of jail. She didn't do anything but run a successful club." She glared at Zimpel and Weismann. "This is bullshit." Kay walked back to the car, leaving the men on the porch.

# CHAPTER 30

AUGUST 14, 1958 · THURSDAY LATE MORNING

Zimpel tapped on the door of the Blue Moon for Walter to unlock it—it was too early to open. He headed for the kitchen to talk with the staff.

"It needs more seasoning."

"It doesn't need any more seasoning, now stay out of my sauce." Sylvia ran the kitchen in Leitisha's place, giving orders in her firm, kind way.

"Inspector Zimpel, please come in. I spoke to Henry. He delivered vegetables twice this week, but he don't recall seeing any other delivery." Zimpel noticed her worried look. His questions weren't about Henry. He was establishing a timeline.

"I got the receipt book out so we can look at the other deliveries."

"Were you back here when they found the gun?"

"Yes, sir. They didn't see me over there by the stove. I was cooking when they came back here, yelling at everyone, telling us to get out. I don't know if they saw me but they—one of them, came in, looked around and went straight to the meat cooler." She pointed towards the cooler, around the corner from where she was working, towards the back door.

"Did you watch them?"

"I did. I know you want to know if they dropped it in there, and we already been talking about it, and I don't know Inspector Zimpel, I just don't know."

"It's ok, Sylvia, we'll figure it out."

Kay waved at Walter from the front door and he let her in. Dust danced in the sunbeam lighting up the front window. "Walter, how are you?"

"Doing fine, Miss Kay, considering. Zimpel's back there now with Miss Sylvia. You two following each other around?"

Kay wondered, too, and headed to the kitchen with its heaven of good smells, sparkling counters, chopped vegetables, everyone working hard to get ready to open.

"Hey Thursday?" Kay stood near him.

"What are you doing here?"

"I took off for an early lunch. Bianco went to the ballgame with a client. I'll be ok."

Zimpel nodded. "But why are you here?"

"Seriously, after that tiff with Saul?" Kay sat at the table, took out a notebook and waited. "He's obviously not doing anything."

She had the bug. He worried she might lose her job.

He pointed to the meat locker. "Sylvia watched the officers come in and find the gun there."

Kay walked over and explored around the locker. "Be hard to hide a gun in here. It's all wrapped meat."

She turned to Sylvia. "You saw them pull it out?"

Sylvia nodded. "They pulled out a package wrapped in white paper and opened it. The gun was inside."

Kay shook her head. "They made it look like meat. Means they disguised the gun at the butcher."

"Who's in the kitchen besides you, Sylvia, Cook, Tildy," Kay paused, "and the waiters?"

"Oh, Joshua, Edward and Albert don't come in here until right before we're ready with dinner."

"I'm thinking about outsiders—maybe this would happen with your regular deliveries. Think back who might have been here in the kitchen yesterday or the day before."

"We got folks in and outta here."

Kay glanced over at Zimpel. "That gun got wrapped in butcher paper and put into that meat locker. When do you get meat delivered? How long would it have been there before someone saw it?"

"We get meat delivered pretty regular."

"When did get your last meat delivery?"

"I got out the delivery book to check," said Sylvia opening a ledger.

"What else is delivered here?" Kay glanced at Cook.

"Oh, we get most supplies delivered, vegetables from Henry's farm, flour and baking goods get delivered every three or four weeks, sometimes we order special for certain spices and oil. Meat is the most frequent. We get it from a butcher down near the docks. He also has a store front in North Beach, Petrini's. Leitisha likes that one the best," Cook said.

Sylvia checked the ledger. "We haven't had a dry goods delivery for several weeks. We had meat delivered on Tuesday, day before yesterday."

"Leitisha was arrested yesterday, on Wednesday."

"Come to think of it, there was a new delivery boy for the meat. He said the other guy was sick. He didn't know where the meat locker was, and Tildy had to show him."

Cook motioned to Tildy. "Tildy, tell them about that delivery boy."

Tildy made a face, looking at the ground.

"Why the face?" asked Kay.

"He was rude. He said," Tildy stopped, put her hand to her mouth looking over at Zimpel, and then at Kay, lowering her voice. "He said things that boys shouldn't say to girls."

Cook frowned.

"Oh honey, you should've said something." Sylvia went over to her and put her arm around her shoulders. "I didn't see him doing that from my place at the stove."

"Anyway," Tildy fussed with her apron, "I showed him the meat cooler and where to put things, but I stood way outside the door. I backed away from him once he got the meat into the locker and I heard it close. I didn't want to be within arm's reach of him." She glanced around. "He ain't no meat delivery boy."

"I'm sorry he was such a . . . such a . . . jerk." Kay walked back to where the meat locker was. She turned to Zimpel. "A package wrapped in butcher paper would look like the meat and go unnoticed for a little while. The tip comes in and the cops find it because they've been told what to look for. Everyone else was busy in the main kitchen and Tildy was avoiding him, makes sense that's what happened."

Zimpel nodded. "Nice work, Kay."

"Thanks. He may have gone after Tildy to distract her, or get her out of the way."

Zimpel turned to Tildy. "Describe him for me? Or did you hear a name?"

"He gots to sign the delivery slip, and someone here has to sign it," said Cook. She looked at Sylvia who had already gone back to the desk.

"I don't like this boy. Here's the slip," said Sylvia. "Hard to make out his name. Can you read it?" She handed the slip to Kay. Zimpel read over Kay's shoulder. Scent of gardenia, a scent he knew well from home.

The name was unreadable. "How old was he?"

"He was about my age. He had on a letter sweater—maybe for football."

"Do you remember which high school?"

"I'm not sure, maybe SI."

Zimpel shook his head. "Saint Ignatius. Nice Catholic school. And the kid plants a gun and talks badly to someone his age? Was he taller than me?"

Kay remembered that Walter said his son went to SI.

"A little." She put her hand up to how tall she thought he was.

"What else? Hair color?"

"He had a blond buzz cut, and," she squinched her nose with a distant gaze. "He had Lucky Strikes in his white t-shirt pocket." She nodded her head at Kay.

"I bet he didn't have them when he was at school." She was impressed with Tildy's observations.

Zimpel's voice was soft. "That's good Tildy. Very helpful. We'll see if we can figure out who he is and what he knows."

Under his breath, he added, "And maybe I'll kick his ass for you."
Finally, Tildy smiled.

# CHAPTER 31

## AUGUST 14, 1958 · THURSDAY LATE AFTERNOON

Zimpel wanted more leads. Frazier was the key to finding the witness. Zimpel needed to obtain clearance for Frazier to work with him, and get some credit. But how to swing it past the Captain. He had heard that Chicago had a lot of sworn Negro officers and wondered how San Francisco got to be more like New Orleans than up north.

The more Negroes came to live in the Bay Area, the more restrictions seemed to come. Certainly redlining for homes, as he witnessed when he was buying his house. The realtor wouldn't sell to the Black family that was in the office at the same time he was, inquiring about houses for sale. "I'm sorry sir, that house has been sold" was the response to every question.

Standing in the doorway, he cleared his throat. The Captain looked up. "Yeah, Zimpel what's on your mind?"

"I want to use Frazier for the Marvin Wright investigation—I have to speak to some folks that don't trust talking to white people."

"Frazier?"

"William Frazier, sir, he's . . ."

The Captain finally got it. "For God's sake Zimpel. First, there isn't a 'Marvin Wright' investigation. We got the murderer—she'll confess eventually. Second, Frazier's hardly a cop. You have police power, get those people to talk to you."

"With all due respect sir," said Zimpel, "We don't have any evidence against Miss Boone except a planted gun and an argument—and lots to say it might have been someone else."

His statement "she'll confess eventually" made him reticent to share any facts with the captain or his lieutenant until he had it in the bag. Giving orders to beat cops to watch the bar, the ABC set up, and the gun plant, all pointed to someone inside targeting her. He didn't want good evidence disappearing. "Either way, we need to do more investigating, and frankly, I need Frazier sir, and he's a good cop with good instincts."

The Captain stared at him for a moment, then waved his hand. "You make me wonder sometimes Zimpel, spending all that time in the Fillmore. Do what you need, but case is closing quickly, so don't get in the way. And no overtime. I don't want Frazier stocking up on overtime because you gave him the green light. He needs to understand he's not an inspector and unlikely to be one."

"Yes, sir, I understand." All too well.

Zimpel called Frazier. "I got it cleared with the Captain."

"Yeah? Am I another boy to be handed around department to department—he own me? You own me?"

"I'll swing by and pick you up first thing tomorrow."

"Maybe you want to do it a little later in the day. Pimps aren't bright and early types."

"Yeah, yeah, we'll go after lunch then. Meet me at the station. And leave the uniform at home."

"Yeah, traipsing in uniform into a whorehouse might cause problems." Frazier hung up.


Leitisha wasn't getting bail. He had a call into the DA. He needed hard evidence to get her released. He drank coffee and smoked, reviewed what he had. He noticed his hair sticking up and scruffed his head. He needed a haircut.

He headed for Pettus's barbershop in the Fillmore. Getting his haircut in a black barbershop was another way he distanced himself from his fellow cops who didn't understand that the barbershop was better than a newspaper for local information. All the news of the neighborhood crossed at the barber shop. Fenton was sweeping out the doorway.

"Fenton, you got time to cut my hair?"

Fenton looked up and down the street, and then in his empty shop. "I dunno Zimpel, I'll see if I can fit you in." The two men laughed. He opened the door and hung the broom on a hook inside. "Nah, come on in. Long as I'm here, I'll cut your hair."

"Hear anything about what happened at the Blue Moon?" asked Zimpel. Fenton draped the white barber cloth over him.

"I heard they arrested her because of some argument she got into with Wright. That weren't nothing, him being hisself, she being herself." Fenton started his work.

"Hear anything else? Like someone might have a grudge against Miss Leitisha?" Zimpel was fishing.

Fenton caught Zimpel's eyes in the mirror. "You mean who might drop a gun on her?"

That fact was not in the paper. From the kitchen to the street, gossip flowed as freely as the gravy in Miss Leitisha's kitchen.

"She's a tough woman, and many don't like how successful she is. Myself? It keeps us all strong, we got good businesses going on around us." Fenton shrugged. "Someone always knocking down the successful Negro."

"Anyone come to mind?" Zimpel glimpsing to see if he can read anything in Fenton's expression.

"She a leader. You think those folks that are eating up the neighborhood want her around?"

"No, but that doesn't narrow down the search."

"I'd look at the folks who want to buy that parcel she's on. It's in the A-2, but some folks are antsy to get going with their building." Fenton took a soft brush to Zimpel's collar to clean the hair off. "When someone like Wright is killed, they are moving folks out of the way. Miss Leitisha, she just in the way."

Others had come into the barber shop with coffee, maybe a paper, having a cigarette, and talking about the news. "Haven't seen Miss Evelyn in a while."

"Oh, she gone. They tore down her rooming house, part of the A-1 renewal plan, so they say."

"What renewal? It's a big hole in the ground, ain't nothin' renewed. They said it was slum, that beautiful Victorian."

"Broke my heart to see that whole row of old Victorians torn down, declared in 'poor condition' by Redevelopment. Tearing down history."

Zimpel thanked Fenton, his theory supported by neighborhood chatter and sentiment.

Zimpel stopped back by the Blue Moon and saw Kay sitting at the bar. He walked in and nodded at Walter, who poured him a beer.

"Leitisha was arrested for murder because someone planted a gun in her kitchen." Kay shoved her glass back to Walter. "As a lawyer, I find that nearly impossible. This can't happen."

Zimpel drank his beer. It happened all the time. Drugs tossed into a gay bar to give them a reason to close it down. Guns slipped into a hand, evidence buried with the dead guy.

"Shows you how dangerous these guys are who want these properties." Zimpel stated the obvious.

"What if I had helped more, stood up for her?"

"They went after her because she's in the way of something they want. Doesn't matter what you did." Walter handed him a beer. "I thought you went back to work."

"I did, finished what I needed to, and came back. Bianco was still out with clients after the ballgame."

"They played the Cubs today. Won seven to four. Maybe he'll be in a good mood tomorrow."

"With me, he's always in a mood to make me work twice as hard as the guys for half the pay." She downed her whiskey.

Zimpel put money on the bar. "Come on, Kay, I'll drop you at home."

Kay started to protest, and Zimpel held up his hand. She closed her mouth and stood to go. Her face was pale. She slowly pulled on her jacket. She was tired and the whiskey weakened her, but she walked perfectly fine to the door. Zimpel reached around her to open it, getting a slight scent of gardenias. Still. At the end of the day.

Standing behind her, he saw a black limo pull away.

# CHAPTER 32

## AUGUST 15, 1958 · FRIDAY

Frazier met Zimpel at Kearny Street and Zimpel headed for North Beach. "Coffee?" he asked without waiting for an answer.

Zimpel parked in a red zone near Caffé Trieste, preferring beatnik animosity to all cops over middle-class prejudice against Blacks. They went in. No one looked at them but the server.

"Officers."

Zimpel nodded, picked up the coffee and put money on the counter even though the server didn't ask, wondering if the guys from Central took advantage of the free coffee. The coffee was really good.

"Last night, I'm at the Blue Moon, and another black limo pulled away as I was giving Kay a ride home."

"You sure you're not her chauffeur?" Frazier laughed, and then nodded at him to continue.

"Been too many black limos lately. Must be LCN but got no reason to say so. I have a license number, owned by Bay Limo."

Frazier shrugged. "I know those limo guys, maybe they'll talk to me."

"Yeah, something is going to clear up for us. We need it now."

"That why we sitting in North Beach? Looking for Eye-talians?" He looked around.

Zimpel wanted to laugh, but didn't. "You said you didn't want to go too early." He started the car. "Where are we going?"

"Head for Potrero. Known this guy since I was kid. I go in, talk to him, see if the girl is really there, figure out a way to ask about the girl without endangering her."

"You know a guy? You going to tell me the connection?"

"Nah. I give you all my secrets, I got nothing."

Zimpel nodded.

They drove to the building Frazier identified. "Pull over here.

Frazier got out, then leaned back into the window.

"Go get us some lunch. This may take a minute. I'm not back in 30 minutes, tell my kids goodbye for me." He gave a big grin that was more ironic than lighthearted.

Frazier's spirit was lively, giving him orders, and wanting to go at it solo.

Zimpel parked and got out of the car. "Nah, I'm going to play backup. I won't get in your way, but I want to be close, and I want to make sure you're ok."

Frazier's smile closed to a tight jaw, but he never expected to be let loose. Frazier nodded without looking back and went up to the door and knocked.

# CHAPTER 33

OCTOBER 20, 1956 · SATURDAY
BEFORE

The streetcar rumbled and rolled on an unusually warm day in San Francisco. Leitisha hurried to the dry cleaner. She wanted her silver dress clean for this Friday because Lena Horne was coming to San Francisco and to the Blue Moon. She loved Lena Horne, who would arrive with an entourage and fans craving autographs. Leitisha wanted to look sharp and be a proper hostess. Part of being the best and the smartest was dressing well.

She'd bought the dress at Bergdorf's in New York. Well, Saul bought it for her. Imagine a colored woman at Bergdorf's.

She had told him she needed a special dress, one that nobody had in San Francisco, and the shoes to go with it.

"Well, let's go shopping," he said. "And find you that dress."

"I can't shop for it, here, I want something no one else has." She loved being audacious, so she set it out there to see what Saul would do. "I want to go to New York."

"Let's go." He smiled sweetly at her. "Tonight!" Saul would do whatever he needed to take care of her. She loved him for that.

Then, what was she thinking? "I can't go, I got the club; I'm not packed."

"You can take a few nights. You can call them from there. You need time off. We'll get Walter and Sylvia to take care of the club, come on." He handed her an empty suitcase. "You can take this or we can get you a new one when we're in New York. We'll fill it full of new clothes. You ever been shopping in New York?"

She looked at him wide-eyed like he was crazy. "Saul, I haven't been out of California since my mama brought me from Mississippi." She laughed.

Saul shrugged. He was a few inches shorter than Leitisha when she was in heels, which was often, but in her eyes he was plenty big. "Come on then."

A limo took them out to the airport, and, after paying a redcap to check their luggage, Leitisha saw no other colored people in the lounge while they waited for the plane. The flight was long, and it was a little nerve-wracking as her first flight, but she didn't let on. They gave her champagne after all. Of course, a limo was waiting to pick them up and took them to the Waldorf Astoria. When Saul, the short, white Jew, walked in with her on his arm, eyebrows went up with the doorman, and then at the reception counter. Leitisha held her breath, sure they were going to say that she wasn't able to stay there. They checked in, he called her his wife, so maybe she was light skinned enough. Or maybe being escorted by Mr. Weismann was enough.

When they got to the room, there was already champagne on ice in a bucket. Saul opened it and poured them each a glass and held his high. "Here's to your first trip to New York City."

They clinked glasses. Leitisha barely spoke. Her eyes took in the room but she kept her grace and wits about her. The view out the large windows overlooked the hustle and bustle of New York City, a gorgeous park that stretched into the distance, with a fiery sunset as a backdrop. She had a beautiful house in San Francisco, but she had never been in a New York luxury hotel.

"Did you hear what the desk clerk said? That Eisenhower was here last month for the UN—the President in this very hotel."

He smiled.

Leitisha took in a breath. "Saul, you're a sweet thing. You're taking good care of me."

He kissed her lightly on the lips, and then winked at her. She never had a man conspire with her like this, treat her so equal with such respect.

It made her feel strong and confident, to have this kind of control. The large bed with its silk linens was inviting, and Leitisha wasn't too tired or overwhelmed to show her gratitude to Saul for bringing her to New York.

The next morning, after breakfast in the room brought on a rolling cart with silver and crystal, they went out, arm in arm down Fifth Avenue. Taxis everywhere, women in minks, limousines, and people bustling with places to go. Street noise, honking, and hawkers was the musical backdrop. Store after store displayed latest fashions, and bigger and grander than any in San Francisco including its City of Paris. It was fall and brisk in New York, the leaves on the trees in Central Park saturated in oranges, reds, and yellows.

"Here we are," said Saul, motioning to the doorman. Bergdorf's. Leitisha felt eyes on her but she never let on. Her friend Josephine Baker had told her about this—about highbrow New York City, the beautiful stores, and you wouldn't see any colored women in them except as servants. Josephine was a special person, and light skinned at that, so Leitisha told herself she was special, too. She held her head high and walked like she owned the place. Saul spoke to several people, and then asked for someone by name.

An older woman, dressed in a tasteful black dress and sweater, came up to Saul and holding both his arms, lightly kissed his cheek. "How you been Saul, been good?" Leitisha wondered who she was, coming up and kissing Saul.

Saul turned to Leitisha, "Nancy, this is Leitisha," and he winked at her. "I made her come to New York without packing. Can you help her out?"

Leitisha wasn't sure what Saul was saying with that wink, but the woman smiled warmly, and put her at ease in spite of her feeling out of place. "I think we can fix her up, Saul. Let's go up to the third floor."

Nancy took them to a private room. "Please take a look. Saul told me what you might like and I hope I got the right size." Leitisha felt self-conscious as the woman's eyes assessed her. If you don't see something you like, let me know and I'll bring in other dresses and pieces. We'll accessorize after you've chosen the outfit."

Saul smiled and watched comfortably on a small sofa while Leitisha tried on clothes and paraded for him. A large, stylish room, with no windows, a sofa and a chair, two three-way mirrors, a dressing room at one end, and a table laid out with champagne and water. They had the room to themselves. Dresses from Dior, Chanel, Fath (but those necklines!) and Balenciaga (not fitted enough for her). She only looked at the price tags when she was in the dressing room. She acted, or tried to because she had no idea how people who are used to this acted, like this was not her first time. Here she was 35 years old and never been to New York, and these dresses cost more'n her payroll for a month.

She picked out a good suit to wear while she was in New York, and the woman brought her underwear like she had never seen. The most amazing bra, girdle and hose, with a lovely black lace garter belt. She smiled thinking that Saul would like that. She got a sensible pair of heels and a stunning pair to wear at dinner—not for street walking.

Because it was fall, she chose a light coat to wear over the clothes, also in case of rain. She got a jaunty little hat—a brown one that would match the suit and the coat.

"Saul said you needed a special dress? How about this one?"

A silver sheath dress shimmered like moonlight. It was the most beautiful dress she had ever seen.

"This is gorgeous."

Nancy smiled. "Dior can never go wrong." She also set down matching shoes and a clutch. "You need these, too."

Saul drew in breath when he saw her in the dress. It glittered silver against her coffee skin.

"Oh, Saul. It's so elegant!"

"Turn around, now walk towards me." He watched her come to him. "You are stunning my dear Leitisha." The woman brought a mink stole and wrapped it around her—oh my lord what a feeling. Leitisha looked in the mirror and said a silent prayer to God. This did not happen to a Negro woman in the 1950s. She must be in heaven.

AUGUST 15, 1958
FRIDAY

Leitisha smoothed her hands on the gray prison dress, the thick black stockings itched under the ugly shoes that didn't fit. Her nails were chipped, and she hadn't slept much since they brought her in. She must have been dozing though, dreaming about her Dior dress. This cell was a far cry from Bergdorf's. The walls frightened her in a way nothing had before.

They booked her for murder. She didn't kill anybody, but that doesn't matter if you're a Negro. They pile it all on your back until it breaks. They hadn't let her use the telephone. She asked to talk to her lawyer, and they laughed at her. "You don't have a lawyer. You're never getting out of here."

Someone had to come for her, someone out there. She worried about the club, and what was going on.

At least she was alone in this cell. When she first came in, she was in a general cell with hookers, drug addicts, and others eyeing her wondering what she did, what she might have, whispering about her as she paced. She could sleep in here without feeling someone going to beat her up. Not that she slept much.

They wanted her club, wanted to tear it down, and move her out. For all she knew, they killed Marvin, and then put it all on her. She would get through this, she would survive it, and she prayed. "Oh, Jesus, did you need to make this burden so heavy?"

She heard a lock click and a door open in the hall. "Miss Boone?"

"Yes?" She stood. "My lawyer called you yet?"

"Nah, we heard from nobody, but we want to talk to you again. You need to tell us what you did now." Two inspectors stood there like thugs instead of lawmen.

This again. She sweat in her pits and between her legs, but didn't show anything on her face. They kept taking her to a room, one of these men yelling at her, telling her to confess, the other talking sweetly, telling her to unburden herself, and sign a confession. They threatened her, told her things they'll do to her. They didn't know her too well, they expect her to confess. Let them come and ask her over and over again. She'd tell them the same thing. She was innocent and they had to let her go. She steeled herself for another go, and hoped they didn't try to touch her.

# CHAPTER 34

## AUGUST 15, 1958 · FRIDAY MORNING

Kay woke up the next morning with an ache behind her eyes. It wasn't the whiskey. She closed the curtain over the rising sunlight.

Ok, maybe it was. Pulling her robe around her, she made coffee, and felt dread, like a flu coming on. Groaning, she dressed for work. She had to go in today, no getting around it.

She went through the medicine cabinet, and the drawers near the sink looking for Bayer for this headache. Nothing. She'd stop by the pharmacy on her way in.

She got off the streetcar near the Fillmore to patronize its stores. The notion that the stores and businesses would be gone depressed her. She wanted to patronize them as long as she could.

As Kay waited in line to pay for her aspirin, the gray-haired pharmacist handed a package to a young man. "Now, Tyrone, I need you to take this over to Miss Fannie. She's too sick to get out, but she needs her medicine."

The young man nodded.

"You know where she lives?"

"On Ellis, sir, right off of Fillmore, yes sir."

"And, if she has the money, she'll pay you. But if she doesn't, give her the medicine and come back here, and let me know, ok?"

The young man nodded again, put the package in his bicycle basket, tied it down and pedaled off.

Kay decided she needed to push more, to make a difference. While she may not stop the razing of the Fillmore, she could do what Zorn was doing, help residents get what they deserved. She caught a streetcar towards downtown and the office.

Frank Bianco stood in her door. "Kay you haven't heard anything I said, have you?"

She hadn't—whether it was the headache, fatigue, or anger she wasn't sure. "I'm sorry Frank, I think I'm coming down with something. I'm waiting for the aspirin to kick in. Something about the bank deal?"

"Kay you've been too preoccupied lately. Are you sure you're up to this work? It's not too much for you?"

His constant implication that women were unable to keep up with men was wearing on her. She worked circles around them at half the price and played music at night.

She felt no urgency to review the agreements she needed to review by this afternoon. The bank's business deal had no meaning to her compared to what was happening in the Fillmore, where lives were at stake. Still, she buckled down so she wouldn't have to listen to Frank tell her how inferior she was.

"Here's the bank deal Frank, let me know if you want to go over the agreements."

"Yes, I want to go over them, but I don't want to be making any appointments with you. I'll let you know when I'm ready."

"Sure, happy to stick around." She decided to push a little.

"Frank."

He cocked his head at her. "There's a question coming and you're not supposed to be asking questions, you're supposed to be working."

She ignored him. "You went to SI, right?"

"Yes, some time ago."

"Isn't there an alumni association?"

"Oh, yes. I'm quite active in it." He perked up. Something to brag about. She'd hit it just right. He was probably president or something and raised money for them.

"What do they do for you? You know, you get your name in the paper or something?"

"I don't know where this is going, but the elite alumni donors get a special place at graduation, and presented each year with the yearbook, and our names are in them." He pointed over to his bookshelf where she saw a stack of yearbooks. "We're honored every year by the school for our contribution. Why do you need to know?"

"Doing some research for a friend about the school, not a big deal. That's all nice." She picked up the current yearbook. "Do you get your photograph in it?"

"No, no, but we're listed towards the end." She flipped the book open.

"Let me take a look?" She intended on walking out with it.

"Sure, sure. It's a very prestigious school, costs a lot of money for parents to send their kids, contributions to the Church and all. Lots of judges started there." He shooed her with his hand. "You'd be lucky to get your kids in there. If you ever had any kids. Now, get to work on the Anderson deal?"

# CHAPTER 35

Walter Jenkins got there first. Sylvia, Tildy, and then the others gathered, standing in front of the restaurant, reading the poster on the door with big red letters: CLOSED UNTIL FURTHER NOTICE. Small type underneath the red letters cited a regulation. The end of the notice was more small type about how the premises were now held by the city, with the signature of The San Francisco Redevelopment Agency.

Walter tried his key and the door opened. What was this about? Redevelopment put a notice on the door but didn't change the locks or lock them out.

"Walter? What's going on?" Sylvia read the notice over his shoulder.

"I don't know Sylvia, I don't know. Something's not right." He flipped the light switch and to his relief, the lights came on. Whatever they was doing, they hadn't turned off the power. He still didn't go in, frozen at the door.

He heard the others talking behind him. "What are we going to do?"

"They come to close Leitisha's because she's in jail."

"I need this job."

"Where we supposed to go now? What does this mean?"

"Take our homes, now taking our work. You think slavery is over? Next they'll be taking our children."

Walter Jenkins read the notice again. A bunch of legal stuff that didn't mean anything to him. He exchanged looks with Sylvia. His insides were jumping like popcorn on a hot fire. He had to do something and standing on the sidewalk wasn't it.

"Look folks, let's go in. We all here, so they can't close us." He stood aside and the crew walked in, bewildered and sad.

Sylvia read the notice again. "Walter, let's find out what this is about. They can't close the restaurant." With that, she went to the kitchen to start her day, leaving it to him.

Walter went over to the house phone. No dial tone. He had to do something before the power was cut, too, and whatever else might happen. Who had authorized the telephone shut-off?

Walter walked over to Pettus's Barber Shop.

"Fenton, can I use your telephone? They're aiming to close Miss Leitisha's and they shut off the telephone. I need to make a call."

"And who's going to pay for that? Miss Leitisha can't even make bail. She's in deep woes."

Walter put a quarter on the counter in front of the mirrors and pulled a card out of his inside coat pocket and dialed a number.

"Bianco and Associates. How can I help you?"

Walter hesitated a minute. He was a bartender. This other stuff, he wasn't sure about. "Hello?"

"Hello. Sorry, is Miss Kay in?"

"You want to speak to Katherine Schiffner?"

Walter hesitated again. "Yes, yes, please." Pettus gave him the eye, minding Walter's business. Walter turned to face outside.

"Miss Kay," Walter said when she came to the phone, "they tried to close Miss Leitisha's place and turned off the telephone."

"Walter, what are you saying?"

"Those redevelopment folks, they swooped in like vultures and put a notice on the door. It isn't right and all of us standing around wondering if we have jobs or what."

"Walter, are you there now?"

"I'm over at Pettus's barbershop. It was the closest telephone."

"They turned off the telephone?"

"Yes, ma'am, but the electricity still works. For now."

"Can you get into the restaurant?"

"Yes, ma'am. They didn't change the locks, just posted the notice. But what does it mean?"

"I don't know yet. I'll get a cab and come to you. I want to see that notice. Go back to the Blue Moon and make sure no one tears down that notice until I get there."

"Yes, ma'am." He felt good for calling her. It had taken a lot out of him, but it was the right thing to do.

Kay swore to herself, so angry with the greed and the men who wanted Leitisha to fail. What Zorn had warned her about—well here it was. Shutting down the restaurant, hoping that no one would push back, hoping to bully their way through. By God, she was going to push back.

"Kay, where are you going?"

Frank saw her in reception with her coat on. She didn't have time to lie.

"Redevelopment put a notice on the door of the Blue Moon, closing it without any process, without any warning. It's not right. I'm going over there to see what the notice on the door says and what I can do."

Frank stood, his mouth open. "Don't you go out that door—we've talked about this. I have real work I need you to do, and I'm sick of taking flak from clients for your carrying on for the colored in the Fillmore—you can't stop redevelopment, but you can lose your job."

"I'll be back. This won't wait." She shook her head and walked out. No other option.

When she got to the restaurant, a truck was parked in front, and Walter was arguing with two large men.

"We was told to empty out the restaurant . . . now get out the way."

Kay stood next to Walter and faced the two men. "What," she paused, swallowing curses, "is going on here?"

One of the men towered over her, agitated.

"We was given instructions to come to this address and empty it out."

Kay interrupted him. "You can't do that. It's illegal."

"What you know?" The second man stepped closer to Walter and Kay.

"I'm a lawyer." She walked toward the second man. She felt Walter's eyes on her back and weight on her shoulders.

"What you're doing is illegal. Now get out of here before I call the cops." She wanted to take a swing at that guy.

"You ain't no lawyer. This here place was closed—and . . ." He put his hand on her shoulder to push her out of the way.

Kay batted away his grip and turned to tear the sign off the door. Her purse slipped from her arm, fell onto the ground, and she kicked it behind her.

She shook the notice in their faces. "You can't close someone down without compensation. You can't come in and steal property from a business. What you are doing is theft. Might even be robbery."

The men's eyes were wide, and they froze where they were.

"You can get arrested and go to jail for this. Do you understand?" The last three words she pronounced slowly.

A crowd gathered around her on the sidewalk and employees were milling about, some coming out from inside.

"This restaurant cannot be closed and emptied because some rich jerk says so." She put both her hands out now and pushed the two men towards their truck.

"Get into your truck. Tell the men that sent you if they try this again, I'm going to sue them for every dime they have." She sweat from anger.

If no one had called her, if they pulled up to a business that didn't know their rights, they'd steal the business. How dare men take advantage to earn a profit? She willed herself to calm, to play though this.

The two men stood, the bigger one staring at her, and then at the crowd that had gathered at the sidewalk and inside the door. Kay was the only white face in the group besides them. She took another step towards the men.

She heard murmurs in the crowd, throat clearing that meant to give her backup. The second man shook his head, pointed at the restaurant. "We gave up our day to move this stuff, and we can't leave until we get it done."

Kay understood what he was saying. With her eyes focused on them, bent down to pick up her purse, felt for some paper money, and put $10 into the hands of the second man.

"Who sent you here?" She dropped her voice.

"Says redevelopm't." The second one pointed at the paper in her hand.

"You didn't see this until you got here. Who gave you the assignment?"

The two men looked at each other, and the one who took the ten hunched his shoulders and glanced around. "Miss, we was tol' at work to come here. They give us the address, and we come. We don't make no decisions."

She noted the name of the moving company on the truck. "You didn't see who your boss spoke to?"

He shook his head.

"What's your boss' name?"

They shuffled again, and finally the big man said, "Murphy O'Brien." The Irish were contractors or movers. Kay noted the name. Getting complicated, all these pieces.

"Thanks. Now go back and have your boss tell the men that hired your company to do it legally next time."

She stood still, her arms crossed now. Finally the big man turned and climbed back into the truck's cab and started it. The second man joined him and they left.

Walter walked up behind her. "Glad they left without a fight. You're strong, Miss Kay, but it could've got ugly."

It had felt like a fight to her. "They knew it was dicey, and decided not to risk it." She stood firm against them. So unfair.

She asked Sylvia for copies of the telephone bill to call and get the service reinstated. She told Walter to call her if anything else happened.

She took a cab back to the office. Two cab rides in one day wouldn't put her in the poor house but she hoped that she didn't have to do that often. Marlene, at the switchboard caught her as she came in.

"Frank said you are to go see him the minute you get back."

Kay's stomach clenched. Marlene's mournful eyes told her enough.

She slipped into her office before Irma fetched her. She wanted a few things if Frank was going to fire her. She quickly filled up a box and took a few files she had, saw the SI yearbook that she had taken earlier from Frank's office and threw it in. Hopefully, no one would search her box.

When she was satisfied she had what she needed, she walked down the hall, struggling to appease her boss, the one that had given her opportunity but at a cost she couldn't afford right now.

# CHAPTER 36

Kay stood in his doorway, searching for something persuasive to say. Frank was on the telephone. "Yeah, I'll talk to you later." As he hung up, he noticed her and shook his head.

"Kay, I warned you, and for your own good, I gotta follow through. It pains me that you can't cut it here."

Kay's temper flared inside her already churning stomach. There was nothing wrong with her work; he didn't like her attitude.

"I told you not to walk out that door, but you made your choice."

Kay chose her words carefully, feeling queasy. He was blaming her when he had the discretion to let it go. "Frank, I'm grateful to you for my opportunity, and I don't mean to be disrespectful." She inched further into the office. Her heart screamed flight. "This was an emergency, and under the circumstances, I was the only person capable of preventing catastrophe."

Frank stood. "With all I have put on the line for you, it's my credibility that is at issue here, it's my reputation. I don't want to hear my clients asking me what I'm doing, letting a girl run all over me and not do her work, taking risks as you go gallivanting off. I want to run a good law firm. But I can't do it with you compromising our quality and our clients with your own ideas. You want to go out there on your own, like you're itching to do, then I'm going to let you. Understand what you're throwing away here."

Kay saw his anger stirring underneath his words. He didn't want to be crossed, or have his judgment questioned. What man did?

He rubbed it in. "I pictured you a partner here, setting the high standards for other women."

Kay didn't believe him. She'd never make partner, but he was on his high and mighty now.

He put his hand through his hair and half an eye on the telephone, which was blinking at him. He finally looked up at Kay.

"You're a good lawyer, Kay, but you've got to learn to play the game right, and this isn't right. Get your things, give your remaining work to Brian, and get out of here. Maybe when you're done saving the world, you can work a real job." And with that, he sat down and picked up the telephone.

"Marlene, get me Mr. McCann please? Yeah, that's the one." He glanced up at Kay who still stood in the doorway. "We're done here."

Still angry, swallowing the comments she wanted to throw at him, and a little scared of what she was going to do, she packed a few more things. She wasn't going to be upset, not yet, or have panic set in, like how she was going to pay her rent.

She now had two boxes of stuff, awkward to carry with her purse and briefcase. She gave her files to Brian, and told him to call her if he had questions. He gave her a sympathetic if lecherous look.

"Told you," he said.

As if she'd go out with him now.

Marlene called her a cab because of the bulky boxes. Her third cab ride of the day.

"Where to Miss?"

She gave the cabbie Zorn's address on Davis Street. Somehow it made sense and a shorter distance so less money.

She hit the bell.

The intercom crackled. "Yeah?"

"Michael, it's Kay."

At the sound of the buzzer, she pushed the door with her shoulder, pulling the boxes inside.

"What's going on?"

With the door ajar, she pushed her hair out of her face, her hat askew and her gloves long relegated to her coat pockets, and awkwardly pulled the second box inside. "I hate to impose, but I got kicked out of my office for being insubordinate." Blessed bluntness, she didn't have to pretend.

Zorn laughed. "Welcome then. Come in and tell me about it. I'll make coffee."

"What's that music?"

"Vivaldi. The Four Seasons. I think this is Fall."

"Appropriate." She started to relax. She didn't even know this guy, yet felt comfortable here, like she could work.

Zorn made some of his delicious coffee and Kay told him about the attempt to close the Blue Moon, the movers, and her subsequent firing.

"Taking property without notice and a hearing? I'm not surprised, but that's a new one. Is the owner still in custody?"

"Yes, they won't grant her bail. Hard to believe this has all happened in two days—almost like she was set up from the beginning. But how did they know that she would get angry at Wright."

Zorn paused. "If they were setting her up, they simply had to wait, and take advantage of whatever happened."

"But who, Michael? Who is doing this?"

"I don't know. You need to figure out who sent that notice and the movers. It stinks, and isn't right, but you know that. What are they doing at the restaurant?"

"We tore down the notice, and everyone went to work. What else?"

"Good. Force them to take real action and not this backdoor bullshit." She heard passion in his voice. "I'm not surprised at their tactics. For the most part, they're dealing with folks who don't have lawyers on call like you. They'd capitulate to that pressure. The Blue Moon should be glad to have you."

Kay had mixed feelings of relief and anxiety, although being in Zorn's office was strangely comforting.

"Yeah, I hope so, but it's still a band-aid on a gunshot wound. I hope it was worth my job." She groaned. "What am I going to tell my parents?"

"Let me give you some advice." Zorn said. "Get busy with what you need to do and you won't have time to fret about what people think." Zorn cleared a surface for her. He had two telephones, and gave her one. "There're two lines on here; here's the hold button. We don't have a lot of help, but we do have some services."

Kay heard him say "we" so she sat at the desk, straightening folders in front of her, and reached for a tablet of paper. "Yeah, let's get to work. I'll get their phone back up first."

"Must have been a mistake," was all the telephone company would say. She called Murphy O'Brien's movers.

"Someone there sent a truck to the Blue Moon. I need to know who."

"Who's calling please?"

"I'm the lawyer for the Blue Moon and someone mistakenly sent two men over. Can you tell me who sent them?"

"Please hold." The line went silent. Then a dial tone. She called again, a busy signal. She'd try again in a few minutes.

Next up was to trace the notice from the Blue Moon.

She called the Redevelopment Agency first, to find out who would authorize such a thing, especially sending movers?

"Please hold."

A few minutes later, the operator's voice came back, "What did you say your name was?"

"Katherine Schiffner."

"And who did you want to speak to?"

Kay sighed.

"I want to speak to whoever put the notice on the Blue Moon."

"I need to know where to direct your call."

"The notice was signed by the agency, not any particular person. Is there someone in charge of the A-1 Redevelopment?"

"There's an entire committee. Who do you want to speak to?"

"Someone authorized the notice. Who would do that?"

"Ma'am, I'm just the operator. I need to know who you want to speak to." She clicked the line. "Please hold."

A few seconds later, the operator came back on the line. "Ma'am, I need to know where to direct your call."

"How about your boss? Can we start there?" Kay's patience, dealing with the movers, losing her job, was entirely gone. She felt raw inside and tired.

"He's not in today." Of course.

Kay shut her eyes, counted to five.

"Ma'am, are you still there?"

"Yes, thank you. What is your boss' name?"

"His name is Mr. Bounty."

Kay wrote it down, and then hung up. Of course there would be no one responsible—close down people's lives and no one is accountable.

Zorn was bent over a box of documents. "Not getting anywhere?"

"Do you have any jazz albums?"

Zorn shook his head. Kay resolved to bring in some music. The music in the background was really nice.

"I need to talk to someone at Redevelopment about this notice, but unless I have a name, the operator won't connect me to anyone."

Zorn straightened up and looked for a card on his desk. "Here, call this guy, Tony Bridges. He's been one of the main guys on the A-1, and I've talked to him a couple times. He'll at least talk to you and I bet he's in today. They are busy. Make sure it wasn't them and maybe we can narrow it down."

Naturally, he had a name. Kay wasn't used to asking for help and getting it.

She dialed Redevelopment again, relief at getting a real person to speak to.

"Hang on, let me look up the address." Hanging on was all she had to do.

"We didn't put up that notice, we don't have authorization. At least, not yet. I don't know who sent those guys with the truck."

"You mean someone impersonated the Redevelopment Agency? Who would have access to your stationery?"

"They probably copied another notice. We have them up on various properties in the A-1 area. I'm sorry for the inconvenience. You can ignore it. For now."

"A bit more than an inconvenience. Hard to ignore two big men who wanted to bully their way into a restaurant and take its furnishings."

"Don't know what to tell you, Miss. Eventually, it's going to all come down."

# CHAPTER 37

## AUGUST 15, 1958 · FRIDAY

A big man opened the door, blocking it.

"Whatchou doin' here?"

Frazier went up a step and stood nose to nose. "Need to speak to Theodore."

Zimpel watched from the side of the building, out of sight but not earshot. Theodore? In a whorehouse?

The big man stepped back, and Frazier brushed past him. Zimpel felt the tension emanating from the two men and he didn't like it.

If he had been present as back up, neither of them would have gone in. Why he needed Frazier. He glanced at his watch to time it. If too much time went by, he'd go in with his gun.

Frazier followed the big man down a long hallway, relaxed his shoulders, expressionless, projecting confidence. Inside he was hypervigilant, his eyes combed the closed doors, his ears heard the slightest sound. Voices, shuffling upstairs, but he discerned nothing definite. The hallway was muffled quiet.

Frazier saw a large room ahead but before they reached it, his guide stopped and opened a door off the hallway. He stood aside and motioned for Frazier to go in.

Frazier raised his eyebrows at the guide.

"Nah, he knows you're carrying. You're a cop. Don't shoot him, ok?"

Frazier smiled his cold smile and went into the room. Unlike the dim hallway, the room was full of light from a glass wall with French doors, a garden beyond. A thick cement wall with glass shards on top surrounded the garden. The room was furnished with two pristine chestnut leather guest chairs, a large desk with a tall swivel chair behind it, and a thick, red, oriental rug. A diminutive man in a creamy suit sat in the desk chair.

"Hello little brother. What brings you here to see me?"

"I ain't your brother." Frazier stood, relaxed.

"Sit down, sit down, sure you are."

Frazier recalled a street in Butchertown, no sidewalk, three big kids and one short one. He had a stack of newspapers he was delivering. "You coming wid us, little Willie Frazier, this is how it's gonna go down."

"I ain't coming with you punks."

"You gonna go fight the white man's war?"

"War is over bro, I'm just making a living."

"I'm making plenty, you shore you wanna do that?"

One of the bigger kids went up to Frazier, then looked back at the short guy.

"Ah leave him be, we don't need to beat him up, the white man will do it fer us."

This delinquent in his fancy office with leather chairs, his whores down the hall in the big room, and Frazier living in an SRO, being the white man's bitch at the police station. Still, Frazier would make the same choice again.

"So what can I do for little Willie Frazier?" He looked like a kid in that chair.

"I'm not the one who was little, Teddy." Frazier wasn't going to call him "Theodore" if he kept up this little Willie shit. Teddy's feet barely reached the floor, the chair nearly swallowed him.

"I'm looking for someone; she might work for you."

"Ah, you fancying something?"

Frazier stood, no expression on his face.

"Ah, you ain't here for fun. Why you packing and standing there all official like you some real cop or something." Teddy stood in his fancy off white suit, and he pulled the cuffs of his white shirt showing off the gold cuff links. "You know they never gonna let you be a real cop, they too scared."

Frazier heard all this before. He'd made his choice.

"Come on, let's walk down to the room where the escorts meet their dates. You shore I can't fix you up?"

"I'm sure."

"And I ain't gonna get in trouble for this?"

"You be in more trouble, you don't let me talk to them. Might benefit you."

"You know what she looks like?"

"She young, with processed hair, little chubby and spent some time with a rich Black man."

"Ohhh, they's all young here, that's the name of the game."

Frazier twisted inside, but let nothing show. He wanted to burn this place down, but not yet. He came for something and he was going to get it. He also remembered Zimpel telling him "smells like roses" and "chews Juicy Fruit." He didn't tell Teddy that. He wanted first crack at her, in case they decided to hurt her before he could get her out of there safely.

He followed Teddy down to the big room, floor lamps, recessed lights to heighten the mood, lounges, overstuffed chairs and an oriental rug. Uptown. The large bodyguard followed until they reached the door and then stood, watching. Frazier now saw that these were girls, not women but girls, giggling and young, way too young. He wasn't sure now how he was going to pick out the girl they needed to talk to.

"Now you can talk, but no touching," said Theodore, laughing, "these'r mine now. You want some'in, you gotta pay for it."

Frazier curled and uncurled his right fist, but kept his arms relaxed and at his side. He didn't want to alarm the bodyguard and risk a shootout among all these girls.

As he observed the room, the girls twirled away like they were minnows and he was a hungry bird. Most of them had processed hair or tight pig tails. Zimpel described the girl as dark, with longer hair, and wore bright pink lipstick. And she had some heft on her in the backside.

A cloying scent of cheap roses wafted. Frazier watched a young girl slink to a lounge in the shadows in the back. Frazier followed the scent. "Can I talk to you for a minute?" he said in a low voice.

The girl, startled, glanced over at Teddy, who waved his hand at her. "Answer his question y'all, for a few minutes and then I'ma boot him outta here."

Her hands in her lap and her eyes unfocused, she sat still. Good chance she was addicted to something as her shackles. Folks enslaving their own.

Frazier squatted down to her face level, and figured maybe she was fifteen or sixteen, with a body that matured early.

"What's your name, darling?"

Her eyes were huge and brown, and the irises shone out at him. He wanted to pull out his gun, tuck her up, and carry her out of there. Instead he sat and waited for her to speak.

"You a police man?" Her voice shook a bit. He noticed she chewed her fingernails.

"Yes. But I'm not here about anything," he paused, "that Theodore might be up to." He lowered his voice, turning away from Theodore, and his bodyguard. "I'm looking for someone who was with Mr. Wright in his Cadillac . . ." He watched her face as he spoke. Her body language answered him.

She pushed back on the lounge she was seated on, crossed her arms in front of her, and looked back down at the floor. Her foot started to kick.

"It was you," he said quietly.

She nodded, still looking down, nearly hugging herself.

Now that he'd found her, he had to protect her. She wasn't safe here or anywhere.

"Come on honey, you need to come with me."

The girl, big eyed now, pulled back towards the wall.

"It's for your own safety," Frazier said quietly, "Because you ain't safe right now."

The girl glanced around her. The other girl sitting on the lounge with her got up and sat across the room.

He reached out his hand, and she pulled her arms in close. "Don't make me pick you up and carry you outta here."

"Are you arresting me? We have a lawyer." A practiced line. She'd been trained.

"I'm taking you in for your own protection."

"You just going to take me?"

"I let you get your things, you'll take off on me. I been around the block before." He smiled at her, but she still looked scared. He was afraid if she didn't leave with him right then that she'd disappear for bringing in the heat.

Theodore was in the hallway when Frazier was walking out with the girl. "You come barging in here, and now you're taking my property. On a Saturday."

"Last I looked, slavery was abolished." Frazier stood still and strong in the hallway.

"Ah, you know what I mean. You can't take her."

"I can. She's a material witness, and I'm taking her into custody for grand jury testimony." There wasn't any grand jury formed, but Theodore didn't know that.

"Who's going to compensate me?"

"Tell you what. I'll refrain from telling vice you got underage girls for sale today, and you back off. You come after me or this young lady, and I sic the puritan, commie hunters after you." George Christopher and his cohorts were going after gay bars in North Beach, why not kiddie bordellos in Potrero?

Theodore stood for a moment and then went back into his office. Likely, he was going to find out how Frazier found him, and maybe move his operations. At least, that's what Frazier would do in his shoes. Frazier didn't know why Theodore let him in to begin with.

"Come on, let's get you out of here."

The goons guarding stared at him as he put himself between her and the guards in case someone got a crazy idea. She was trembling, but walked herself out.

He saw the car pull around and he steered the young girl into it.

"Who's that?"

"A friend. Let's go."

Where was he going to put a drug-addicted juvenile and a flight risk, and who needed clothes and a toothbrush?

Frazier put the girl in the back seat, and then got in after her.

Zimpel turned to look at him and the girl. "We have a guest?"

"Yes, meet . . . I'm sorry, dear, I didn't get your name."

"Madie."

"Got a last name?"

"Gunther."

Zimpel pulled away. "Well, Madie Gunther, we'll see if we can explain to you that Frazier here saved your life."

# CHAPTER 38

Zimpel headed for 750 Kearny to record the girl's responses in the interview room so there'd be no argument. As he glanced at her, she stared out the window with no volition.

Frazier tapped him on the shoulder from the back. "You can't take her there." He had read Zimpel's mind, or at least the direction of car. "She ain't safe. Same folks that framed your gal gonna make sure we don't have a witness."

"You takin' me to jail?" The girl scratched her arm.

"Not exactly," said Zimpel. Frazier was right about taking her to Kearny Street. "Where do you suggest?" he asked catching Frazier's eye in the rear view.

"No," said Frazier. "I don't need the trouble that would bring me."

"Children's Bureau?" asked Zimpel.

"Oh, yeah, for Colored? Nah. Same problem as 750."

Zimpel turned off and headed for the Fillmore.

The girl, Madie, slumped in the passenger seat. "Now what?" She sensed a change in plans.

"We're taking you to stay with friends, to keep you safe."

Her brown eyes turned to him. "Ain't nobody my friend. They all bad guys. I pass from one to 'nother." She gazed back out the window.

This girl's life was already difficult, and now they put her in more danger.

"Madie, how did you meet Mr. Wright?"

"Who?" She sat up in the seat.

"The man you went to the Blue Moon with, who bought champagne, who had the Cadillac deVille."

"Like I always do. Mr. Theo says to go, and I go." Madie regarded Frazier as she spoke.

"How'd you get to Mr. Theodore?"

"My mama worked for him."

"She doesn't anymore?"

"She dead.." She drew out the word.

Zimpel winced. In the rearview he caught Frazier working his jaw. "And it was Mr. Theodore that took you to the man with the Cadillac?"

"No, it was another man, a white man, he brought me, had a big ol' limo."

"Where did he take you?"

The girl wiped her nose again. Zimpel handed her his clean handkerchief. God bless his mother who insisted every man had to have a clean handkerchief in his pocket. She stared at it and him before she used it. So damn young.

"Took me to a street somewhere, said wait here, man come by in a Cadillac, and will pick you up. 'Bout few minutes later, man came by, said git in, so I did."

Zimpel maneuvered around a garbage truck and headed along Divisadero Street. Divisadero followed a three-mile corridor, the original path from the Mission Dolores, the first site the Spanish settled 200 years ago, to the Presidio. It was considered romantic, which brought irony to the moment, another sign he was getting closer. He drove into the Fillmore and pulled up outside the Blue Moon.

"This where the lady threw me out."

"Yes, I know, but you'll be safe here."

Madie gave him a side glance.

Zimpel knocked at the door. Walter unlocked it and let them in. Frazier was right behind him with the girl in between, hopefully hidden.

Walter held the door, locking it behind them, his eyes following the girl.

"I know her."

"Yes you do," said Zimpel. "Sorry to burden you, but we brought her here because we don't have anywhere else to take her."

"They tried to close us today."

Zimpel ran his hand through his hair. He was having a hard time keeping up.

"What happened?"

Frazier leaned against a wall, and settled in to listen.

"I got here early this morning and there was a certificate on the door, said the restaurant was closed, and it was signed by Redevelopment. I unlocked the door, and the lights worked, but the telephone was dead. I called Miss Kay . . ."

Zimpel got a bad feeling about all of this. Too many things were converging on them.

"She came down, and good thing. Two big guys showed up with a truck, ready to haul out the restaurant."

"What do you mean 'haul out'?"

"I mean take the tables, the chairs, the china, everything. They were told to empty the place."

Zimpel shook his head. "I don't understand—just take her things?"

"Yeah, the notice was on the door—they didn't know. Anyway, Miss Kay was at work. She came down and got them to leave."

"She came from work and dealt with it?"

"Yessir, and it's a good thing. Not sure what I could've done . . . . Anyway, come in with the chil' and let's see what we can do."

Walter walked to the kitchen, Zimpel and Frazier followed. "Come on back," said Zimpel. "I'll show you the drop site."

They all came into the kitchen. Sylvia scanned the group, nodding at Frazier, and then stopped at the girl.

"Sylvia, I hate to burden you, but Madie here needs a safe place to stay, and I didn't trust the Children's Bureau or Juvie, or frankly anyone."

Sylvia wiped her hands on a towel and came over to Madie. She touched the girl's arms and took her hands. "We got her today, no problem. Where she going sleep?"

"Let me work on that," said Zimpel.

"Tildy, get them some sweet tea, and put some bread and jam out for now? Y'all can taste my smothered chicken in a bit. Sit at the big table."

They sat down, happy to have some sweet tea, and ate the bread, smiling all around the kitchen, feeling at home. Madie drank the entire glass of sweet tea. Tildy hovered over her, and poured her another, her curiosity making her stare at the girl she knew must be a prostitute.

# CHAPTER 39

## AUGUST 15, 1958 · FRIDAY NIGHT

Kay walked home from the streetcar, uneasy about her changed circumstances. Zorn was sweet and all, letting her use his office, but how was she going to pay her rent? She hadn't been hired by Leitisha or the Blue Moon, even though all the work she was doing was for them. She'd gone from successful lawyer to unemployed in a day, and she'd be hard pressed to get another lawyer job, especially when her reference would likely be poor.

A car engine started. Feeling watched, she hurried her steps, as much as she could in heels. She pulled her coat tighter. The fog blocked the faint twilight left in the steel-gray sky, chilling the air. The street was empty except for a cab. Now that she didn't have a job, she wasn't going near a taxi.

Streetlights reflected off the parked car windshields, hiding anyone inside. She dropped her keys nervously when she reached her building. She rang for the elevator and it came empty. Mr. Louis must have gone to dinner.

Flicking the hall light on, she peered out her picture window. A man in a long black coat and hat stood in the light of the streetlamp and stared up at her window. She had been right. Her stomach tightened, her mouth dry. She slunk out of sight and hit the light in the hall.

If he was standing under the streetlight, he wanted to be seen. He wanted her to know he was there. Gave her goosebumps. She picked up the telephone. No dial tone.

Of all nights for the telephone not to work. She snuck another peek out the window, her apartment now dark. He was still there, looking up at her window. She shivered. This was a threat.

Was this what Zorn warned her about? Or the kind of trouble Zimpel worried about?

She picked up the phone again and jiggled the switch hook, trying to get an operator. She dialed zero listening to the clicks, but no dial tone, no operator. Still dead. Taking a breath, she went out into the corridor scanning the neighbors' closed doors. Who might still be awake? She listened carefully and heard a radio from across the hall so knocked lightly on the door. Between work, and playing music at the Blue Moon, she hadn't gotten to know her neighbors.

She heard a woman's voice behind the door. "Who is it? You know it's late?"

"I'm so sorry to disturb you and I hope I didn't wake you. It's Kay Schiffner, I live across the hall."

The door opened as wide as the chain with a clunk. Through the crack, a woman's pale face peered out, no makeup, curlers, wearing a quilted housecoat covered in pink roses.

"You didn't wake me, I was up. What do you want?"

"My telephone isn't working." She feigned calm. "May I use your telephone? I need to call my mom and tell her I'm all right."

The woman sighed. "You look all right." She closed the door, pulled the chain and let Kay in. "You might as well come in." A large yellow cat meowed and Kay started.

"Oh, that's Cooper, you know, like the actor."

Kay, "Who?"

"You know, Gary Cooper. He'll be ok, so long as you're not wearing stockings." The woman glanced at Kay's legs, which had stockings. "You best be careful. He loves to tear them up."

"Ok. Hello Cooper," said Kay, eyeing the cat. "I'm Kay." She turned to the woman in the housecoat. "And what is your name?"

"I'm Mrs. Johnson—uh, Lucy." She smiled. There was a cigarette burning on the kitchen table, Kay smelled coffee, and the radio was on. Figurines adorned every flat surface of the apartment. Antimacassars lay on the backs and arms of the worn furniture. The kitchen cupboards were open shelves, stacked with turquoise melamine. "Uh, what did you want?"

"To use your telephone?"

"Oh, right. It's there in the hallway, help yourself. Would you like a cup of coffee?"

"Actually, I'd love one."

"Anything in it?"

"No, black is fine," said Kay heading for the telephone, eyeing the cat who eyed her back. He stretched out slowly, then walked up to her. She pushed at the cat with her foot and felt the claw in her stocking. Glancing down the hall, she kicked at the cat, who howled.

"Cooper? Come on Cooper, let's listen to our radio program."

Kay called Zimpel at the police station hoping he'd be there.

"Southern Station."

She turned her back to her host. "I'm looking for Inspector Zimpel?"

"Hold on."

Mrs. Johnson came up and handed her the cup of coffee. Kay mouthed thank you and turned away to avoid her hearing. Mrs. Johnson stared at her and went back into the kitchen. Kay was sure she hovered near the door.

"Zimpel."

"Thursday. You're there!" Did the man live at the police station?

"Yeah, I was . . . chasing something down. Kay, what's wrong?"

How did he know something was wrong? She started to whisper, as her neighbor was eavesdropping. "There's someone watching my apartment."

"What? Speak up, I can't hear you."

She raised her voice a little. "I'm at a neighbor's apartment. My phone's not working. Was calling to say, 'Hi mom.'" She paused, hoping Zimpel would get it.

"What? Oh, I see. You don't want the neighbor thinking that you're calling a cop?"

"Yeah, that's right," said Kay.

"Can you tell me why you're calling?"

"I'm at my apartment, and someone else knows I'm here, too, and," she lowered her voice and turned her back to the kitchen. "They are watching me. Now, outside."

"Ok, I know the way by now."

Kay realized this was the third time he had come to her rescue in the last couple weeks.

"What's the number?"

"501."

"I was about to get out of here. I'll come by and check it out on my way home."

"That would be great. I'm afraid they followed . . ."

"Yeah. Have to teach you a few things about losing a tail."

"A tail?"

"Never mind. See you"

"So how's your mother?" Mrs. Johnson was leaning on the kitchen doorway, holding her cigarette.

"Oh, she's proud of me, moving out on my own."

"Is that so?" Mrs. Johnson took a drag on her cigarette. "I'm surprised. When I moved out of my parents' house, I got grief, you know, you'll never find a husband. They'll think you're a loose woman. Then I finally do get a husband, and he drops dead of a heart attack." She shrugged and let Kay back out.

Kay handed her the coffee cup. "Good to meet you. Thanks for your hospitality, and I'm sorry to disturb you."

"You feel free to drop by anytime," said Mrs. Johnson. "Nice to have you as a neighbor."

Would it be so nice if she knew she was being watched?

# CHAPTER 40

Kay avoided the elevator that opened in full view of the glass front door. Instead, she took the stark, dusty stairwell that opened into a hallway off the back of the lobby.

As she descended she realized her skirt hampered any quick escape. Now that I'm not going into an office every day, I'm wearing pants. The reality of "not working" hit her again and she sucked in a breath. It'll work out, she told herself. Maybe Frank will take her back when this mess is over.

Maybe she didn't want to go back.

She slowly opened the door into the brightly lit lobby, hit the switch, and the lobby sunk into streetlight shadows. She crept towards the mailboxes, away from the window and counted to 100—to give herself some patience and give Thursday time to get across town.

A man walked towards the door. She turned from the window, her heart beating in her head. If she went back up the stairs, he would see her across the lobby. For now, she was hidden in the darkness.

She heard him jimmy the door. She held her breath. After a few moments, the locked clicked and an elderly man walked into the now unlit lobby. The man walked over to the switches and turned on the lights. He went to the mailboxes.

He stared at her. "You were sitting here in the dark. Can I help you?"

Kay glimpsed behind him, causing the man to turn around. "Oh, no. I'm waiting for a friend to come and pick me up." She realized she'd been holding her breath, and she coughed a little.

"What happened to the lights?"

Kay shrank further into the mailboxes.

The man hit the elevator button. "Be sure to stay inside here, where it's safe until he comes." He gave her a bugged-eyed glance and the elevator doors opened.

"Good evening Mr. Reynolds."

"Good evening, Louis."

"10th floor coming up sir." The elevator doors closed. Louis was here?

She heard a tap on the door and jumped. Zimpel stood on the other side of the glass. She opened the door, pointing behind him.

"He stood there, in a long coat and a hat staring up at me. Under the streetlight to make sure I saw him. He came up to the door but it was locked of course. Then another tenant unlocked the door so he must have backed off." She was out of breath again.

Zimpel peered out at the night. "Why didn't you turn the lights off while you waited?"

She was suddenly bone tired. This had been a long day.

"Come on, let's go up to your apartment, maybe he'll come back out. Those kind of guys don't give up easily." She felt Zimpel's hand on her back.

"What kind of guys?"

Zimpel realized he had alarmed her. "He's working for someone—he ain't the guy who's after you."

"Yeah, well. I want the guy that's after me. That's the one who killed Marvin Wright." She wrapped her arms around herself, chilled. "And maybe sent the truck to the Blue Moon today."

"I heard."

"How . . .?"

The elevator came. "Miss Kay."

"Hello, Mr. Louis. So you are working tonight?"

"Yes, ma'am. I took a little time to eat some supper. I apologize if I missed you when you came down."

Kay waved her hand. Zimpel sensed her discomfort. She hadn't meant to make Louis feel bad.

Zimpel stepped out of the elevator first and looked up and down the hall.

Louis put his head out. "Everything all right?"

"Yes," said Kay. "Thank you." She didn't explain why Thursday was there or who he was. She didn't want the apartment management to know she was being stalked.

"Here, 501." Kay unlocked her door and they went in. "Unfortunately, I don't have much to offer . . ."

"I came prepared." Zimpel pulled a six pack of Anchor Steam out of a bag. "Big times."

"That will do." She walked to the window and looked out. "You always working this late?"

"Got things on my mind." He should tell Kay about Madie the witness, but maybe after they deal with the wise guy.

"You have a church key?"

Kay walked back to the kitchen. "I don't have much, but I do have that."

Zimpel popped open a beer and handed it to her. She took a healthy swig. He opened one for himself. "So tell me about Redevelopment trying to close the Blue Moon today."

"It wasn't Redevelopment."

His eyebrows went up.

"I called and they checked. Someone forged their letterhead, and then hired these thugs. Ok, they were union guys who needed a job. Still, I was outraged." She told him about the notice and the truck pulling up.

"Walter called me at work." She said, smarting again at the loss. "If I hadn't arrived immediately, these guys would have hauled everything away, the tables, the china, everything."

"Hauled it away?"

"They were instructed to pack it all up. Can you imagine if I hadn't been there? If someone gave in to them?" She wasn't sure how she got so resolute.

"Good you got away from work."

"Oh. That's the other thing." She took a breath, this was the hard part.

Zimpel glanced up at her.

"I got fired. For leaving and for going to the Fillmore."

Zimpel stopped, turned. "Ok, I admit, I wasn't listening carefully. What did you do today that got you fired?"

She went through it again, now telling him what Frank had said to her, and then ending up at Zorn's office.

"Seems you have made a choice."

"Maybe, I don't know." She did though, and Zimpel was right. She felt relief to not have to play the macho game with those men no matter how much she needed the job. "Anyway, I didn't have time to leave a message for Edelman, the lawyer Saul hired to represent Leitisha. It was a moment that had to be reckoned with immediately."

"You did that, you saved the restaurant. You're good at what you do. You need to be doing it for folks that appreciate it."

"I need to get paid for it." Then she looked out the window and remembered why Zimpel was here. She yawned.

"You had a helluva day." Zimpel sensed a shift with Kay. Losing her job that gave her independence and stability might make her more reckless, more vulnerable. He didn't tell her about the girl and hoped that Sylvia would deal with her tonight. He had to figure that out before someone got wind he was holding an underage girl.

"Yeah, I guess that's why I called you. I'm about at the end of my rope today. So who is this guy?"

Zimpel pointed to the front windows. "Is that him?"

"He's there again. Oh my God." She shut off the one light she'd had on in the back of the apartment. Zimpel watched her silhouette against the window. "I swear, he stood under the streetlight staring at my window so I would see him."

Zimpel pulled her from the window. "To scare you."

"Scare me? For what?"

"Did you see his face?"

"I only saw him close up for a second downstairs." She shut her eyes and gestured at her cheeks. Zimpel almost smiled. "Reminded me of a . . . of a bloodhound, jowly. Why?"

"I think I know that guy." Zimpel squinted down at the street.

"And?"

"He's a mob guy, LCN. Bunch of them came in from Chicago, others are local. Cahill, who recently made chief, he was a homicide inspector, along with me. He solved a big case that involved the LCN."

"LCN?"

"La Cosa Nostra."

"The mob, like organized crime . . . here?"

"Oh, yeah, like a rat infestation. I brought a couple photos. Maybe you'll recognize one." He pulled some photos from his inside suit pocket. "Here, is this the guy downstairs?"

"You already brought photos?" She smiled at him, made him feel good she recognized that he was thinking ahead.

She reached for the photographs. "Why would a mob guy be following me?" He liked that she was more curious than afraid.

"Now that's the sixty-four-thousand-dollar question, isn't it?"

She walked to the hallway, flipped on the light and scrutinized the photos. "I can't be sure. This man might be him. Who's this fancy dressed man with him?"

Zimpel looked over her shoulder. "That's Michael Abati. He's a boss guy, born in Sicily, and moved out from the East. Not Chicago. The guy downstairs, he's just a soldier. I think he's Vito Carelli, came in with a guy name LaRocca."

"Like the seafood company?"

Zimpel smiled. She was a pretty good detective, making connections. "They have legit businesses to wash their money."

"Wash money? Maybe that's what's going on with redevelopment? There's a lot of money involved with this development."

That was exactly what he was thinking.

She leaned on the doorway, yawning.

"You need some rest."

"Maybe I can, if he's gone?"

He turned back to the window. "I'll call someone and have him picked up. We can at least eliminate his watch tonight." He pulled on his beer and then remembered her phone didn't work. "Let me call from my radio downstairs."

She picked up the phone and it was still dead.

"You want me to leave these beers here?"

"If you need some at home, take them. Otherwise, they'll be here if you need one later."

Zimpel liked the idea of being back later, and left the rest of the six pack in her Frigidaire.

"You going to be all right?" While he asked, he glanced up and down the street, and then he turned to look at her.

"Sure."

"Here's my home number. You see Bozo again, or Bozo's brother, you call me. From the neighbor's if you have to. And get that phone fixed. We want these guys so if you're drawing 'em out, we might as well go get them."

"Great, now I'm bait." She yawned again.

Zimpel shrugged. "Better than being chum."

Kay hesitated. "Do you want another beer? Is he going to break in here?"

He considered the beer in her fridge and the view from her window. Her anxiety was like a third person sitting between them.

"No, we'll pick him up. It'll take them a while to bail him out. You'll be okay."

"Thanks for coming by. You're a good friend."

He gave her a smile, and let Louis take him down in the elevator.

He could have used another beer and a bathroom, but that wouldn't have been right. He'd piss in the gutter if it came to that. The wise guy had gone when he reached the street, but he'd report it anyway, and pick up the guy if someone saw him.

He drove his car farther down the block out of her sight, but where he had a view of the front of her building. He'd sit there for an hour or so and watch the watchers.

# CHAPTER 41

Zorn had told her to work out of his office until she figured out what to do. Saturday was a normal workday for her, and with Leitisha's situation urgent, Kay wanted to work.

She was grateful not only for the office but also for someone to share her questions and discovery with. Zorn knew the regulations and the people at the Redevelopment Agency. He had given her a set of keys. They felt good in her hand.

As she came in the front hallway, she heard Lester Young, "You Can Depend on Me" from the Jazz Giants that came out two years ago. The pianist was Teddy Wilson. Great album. She was having influence on Zorn already.

"Michael?" She called out to the back so he'd know she was there.

"Coffee?" he yelled back.

"Yes, please." She smiled, feeling comfortable in this strange environment, ordering coffee down a dark hallway, and feeling in control.

A couple minutes later, he walked into his office area with two steaming and aromatic mugs of coffee. The smell must affect the taste, dreamy good.

He set her mug down. "Like the album I bought? Garage sale on the way into the office."

"Who gets rid of such a good album at a garage sale? I love it and this cut is great." She had intended on bringing in some music, and here he did it for her.

"Yes, I'm enjoying it. Let me show you what I connected with the information you gave me on Wednesday."

She had dropped it off late Tuesday, but listened rather than make the point.

Zorn sipped his coffee, then carefully set it down. He ran his eyes and hands over the mound of paper on his desk, then pulled several sheets from under the pile while resting his hand on the pile so as to not start an avalanche.

"I looked at the property that transferred ownership from Marvin Wright's estate, with no eminent domain proceedings, or irregular ones in any case. At the same time, there was a payment of money to Redevelopment to help with 'expenses,' yet it didn't have an attribution."

He paused and carefully pulled another piece of paper from the pile. "And I told you that I was tracing some of the money . . ."

Kay leaned toward him then, remembering his "funny money" comment.

"Here's the financial statement that Mid-City gave to Redevelopment to qualify for bidding. Check this out. They look flush."

Kay reviewed the financial and indeed there was a lot of money showing in the balance sheet. "So this is why they are getting priority?"

"Hard to say."

"Still, I'd like to know how they bypassed the procedures set in place."

"Yeah, that would be good to know. Maybe we can find out in our lawsuit."

"That might take too long. I need to safeguard Leitisha's property, at least until she's back and can defend herself."

This process felt so wrong, even if she didn't know eminent domain law, even if Michael hadn't told her it was irregular, she couldn't let it go.

# CHAPTER 42

Leitisha leaned back on the hard surface of the bench in her cell. Exhausted from the continual barrage of questions from those cops, determined to get her so hungry and sleep deprived that she confessed, she sat still to recover. I can put up with it until it's over. Saul will get me out, been here three nights now, and they aren't letting him.

She'd been through worse and they hadn't beat her yet. The great jaws of white society eat up Black people. They get swallowed and nobody knows, they "been 'et" as her daddy would say. That was her fear, to simply disappear.

When she was a teenager, when talk of war began, her daddy was out of work and her mama was pregnant again. Her mama's brother had already gone out to California because there was work there, and no Jim Crow and no lynching. She had never seen a lynching but John Henry, her cousin, had seen one. A young man, hanging from a tree. Angry mobs. In Mississippi in the early 1940s, there was no safe place for a colored man.

Her daddy decided he was headed out to the shipyards in California, to Kaiser Shipyard—they needed a lot of labor, and maybe they make a life out there and his kids would be safe, get educated. His grandparents were slaves, his parents, sharecroppers. He tried to learn a trade but no white man would take him on as an apprentice and teach him. He learned about tools and building but wanted more for himself and his kids.

Leitisha remembered when he talked to mama about it, she cried. She was scared to leave. Daddy would go on ahead, get the job and prepare for his family coming. She had never been out of her small town, taken the train, much less navigated a white world that terrified her more than going to hell.

They didn't tell anybody they were leaving except their uncle who took them to the train. Leitisha helped mama with the packing and the kids, two little brothers and a sister. And there was one on the way. That trip across the country without their daddy was hard. They had to ride in the colored train cars where there weren't enough seats. The kids sat on suitcases. They packed food, but it took so long and no place would sell them food so they were hungry. It was hard to sleep with all the noise and moving around, loud conversation and jostling, never mind having a bathroom or water to wash. By the time they got to California, they were all exhausted and worn.

She remembered feeling lost in the train station, all those people and they didn't know how to reach Daddy or Mama's brother. They had to wait and eventually they got fetched. They stayed with another family in Oakland. Redlining, which she didn't understand then but did now, made it hard to rent or buy in the Bay Area.

In 1942, they moved to Marin City—housing for Negroes near the shipyards. Daddy worked in the shipyards in the early days, hard work but good, and better than sharecropping.

Leitisha sat up, thinking she heard a noise, but nothing came down the hall at her so she settled back into her memories. Daddy was at Port Chicago when all those military men, mostly colored enlisted, were killed.

A crew of sailors had taken over loading munitions at Port Chicago Naval Magazine—on Suisun Bay, there across the bridge, it was in the 40's, during the war—in July she thought, 1944.

At a barracks, half a mile away, Irvin Lowry, he was a friend of Daddy's, heard an explosion. It shattered his window and threw him across the room. It also killed 320 men—202 of them Negroes.

Daddy, Lowry, and others spent two days collecting body parts of the men they had worked with. Lowry was the physical instructor of the recreational staff. He worked out with these guys, bowled, played basketball with them.

Daddy wouldn't go back to work at the shipyard after that. He decided he'd open a barbecue and cook for folks, his folks, Black folks, and to hell with trying to unionize, and work in these big companies. He found a cute place, small brick building, got some help getting the permits, and started cooking. It was smoky, and rough, but the meat was good, and he had a steady flow of customers. Leitisha grew up working there, sliding her butt away from the hands that reached for her as she brought slabs of ribs, coleslaw and beans to a table. She swore she'd have her own place, with finery and class.

Leitisha heard a key in the lock, and a steel gate slide, shut her eyes and said a prayer. Dear Jesus, please help me convince these white men I haven't done anything. Amen.

Kay's fact finding revealed a disturbing story. Mid-City Development was on the receiving end of property in the A-2, a part of the redevelopment plan that wasn't implemented yet, all near the Blue Moon. The president of Mid-City was a guy named Mullin. He was in the filed papers, giving affidavits, presenting financial information, and attesting to "readiness" to build.

Zorn was in court or she would have discussed these facts with him. Mullin was the key, and if she asked him a few questions directly, maybe she'd get closer more quickly as to who was targeting the Blue Moon. A lawyer showing up in his office ought to be enough to shock him into telling her what their intentions were. She would make it clear they had to pay big to get the Blue Moon.

Her palms were sweaty going up in the elevator and she wiped them on her tweed skirt as if she was smoothing it out. A man got off on the 9th floor and the other woman in the elevator stared at her. She stood still and watched the elevator floor indicator until she got to 20.

She walked up to the receptionist. "I'm here to see Mr. Mullin." The receptionist had permed hair and red nails with matching lipstick, perfectly applied, dressed in a midnight blue suit that she filled out spectacularly. Kay's hand went to her chest. She'd never be comfortable showing that much cleavage. Clearly lots of maintenance and equally clear why she was on the desk.

The girl gave her the once over. "And your name, please?"

"Kay Schiffner. Tell him I'm the lawyer." Maybe the novelty of a woman lawyer would work.

The reception glanced up at Kay while she listened on the telephone, "Yes, I'll tell her."

"His secretary said he's in a meeting and can't be disturbed. Did you have an appointment?"

Of course she didn't, and they all knew that. They just wanted her to go. "How long is the meeting?"

"She didn't say. Who did you say you were with? I'll leave him a message for you." She poised with a pen.

"Thank you. I'll get you a card, but would you mind if I use your restroom, please?" Kay gave her a sweet smile and dipped a little. The receptionist smiled and pointed down a hallway. Kay went towards the restroom then diverted down another hallway, looking at names on the door. She glanced back at the receptionist chatting away on the telephone board. It was a busy place.

"Can I help you?" asked a secretary, dressed in a tight pencil skirt and heels.

"Oh, thank you. I was directed to Mr. Mullin's office, but I must have misheard the direction." Kay gave her a big smile.

"Oh, you're going the right way, keep going down this hallway, he's in the corner," she winked. "Of course."

Kay walked farther down the hall, astonished at all the paper and hustle, bustle of the office. Certainly a sign of affluence and money. Half the floor was taken up with drawing boards, men in suspenders, smoking and talking. None of them paid any attention to her. Guess they think I'm another secretary.

She reached the corner office, where a brass plaque announced: Bradley Mullin, President. The door was shut. She hesitated and then knocked.

"Yes, Lorraine, what is it?"

"Sorry, I'm not Lorraine, my name is Kay Schiffner," She opened the door.

Kay recalled him from the hearing. He was attractive, in a movie star way, square jaw, salt and pepper hair parted on the side, athletic physique. He wore his gray suit pants that fit perfectly and the white sleeves of his heavily starched shirt rolled up once, like the models in Vogue. He stood behind a huge, pristine desk. A skinny man with sallow skin stood next to him, like his weaker, sick twin.

"Mel, we'll have to finish this later. Apparently, this pretty lady needs my attention." Mullin turned a movie star smile on her and gestured for her to sit. This took her off guard. She expected him to be hostile. The room smelled of cigar and she noticed one burning in the ashtray on his desk. She didn't sit.

The skinny man gave her a startled look, his arms suggesting a praying mantis. "Thanks, Mel. We'll talk later about that plan." The man scurried from the room. Mullin stuck his cigar in the side of his mouth and leered at Kay.

"What can I do for you, honey? You looking for a job?" His eyebrows actually went up and down.

Kay put her hand out. "Kay Schiffner, Mr. Mullin. I'm an attorney." She let that sit a minute. His face twitched as he reluctantly shook her hand. "I wanted to ask you about your development contracts with the city, and how you got them without bidding."

"What? Who do you represent?" His posture went rigid. He stepped back.

"I represent Leitisha Boone, and the Blue Moon. She's been accused of . . ."

"Why did you come here? I've got nothing to say to a criminal lawyer."

He knew about it? A busy man like him? "I'm not actually doing the criminal case, but I'm working with . . ."

"They sent a woman to deal with me?"

She wasn't melting under his gaze. His charm dissolved to fighting mode. Kay counted to five. "Who are 'they'?"

"Never mind. Why are you here?"

"You're the developer. You had some interaction with Marvin Wright that might . . ."

"Interaction?" He said. "What does that mean?" He picked up a cigar stub and the long ash fell to the floor. The smell thickened the air, like a shroud around him. She noticed a wedding ring and glanced at the photos on the desk. A blonde wife with styled hair and a preppy looking teenage son.

She started in, to see how far she could go. "Did you know Marvin Wright?"

"Sure I knew him. Everybody knew him. He threw his weight around like everybody owed him something, like we didn't work for what we have." He pointed his cigar at her. "You best stay out of this and leave it to those who know what they are doing."

"I actually do know what I'm doing." She was calm. Even though she wasn't a trial lawyer and hadn't even been allowed in the room to negotiate a deal, she embraced taking on an adversary like this.

He took a step towards her. She stood firm. His threatening stance showed fear. She pressed him.

"Did you discuss with Marvin Wright his refusal to sell his property to you—as part of your plan to redevelop the Fillmore? Did you fight with him?"

A storm swirled his face. "I don't have to tell you anything. Get out of here." Bingo. She'd hit a sensitive spot.

"I'm aware that he was not happy to sell out, and that eminent domain proceedings would have to be instituted, but he had good lawyers . . ." She continued to push.

"That colored man didn't know what was good for him or this city, and look what happened to him."

"You have something to do with that?"

He turned cold on her.

"I'm a businessman, and I know what's good for this city and my business." He put the cigar stub back in the ashtray—one of the few things on his desk. "There's a slum in the Fillmore, all run down with drug addicts and whores, and needs cleaning up. That's what I'm doing."

"What about the nice clubs and restaurants and the 300 small businesses? What about people's homes?"

"What did you say your name was again?"

"Kay Schiffner." Something she was saying was hitting, she wasn't sure what.

"Well Miss Schiffner, you're trespassing and you need to leave before I call security."

"I'm a lawyer, just doing my job for my client. This is a business office, a natural place to find you and discuss business."

"Ha, your client," he laughed. "What happened is Mr. Wright wanted to buy out your client, he made her mad, and she shot him. They found the gun in her restaurant. End of story."

How did he know about the gun? She didn't remember it in the paper.

He dusted imaginary lint from his shoulder. "You need to mind your own business. Not a place for a woman."

"Neither is jail for an innocent woman." Now he was making her mad.

"She should've minded her own business, too."

"She was minding her own business, and doing well, until you and the other developers started pushing her and others around for your own profit."

The phone rang and he picked it up. "We're through here, you need to go." He pointed to the door.

"We're not through," said Kay, leaving his office. "Not by a long shot."

# CHAPTER 44

Damp with sweat, mouth sand dry, Kay walked from the confrontation back to Zorn's, her adrenaline pumping. She went back to searching for a trail of money leading to the company.

She worked late into the night and back at it the next morning. Zorn was at court all day, so she had the place to herself. She wasn't quite up to making her own coffee though, and missed it. She did put on the Lester Young album, and wished she had some Amad Jamal. Still, "I Guess I'll Have to Change My Plan" worked for now.

Kay drove her own deadlines, set her schedule, and chose what to do. All new to her. Seeing how her work impacted others—if it wasn't for her, the Blue Moon would have been wiped out by those movers—helped her understand that her position with Bianco was worse than a compromise, it perpetuated the very situation she hated. You can't succumb to the authority you're trying to oust, and win.

Connecting the dots was tedious and slow. She wanted to keep working but she had promised her mother, more than once, she'd come for dinner. She didn't want her calling the Bianco office and finding out she'd been fired, so she called her and told her she'd come tonight.

"That's good dear. You're always working too hard."

Calling it a night, Kay touched up her makeup and took the streetcar to her parents' house in the Richmond, with its wide streets and middle-class professionals like her father.

Her father worked for Pacific Mutual Life Insurance Company, one of the thriving companies in San Francisco, and she knew he was proud of his work. Her mother had an office girl's job for a while before she was married.

As Kay came in the door, her father was reading the newspaper aloud to her mother who was in the kitchen.

"What?" her mother yelled from the kitchen. "I can't hear you."

"It says here that the new Negro ball player was complaining about being in San Francisco."

Kay listened to the exchange. "Maybe it's because when he tried to buy a nice house in St. Francis Woods, he discovered that it was redlined against Negros? That article was also in your paper." She flapped at the page he held open.

"Oh, why do you always have to bring up the negative, Kay?" said her mother, from the kitchen door. "Come in and help me get the food on the table?"

Kay was too tired to argue. Her mother pulled a browned pork roast from the oven, the smell filling the kitchen. She spooned out the pan roasted potatoes. The canned green beans and apple sauce warmed on the stove.

Kay wondered what her mother would think of the fresh collard greens she ate at Miss Leitisha's, or the cornbread. And the whiskey.

"Kevin, come down for dinner!" She turned to Kay. "He can't hear anything with that music playing."

Her brother came down the stairs two at a time, thudding, his hair slicked back with his Elvis look. He gave Kay a nod and swiveled his hips at her, "I don't want my heart to be broken, it's the only one I got . . ."

"Nice Kevin."

"Maybe I should take up guitar."

"Oh, no, not that rock and roll stuff," said her father, folding down his newspaper and coming to the table. "I've had enough disappointment this year with the Giants, coming all the way from New York with the best hitter in the league, and it doesn't look like they'll make the series in spite of that rookie Cepeda."

"Am I a disappointment because I play jazz?" Kay was half serious when she asked him.

"I don't know why playing in the Fillmore is so important to you." Her father used his logic voice.

"Because it's the only place they let Black people in this town go to a restaurant and they want to play and listen to jazz, and so do I."

"You can play music at home, at church, or some other place," said her mother.

"What did you expect me to do with all those years of piano lessons? Entertain my gentlemen friends?"

"Why not? You always loved entertaining."

Kay ignored the comment.

"I never practiced when I was young," her mother said. "We couldn't get you off the piano to go to school."

Kay passed the green beans. Kevin wrinkled his nose.

"And you played Tommy Dorsey and Billy Eckstine records. Learning to play jazz was not a leap for me. I love the piano and would play against the records and practice for hours. You thought that was great."

Her father nodded. "Yes, we didn't exactly bring you up on Beethoven or Brahms, your mother and I, we love the big bands." He smiled at her mother. "I even have some Duke Ellington, now there's a band leader."

He looked at Kay. "See how democratic I am?" He held his plate out for more pork roast. "But that doesn't mean that I like you down in the Fillmore." He frowned.

"There's no place else to play jazz. Jazz came from the blues—that's Negro culture." Her father winced. "Mainly what is played in the Fillmore is the blues. It's urban players that took it to other levels, with the improv that is jazz. Ask any jazz man, Black or white."

Kay's mother shook her head. "Kay, let's not . . ."

Her father changed the subject, as he did when he was done talking about a topic. "Kevin, when is practice for you this week?"

A loud pop and then shattering. Kay's mother gave a little scream.

Kay pushed her chair back.

Her father stood. "Stay here." Kay was already in the front room.

"Jake, what was that?" Kay's mother had her hand to her mouth. "Is a window broken?"

"Fire!" Out the picture window, flames danced up and down on the lawn.

Her mother and Kevin watched from the kitchen doorway. Her father was already dialing the telephone. Beyond the flames, neighbors gathered in the street and a few cars stopped.

Her mother held a Kleenex, teary-eyed with fear.

Her brother's eyes were wide. "What's going on?"

"I called the police and the fire department," her father said.

Kay pulled open the front door. The acrid smell choked her. The sooty smoke made the scene surreal and made it hard to see. As she wiped her eyes, Kay realized that it was a cross burning. A cross was burning on her parents' lawn. Guilt flooded her.

"Kay, come back in. My god, what if they're still . . ." Her mother held back, her hands at her face.

"They're long gone, mom, they scare and flee—cowards." The wind licked the fire and Kay worried it would burn into the garden and then the house. She pulled the garden hose from under the house and turned it on, flames flaring up when she sprayed.

"Is this what happens when you spend time with the Negroes?" Her father asked, taking the hose from her.

It had to be her. She was the target, and this was the easiest place for her to be found. She scanned the street but she was right, who did this was long gone. But who?

The cross, wood at its base, was stuck crudely in the ground, leaning as if it was going to fall over, giving off a pungent smell and black smoke.

Their neighbor, Mr. Simpson, had a pail full of dirt. "This'll work faster than water on that kind of fire." He tossed the dirt at the bottom of the cross and went to get another shovelful. Kay saw broken glass on the sidewalk and onto the lawn.

"Be careful of the broken glass."

"What's going on here, Kay?" asked Mr. Simpson.

Kay glanced at the crowd gathered. "I'm being a fairly effective lawyer." The smell was sickening, in her hair and on her clothes.

"What kind of case prompted this horrible reaction?"

This would never have happened if she had stayed on at Bianco.

Her father found another shovel and alternated with Mr. Simpson putting dirt on the fire, which had died down a lot with the two men covering it. Soot hung in the air and on the surface of the house, the porch, on everyone's hair.

A fire truck pulled up, and a fireman, in his waterproof slicker, took a hatchet, whacked at the cross so it pulled out of the ground and fell towards the street. Several other firemen doused the remainder of the fire with fire extinguishers.

"Thanks." She caught a fireman's eye.

"Second one tonight," the fireman said to her, still holding the fire extinguisher.

"There was another burning cross?"

"Yeah, and another a few weeks ago. Someone's on a rampage."

"Do they seem like they were done by the same people?"

The fireman gave her a curious look. He regarded the cross laying in the street. "I hadn't thought about it, but, the one earlier one tonight? Yes, I guess so. They were both 2 x 4's painted with some kind of thick tar, like roofing tar, and used a post hole digger to get it into the lawn." He pointed at the hole, which had a distinct conical shape.

Kay nodded. "Look, I know this is odd, but who was the other person that had this happen tonight?"

He shook his head. "I don't know their name."

"My name is Kay Schiffner—this is my parents' house. Someone, I think

. . ." Just then a police officer walked up.

"What's going on here?" He shook hands with the fireman. When Kay stuck her hand out, the cop hesitated, and then shook it expecting something less than what he got.

"I was telling Mr. . . ." she looked at the fireman, obviously wanting to know his name.

"Mark Redman."

"Kay Schiffner, yeah, I said that, ok." She was alternatively mad about the burning cross and flustered by the fireman. "I was asking Mark, who said this was the second cross tonight, who the other person was that . . ."

"Oh, this stuff happens all the time, I wouldn't worry about it . . . it's some crazy people."

"Uh, officer, I think it's related to my work as a lawyer."

"You're a lawyer?" asked the cop. Mark the fireman looked at her a little differently.

"Someone threatened me. I want to know if the other cross burnings were related to the people who threatened me." Did someone really go after her? And put her family in danger? Anger and guilt all swirling. After standing up in the hearing, anyone who believed she was in the way could have done it. Mullin threatened her but she couldn't picture him doing something like this.

Kay's dad came over and introduced himself. The cop seemed more comfortable talking to Kay's dad so the two of them stood to the side. The fireman went back to the truck to pack up.

Kay shivered and wrapped her arms around herself. She wanted to know who the other person was—and what they had done to get a cross burned on their lawn. She walked over to the truck, determined to get an answer. "Would it be ok, if I called you later, and asked you about this? It might be relevant to my case."

"Sure," Mark said eyeing her to see if she was serious or flirting. He pulled out a pen but had no paper.

"Hang on." Kay went inside and pulled the pad by the telephone in the hallway. "Here, here's my number," she handed him a slip with her number, "at the office." She kept it business like. She hadn't given her telephone number to a man in a long time. And then it was Zorn's.

"Ok, I'll call you. Too hard to get me at the fire station. Never tell where I'm going to be. I'm off Fridays and Saturdays. . ." No mention of a wife. He gave her a warm smile.

"Thanks, I need to figure this out."

"Yeah, and be safe, hear me?" He walked back to the fire truck, glancing over his shoulder at her. She went back into the kitchen.

"You ok, Mom?"

Her mother nodded, keeping her hands busy putting away the food and washing dishes. Kay went over and gave her shoulders a squeeze. Her mother gave her a wan smile.

"Kay, I don't know what you're doing, but you need to stop. This is dangerous." Her mother blamed her, too.

Kay felt terrible. She was good at letting people down. Leitisha, Frank Bianco, and now her parents.

Her brother was eating a large bowl of cereal.

"All you ever do is eat?"

"What? What's wrong with eating?" He shook his head and went back to reading the back of the cereal box.

# CHAPTER 45

Zimpel stopped and picked up a six pack on the way home. He preferred Anchor Steam made in San Francisco. He worried because they were having financial troubles, and everyone was drinking that light beer made in big factories, which tasted like piss to him.

He put the beer in his ice box and pulled one out, took the church key he kept on the table next to his armchair, and popped open the bottle. Cigarette ashes dusted the table's surface, piled with books and bills. He spent most of his time sitting there when he wasn't sleeping. It was comfortable.

Since his wife left him, he couldn't handle having a housekeeper and the dust got bad sometimes. But not bad enough to clean. Or he was working or drinking beer or sleeping. His brain churned facts about Marvin Wright. There were a lot of pieces and no connections. He'd keep agitating until he saw a picture. He turned on the TV, then lit a cigarette. The beer was cold and tangy. It felt good in his mouth.

He leaned forward and kept switching the channels, but it was all reruns and he was too restless. He leaned back, took another swig of beer.

He turned on the radio. Willie Mays was still his favorite player and he didn't care where he played. Today's game was over, the Giants had won. He switched off the radio.

He glanced up at a map of the city on the wall. There was nothing else decorative. His wife had taken what she wanted and gone back to St. Louis. They had met when she was out here for college, but in short order, she decided she hated San Francisco. She didn't like his police work, always nagging him about being home, complaining the city was too crowded. She wanted kids, a lawn, a house in the suburbs, and he was a city guy. They had been so much in love.

They met when he was recently home from the war. He became a police officer, and his ambition took him all the way to homicide. It wasn't her idea of what married life should be. She was from a nice Midwest family who managed to get the marriage annulled because they didn't have any children. A fat contribution to the Catholic Church no doubt. They didn't want the taint of divorce on their daughter. He liked it better now that she left. The pressure was gone, and the tension, too.

He sighed deeply and pushed himself out of his chair.

The world was a strange place. So many dividing lines he couldn't keep them straight. Church, no church, kids, no kids. Black, white, money, no money, and more.

His colleagues were all about keeping out the "short" Chinese by putting in a height requirement and keeping out the Blacks by making shit up. A Black homicide inspector right about now might get answers where he didn't.

How were you supposed to get information from a community that you treated as second class? Of course they were hostile. You would be, too. He took a swig of beer.

Kay's questioning in the kitchen was focused and helpful—she managed to get some good information out of Tildy. He fretted over Kay's boldness. This was not safe work. Marvin Wright's murder exposed the money at stake and the willingness to do anything to obtain it.

He gazed out to the street wondering what Kay was doing when the phone rang.

"Thursday, it's Kay."

She had his home number?

"Sorry to call you at home but I was glad you gave me your number." She was reading his mind now.

"It's fine." He didn't like the sound of her voice. "What's wrong?"

"How'd you know something's wrong?"

"You only call me when something's wrong. Just tell me." He grabbed his keys from the table.

"I was home with my parents for dinner, like I do." He waited for her to continue. "And we heard an explosion or a pop or well, I don't know how to describe it, but it was on fire."

"What was on fire?"

"They burned a cross on my parents' lawn."

Zimpel paused a moment. "You sure? It was a cross burning?"

He heard her impatient sigh.

"Ok, it was a cross. Tell me what happened."

"We heard it first, a small explosion, and then a bright fire. I ran out, got the hose, but it was smelly oil, and water wasn't much good. There was broken glass all around. Dad called the fire department, and by then we had the shovels out, and we were dumping dirt on it, making a mess of the front yard. Took the fire department a few minutes and they finished off the fire with fire extinguishers. One of the firemen said this was the second one tonight." She paused, a bit breathless.

"Cross burnings?"

Again the sigh. "Yes, yes, that's what we're talking about."

"Ok, ok. I'm coming over. Are you still at your parents?"

"Yes." He heard hesitation in her voice.

"You called me. I'm a cop. I want to see, ok? It'll take me 10 or 15 minutes to get there. Ok?" Zimpel pulled on his leather coat, took the last sip of beer from the Anchor Steam, and locked the door behind him.

Why had she called him? She wanted a witness to assess it with her, because in the aftermath, it seemed impossible that this happened to her, at her parents' home.

Her mother made coffee of course, so now they were all awake and agitated.

"Why did you call this police officer?"

Kay wasn't sure what to tell them. "He's a friend."

"You're friends with a cop?" her father asked.

"Well, you liked the fireman didn't you?"

"Honestly, Kay, sometimes I feel you fight me for the sport of it."

Kay helped her dry the dishes because she needed to be busy. The front lawn was a mess, dirt, water, what the cross left behind, and broken glass. The cops had made a report and taken photographs, but none of the neighbors had noticed anything as it was during the dinner hour and they were all inside. That seemed odd to Kay.

Zimpel pulled up and rang the doorbell. Kay's father opened the door and stood for an awkward minute.

"Hi, I'm Thursday Zimpel, SFPD." He held out his hand. When Mr. Schiffner didn't take it right away, he said, "I'm a friend of Kay's."

"Oh, oh of course. Please." Then Kay's father shook his hand and invited him in.

Kay stood in the foyer with a flashlight. "I'm afraid there's not much to see—it burned, we threw dirt on it, and the firemen finished it off."

"Let's look." Zimpel walked out to the lawn.

Kay shrugged on a jacket over her dress. Her father stood on the porch.

Zimpel stepped carefully around the cross, black, sticky, and smelled like burned rubber, it was covered in foam from the fire extinguisher. He squatted down, took out his handkerchief, and pulled a piece of the cross from under the dirt. He motioned to Kay and she shined the flashlight on it, revealing a faint stamp on the wood. "This is from Beronio's, off of Army Street."

"How can you tell? And what does it matter?"

"This mark is part of their logo and name here. I recognize it. Beronio is pretty high-end. Before the war, they were on the waterfront, been here a long time. They might remember a customer that bought a bunch of 2 x 4s without plans or any other materials."

He moved one of the pieces of glass with his foot and motioned again for Kay to shine the flashlight on it. He picked it up with his handkerchief and smelled it. "Gasoline. Looks like a Ball jar, filled with gasoline and poured on the cross. Once it was lit, he tossed it or it burst from the fire."

Kay shivered in the fog.

"Let me take you home," said Zimpel quietly. "You're not taking the bus tonight—not after this." He searched up and down the street.

"What? You think they'd go after me?"

"They did go after you." His hand swept the yard. "I told you it was dangerous." He shook out his handkerchief. "I'm going to make sure they don't get near you."

Kay glanced at him. "Did you come here to give me a ride home?"

Zimpel searched the ground. "Seeing things helps keep them in your mind, gives you information, like the lumber company, that you might miss otherwise. That others might miss." He turned towards the house. "Come on, say goodnight, and let's get you home."

# CHAPTER 46

"You have a visitor."

The guard banged her door. Leitisha jumped, with a hand on her heart. Breathe, she told herself, breathe. This is how they wear you down. "Who?"

"You don't want to go, I'll tell 'em."

"I'll go, I'll go."

"You know the protocol. Stand still inside the door with your hands out so I can cuff them."

Leitisha stood, wary of the guard. Several of them had said what they could do to her, in low voices, in her ear. Horrifying. She stayed inside herself and did not react. She gave them no reason to come after her. No reason but their prejudice and their appetites.

The guard cuffed her and glanced down at her ankles. Shrugging, he led her out of the cell. No shackles today.

She was kept in her own cell away from the general population, but also away from light and exercise. It was making her crazy, this isolation, and she didn't understand why there was no arraignment, no bail.

As the guard led her through a door, she saw a white man sitting in the room. Tall and thin in an expensive suit, with a $5 haircut, perfect shave, cuffed shirt. Had to be a lawyer. Finally.

He stood as she entered the room. "Miss Boone."

She tilted her head at him, standing in the jail dress, no makeup, her hair tied up, knotted and unruly, but she stood tall. She knew who she was inside.

"My name is Joel Edelman. I'm your lawyer." He eyed the guard. "I need to speak to my client in private."

"I ain't supposed to leave." The guard shifted from one foot to the other.

"Yes, you will leave. I get to speak to my client without you listening in. I don't think she's going to hurt me in handcuffs." Edelman's demeanor was like a hand pushing the guard out the door, a man used to giving orders. The guard left.

Leitisha couldn't believe they even discussed that she might do harm to someone.

"Please, have a seat." Edelman flexed his arms, tugging at his shirt cuffs to straighten the sleeve under his jacket. "Saul sent me to see you."

"Why am I still here, Mr. Edelman? Why did it take so long for you to see me?" She gestured and the handcuffs clinked on the table. They hurt her wrists.

"Now Miss Boone, these things take time. The charges against you are serious."

"Don't patronize me Mr. Edelman." She sat still, her spine tall. She wasn't going to show no white man her deep anxiety. His face held that look that white men get when they want you to be grateful for a lukewarm dish of nothing.

"I'm a businesswoman of many years and I've been colored all my life. You need to talk to me straight across and not down."

If her voice had been a knife, it would have cut a neat slit in his designer suit.

Put off by her terseness, she watched Edelman's body language backing off from her. The convict dress was convincing him.

"Miss Boone, I assure you that Saul and I spoke, and we are doing everything we can to get you out of here. We have asked for a bail hearing."

"I haven't had an arraignment. This is the first time I get to talk to a lawyer. I been in here for over two weeks. That ain't right." She had surprised him with her perception.

"Colored folks know about these things, Mr. Edelman. We been on the wrong side of the law whether we did anything or not. This," she pointed to her face with her bound hands, "is crime enough for some folks. You get my meaning?" She wasn't letting him off the hook. What was Saul thinking hiring this highbrow man who hated being here for her.

"We need to respond to the evidence they are putting forth." He adjusted his sleeves again.

"They don't have no evidence. All they got is a desire to convict."

"Let's talk about that for a minute Miss Boone. They say they found a gun in the kitchen in your restaurant, the gun that was used to kill Mr. Wright." His face was stiff.

"Yes, they found a gun there." She sat with her back straight, and said nothing else.

"How do you explain that?"

He was being so dense. "You sure you're my lawyer?"

He leaned back in his chair, working his jaw. She noticed tension in his neck.

"That was planted. I don't own a gun." She waited. "Ok, how's this. I didn't kill anyone and would never. Start with that premise and we'll be fine. Are you assuming I killed him because I am a colored person?"

She finally got him to blush.

"No, no, of course not." Now flustered a bit, he straightened up, adjusted his jacket, and pulled out a fancy fountain pen and a pad of paper.

"Let's work on the facts, for now. We'll trace that gun if we can get the information from the police . . ."

She interrupted him. "Haven't you talked to Inspector Zimpel?"

Again, she caught him.

"No," he recovered. "Not yet." He waited.

"Thursday is my friend, and he was the inspector assigned to the crime. He didn't even know they were going to arrest me, which shows they're aiming to frame me. He has the real facts." She took a breath, clasping her hands in her lap.

Her strength was waning but she wasn't going to show this lawyer any weakness.

"They want me to confess, and pull me into a room every other day or so to see if I'm ready. They keep the lights on so I can't sleep. Others threaten me, tell me what will happen if I don't confess." Then she looked him straight in the eye. "I didn't kill him and I am not confessing, but if you don't get me out of here, if they kill me, no one would do nothing about it."

"Look, no one is going to kill you, and I'll talk to them about how they are treating you." He started to write. "Zimpel you say?"

# CHAPTER 47

A Pontiac convertible with fins stopped at the light, the driver's hair swayed back, his arm around his girl, a blue scarf tied at her chin. Buddy Holly's "Tell Me How" blasted from the radio. Kay shuddered a bit, warding it off. Girls in sweater sets from I. Magnin's and poodle skirts, a look her mother wanted for her.

Tonight she wore a black sheath dress and peek-a-boo heels, with a small hat and a light jacket. She walked towards the Fillmore from the streetcar stop, the sun setting behind a thin covering of fog, reflecting orange and pink light across the horizon.

She had a date with the fireman, exactly the type of guy her mother wanted her to see. Local family, good job, all the manners, a nice boy. When he called her about the crosses, he pushed her to have dinner with him, so she said yes. Just made it easier. She needed information from him anyway, so why not?

The fireman wanted to go to a bowling alley, but she had no desire to go bowling. Instead, she gave him Jimbo's Bop City address and told him she'd meet him outside there for dinner. He didn't recognize the address because if he had, he would have questioned her choice. He wanted to pick her up, but she told him she worked long hours and would come from work. He wasn't used to dating career women.

She was calling the shots tonight. Her romantic interests took a low second place next to her desire to get Leitisha out of jail and learn about the other burning crosses. Whoever felt threatened enough to burn a cross on her parents' lawn was leaving a trail, and she was going to follow it.

Right on time. Mark, the fireman, wore slacks and a sport coat. She was glad he had dressed up so he wouldn't look out of place.

He took her hand, smiled at her. "Nice to see you."

"You, too." She took her hand back.

He glanced up at the sign and the people going inside Jimbo's. "You want me to take you into a colored bar?"

"Actually, Jimbo's doesn't serve any liquor, just great food, and has wonderful music." And I'm taking you." Kay gave the doorman a quick kiss.

"Evening Ty." The doorman gave a smile to the tall white guy who raised his eyebrows. The restaurant was packed, and Kay was already nodding to the music playing in the back.

"These people are all dressed up," he whispered to her.

"Yes, of course." She looked him in the eye. "It's always like this. Your first visit to the Fillmore?"

"Well, except for work . . . we've had some fires down here but that was different."

"Yeah it would be. Come on, let's sit at the counter and you can taste Leslie's fried chicken." She sat down at the counter leaving the fireman to decide what to do.

"Kay, so nice to see you. Who's your friend?"

"Good to see you, Althea. This is my friend Mark Redman. He's a fireman."

"Oh, isn't that nice. They's all handsome like you?"

Mark's head swiveled. By his nervousness, he'd never been one of few white people in a club.

"Mark, Althea's a doll and she'll get us fed." Kay's attention strayed to the back room.

Althea glanced up and down the counter to make sure everyone had what they wanted. No one waited a minute under her watch.

"Who's here tonight?" asked Kay.

"Well later, we'll have a full house. Right now, it's the house band and

Federico is playing piano. There's a kid from the neighborhood, his name is Johnny Mathis, and he's supposed to sing tonight."

"Can we have glasses with ice, Althea, and don't tell Jimbo?"

Althea had a beautiful laugh and put two juice glasses with ice in front of them.

A big sign at Jimbo's said: "No liquor sold or served," but those that came regularly knew how to get around it. Kay pulled a small flask from her bag and poured a little whiskey in each of the glasses. She pushed one over to Mark.

"You're a regular here?" His eyes followed the entire transaction.

"Look, I didn't bring you down here to show off." She laughed, and he smiled finally. "I want people to understand this way of life, that it's a good way, not what they say—that there's crime, or trash. It's vibrant and delicious."

Althea set steaming plates of fried chicken, greens, and mashed potatoes in front of them. Mark's eyes lit up. Didn't look like his appetite was discouraged from being in a Negro restaurant.

He held out his glass, and Kay poured more whiskey into both their glasses. Mark the fireman was starting to relax.

"So your parents let you come down to the Fillmore?"

He believed she needed permission. "My parents have no idea how long I've been coming down here on my own. I finally moved into my own apartment after law school."

Mark's eyebrows went up again. Obviously, he assumed she lived with her parents, because that's where he'd met her. She was a full-time lawyer, she lived alone, and she hung out in colored clubs in the Fillmore. She might be conveying the wrong message here.

She made a note to get him to go home at a reasonable time, and to watch her intake of whiskey.

"So tell me about the 'cross burning' incidents?" She'd get what she wanted.

"Yours was the second that night." The meal nearly had his full attention, and it interrupted his story. "The one before yours was an older guy and his wife." He paused with a forkful of food. "There was another one before these two that I know about recently. Why do you want to know?"

"I want to know who's trying to scare me." She sipped her whiskey.

"Everything ok here?" asked Althea, who had a cat's curiosity for eavesdropping. She caught Kay's nod and her eyes lingered over the fireman before she turned to wait on someone else.

"There's an investigator with the SFFD. I'll talk to him and . . .let you know what I find out? Let you know over the weekend?" He was angling to stay in touch with her.

"That would be so nice of you. Tell me about the other cross burning that night. Was it like ours?" Kay wanted more facts, not another date.

"Let me think. The place before we came to your house, same night, same kind of cross."

"What exactly was the same?"

"2 x 4's, tar stuff to make it burn and that nasty smell." He wrinkled his nose.

When did a fireman get fussy about burning smells? "Who were they? What did they do?"

"Hey, slow down a minute. Third degree."

"Sorry," she said, curbing her impatience. "Just getting it all complete. Blame it on the lawyer in me."

"Ah, right. I forgot you were a lawyer."

Of course, he would forget. "Would you like something more to drink?" Kay held up her flask. Maybe he needed some more booze to get him talking.

"Can you get a beer in here?" Mark was smiling at Althea, which amused Kay.

"Jimbo don't serve no liquor." Althea leaned over the bar. "I might could find you one?" Now she was looking directly at Mark.

Mark's eye followed her. "Could you?"

"Sure, Sugar." Althea dug around in the Frigidaire, and pulled out a

Budweiser. She opened it slowly and poured it in a glass and handed it over, nearly caressing it.

Kay smiled, and Althea winked at her.

"So what was the other family like?"

"I don't know what the husband did, clearly they were shocked. The wife cried; she was scared and her husband was comforting her. No kids, all grown I guess."

"Can you tell me their name? Or where they live?"

"I remember addresses from emergencies but not people's names. What we focus on I guess, you know, what building is burning." He recalled the address, out in the Avenues, Sunset District. She wrote it down in the notebook she kept in her purse. "It was a modest house, stucco, so the burning cross wasn't much of a risk."

"What was the one before that?" Why hadn't he written the information down or remembered it enough to know who the people were?

Mark took another chug of the beer. "The other was maybe a month ago at a Negro lawyer's house, Poole. I remembered his name because he's a district attorney in San Francisco. I understand why they might burn a cross on his lawn, as he's stirring stuff up, Negro lawyer and all."

Kay swallowed and said nothing. It was ok to burn a cross on a man's lawn because he was a district attorney and "stirred things up?" Or because he was a Negro?

Mark the fireman didn't notice her tension. "That was out on Ingleside Terrace. The cross was different, two thin pieces of wood, not 2 by 4's, come to think of it. It looked more like a prank."

"A prank."

"Yeah, at least that's what the . . . lawyer said."

What had she stirred up that incited the fear mongers and their burning crosses? She made more notes in her notebook, including the 2x4's. Mark's eyes followed her, and she pointed at his clean plate to get his attention off her. "So what do you think of the food?"

"You were right. It's delicious."

Althea smiled at him again when she picked up the plates.

"Hello Kay?" The bandleader stood near her stool.

"Ah, Federico. You forgive me?" She searched his face to see if he was angry with her still.

"Ah Sweetie, we all have our nights. I know you can play. You didn't need to play that night." He touched her arm. "You'll not run out on me before you play a few?"

"Not on your life." Her entire being relaxed, felt like home.

"That's wonderful." He pointed at the stage. "Sit in after this number?"

"Sure, I'd love to." She'd redeem herself tonight.

When the song ended, Kay patted Mark's hand, who had no idea what was going on. As she approached the stage area, she shook each band member's hand, grateful they welcomed her after her fiasco the other night. "What're we playing?"

Even the drummer who had tossed a cymbal at her was smiling now. He glanced at the fireman at the counter. "You know 'I'll Close My Eyes'?"

Kay nodded and laughed at his gesture. Kenny Burrell and Mal Waldron had put it out last year. A piano tune. They had definitely forgiven her.

Kay received nods from the band and applause at her solo. Then they played behind the lovely voice of a young man from the neighborhood, Johnny Mathis. The kid could really sing. Had a nice hit, "Chances Are," and got a good ovation from the crowd.

She saw Mark and Althea talking and nodding up towards the stage. Afterwards, Mark offered his arm as they got ready to leave. "You can really play."

"Thanks."

"Let me give you a ride home."

"No, I'm ok. I need to run a quick errand." She stepped out of his reach.

"At 10 o'clock at night? I should see you safely home."

She knew that it wasn't right taking off without an escort home. Oh well, she wasn't going to worry convention right now.

"Oh nonsense, I find my way home from here all the time. Don't worry.

I had a lovely evening, and I hope you enjoyed yourself." She shook his hand and turned out of his view before he steered her towards his car. She wanted to find Zimpel.

As she crossed over to the Blue Moon, a black limousine pulled away from the curb and turned into the alley.

# CHAPTER 48

## LATE WEDNESDAY NIGHT

Zimpel saw Kay sitting at the bar and nodded hello. The club was about half full and not as vibrant as when Leitisha was walking the tables.

Walter glanced from Kay to Zimpel. "You two following each other around?" He poured a beer for Zimpel.

Neither Kay nor Zimpel responded, both lifting their glasses, avoiding the other's glance. Zimpel noted she wore a stylish black dress and jacket that didn't look warm enough for the fog outside.

"What we gonna do?" Walter wiped his meticulously clean bar, his head moving from Kay to Zimpel.

"What do you mean?" Zimpel took a deep swig of beer. He felt Kay's eyes on him.

"I thought we were having a meeting now that you're both here." Walter said. "You been doing nothing but worrying about Miss Leitisha. You're not sleeping none either, neither of you, cause you're always here, late at night, and you both working during the day." He pointed at Zimpel. "And you're drinking too much beer. You eat anything today?"

Walter didn't wait for an answer but ducked into the kitchen for a moment and came back with a steaming bowl of deep brown rice with shrimp. He set it in front of Zimpel with a linen napkin and silverware.

"Sylvia made some jambalaya—everything in there is good for you, now eat some."

The smell alone gave Zimpel solace.

Walter shined another glass that didn't need shining. "At least she had the good sense to eat."

Walter seemed to know everything.

Zimpel turned to Kay. "What did you eat?"

"I ate at Jimbo's." She paused. "I had a date."

"Oh?" Zimpel dug in, eating half the bowl, then took another swallow of beer.

"With Mark the fireman—I met him during the cross-burning."

"An odd way to find romance." Zimpel shifted his weight.

Kay laughed. Zimpel eyed her glass as she pushed it towards Walter.

"I wasn't looking for romance, but information. And Jimbo's fried chicken—and Althea—soften up even a fireman."

"Mark the white fireman warmed up to Althea?"

"Oh, come on Thursday, you'd have to be six weeks dead not to warm up to her. She has the magic." They laughed. Walter pretended not to hear.

"So did it work?"

"Yes, I got some good information."

Zimpel turned to her and their eyes met. His stomach churned, and he wondered if it was the jambalaya. "What?"

Kay gave him a side glance. "Before I give it to you, I want you to promise me that we'll go together to follow up on this."

"Kay, I can't promise that—this is cop's work, dangerous business, you had a burning cross on your parent's lawn for chrissake." Stubborn and fearless. He didn't bring up the wise guy watching her apartment.

"Look, you can't keep protecting me. I'm a lawyer and a woman at a time when that combination is unusual and unwelcome. I'm already a target. I'll be careful—now do we have a deal?"

Zimpel cringed inside; she was being watched. She had stirred a hornets' nest, and the burning cross showed they, whoever they were, had her in their sights. This was cop business.

He would agree to get the information, and when he followed up without her, he'd deal with the consequences.

"Walter?" Walter refilled Kay's glass.

"What else aren't you telling me?"

She could read him, and that made him sweat. He wasn't going to tell her much, but he did need to ask her about the girl, where she could stay.

"We brought the girl, the one who might be a witness, here. We need a safe place for her to stay."

"Where is she staying now?"

"With Sylvia. She witnessed the murder," he spoke in a low voice just to her, "and that puts her and everyone around her in danger."

"All these women in peril, Thursday. So my apartment?"

Zimpel drank more beer. "She can't stay with you, they are watching your apartment."

"The LCN is after her?"

"Maybe the LCN, or someone connected to redevelopment, or someone pissed off at him for being their landlord."

"Where did you find her?"

"Never mind, but that wasn't safe either."

Kay sat back sipping her whiskey. She didn't like it when he kept information from her. And half of this was happening to her.

He glanced around to see if anyone was paying attention to them. No one was.

"She won't run away?" Kay asked.

"She might—I might if I were her. She's not in great shape. They drugged her to keep her compliant, and she probably needs a doctor, but Sylvia has been feeding her and then getting her to work, to help her self-esteem. Not sure what you can do with someone that has been so beat up by life."

"Maybe she can stay at Michael's?"

"At Zorn's?" At another single guy's place. Didn't sound like a good idea.

"Yeah, his office and his home are in the same building—well it's a cot and a kitchenette, I wouldn't call it a home. But he keeps everything secure, you need to be buzzed in, and there are double doors. I'll give him a call."

"Yeah, do that." Zimpel wanted to give her something to do instead of telling her no. He was only a little ahead of whatever they were after, hoping he was moving in the right direction.

Tonight, a blues band performed with a singer she didn't know. Maybe playing might focus her restlessness. Walter was right, she hadn't been sleeping. Neither had Zimpel from the looks of him. And he's not eating regularly. He'd inhaled the jambalaya.

"So what's the plan? How are we going to deal with this?" Walter was wiping down each bottle as part of his closing ritual.

"We're going to find the sons of bitches that shot Marvin Wright, Miss Leitisha will get out of jail, and we'll somehow stave off Redevelopment until we can't. Then we'll all live in the Bayview." Zimpel smiled at Walter and pushed his glass across the bar.

Walter gave him a side glance like he was crazy. "You wrap it all up just like that."

"Frazier has a lead, and we'll figure out who planted the gun."

"He don't learn that they don't want colored cops."

"Well, I want him, and he's got some angles others don't have."

Walter shrugged. "We running out of time."

Kay felt the urgency, if not the energy to keep going. "He's right. Maybe we should go talk to them tonight?"

"Them?"

"The other folks that had the cross burned on their lawn."

Zimpel looked at this watch and then at her. "It's too late to cold call someone." Her eyes told him she was spent. "You're too tired, we'll do it another night."

"I can do it."

She slumped, fatigue in her posture, and wrapped her arms around herself. She needed a coat.

"Come on, I'll drive you home." Zimpel didn't want her exposed with that fearless attitude and all that booze in her. Something bad out there had its eye on her.

"I'm fine, I'll take a cab."

"You're so stubborn." He worried she might still take the streetcar.

"If I wasn't stubborn, I never would have become a lawyer."

There was truth to that.

# CHAPTER 49

Kay hopped on the streetcar and headed to the Blue Moon with the yearbook she had taken from Bianco's office. If Bianco missed it, as an alumni he'd paid enough to get another. She needed it more than he did.

She and Zimpel were meeting at the Blue Moon to call on the other family that had had a cross burned on their lawn. She knew he was mad that she wouldn't give him the information, but this was her find and she wanted in.

Zorn was generous with sharing the work he had; there was no end to it. She was starting to make a little money helping with his cases. She'd need to find some of her own clients soon though. There was only money if they won because unlike Bianco and Associates, Zorn's cases were mostly contingency fee and not hourly. He was only paid if he won the cases and was paid out of the proceeds. And winning took time.

The day was gorgeous yellow and blue, like San Francisco can be. Bright, clean, and cheery. The streetcar started with a clunk. She watched folks going about their business, headed for happy hour, or running errands, carefree and secure. She didn't want their life; she wanted her own: to play jazz and the world to be fair.

It was worth her job to prevent those men from emptying out the restaurant, even though it made her queasy considering her rent and meager savings. And she hadn't yet told her parents. Time enough. She got off at Fillmore and Geary and walked to the Blue Moon.

Walter looked up from the bar. "You have a purpose to your stride today, Miss Kay."

"Indeed I do, Walter. I need to see Tildy, then I'll come see you." She headed for the kitchen but stopped at the door out of respect for Sylvia's domain.

"Sylvia, may I speak with Tildy a minute?" Tildy's head popped up from peeling potatoes at the table.

"Good evening, Kay, come on in. We're in good shape tonight." Sylvia's voice was velvety and calm.

Kay set the St. Ignatius yearbook on the table. Tildy wiped her hands on her apron, gave her a wide-eyed look, then reached for it.

"You want me to see if that boy is in here." Kay nodded at her and Tildy carefully opened the book.

As she paged through it, Kay wondered what Tildy thought—all those white kids getting that elite education from the Catholic Church. The kids whose parents had the money to send them, and the kids that had enough schooling to satisfy the academic entrance requirements.

Sylvia poured some iced tea and brought it to Kay. "I know you'll have something stronger later, but this will keep you until you get out to Walter." Sylvia gave her a sly smile. "Are you hungry? You want a bite?"

"Thank you, I'll wait a bit." The sweet tea did taste good, the glass slick with condensation. She noticed the new girl in the corner who was scrubbing pots in a dress that looked a bit big for her. She caught Sylvia's eye and glanced over.

"That's Madie. Zimpel asked us to keep an eye on her, and while she hasn't been feeling great, she decided to pitch in and help."

Madie looked over her shoulder at Kay, her arms deep in sudsy water, and appeared young and old, and deeply sad at the same time. Kay realized who she was, the girl she and Zimpel talked about. The girl in the Cadillac, and in the Blue Moon, with Marvin Wright. Kay's eyes went back to Tildy looking at the yearbook. These two young girls, witnesses to terrible actions.

Tildy carefully paged through the yearbook, and then put her finger on one page and then went to the back where the class photos were.

"Here, this is the boy." She pointed to a page about the football team, and then his senior photo with his name underneath, showing Kay both photographs. "I'm sure of it." She met Kay's eyes, and Kay remembered how mean he had been to Tildy. Kay turned the book around to look. Doug Mullin. The name was familiar but she made no connections sitting there in the kitchen.

"Thank you Tildy, great work."

Tildy beamed and picked up her work again with the potatoes. "I didn't like that boy."

"I know, and if he's the one that set up Miss Leitisha, we're going to make him pay for it."

"Thanks, Sylvia." She picked up the sweet tea glass, but Miss Sylvia waved a hand, and she left it on the table. As she left, she glanced at the girl, Madie, who was scrubbing a large pot.

"Walter, whiskey please." She sat and laid the yearbook on the bar. Other than a couple at the end, she was alone.

Walter glanced at the yearbook and set her glass in front of her. "My son goes to that school." He pointed at the yearbook.

"I remember you mentioned it." It still surprised her.

Walter polished an already sparkling glass. "I saved my money from the shipyard work. The missus and I, we worked hard with William, got him tutors, worked with him at home. Bernice is a nurse."

"That was a great thing to do, to get him into there."

"An education's the only thing that going to get the Negro out of the cycle, the ghetto."

"This isn't a ghetto, Walter."

"No, miss, but they is taking it away from us, and we got no place to go 'cept down. If William has an education, he'll have more control, more choices. I want him to go to college, and he'll get to go if he graduates from SI."

"Yes, he will Walter, that's amazing. Maybe he knows this kid that Tildy identified." She tapped the yearbook. How hard was it for Walter's son to go to a school with people like Doug Mullin?

"Well, you can ask him because he'll come down here before he goes home. Should be here any minute."

# CHAPTER 50

Kay had just finished her first drink when a tall, good-looking teenager came into the restaurant. "William, this is Miss Kay." Walter's hand was at the young man's back.

"Pleased to meet you, Miss Kay." William held his hand out to shake hers. Confident grip, but reserved. He tilted his head at her. "You're the piano player that's friends with Miss Leitisha."

"Yes, thank you for remembering." For all the times she had been there, she had not noticed Walter's son. Nice that he knew who she was, but why didn't she know him?

He gave her a smile. He opened his satchel and pulled out a notebook.

"William, can I ask you something?" He turned to her, his face open. "You know a kid named Doug Mullin?"

"Oh, yeah, I know him." His face went flat. "He's a football player, like me, and well, what do you want to know?"

Walter's son plays football, too?

"Tildy identified him as the guy who delivered the meat—the day the gun was dropped in the kitchen."

"He's the guy that bothered Tildy?" William's nice boy demeanor changed like fast weather, and his knowledge surprised her again. She saw him exchange glances with his father. There was something more.

"Yes, that's the guy. What else do you know about him?"

William shrugged like boys who don't want to tell. "I don't like the way he treated Tildy. He's rude." William fumbled with his backpack to get a pen, to do something else. He had set his notebook and textbook on a table to the side of the bar.

"Is he a good student?" She pressed him, aware that Walter was hovering.

"Not particularly. He skips school sometimes and gets into trouble—he doesn't do his homework."

"What kind of trouble?"

William glanced at his father. Walter glanced back and nodded at him.

"I heard he got arrested." He glanced back at his father. "He broke into a restaurant and was drinking, being crazy. They took him into jail and his dad was really angry. They suspended him from school and from the football team for a while, but he's back in now."

"What does his daddy do?"

"He's some big businessman, not sure what he does. Drives a fancy car, wears the nice suits and all."

William again glanced at his dad and then Kay. "He also hangs out with the gear heads, that go hot rodding."

Kay had no idea what that meant. "So what does a 'hot rodder' do?"

"They race cars late at night, sometimes at Ocean Beach and other places where they can get away with it until the cops come."

With this admission, Walter stared at William for a moment.

"They got money, not sure why Doug acts all crazy like that. Seems sad to me."

"Thanks William, that's helpful." Kay considered a connection between the boy getting arrested and planting the gun.

"How are you liking the school?"

"Oh, it's a good school, I like the learning part. Sometimes being one of the only," again he looked at his father, but Walter had gone behind the bar to wash some glasses. "the only Black kids, people say things behind your back you gotta ignore. Sometimes people are nice because they think they ought to be, not because they truly are. But there are good people there. I got some friends. My parents have worked so hard." He stopped again. "I gotta break out, that's my job here. You're a lawyer right?"

"Yes, amazingly enough. And speaking of being 'only,' not a lot of women lawyers out there."

He nodded. "I'd like to be a lawyer."

"You'd be good at it, William, you notice things. Cecil Poole's a well-known," Kay paused. William had said "black"—some of the younger kids, the civil rights leaders, were using "black" instead of "Negro." "Uh, Black lawyer. If you want to meet him, I could introduce you. And there are others in San Francisco. I know a guy, Willie Brown, who recently graduated from Hastings, where I went to law school."

"Oh, I would love to meet them." He smiled again. "Thank you."

She could at least do that for him, for Walter.


Zimpel needed folks to trust him if they were going to give him information, and that took time and being there. He didn't blame the Fillmore for distrusting a white cop.

He pulled up in front of the Texas Playhouse. Inside was a series of beautiful portrait paintings shaped like medallions. The lace fringed tablecloths dressed with tall candles gave class to the place—not like the Blue Moon, but still nice. He sat at the bar, embedded with silver dollars. "Hi Zeke, can I have an Anchor Steam please?"

"Yessir Mr. Zimpel, how are you tonight?"

"I'm good Zeke, how are you doing. Zimpel never corrected his title with Zeke.

"Oh, doing fine, I guess." Something in his voice said otherwise.

"Something up?"

"That Redevelopment, they is eyeing our apartment building. My wife and I, we lived there 16 years, all our friends are there, they is saying that it is rundown and got to go. What's going to happen? Where we goin' go? Out to Bayview? I like it right here, I can walk to work, we got the grocery; it's safe. Why they got to tear down everything?"

Zimpel shut his eyes for a minute and took a pull on his beer. Hearing the same story over and over again. He counted to five and then to ten. "Because they are greedy assholes, Zeke, that's why."

"Hmmm. You a bit cynical tonight, Mr. Zimpel."

"I'm a cop, Zeke, I think it's part of my job to be cynical."

"Yessir. You get set in your ways, don't want these changes that are coming, I don't want to move. Who are they to say that this is bad for the city? City never comes here. This is the Fillmore, for colored folks."

Zimpel sighed and drank his beer. "You hear things working the bar? Something about Marvin Wright?"

"Like what? Like Marvin Wright talking with someone about his properties? Talking to Redevelopment folks? Like a big white guy and his Italian friend? Like maybe selling to them, but they ain't paying enough?"

"Yeah, like that."

"I don't recall anything like that. I try not to hear too much." Zeke was a conservative, church going, hardworking man and wasn't going to talk about certain things because it wasn't safe. Zeke confirmed what Zimpel already knew. Marvin Wright was in the way. And so was Leitisha. Two for one bargain. He'd bet his house on it.

Zeke went to serve a young couple farther down the bar. She wore a green taffeta dress, a flower at the breast, strapless, with a gold chain necklace. Her hair was short and curled and her smile was wide. The man wore a hat with a white band, glasses, tie, and a gray suit that fit him well. The couple cooed at each other and clinked their glasses. Zimpel smiled to himself. Good to know people still fell in love and had a good time when the whole world was disintegrating.

He felt the mob presence in the destruction of the Fillmore but it was like chasing ghosts, couldn't grab hold.

Deciding he'd put it off long enough, he walked over to the Blue Moon.

# CHAPTER 51

"So, on your date with the fireman . . ." He pulled on a beer.

"It wasn't a date." Walter poured Kay a whiskey.

He let it go. "What this?" Zimpel pointed at the SI yearbook on the bar.

"Last year's St. Ignatius yearbook. Tildy pointed out the boy who did the delivery the day the gun showed up."

Zimpel rolled his eyes. "You could have told me. That's more important than you seeing . . . What did she say?"

Kay opened the yearbook and showed him the football photos and the headshot. "Doug Mullin."

He noted the face. Why was he delivering meat to the Blue Moon instead of the regular guy? After school job?

"Where did you get the yearbook?"

"Frank Bianco, the, my ex-boss—he had the yearbook. He's on the alumni board."

She was hellbent on investigating this on her own and had the resources and smarts. All he saw was danger. He'd try a different tack. "Why don't you give me the address of the other house where they had a burning cross and let me chase this down, so you're not out there exposed?"

"I am already exposed and no. I told you what the deal was. I hated seeing my mother's face as that cross burned. I'm in on this."

Damn determined woman.

"What else did the fireman say about the other cross-burning?" Zimpel asked.

Kay pulled her jacket from the back of her chair and grabbed her notebook from her purse. "Mark said the burning cross had the same 2 x 4's, same tar substance that burned and stunk horribly, same method of getting the thing into the ground, like a fence post thingy."

"Fence post thingy." Zimpel smiled.

"Hey, I'm a lawyer, not some construction expert."

Sometimes he forgot she was a lawyer and other times saw that solid strength in her.

"They were another family, like ours, middle-class, out in the Avenues, with the same type of burning cross on their lawn." She paused for effect and saw the interest in his eyes. "The same night," she emphasized "night," "as the burning in our yard."

Zimpel nodded at her. She wasn't going to give him the address until they were actually going out there. She wasn't going to be left out.

"Who targeted and scared two white families that night? Who did we scare so much that they wanted to scare us back? And there was a third cross-burning that happened a lot earlier with different materials and doesn't match ours and the other families' incident." She finished her drink.

"What was the other one?"

"It happened to Cecil Poole—the Negro District Attorney, and that makes more sense—if these kinds of thing ever do—because he's a public figure. And the sticks there were flimsy, not dug into the ground. He called it a prank. Ours and the other one that night were nearly identical materials, as if the same people did it, one after the other."

"Same symbol, if not the same person." Zimpel said.

Finally, they were on their way. She was conducting this investigation like she worked her corporate transactions, going after each piece that needed to be completed to close the deal.

"Why did you let me come on this interview with you?"

She glanced over at him. He was divorced, but that was all she knew. And that he spent a lot of free time at the Blue Moon. And with her.

"I didn't 'let' you do anything. You gave me an ultimatum."

"True."

He frequently checked the rearview, watching for someone following them, a "tail."

"Tell me the truth about these guys, these 'LCN.' Seems plausible this is . . ." She paused, "connected to redevelopment." She felt it was right as she spoke it.

Zimpel's eyebrows went up. She had scored.

"Ok, here's the truth."

Her stomach tightened.

"I've been following these, these mob guys, there's an up-and-coming mob guy, Jimmy Lanza. He's investing in businesses, trying to wash his money. He may be working with this guy Abati, he's the crime boss . . ."

"The flashy dresser . . ."

"Yeah, but he's been hard to get. They're all hard to get. There was a bust in New York when they held a national meeting last year, but the San Francisco members got away."

"A national meeting?"

"Why they call it 'organized' crime. Anyway, we're watching them build up a big organization. Working with FBI, ATF, all kinds of folks." Kay watched him talk as he drove. "You know, I shouldn't be telling you all this."

"Hey, like you said, I'm risking my life chasing down this killer for Leitisha. This information protects me as a citizen of San Francisco."

"Yeah, yeah, keep it to yourself, OK?"

They pulled up to a bungalow near Ocean Beach. There were lights on in the kitchen. As they approached the front door, Kay glanced at his beltline.

"Yeah, I got my gun on. I always do."

Zimpel tapped lightly and in a couple of seconds a light came on over the front door.

A tall, lanky man stood in the doorway. "Can I help you?"

Zimpel had his ID in his hand and showed the man. "I'm a homicide inspector with SFPD. Can we ask you a few questions?"

"Homicide Inspector? Sure, come in. My wife's asleep, if you don't mind

. . .?" He pushed his horn-rimmed glasses up his nose.

"No, no," said Zimpel, lowering his voice.

The man led them into the kitchen. Kay smelled coffee. A typewriter sat on the kitchen table, paper strewn about, and a pipe in a large ashtray. The man gathered up the papers to clear some places at the table.

"Yes. Why are you here?"

Zimpel cleared his throat. "I didn't get your name—we got your address from the firemen who told us that you had a cross burned on your lawn the other night."

"Oh, that. Sorry. I'm Jeff Giamatti." He shook hands with Zimpel, and, after an awkward moment, Kay put her hand out.

"Kay Schiffner." Giamatti?

"Are you a cop, too?" He scrutinized her.

"No, I'm a lawyer—I work—I worked at the Bianco firm."

Giamatti cocked his head at her and shook her hand. "You work at the Bianco firm?" He had a shank of hair that fell into his eyes and he brushed it back.

"Well, I did until last week."

"My son works there. He's a lawyer"

"Brian." Of course, her talk with Brian about the graft. This was Brian's father? He wasn't wearing a Rolex. She saw Thursday glance at her. "Brian gave me Michael Zorn's number."

"Zorn, yeah, good guy." Giamatti nodded absently, pushing up his glasses, and brushing hair out of his eyes. He gestured for them to sit at the kitchen table.

Kay noticed marked up pages. "You're a journalist." She forgot she was going to let Zimpel lead. "You found out something about redevelopment and bribes." Her conversation with Brian came back to her.

Zimpel watched them, his interview hijacked.

"Yeah, that's right."

Kay saw a connection. "Do you think that's why a cross was burned on your lawn?"

Giamatti shrugged. "I write all kinds of things people don't like. I hated McCarthy and got hate mail. I hate bigotry, people spray stuff on my house. I think there's mob money in redevelopment and said so. Take your pick."

"Why do you think there's mob money in redevelopment?"

"They need a business to wash their money, and real estate and construction is a good way—lots of methods for hiding it through investment companies, unions and the like." Giamatti absently picked up his pipe and tapped it out.

The pipe smell conjured her father reading the paper that Giamatti worked for.

"Recently, small businesses have been pressured to pay into a protection racket. I can't use anyone's names or even identify the neighborhoods because there will be retaliation." He laughed a little. "The only protecting they need is from these so-called 'protectors' and if they're doing that racket, there's some big boys washing some money through this redevelopment. Use bad money to build, how they do it. Some of them own olive oil companies. LaRocca sells fish and crab."

"But why would they burn a cross on your lawn?" Kay asked.

"To make it look like something else, to make it seem racial. Focus the sympathy on civil rights to take the attention away from them? I don't know." He shook his head.


"Can you describe the cross?" Zimpel had a hunch. Beronio supplied some of the contractors taking the houses down, safety braces and the like. Wouldn't be much to get them to go after folks trying to stop their work.

Giamatti glanced off as if picturing it. "Stinky, had tar and gasoline to ignite it. I called the fire department and then shoveled dirt on it."

"What was it made of?"

"I saw that they were decent 2x4s, and had the 'Beronio' logo on them, which was strange."

"Why was it strange?"

"Who would spend good money on decent 2x4s just to burn them?"

Giamatti reached for his pipe.

"Are you working on anything particular that would pin down who might want to scare you?" Zimpel leaned forward. He took a small pad out of his inside jacket pocket and made some notes. He felt a connection.

"The last couple of months I've been focused on the Redevelopment Agency and criticizing their bidding process. It looks set up. How are they moving people out of the Fillmore, tearing down the apartments and businesses without any replacement? By promising the property to these developers to make their big bucks, there's no room for anyone to move back. And the developers help 'fund' redevelopment. Their ads are lies. They have no intention of replacing that neighborhood with anything that the Negroes could move back into."

Kay felt gut punched. "What?"

He nodded at her.

"But they are giving the businesses certificates for 'like property' when redevelopment is over."

Giamatti shook his head. "Know any that got any property in return? It's a giveaway on the backs of these businesses."

"I did some digging at Redevelopment to research what was happening to Marvin Wright's properties. One of the developers obtained one of Wright's properties directly. I can't figure out how they did that legally," Kay said.

"Huh. They aren't supposed to do that, but it doesn't surprise me," said Giamatti. "One of the guys we identified as part of the rackets was seen at Tadich's with one of the Redevelopment Agency bigwigs, and some of the union guys. Do you know which developer?"

"Mid-City."

"Mid-City is all over this stuff."

"I confronted their CEO, and he seemed like he had something to hide."

"Well, that was gutsy of you, with his chauffeurs and fancy everything. How did you manage to talk to him? He won't give interviews."

"I went to his office and walked in."

Thursday cursed to himself. She was back out there, inviting danger. No wonder they burned a cross. They were following her then, catching her at her parents' house. He didn't like this.

"That might explain the cross on your lawn," said Giamatti.

"A CEO would do a hoodlum thing like that?"

"With his money, a guy like that can get anyone to do anything."

"Resort to burning crosses on people's lawns? My parents?"

Giamatti nodded, "Maybe so."

Zimpel saw Kay make the connection to her parents' house.

"You know some names of these guys you saw at Tadich's—connected to redevelopment?" Zimpel scribbled in his note pad.

"Yeah, I got names. Why they're pissed off at me." He ran his hand through his hair and the flopping cowlick stood up. "I got some photographs, too. But this is journalism. I don't want to endanger my story."

"Your story? What about your family?"

He nodded, "Yeah, yeah, that's why I have to nail it all down before it leaks, if they don't break me first."

Giamatti turned to Kay. "What about you. Why would they target you?" He laughed. "Besides the fact you stirred a hornet's nest by cornering a CEO?"

"I'm a lawyer and I'm helping Leitisha Boone keep her restaurant open."

"A lawyer? That explains a lot. And the club owner of the Blue Moon, she's a tough lady." Giamatti nodded at Zimpel. "Couple of tough broads, yeah?"

Thursday didn't think of either of the women as "broads" but kept that to himself. If Giamatti knew Leitisha, maybe he knew some more usable facts.

"What do you know about what's going on with the developers?"

"Mainly trying to trace the money."

"Find anything interesting?" Zimpel wanted that information.

Giamatti nodded. "I'll make you a deal. I'll send you what I have. You find something is going down, I get a call. I want this story. I want to get these jerks."

"Sure, we can work something like that out." Zimpel stood up. They got what they came for. He was seeing the trail start to light up.

"Ok," said Giamatti. "I'll get some photos and names together. What do I do with them?"

Zimpel handed him a card. "I work out of 750 Kearny. You can send them over there."

"And keep my name out of it for now? Until I get the story?"

"I'll try. I think you've had enough trouble."

"Yeah, for me, not so much, but I worry for the wife, she gets so scared. My kids don't live here now, but still, they don't need this worry."

"Well, Mr. Giamatti, thanks so much. Sorry to disturb your evening." Zimpel shook hands with him again.

"Not a problem. I write most nights, it's the quiet time. During the day, I'm out investigating and researching." He turned to Kay. "I'd be interested in hearing what happens with the Blue Moon. Might want to write about it."

"I'll stay in touch."

As they walked to the car, Kay pulled her sweater around her and shook her head.

"What's wrong?" Zimpel opened the car door for her. Inside he was worried. She had confronted a developer.

"Everything keeps coming back to Redevelopment. And then, this thing with, what do you call them, the LCN, the mob guys."

"And you called on the CEO of a redevelopment company and didn't tell me?"

"He was quick to throw me out of his office. I can't imagine he paid it much attention afterward."

"The amount of money involved, he's going to pay attention."

Zimpel stopped the car in front of Kay's building, "Here you go." He got out and opened the door for her, checking up and down her street. He didn't see anyone loitering that might be watching her.

She followed his eyes, inspecting the street herself. Someone didn't like what she was doing. "We've made some progress. We know who the kid is that planted the gun, and there's a money trail."

"Get in there and lock the door," Zimpel said. "Let me do my job? And stay out of trouble including calling on CEOs? Here's my home number again." He handed her a piece of paper with his number on it. She was getting to be a burden on him and on Zorn. She needed a breakthrough for Leitisha.

# CHAPTER 52

## AUGUST 22, 1958 · FRIDAY

"It's Friday. Let's walk up to North Beach for a sit-down lunch. I'll buy."
Zorn had won his trial and was feeling gregarious.

"That sounds great." She hadn't eaten a real meal since she'd got fired,
save for Jimbo's. Too worried, and no time to cook.

They walked through Washington Square Park past the famous Fior
D'Italia. "Have you eaten there since they moved?"

"I liked the Broadway location better, but the food is still good, and the
place is elegant."

Kay stopped behind Zorn. She recognized Frank Bianco with several
associates from the firm, including Brian Giamatti. She didn't want them
to see her.

"What's wrong?"

She nodded at the group going into the restaurant.

"Ah, that's your former boss?"

"He takes the men to lunch regularly."

"But not you?"

"Nope. I was always working, this had to get out, or that."

"Well, forget about it now."

"Easy for you, I need to pay my rent."

"Oh come on. I'm buying lunch."

"Oh my god, that's Michael Abati."

"Holy Christ, keep your voice down." Zorn whispered leaning across the table. "How do you know who he is?"

"I've seen his photograph." Was it Abati who ordered the man to watch outside her apartment building?

Zorn kept his voice low. "Ignore him and look at the menu."

They sat in the window of DaVinci's, a restaurant in North Beach owned by Vinnie Bianco, a lifelong restauranteur and, ironically, Frank Bianco's brother. He came straight to their table. "I could hear you across the room, for the love of God, hush. Let's get you some lunch."

"Vinnie, he's not even looking. Why is he eating here?" Kay didn't understand why he was so upset.

"He likes the risotto like you do? I heard you got fired by my brother. Still you eat in my restaurant and get me into trouble."

They were all talking in loud whispers.

"Your brother didn't like I was helping my friend Leitisha Boone—who owns the Blue Moon?"

"Yes, I know that place."

Kay was grateful that he knew of it at least.

"Some bruisers showed up claiming they were with Redevelopment— but they weren't—ready with trucks to cart off her belongings, everything, as if the restaurant wasn't open, wasn't in business."

"He fired you for that? You should have gotten a medal. Times are difficult right now, for all of us." Vinnie jumped up from the table, and in a voice a little too loud, "Look, you want some more wine? Some tiramisu? Let me know. I'm needed in the kitchen, now. You let me know." Vinnie took off.

Kay leaned into the table, with half an eye on Abati. "Why was he so nervous?" Kay knew him through Frank. Michael had his own connection to Vinnie, which is why he wanted to eat there.

"Has a lot on his mind. Let's have a coffee."

When the waiter came back, she said, "I'll have an espresso and let's get a tiramisu, why not, eh?"

"Make that two," Zorn told the waiter.

Kay saw that Vinnie gave them a big discount. "Vinnie's been your client?"

"You could say that."

"Not his brother, the lawyer, but you as his lawyer?"

"It can get complicated."

They walked back to the office with Zorn on the street side.

"So what was Vinnie alluding to?"

Zorn scanned all around him before he spoke. "I have a buzzer on my door for a reason." He glanced about again. "What the LCN has been doing with businesses is that they ask for 'protection' money—you know, some kickback from the businesses."

"Thursday and I met with a reporter who was talking about the same thing. Is that what's going on? Mayor Christopher did a big crack down on all kinds of criminal activity."

"That was for show—to please the anti-commie groups who believe that gambling and prostitution is done by communists instead of your everyday Joe or Jane."

"But seriously, that's extortion. This is the modern era, not the 30's for god's sake." There was still something unsaid, something bad. She wanted him to tell her.

"You need to be more discreet—you're setting yourself up for trouble."

"I'm discreet enough," said Kay. "They don't notice me."

Zorn's eyebrows shot up. "You'd be surprised."

# CHAPTER 53

Another perk about working at Zorn's office was his Hi-Fi in the back with speakers everywhere, and they took turns playing albums. She started with Duke Ellington—*Ellington Uptown*—and "Perdido" was playing at the moment. Michael's taste went a little more classical, but he didn't mind the jazz influence. In fact, he bought jazz for their collection. The music kept the stress in check and kept her working.

That afternoon, she drafted pleadings to file in Zorn's class action suit. Since he was paying her by the hour, she might make her rent after all.

She wanted to ask him about Madie staying there, but first she had to know more about him, his attitude towards young girls. Zorn was around her age, and not bad looking, if a bit of a slob, at least in the warehouse. She'd heard his father had made a lot of money and set up a trust fund for him, so he didn't have to work but did anyway. Extremely hard. All in all, a decent catch, her mother would say.

She'd only seen him work, never play. But he must go out.

He didn't flirt with her, or make the kind of remarks she'd become accustomed to from the male associates at the firm, or guys generally.

"Michael, do you have a girlfriend? I don't mean to pry . . ."

"Why? Are you interested?"

She blushed. "I'm so sorry, that wasn't what I meant."

"Oh no, I'm not good enough."

Ugh, that felt awkward. She wasn't asking him what she wanted to know.

His laugh was genuine and put her at ease. He waved a hand at her, "Relax."

"It's just that you're here all the time, and I don't see any sign of a social life. Wondered if you had one."

"'Bout as good as yours, I might say." He side-eyed her.

"Yeah, ok, but I do get to the Blue Moon and some of the other clubs to play music. I get out." Her mind went to the sax player. And Thursday.

"I have friends. The work consumes me."

"No, come on. You must do something?"

He rested his arms on his knees, searching her face. "Not sure why you're pressing this."

He's wondering if he can trust me.

"This is George Christopher's San Francisco that promotes post-war macho America," he said quietly. "That sets up bars like 12 Adler to lose their liquor license because gay people congregate there."

"You're a fag?" She didn't mean it like it came out and he winced. "I'm so sorry, Michael, I didn't mean it like that, I don't care." She walked over to him and put her hand on his shoulder. "You surprised me and I blurted. I'm sorry."

He patted her hand. "I have to be careful or I'll lose my trust fund. My dad doesn't care that I'm a lefty suing people, but if he found out I liked guys, he'd find a way to cut me off."

She sat back down. "That's terrible. You can't be yourself with anyone."

"That's how it is out there." He reached for his coffee. "So I go to Vesuvio's, sometimes I go to the Tin Angel or the Black Cat. No one sees me there but the patrons. No one who I work with or my family, or any of my clients, God forbid, knows I go." He raised his head to her. "Except you. Now."

She had crossed a bridge of trust. High praise, especially from someone she practiced law with. "Well, it's still bad that you have to hide, but I'll make sure that the secret stays safe."

She giggled.

"What?"

"So, I guess I'm safe, too, right?" They both laughed.

Kay was working on a petition for two companies that had been given a certificate in exchange for the city taking ownership of their business. She learned eminent domain law from Michael, and how to trace the parcels through the Redevelopment Agency. Once they'd made that connection, they would draft and file a petition for real value, not some empty certificate to be traded at some undetermined time in the future.

She now also had time to trace Marvin Wright's properties through Redevelopment. So far, his estate still held the property underlying the Blue Moon, despite the fact that someone wanted it badly enough to bribe an ABC cop and fake a Redevelopment order.

She believed that Marvin Wright's death was connected to his property and that's where the answer would lie. Then she remembered the girl.

"Michael?"

Reading a file intently, he was on maybe his tenth cup of coffee for the day. He pushed his glasses back up on his head, squinted and looked up. "Yeah?"

"Thursday found a potential witness to Wright's murder."

"Your cop friend? That was lucky. Who?"

"She's an underage prostitute addicted to drugs, and now that they have her, she's a target." Kay dumped all of the information on him at once.

Now he sat upright. "That sounds terrible. What do you mean, "have her." Where is she now?"

"She's at the Blue Moon, but they need somewhere secure to keep her."

"What about Kearny Street?"

She shook her head. "Whoever set up the gun drop at the Blue Moon is inside somewhere, maybe at the police station or the DA's office. We don't know. So Thursday is keeping her safe until he figures out who it was, showing her photographs and all."

Thursday had explained to her what Frazier had done, and why a young colored girl was expendable, telling her he and Frazier didn't know why

Wright's killers had let her live.

Kay glanced around Zorn's office.

Zorn watching her, now stood up. "You want her to stay here?"

"She can't stay with me, I've been watched by someone who works for Abati, apparently."

"Wait a minute. You didn't tell me that? How do you know who Abati is? Oh, never mind. The cop told you. We saw him at lunch." He paused. "He was watching your apartment?"

She nodded. "Someone he hired, we think. Thursday, my cop friend, recognized the guy."

"You stirred some shit. You need to watch your back."

His hands were on his hips and he wanted to say more. She braced for a lecture. Kay hoped he wasn't going to evict her because she was being followed by the LCN.

Instead, he said, "Now tell me about the girl."

"I don't know that much. I saw her the night she came in with Wright."

"The night he was murdered?"

"At the Club. She seemed out of it and young. Now, she's washing dishes at the Blue Moon because Sylvia doesn't let you sit around. She was drugged to be compliant so she's dealing with that."

"Christ, to be compliant and be a slave. Where's her mother?"

"I don't know. I don't know that much about her. Just that she has to be safe so when they find someone for her to identify, she can."

"Shit. How long does she need to hide out? I'm not sure I can keep her safe here for long. It's not like I'm not watched, too."

"Until we find someone for her to ID, I suppose."

"I need to make more coffee." Zorn's solution for everything unsolvable.

Kay stretched, feeling the long day in her tight shoulders. Grateful for the work, she stayed to finish the latest version of a petition and dropped off the revisions with the secretarial service on her way home, arranging to pick them in the morning. Michael had gone to a dinner meeting and was out when she left.

Given the late hour, she knew she should take a cab home but wanted air. She needed to walk and let her mind go elsewhere. It was a warm night, calm and still. Earthquake weather.

Leaving the building, she walked up Washington to Montgomery Street for the streetcar. A cab drove by. A couple walked up Montgomery on the other side of the street. The Financial District emptied after eight. Streetlights and restaurant windows lit the blackness, casting long shadows.

A limousine turned the corner slowly, like a shark swimming. It came up next to her and she glanced at it wondering who was inside. It drove ahead of her, and then pulled over to the curb. Kay watched with curiosity until she realized that a large man in a trench coat made eye contact with her and raised his arm.

"Hey," was all she managed to get out before she turned and ran up California Street. They were after her. What the hell? She heard steps behind her, then someone grabbed her arm. She pulled forward, struggling to yell, when a cloth was pushed over her nose and mouth, smelling chemical and sweet gone bad. She struggled and tried to pull her head away from the smell, but a hand held it firmly. She felt herself melting.

# CHAPTER 54

She woke in darkness, headachy and disoriented, the smell of tires all around her. She heard a honk and her hip hit something sharp. She was in the trunk of a car.

A sharp pain stung her when she pulled her arms. Her wrists were bound in front of her with rough twine. "Need to get out," she thought. Woozy, she felt around for a sharp edge. Metal along the trunk opening would do. She rubbed the binding on it, and her skin at the same time, burning and scraping. Bumps in the road jostled her, causing the metal to cut into her arm. She bit her lip and kept at it, focused on nothing else until one strand, then another broke. Until finally she pulled her hands apart.

Untying her feet with difficulty in the cramped space, she felt bruised and dizzy, her headache screaming. She listened for voices and car noise, trying to figure out where they were and how long she had until they came to get her.

Zimpel and Zorn were right. She had been careless and felt stupid.

Turning her lawyer mind to the situation, she remembered that when she was a kid, her mom had once told her to get something out of the car trunk and she had had to reach way in the back, almost had to climb in. Her little brother, being the dork that he was, pushed her in and shut the trunk. Trick was, he didn't know how to open it. She banged on the lid but her brother either didn't care or was too pleased with himself to go get help.

So she had figured out how to open it from the inside. Hoping that this car trunk wouldn't be much different, she started to feel around where the latch might be. She worked the lock, feeling the mechanism. Damn. The car slowed down. Her heart raced. This is it. They are going to open the trunk and drop me in the Bay. Sweating, panting, she had the urge to pee, fought it back and worked the lock again.

She willed her brain to work, to remember, to get it open. A pop, and the trunk flew open, cool air rushed in around her, the car still moving, but slowly. No cars behind, she projected herself out with a roll, hitting the cement hard, feeling the scrape but continuing to roll. Then pushed to her knees, scraping them some more, and started running. Her shoes and purse were gone. The cement was rough and cold on her feet. She turned a corner, staying in the shadows of the streetlights, when she heard the car screech to a halt and the doors fly open.

No time. She threw herself under a large hedge, ignoring the branches poking and tearing at her, pushing with her back until she was buried inside it, and lay still. She tried to hold her breath, her chest heaving with effort and fright. She had no idea if they had seen which way she'd run. Surely they could outrun her, she had no shoes, and they had the chemical, whatever it was. She had to become invisible.

In dark silence, she listened intently for the sound of another person, a car, anything, and tried to swallow her breath. Her heart beat so wildly she was sure they could hear it. Still woozy from whatever they'd drugged her with, she used that to shut down a bit. If they found her, maybe she'd be asleep and wouldn't know it if they threw her into the Bay.

Car doors slammed, voices sounded far away, indecipherable. She drifted in and out of consciousness. She pinched herself hard—stay awake. The limousine drove by slowly. They were looking.

She waited until it was completely silent. She pulled herself out from under the hedge, small branches scraping her, twigs breaking, scratching her legs. Everything hurt, was asleep or bleeding. Her wrists seeped blood from the twine and cutting. She had no idea where she was, no obvious landmark. The only thing to do was to get up and walk somewhere. It took three tries to stand up.

They must be searching nearby. Her head throbbed. Rubbing her neck made it worse. The inside of her sinuses felt burned and her mouth tasted the sickly sweet remnants of whatever it was they had drugged her with. Her stomach bubbled, dizzy. One hand on a tree, she retched, vomiting into someone's garden. Her stockings shredded, grease and dirt smears on her dress and bits of blood everywhere, she needed to get out of there.

She unsnapped her garters, pulled off her stockings, looking around to see if anyone saw her with her skirt up. Balled up in her hand, she used the stockings to rub some of the dirt and blood off, not very effectively. Cement cold to her feet.

Fog swirled, turning the night chilly in a part of the city she didn't know. Not a car drove by, not even any inviting house lights.

The fear was enough to make her sick and crazy, but mainly she was angry. Mad because she had been caught unawares. Someone had actually kidnapped her.

She walked a bit, limping, and then leaned up against a wall and tried to get her breath. She was so tired and her muscles did not want to work.

She'd been shoved into the trunk of a limo. Did Abati order it? Or was it the man watching her apartment? She tried to see his face, the man making eye contact with her. It didn't come, but it would.

Seemed incredible that she had been kidnapped by what they call the LCN, like a bad movie. Stuff like this didn't happen to lawyers, people that held jobs, ordinary people. This was modern times. We had televisions, fast cars, airplanes, all the wonders of the world.

She wanted a telephone. She scanned the street again. She didn't know how long she had been in the trunk or how long they'd been driving.

She saw a street sign, Mandel Avenue. She walked down a hill and after a few blocks, there was a park of sorts.

"You look lost miss."

"Oh, God," said her heart. A greaser guy in a leather jacket stood on the sidewalk, staring at her. She wondered if he had a switch blade. She heard that greaser guys carried switch blades.

"Not exactly," she said. "I think the cab dropped me off on the wrong street." She wasn't going to ask for help until she knew what he was about.

"What street are you looking for?" The guy asked, like he didn't believe she was looking for anything. He leered at her. She turned and started to cross the street away from him.

"Do you know if there's a pay phone around here somewhere?"

"How did you get here? Girls dressed like you don't usually end up in this neighborhood." Kay's hackles twitched. He was walking towards her now.

"And you don't have any shoes on. What happened to your shoes?"

She wanted him to stop. "What, are you the neighborhood greeter or something?" Self-conscious of how she looked, she pulled her fingers through her hair. "How should I be acting?" Her legs found some footing.

He shrugged. "Well, being dirty and barefoot, you look like you should be soliciting to feed your drug habit." He laughed.

She continued walking down the hill on the other side of the street. Two more guys walked up the hill at her.

This she didn't like. She'd gotten away from the LCN only to be knifed by neighborhood thugs. She needed a telephone.

"More greeters?" She turned to her shadow, hoping to ally with him against the two men.

"Hey Jake," said one of the two guys. "Who's your girlfriend?"

They knew each other.

"She's visiting, on her way to a pay phone. I think she's lost." The other two were closing in.

"Oh yeah? Well maybe we can help her find her way." One guy elbowed the other.

"Evening, gentlemen," said Kay, surprised that her voice didn't waiver or shake. Inside she was Jello. "You doing ok?"

"Yeah, we're fine," said the other one looking her up and down. "You're fine, too, if a little disheveled."

"Disheveled?" She glanced at the guy now behind her, apparently his name was Jake, like her father, and considered the other two. The other men were under the streetlight. Longer hair, a little beatnik beard, a bag that looked heavy, maybe books.

"You guys aren't some greasers. You're a bunch of," Kay examined them, "poets." She guessed but knew it was right.

The three of them laughed, still elbowing each other. "What gave it away?"

"Greasers would never say 'disheveled.'" She had noticed they were all carrying bags or notebooks.

"Greasers?"

"I don't know, the leather jacket. I'm out here on my own. Tell me your names." She didn't want them to be anonymous. She wanted the advantage.

"Jake Holmes."

"Hmmm, Sherlock, ok, I got that."

"Milt Funston," the shorter kid nodded at her.

"Jack Micheline." He was stocky, deep voice, a little drunk now she let herself look at him, pretty cute with his flipped-up hair and all. He stuck his thumb out. "I'm visiting these guys." He had a New York accent. "We were all part of a poetry reading tonight. We have chapbooks out." He pulled one out of his bag and handed it to her. "Here, have one."

"I'd offer to pay for it, but they took my purse."

"Who's they? Did you get robbed?" The grins turned to solicitude.

"I got kidnapped tonight, escaped from the guys' trunk, and found myself here. Where the heck am I?"

The three guys, wide-eyed now, all spoke at once. "Are you ok?" "You're injured." "Who did this?"

"I'm bruised up, but I'm ok."

"How did this happen?"

"I'm working on a case, I'm a lawyer, and it's controversial. I guess someone doesn't want me working on it."

Gape-mouthed, the men surrounded her, looking outward. "A lady lawyer, who knew? Come on, let's go down the hill and make sure you get your call, and someone comes and gets you. This isn't right."

Her greaser boys were now her bodyguards.

"There's a telephone at the gas station at the bottom of the hill. We just came back from North Beach, we were at City Lights."

"I've been there, Ferlinghetti's place?" Any car she saw, she twitched.

"Yeah, that's it," Milt said. "You should come hear us read sometime."

"Deal, if you all come hear me play piano at the Blue Moon." Kay wondered how long she'd be able to say that.

"What? A kidnapped lawyer who plays piano?" Now they were impressed.

They reached the gas station.

"Come with me," said Jake. "Hey Robert."

The attendant, about the same age as the guys, looked over. "Yeah, fuck off, no more handouts tonight."

"Help a pretty lady in distress." He turned to Kay. "This is . . .?"

"Kay, nice to meet you."

The attendant smiled. "Oh, that's different. Sure, that I can do. What can I do miss?"

"Can I use your telephone?"

"Sure, no problem. It's in the office. Local call right?"

She also wanted to use his restroom but not in front of all these guys. She went in and hit the operator and asked for Southern Precinct. She was sure the operator would stay on to listen.

It didn't take long to get Zimpel on the line. He was always there.

"Zimpel, it's Kay." She was working bravado into her voice, but she saw her hands shaking.

"What's up?"

"Don't say I told you so."

"What happened?" Now he was attentive.

"I got kidnapped tonight. Black limo, late after work."

A dead moment before he spoke. "What? You got kidnapped? By who?

Did you say a black limo?"

She felt his concern in the pit of her stomach. Everything that he and Zorn had said was true. She held the phone with one hand, and held her stomach with the other, shaking from the cold.

"Yeah, escaped out of the trunk, I'm still in the same neighborhood where I got out—I don't want them coming back. I don't have my purse, or my shoes.

"Do you need an ambulance?"

"No, no, I'm bruised, but fine. I don't even know what neighborhood I'm in." She gave Zimpel the address.

"Somewhere in Silver Terrace, OK sit tight. Are you safe to wait?"

"This gas station looks safe. I seemed to have attracted a band of poets that are protecting me."

"What? Poets? You're not making sense."

"I'm not surprised. They drugged me. Come and get me, I need to report a crime." She felt giddy with relief and fear at the same time.

"On my way."

How many times had she called him to rescue her?

# CHAPTER 55

Zimpel picked her up at the corner of Mandel and Silver Avenue. He noticed the bare feet and dirt, then the blood and bruises.

"Holy Mother, Kay."

"Yeah, I know, I look terrible. I'm ok."

Her appearance brought up all his fears like a bad burger.

"Get in the car, I'm taking you to the hospital." He handed her a blanket he had brought and she wrapped it around herself. She was shaking from the cold or otherwise.

"I'm fine." Her newfound poet friends waved goodbye. "I know I look terrible, and my head is killing me from whatever drug they used."

"Drug?" He drafted a crime report in his head.

"How was he going to get me into the limo otherwise?"

"Limo?" The image of the black limo, the one he saw pull away from the curb when he and Kay were in the Blue Moon, the one that carried Marvin Wright's killer, was vivid.

Kay told him the details of her ordeal, including the story about how she got out of the trunk. She balled up her hands so they wouldn't shake.

Zimpel gripped the wheel tightly. "Are you actually doing all right?"

He asked that too many times.

That she was scrappy enough to get away made him proud, but he was also furious and afraid for her.

"Where are we going?" asked Kay.

"I was going to take you to a hospital. You don't know what those drugs were, and you jumped out of moving car."

"I told you I don't want to go to a hospital." Resoluteness in her face, a fighter. Stubborn.

"I'm fine. I mean I feel a little dizzy still, I'm dirty. I lost my purse, and they scared me. But I'm safe now, and I can replace everything, including my stockings." She still held the wadded stockings in her hand. "These guys didn't kill me this time."

"Yeah," said Zimpel, attention to the windshield and the rearview. He didn't want to hear her say it. "This time." He saw how they'd cleared a path and Kay was in the way.

"Oh, shoot, I lost an earring, too." She fingered her ears. "I liked those pearl clips, they were a gift from my mother. What a night." She removed the other one and realized she had nothing to put it in. No purse, no pockets. "Here." She handed it to Zimpel as he drove. He glanced at it and put it in his pocket.

"Evidence," she said. Along with her purse and her shoes.

"What's that you're holding?"

She put the chapbook the poet had given her and her wad of stockings on the floor. "The guys at the gas station, they were poets and they'd had a reading tonight." She wrapped the blanket tighter.

"Ok, so where do you want me to take you?"

She did not need a hospital. "Shouldn't we be doing something to catch them?"

"Maybe you need to go home and at least get some shoes."

Her feet were bare, muddy, and covered in leaves and grass. "I guess I'm in shock."

Thursday just glanced at her and back at the road. She laughed, realizing she was bloody, filthy, and cold. "Maybe I should have been a cop rather than a lawyer."

"We can go to Kearny Street and look at some photos. Did you catch a face?"

She noted he was driving right to her house. The car likely knew the way by now.

"I'm not sure."

"It's worth a chance. Your eye may have seen something the mind doesn't remember—until it sees it again." Thursday was humoring her. Considering her appearance, that was sweet.

"I saw one guy's face."

"Yeah?" He glanced at her and turned back. She looked terrible.

"Yeah, he looked me right in the eye before he came after me."

Zimpel didn't like that, meant the guy knew she saw him, too.

"You have to show me photo arrays including others, right?"

"I think I know the thugs that did this. Obviously LCN," he said.

"Don't tell my parents."

"That's your issue." He couldn't leave it. "After this, you should leave town—or go stay with your parents, to be safe." How was he going to keep her safe, and Madie, and get Leitisha out of jail? His insides burned with fury and worry. There was an answer somewhere to all of this but he wasn't finding it. He needed to keep folks out of harm's way. And even there he was failing.

"I'm not going to my parents, they burned a cross on their lawn! They, whoever 'they' are, aren't going to chase me out of town."

"No, right into a limo trunk." He had to make her understand. "You need to protect yourself. First the thug watching you, then burning cross, and now this." He shook his head. "Kay, they'll kill you."

Kay shook her head. "If they want to badly enough, I'm not sure how I could prevent it."

His throat tightened and he coughed. She was right.

She turned to him. "I mean, I'm not the damn president of the United States. I can't be guarded all the time." She sighed and rubbed her arms.

He nodded, eying her while he drove. Her face was pale. He was glad he'd brought the blanket. She had wrapped it around her legs. He pulled up in front of her apartment building.

As she stood at the door, she realized she didn't have her keys. They were in her purse. Which she didn't have. She knocked on the door to get the doorman's attention. A face appeared in the glass and then the door opened.

"Hello Kay, what happened to you?" Mrs. Johnson wore her familiar house coat, a laundry basket under one arm, a cigarette in the hand that held the door.

"I don't have my keys. I was hoping Mr. Jeff or Louis would be in the lobby." Kay pushed on the door, self-conscious of her bare feet and general grime. "I'll need to get a key to my flat."

"Mr. Jeff is helping Muriel with her groceries. Did someone rob you and beat you up? You look terrible."

"No, I," she had to make up something. She didn't want her building to know she'd been kidnapped. "I had a bad fall on some slippery grass."

"Lucky I was doing laundry and just coming up." Mrs. Johnson glanced beyond Kay to the street. "Is that your mother out there in the car?" She didn't wait for an answer but pressed the button for the elevator.

Kay waited for Mr. Jeff to come down. "Are you ok?" he asked Kay.

"Mr. Jeff, my purse was stolen . . . and I had a bad fall."

"My you look awful, I'm so sorry. Let me get you a key. He went to his desk, unlocked it, and found her a key. Kay grabbed it and went to the elevator, not wanting any more conversations about what had happened.

First she stripped off her clothes and put them in the garbage. After using the bathroom, she washed off the blood and dirt, slipped into a pair of black slacks, pulled on a sweater, wrapped a scarf around her neck, and went back down. Mr. Jeff was back at the desk.

"Thanks again," Kay waved and went out to the car. Revived by the warm, clean clothes, she walked steadily, no longer dizzy.

"This may sound odd, but I need to eat something. I'm hungry."

He shook his head. "You've been in shock. That's a good sign you're coming out of it. You need some warm, delicious food, preferably fried." He raised his eyebrows.

"Jimbo's?" they said at the same time. "Jinx!" And they laughed, making them both feel better.

The neon "Jimbo's" sign shone through the fog. The triangular sign on top of the door read "The House that Bop Built." When Kay and Zimpel arrived, the place was packed and noisy, music wailing.

"Althea."

If Althea considered it unusual that the two of them showed up so late on a work evening, she didn't show it. "Well good evening you two, I got a place at the bar for you in a minute." She caught Kay's eye. "You all right Kay? You got some scrapes."

"Oh, it's fine, had a little fall." Her hands were still ice cold. "What's going on? Wild sound from the back."

"Ah, Willie Mays is in the back room and they's listening to a young saxophone player. Name is John Coltrane, and he's making everyone crazy."

# CHAPTER 56

"Oh, let's go listen while we wait." The normal pull of the music hit her intensely as they reached the back room. Kay took to hard bop like a person to water in a desert. She breathed it in and her worries subsided.

"That sax is out of this world!" He was playing "Stardust," an old Hoagy Carmichael song. They watched the young man, intense, tall, in a tweed jacket and white shirt. John Coltrane. New sound, so spiritual. Someone to remember. Her hands itched to play.

Althea, true to her word, got them two seats and took their order. Zimpel glanced around the room and Kay took his sleeve and pointed. Willie Mays sat over on the side with Jimbo Edwards, watching the music and eating chicken.

Zimpel said, "He's one of my heroes."

In spite of the sign that said, "No liquor served on these premises," Zimpel pulled out a flask. Lucky for Kay, he had filled it with Irish whiskey. She took a big swig and let it burn down her throat. The taste of whatever poison they had given her was finally wearing away.

They each had a plate of chicken with good sides, greens and sweets, washed down with the rest of the whiskey, then got back in his car.

Although it was after midnight, Zimpel drove over to Southern Station to make the report and look through mug shots and photo books.

"He attacked me from behind with the chemical, whatever it was. There was only the one guy. I looked him straight in the eyes right before he chased me. Now I can't remember his face. I see his eyes though. I never saw the driver or anyone else in the limo."

"Just humor me?"

Tired from the ordeal and the food, she started going through the photographs. Used to the methodical detail of legal research, she started with the first book and worked her way through the stacks that Zimpel had set out for her.

"Thursday?"

Zimpel got up and leaned over her shoulder to look at the photo Kay pointed to.

"This guy. This is the guy that was outside my apartment, right?"

Zimpel peered down at the photo, their faces inches apart. "Yeah, that's the guy. Is that the guy from the limo."

She shook her head, "No, they aren't the same."

His voice was hoarse. He turned to Kay. She felt his breath.

"You," he paused. "You scared me tonight."

"I scared myself." Not enough to stop.

"I'm feeling responsible here, and I screwed up."

She patted his arm and he sat back in his chair. She felt him near still.

"Contrary to current thought, the man is not always responsible. I make decisions, and the consequences are mine alone." She didn't want him carrying any blame for her. "Not that I'm not appreciative that you keep saving me. It's lovely and irksome at the same time. Do you understand?"

Zimpel smiled at her. "Yeah, I get it." He liked that she took responsibility and was her own person. That didn't help him get beyond wanting to keep her safe though.

"So," she drew his attention back to the mug shots. "Didn't you pick this guy up? What was his name?"

"Vito Carelli. Yeah, but he made bail right away."

"I love how mobsters can make bail within minutes and Leitisha, because she's not white, sits in jail." Kay sighed. The system was so lopsided. "Did we learn anything from him?"

"Nah, he wasn't going to talk, no reason to, but we know who he is and who he works for—Michael Abati—which is enough to make us nervous. And pay attention."

"We can assume that whoever picked me up also works for Abati, right? I mean, I wouldn't have one guy following me, and then someone else kidnap me?"

"Not sure." Zimpel had talked to Carelli before they let him loose. Told him that if he didn't stay away from Kay, he was going to find some real trouble. He wasn't sure it was Abati who had kidnapped her. If it was, Zimpel now had a personal grudge against him.

Kay kept looking through the books but didn't see anyone she recognized. She was resting her head in her hands when it came to her. A smell. The memory was faint but distinct. A smoky smell—she remembered it clearly. Was it on the guy when he held her before she passed out?

Zimpel stood in the door watching her. "You ought to call it a night. You've had enough today."

She felt her head drooping. "I admit that I am pretty tired. But I remembered something else."

"What?"

"I don't know what it means or even if it's a clue or what. But there was this smell, a smoky smell, like . . ." Her brain was so tired but she pushed. She knew that smell. "Oh my God."

"What, what?" He was standing with car keys in his hand, files under his arm, ready to take her home.

"It's a booze smell, maybe scotch, smoky. What do they call it? Peaty? That's what I smelled when I was out of it. I don't know if I smelled it on the guy or in the trunk, but no mistaking that smell."

Zimpel nodded, "I like it. Scotch tasting. My kind of assignment. I know where to go. You up for this? We'll call it a nightcap." Against his better judgment, but nothing about this case was right. He was going with it.

# CHAPTER 57

AUGUST 30, 1958 · SATURDAY, EARLY MORNING

"I'm supposed to be taking you home. You've been kidnapped, eaten at Jimbo's, and it's nearly 2 a.m. I am a bad person."

"Shut up and let's go. I won't be able to sleep anyway. Let's see if this helps." She was wide awake now, a second wind kicking in. Or maybe a third.

They pulled up to Tosca's in North Beach.

Tosca's, started by three Italians after the First World War, was on Columbus Avenue in North Beach, San Francisco's Italian neighborhood. It became famous for its "house cappuccino," trendy during Prohibition, which contained brandy.

Zimpel parked at a fire hydrant. "But it's closing time," said Kay.

"Yeah, perfect," said Zimpel, opening her door.

Zimpel caught the eye of the bartender cleaning up. "Nick Landis, meet Kay Schiffner."

"What's a nice young lady like you out so late with the likes of him?" Nick asked, winking at her. His implication was anything but "nice." She was in slacks with no makeup.

But she wasn't some young hussy coming into a bar late: "I was kidnapped tonight by someone from the LCN. So we're here because I remembered smelling something after they drugged me. We think it's a scotch. Obviously, Zimpel believed you might help."

Nick bowed. "I apologize." Meaning he had thought she was a hussy. He glanced at Zimpel. "So this is police work?"

"Yep, straight up," said Zimpel.

"Let's go to it," said Nick. "Joey, lock the doors. We got some work to do."

Kay felt someone walk behind her, a small man in a white apron, and heard the door click.

Nick proceeded to line the bar with a number of bottles and glasses. He lined them up just right, and then poured a glass of water. "Do you want ice?"

Kay shook her head. "I drink it neat and I want it more for the smell."

Nick's eyebrows went up. He poured a little whiskey in each glass and motioned for her to come over.

Kay carefully picked up each glass, sniffed it, and took a sip. When she got to the end, she picked up a glass and downed it. "It wasn't this one. Sorry, thirsty work."

Zimpel smiled. Nick shifted from one leg to the other.

"None of them matched the smell." Kay began to doubt what it was she'd smelled. Maybe it was all in her head.

Nick glanced at Kay, and then turned to the wall of bottles behind him. "Tell me again what it smelled like."

"Extremely smoky, like grass on fire or something. Hung strong in the air like a perfume."

Nick looked at her again. "Hang on a second." He went out a back door.

"Maybe this is stupid and I didn't remember anything important."

"You heard the man, hang on," said Zimpel. "If we're going to find it, this is place. Nick knows everything about drinks, bars, and scotch whisky. Everything. Hang on."

"Even if he doesn't know much about women?"

Zimpel raised his eyebrows and sat at the bar with a bottle of Anchor Steam in his hands.

Nick came back, a little breathless. "I got a few bottles I brought back from Scotland. Our license lets us bring in some imports, so I bring bottles for certain folks. That can afford it."

"Oh, don't . . ." This was too much, opening all these bottles for her.

"Oh, yes. Someone kidnapped you? I can't think of a better reason to open a bottle of scotch. What do you think it was made for?"

He looked a little afraid of her.

Nick set up three sets of two glasses on the bar and poured scotch into each of them.

Kay reached for the first of the two glasses. Before she had it to her lips she knew that was it. The smell. "This is it," she said. "This is exactly the smell I remember." The smell made her cringe thinking of the man, and shiver from cold or fear, she wasn't sure which. "The guy who grabbed me smelled of it as I collapsed."

"Smells are powerful," said Nick, eyes wide. "Good nose. That's Lagavulin, a famous Scotch, made in Islay since the early part of the 19th Century. Not too many people drink that scotch around here. I only have one customer that does. He has me get it for him when I can."

"And, who is it?" She was losing patience now, tired.

"Brad Mullin. It's his favorite."

Kay gave Zimpel a pointed eyebrows up and nodded. Zimpel stood.

Landis gave them a puzzled look. "Has to be someone else though. That guy's not a bad guy, just rich. Lives over in Pac Heights." He scratched his head and ran his hand down his end-of-day whiskers. "Should be a pretty good ID because not too many folks can obtain or afford this."

"I, uh . . ." Kay turned to Zimpel.

Zimpel nodded at her, stopping her midsentence. "Thanks, Nick, very helpful. We catch the guy with the scotch, we're good." They laughed.

Nick poured the shot glasses full and pushed them towards Kay and Zimpel. "We need to make sure this is the one, then," he paused, "commit it to memory. Ready?" He held his glass up and took the shot.

Zimpel wiped his mouth. "I need to get this lady home, now."

Kay had enough. Too much memory in that smell. She didn't touch her glass.

"Sure, glad I could help." Nick unlocked the door, let them out, and locked the door behind them. The street was deserted.

"Zimpel, Brad Mullin is the contractor I went to see."

Zimpel nodded. "Maybe he made it personal."

Kay stopped, realization showing plainly on her face.

"What is it?" asked Zimpel.

"Mullin. The kid that Tildy identified, that Walter's son told me about. The football player who delivered the meat on the day the gun was dropped. His last name is Mullin." She scrunched her mouth, the taste still there. "The picture is starting to clear up."

Due to the late hour and the whiskey, Zimpel wasn't sure if it was coming together or getting more confusing.

# CHAPTER 58

## AUGUST 30, 1958 · SATURDAY, MIDDAY

Later that morning, after getting some sleep, Kay was sore, bruised, and groggy. Had she really been kidnapped?

After coffee and some aspirin, she called Michael Zorn and told him what had happened. "I was going to come in and do some more work, but I think I need to pass."

"You were what?"

"Thrown into the trunk of a car after being drugged with something."

"What? Who did this?"

"No one spoke, and I only saw the one guy right before he held something over my nose."

"Holy mother, that's terrible. Are you ok?"

"Yeah, bruised and all, but nothing serious."

"What happened? How did you get out?"

She heard the concern in his voice, and she realized how close she'd come.

"I cut the ropes on my wrists," she glanced down at the sore, red bruises, "and opened the latch from the inside. That wasn't the big deal. It was rolling out of a moving car that was tricky."

In telling the story, she saw how she had distanced herself from it.

"What? Sounds like something out of a movie. I'm not sure I want you working with me—you're pissing people off."

Kay was alarmed. She needed work. "I just . . ."

He laughed his easy laugh. "I'm kidding, it's what we do. We make people mad. But please, this does worry me. Have you seen a doctor?"

"No, no, I'm ok. Zimpel found me, I made a report." She wanted to tell him about the scotch, but that would wait.

"You need to listen and we both need to take precautions. This is serious. You can't be cavalier."

The knot in Kay's stomach loosened a little. "No, no, you're right."

"Besides, I'm surprised I got along without you—you do good work, and fast. Just take it easy today."

"I don't know, there's so much to do. Speaking of which, the young girl that's a witness. I told you about her."

"Tell me the story again?"

Kay tried not to be impatient. There were a lot of moving parts right now.

"She is, or was, a young prostitute, and was with Wright the night he was murdered. She's been hiding out at the Blue Moon, but that's probably not a good idea since between the ABC, Leitisha's arrest, and the moving vans, the Blue Moon is being watched."

Zorn sighed. "Geez. I'm going to be hiding out two women who are being chased by the LCN or worse. I might have to get an armed guard." He laughed his funny laugh again. "So, you want to hide her here?"

"Just until we can figure out who it was she saw, and then we can get some protection." There were too many targets, like a line of pins at a carnival.

"You say 'we'—you thinking of joining the force and being the first woman detective?"

"No, no, being a lawyer has been hard enough. Zimpel gives me trouble for saying 'we'—he feels I'm interfering. It's that I'm trying hard to protect the club, and eventually get Leitisha out of jail. Finding another plausible suspect seems the best way to do that. Maybe it's the LCN, since it seems they're the ones who've been after me. I guess I shouldn't have talked about Abati after all."

"You shouldn't ever talk about Abati, at least not in public. Sure, she can stay here. There's a room I don't use. It's a warehouse after all, so there's lots of room. Can she read?"

Kay blinked, confused. Another room? A warehouse? She hadn't gotten past his cot and a sink. "What about a bed?"

"I'm sure I can come up with something for her. But if I don't keep her busy, occupied, she'll take off. I'm not a prison. How do I keep her here? That's why I asked about whether she could read."

He was thinking of everything. "I don't know what her schooling was. Are you thinking she could do some document work?"

"Let me see what she knows, and if she can be engaged. Otherwise, she may get too agitated, or scared, and split."

"I'll let Thursday know and call you back. I don't know when I'll be in. I'm feeling pretty exhausted."

"Stay home, I can give you something to do there if you get bored. We're on schedule for next week's filings and court appearances."

Zimpel saw he had a message from Kay, and he smiled. She'd been through a lot but was still working. He called her at home.

"Michael's able to house her and may even be able to give her some work."

"I'll bring Madie over there in a couple hours, although Sylvia may miss her. Will you be there?"

"Maybe. I may head in later. I'm pretty tired and sore this morning."

"I'm not surprised. You sure you don't want to see a doctor?"

"No, I don't need anything but rest." He heard that stubbornness that made him crazy, and the strength he admired.

"Madie going to be ok with him, and it's safe there?"

"It's messy, he's a slob, but yeah, it's a fortress, and there's apparently more room than even I have seen. He said he had something to fix up for a bed."

"He's not . . ." Zimpel hesitated. Neither he nor Frazier, both single, wanted an underage girl at their houses. What made Zorn take her?

Kay snapped at him, not getting his question. "He's not what?"

"She's an underage girl and prostitute . . ."

"Oh lord, no." Kay laughed. "She'll be safe."

"What does that mean?"

"Just trust me on this. She'll be well protected." Zimpel understood then. Understood why Kay didn't tell him and understood why Zorn wasn't making a pass at Kay, impossible not to do in his mind.

San Francisco's mayor, George Christopher, targeted gay bars as well as the burlesque and strip joints. Zimpel knew cops dropped drugs so there would be cause to yank their liquor license—a death knell and a practice he disapproved of because it wasn't honest, wasn't police work. It was politician's work. Still, no one would willingly share information with him that would get them arrested.

He knew a few poofs in the service and many who stayed in San Francisco after the war like he did, and much for the same reason. Wanting some tolerance.

"Thursday?"

He grunted to let her know he was there. "Yeah, she won't come empty-handed. Sylvia fixed her up with some clothes and toiletries."

Sylvia went above and beyond. Zimpel believed that the kitchen staff saw Madie as Leitisha's way out of jail, and treated her well, even by making her work. While Madie had some drug sickness, the closeness of the staff and their help was what was keeping her from running off. He hoped moving her to Zorn's didn't trigger some escape response.

"In the next day or two, I'm going to need to get her in front of some photos. Maybe I can sneak her into the station, and we'll go from there. Which brings me to another problem. I spoke with the lawyer Saul hired for Leitisha. His name is Joel Edelman."

"The one who works for Teasbury?"

"Yeah."

"They represent developers, according to Michael."

"Might explain why I don't have a lot of confidence in him—he was distant, almost dismissive."

"He's a rich, snooty lawyer. He's going to be distant with you."

"But he was a jerk. You'd think he'd at least listen to the evidence I was giving him, even if he doesn't trust the police. Or that I am her friend." Edelman didn't care about the evidence, which worried him.

"What did he say about an arraignment, her right to a speedy trial?"

"Edelman says he wants to see what they have first, to get her out on the merits." Except he didn't want any merits evidence.

"That's exactly backwards. Clear he's not going to do anything. It's up to us." He felt her pause and pictured her brow in thought. "Something is off here. His firm represents the developers, so there's a conflict. It doesn't surprise me that he wants to keep her on ice until she loses the restaurant. What was Saul thinking hiring this guy for Leitisha?"

Zimpel had a suspicion he kept to himself.

"I'm sure they're friends, it's how he does things. Works within his inner circle." Zimpel said, but believed it was something else.

"Saul knows what kind of man Edelman is, and not the kind that would warm up to Leitisha." Kay wasn't buying it either.

She was right. Just the kind of man Zimpel would keep away from Leitisha.

"I'll take Madie over to Zorn's. Thanks for everything. You rest."

# CHAPTER 59

By late afternoon, after a nap, a sandwich, and some aspirin, Kay felt better, and itched to work. The call with Zimpel about Edelman stuck with her, and she decided she didn't need to call him because he was in no hurry to get Leitisha out. It had been weeks, and it was clear he had a different agenda.

If Kay showed the gun had been dropped, that would be enough to get Leitisha out of jail, or at least get bail. If she could get her out of jail, Leitisha would understand that Kay was on her side.

They had identified the Mullin kid as the drop guy in Leitisha's pantry. If the kid's dad was involved with redevelopment, and she had pissed him off enough to have him attack her with the cross or the kidnapping, then maybe there was a connection between him and the kid dropping the gun?

No one saw him plant the gun, though. All they had was Tildy telling them that he went into the meat cooler, and was the only new delivery person that day.

William said that Mullin liked to hot rod and occasionally got into trouble. Maybe she could find him at a race, confront him while he was doing something illegal, and see if he would tell her about the drop in exchange for her not calling in the cops. Long shot. She needed to figure out where and when he would be doing this racing. She jiggled her telephone to get it to work.

"Hi Mom, is Kevin there?

"Kevin? Why yes, he's in his room—so how are you?"

"I'm fine." She still hadn't told her parents she'd gotten fired from Bianco and was now working for Michael Zorn. "Everything's fine, just wanted to ask him a quick question."

"Well, what is it dear?"

"It's a . . ." Kay paused, not wanting her mother as a go-between. "A music question, you wouldn't know the answer."

"Oh very well. Why don't you come around for dinner? Sounds like you're working too hard."

"Sure, I'll do that. Thanks, mom."

Kay heard her mother yell up the stairs. "Kevin, turn down that music. Kay wants you on the telephone." Kay heard the phone receiver drop, and "Jailhouse Rock" in the background.

"What?"

"No 'hello'—no telephone etiquette?"

"Why are you calling me?" She guessed she disturbed him.

"I'm working on a case, and I need to know where high school kids might go hot rodding, you know, racing."

"I know what hot rodding is. What kind of case?"

"I figured you did. Never mind the case. Where would they be and when would they do it?"

"How would I know?"

Kay rolled on her feet, impatient. "Help me out here Kevin, don't make me beg, ok?"

Silence.

"Kevin?"

"If mom and dad even knew that I knew this stuff . . ."

"Kevin, I went to high school. If mom and dad knew the stuff I do now . . ."

"Like what?"

"Never mind, come on . . . tell me. I need to find this kid."

"Well, if they're racing in San Francisco," Kevin lowered his voice.

Kay hoped their mother wasn't listening. She didn't want to explain any of this.

"I mean, if he likes to illegally race cars, I heard that if you go out to Ocean Beach sometime after 11 but most likely around 2 a.m. on the weekends, they race up and down there."

"Ok, anywhere else?"

"I heard there was a place down the Peninsula. There's a place in Oakland . . ."

"Have you ever seen them?"

"What? I plead the fifth!" He laughed.

Great, lawyer jokes from her little brother.

"I swear to God if you tell anyone I gave that to you, I'm dead meat." His tone was serious now.

"Oh, yeah, there's a zillion high school kids at these things and they are going to think that you gave it away? Come on."

"I'm serious, Kay."

"So am I, it's not going to happen, relax." She paused, thinking she should be more like a sister. "So what are you doing tonight?"

"I'm going to an Elvis sock hop at the roller rink—meeting Judy Saber. Cool right?"

"Right, thanks." They couldn't be more different. "Don't tell mom what we talked about. I told her I was asking you about music."

"I'll be fine," he said. "She doesn't want to hear 'bout music."

If she was going to find kids racing cars at Ocean Beach, she would need some wheels herself. Barb had a car and might be up for a late-night adventure . . . if she hadn't written Kay off as a bad friend.

# CHAPTER 60

"Barb?"

"Kay! Is that really you?"

"Yeah, I'm sorry, it's been a while."

"I understand." Barb's tone made Kay feel guilty. "I've been busy, too. Dad said he ran into you at some hearing."

"Yes, good to see him." Kay took a deep breath. She had to work up to this.

"You bury yourself in your work. I hardly see you. Everything ok?"

Kay avoided the talk about work. "Everything is fine. How are you doing at City of Paris?"

"Everything couture, you know, fashion . . . and the clothes! I'm having a blast, but not on the love front. Can't seem to get a steady date. I'm not sure it's the right job for me. Men bring their wives in, but it's hardly a place where a nice single man would be."

Barb was obsessed with "getting a man." She could talk on the telephone, paint her nails and do her hair all at the same time, expounding for hours on her favorite theme: husband hunting.

Kay laughed. "What are you doing tonight?"

"Tonight? I don't hear from you for a couple of months, and you're giving me a last-minute invite?"

"I apologize, something came up but if you're busy . . ."

"No, I'm not busy, but I look a fright. It'll take me a while to get dressed up. Where are we going?"

"I wouldn't get too dressed up. We're going to watch high schoolers race cars illegally on Ocean Beach."

"Is that some kind of joke?"

"Sorry, no, actually, it's . . ." Kay was going to have to explain that this wasn't a social outing. Awkward after so long. "I need your help for a case I'm working on. I need to find this student, who is a witness to something. I'm told that he may be there."

"Well, exciting, some detective work." Barb paused. "So Kay Schiffner on the case! Sounds intriguing." She paused. "And you want me to drive is that it?"

"That's it." Kay realized her request was rude but was hoping their friendship and Barb's curiosity would win her over.

"Now that you're renting an apartment, and you're on your own, you need to get yourself a car. So what kind of case is this?" Curiosity won.

"I'll fill you in after you pick me up—I heard they start late so come around 9, and we'll get a bite to eat first."


Kay dressed in a black skirt and tights with a pullover. If she got in a situation, she wanted to be business-like but also comfortable.

The phone rang. Mr. Jeff saying that Barb was downstairs in her sedan. Kay had intended on letting Zimpel know but she'd tell him later.


Bright moonlit waves gently hit the shore. Kay loved that San Francisco has many faces, including a beach at the edge of the Avenues that stretches for miles.

It was nearly midnight. She and Barb had driven out past Geary, turned around and pulled into the parking lot in front of the Cliff House to see what was going on.

Soon kids and cars crowded the parking lot off Ocean Beach. Cars steered around the parking lot, screeching donuts. Radios played and girls in ponytails, sweater sets and skirts sat in cars or stood in groups talking, their clean-cut looks deceiving. Guys with leather jackets and greased back hair smoked cigarettes and talked back and forth, milling around their cars. Kay and Barb parked close enough to observe. They heard the music and occasional loud comment.

Kay kept looking for Mullin among all the kids. There were so many, she wondered how their parents didn't know they were out at the beach.

"There, he's there, that's him." She pointed. "Good, he's here." She went to get out of the car.

Barb put a hand out. "Look, why don't you watch him for a minute before you dive in, see what's going on?"

Barb's patience surprised her but she was right. Kay nodded. From where they were, they saw him pretty clearly.

A cigarette dangling out of his mouth, the Mullin kid stood next to a fancy car, which she suspected was his father's. Definitely a jock type with broad shoulders. The girls were swooning, two or three hovering to talk to him. Then he had some words, not all of which she heard, with another guy, gave a whoop and got into his car, revved it up, and squealed out of the parking lot.

"Damn, there he goes."

"He's going to race," said Barb. "See the other guy." She pointed. "God, what losers, their ego is all tied up in fast cars."

"How do you know all this?" Barb was proving to be an expert—telling her what to watch, and then explaining what was happening.

"I used to date a guy who liked to race—drag racing mostly, not just street racing.

"So even better you joined me."

"Why? Because I know these guys are losers?" She poked Kay's shoulder. "Maybe if you called me for a drink once in a while."

Kay grimaced. "I'm sorry. I'll be better." Why hadn't she asked her to come to the Blue Moon?

Barb and Kay got out of the car to watch. The two cars raced neck and neck, going faster and faster, down the road.

"If someone was coming, they'd have no time to get out of the way. That's nuts." They race like this and no one calls the cops.

"They don't go that far down, and someone watches on each end to stop anyone from going up the road. Mostly no one is out right now." Barb walked out on the road. "They'll circle back, or at least the winner will, some money will exchange hands and some girl attention will be had."

"Let's get back to the car." The wind blew the fog around; it was cold.

They didn't have to wait long. The two racers peeled back into the parking lot. Doug Mullin smiled getting out of the car. Money exchanged hands as Barb predicted.

Kay was ready now. "I'm going out there to talk to him. Something happens, drive into the middle of it and pick me up. You ok with that?"

"I'll pretend that whoever gets in my way is my old boyfriend."

Kay laughed. "You could say that about a lot of guys."

"They have to be good for something, eh?"

Kay headed to where the kid was leaning up against his car. Loud music played, Jerry Lee Lewis. The girl hanging on him gave her a dirty look.

He reached into his car for two bottles of PBR, handed one to the girl who looked younger than he did and then gestured at Kay with the other can. "Wanna beer?" The win made him gregarious.

Kay shook her head. "Not right now." He eyed her curiously.

"Let me ask you something."

"Sure." He leaned back on his car and smiled at the girl.

"You made a meat delivery to the Blue Moon."

He opened his beer with a church key on his car key chain, took a swig of beer, wiped his mouth and said, 'I don't know what you're talking about.' His smile faded.

"You dropped a gun in the pantry while you were there. Help refresh your memory?"

He hugged the girl, took another chug of beer and turned away from Kay. "I got nothing to say to you."

She went at him again. "We already know you set up Leitisha at the Blue Moon—you were identified. I need to know who's trying to frame her."

"I don't know any lay-tisha, and we got better things to do, if you don't mind." He tossed the empty beer bottle at her feet. It broke on impact so she had to jump.

Kay was about to tell him that she did mind when she heard sirens.

"Shit, Doug, here come the cops, let's go." The girl pulled at him. Kids jumped into cars, engines revving. Mullin pulled his key out to start his car but it wouldn't turnover. He ground the starter.

"Damn, it was working great." He got out and opened the hood. He fiddled with something and tried to start the car again. The girl glanced first at him and then at other cars leaving.

"Hey Doug, sorry but I need to leave. Cops catch me, I'm dead meat at home. Hey, wait up . . ." she called to the other kids, and hopped into a car and left him.

"Victory is fleeting . . . now he's the loser," observed Barb, who had driven up close to Kay. "Should we go?" she asked nodding at the approaching sirens.

Kay saw this as an opportunity. She noticed Mullin begin to panic, and he glanced at her; the sirens were getting closer and they could see the police lights. One more intersection and they would be there.

# CHAPTER 61

Kay gestured at the car. "Let's push your car away from the broken beer bottles and mess, now."

He shrugged in response, and the two of them pushed the car to the other side of the parking lot. Barb followed in the car.

"You got any more beer in your car?"

He nodded.

"Give it to me." He handed her the rest of the six-pack and she motioned to Barb to open the trunk and she put the beer inside. Just as she slammed it shut, two cop cars pulled up into the parking lot and one headed for them. Kay saw the other pulling in front of cars that hadn't gotten out yet, and other black-and-whites had pulled over several cars on the side of the road.

The black-and-white stopped behind Barb's car.

"Good evening officer," said Kay said to the cop driving, not getting too close. "You just missed them. There were maybe 50 kids here. They all pulled out when they heard your sirens."

The cop on the passenger side got out, eyed the three of them. "Let me see your driver's license." Barb and Kay handed the cop their drivers' licenses. Mullin held back. The other cop got out and stood to the side watching.

"So what are you doing here?" The first cop used his flashlight to read the licenses.

Kay spoke up quickly. "He came to rescue us. See, our car stalled at the light and wouldn't start again, and he's good at fixing cars so we called him to come help us. Then all this racing stuff happened so we tried to stay out of the way."

The cop gave her a side look, and then looked at the kid.

"Why were you here in the middle of the night if you weren't racing?"

Barb spoke up. "We were going home from a late movie, and the car stopped and it wouldn't start again, like she said."

"What was wrong with the car?"

The kid finally spoke. "They had let the battery die down. I guess they had enough to get it started once, but it wasn't recharging. So I gave them a boost, and now they should be good to go until they get it fixed. It took me some time to get over here so they got stuck for a while."

The kid was good at lying. Kay suspected he had done his share of it. The cop clearly didn't believe any of them. "Let me see your license," he said to Mullin.

Mullin fumbled for his wallet.

"Officer, if you wouldn't mind, please contact a friend of mine that's a police officer and let him know we're ok?"

"Who's that?"

"Inspector Thursday Zimpel."

"He's a friend of yours?"

"Yes." She decided to leave it at that.

"Hang on." He went back into the car and got on the radio. Kay turned to Mullin. The kid was shaking, still holding his license back.

After what seemed like a long time, the cop handed back their licenses. "Now all of you go home, especially you, young man. I'm betting you're underage and if you weren't with these ladies, I'd haul you in with the rest of them."

"You got lucky kid." The cop went to get into his car. Kay hoped the "kid" now would be grateful and talk to them.

Kay turned to him. "What about your car?"

Mullin ran his hand through his hair. "I need to figure out what's wrong with it. I can't leave it here." He looked back inside the raised hood. "Something must have come loose while we were . . ."

Kay saw a familiar car approach.

"Thursday, how'd you get here so fast?"

"Cop called me first, and I told him to delay so I could make my way over here and make sure you were ok. Out a little late tonight?"

Zimpel moved fast when he heard that Kay was out at 2 a.m. after all she'd been through. He had to put an end to this recklessness. Her risks made him ache.

"What happened?" Zimpel glanced at the woman with Kay who watched him closely. Zimpel assumed the car was hers.

"We were out and happened across some car racing." Kay glanced at Mullin.

She'd gone out to find the boy who planted the gun. Why didn't she tell him what she was going to do?

"I see. You almost got swept up in the arrests. I heard they picked up over 20 kids." He made sure Mullin heard him. He studied the kid, watched him fiddle with his car.

"I'll follow you home. I want to make sure you get there."

"That's not necessary, Barb's going to . . . uh, Barb, this is Inspector Zimpel."

"Oh, this is the cop with the day name?"

Zimpel grimaced. Still, he was pleased that Kay had talked about him.

Barb smiled and put her hand out. "Hi, I'm Barbara Kimball. And I am truly pleased to meet you." Zimpel took her hand, realized she was flirting with him like it was a sport. Maybe it was to her.

Zimpel turned to Mullin, who avoided eye contact with him. "You're the kid who planted the gun at the Blue Moon." He hit him between the eyes with it, now that he understood what was going on. But Jesus, Mary and Joseph, she should have told him what she was doing. Woman was obstinate.

Doug Mullin's shoulders slumped.

Zimpel had done this a thousand times. He kept his voice modulated and friendly. "You walked into a kitchen where everyone knows each other, and shortly after you left, their employer was arrested." Zimpel waited patiently. "It wasn't exactly a sneak attack."

The kid glanced right and left, and shifted his weight.

"You can tell me who told you to do the delivery, or not. Up to you. But planting evidence is a crime—this is a crime." Zimpel waved his arm to take in the parking lot. "You're not exactly on a good path here, and you have the chance to turn that around." Zimpel hoped the kid was smart enough to know it got ugly after this. "I'll take you in like the rest of them." He waited.

The kid, agitated now, his hands going for his pockets, and then out. Glancing at Kay, and then at Barb, he saw there was no reprieve. He started to nod before he spoke. "I was asked to make a delivery."

"Why were you asked to make a delivery?"

The kid didn't answer right away. Zimpel assumed he was deciding if he could lie his way out.

"I had . . . ." He finally spoke. "gotten in trouble. My dad's lawyer bailed me out."

Kay's head was calculating. "What does your dad do?" She wanted this answer now.

"He works in construction, builds big buildings."

"What's the name of his company?" Kay asked the kid. She had already made the connection.

"Mid-City Development."

Kay made a noise, and Zimpel took the lead back.

"What did you do?"

Kid's chin was tucked down. "I don't want to tell?"

Zimpel nodded at him. "I'm sure I can find out."

The kid leaned against his car, his arms tightly folded across his chest.

"Some friends of mine and I, we were hungry and got into a restaurant that was closed."

"You broke into a restaurant." A kid who has everything at home.

"Well, we figured out how to unlock the door." Kid squirmed.

"Which restaurant?"

"San Remo."

Zimpel groaned at the multiple layers of stupidity. "That's a cop hangout."

"Yeah, well, I figured that out."

"A cop didn't ask you to drop the gun?" Zimpel hoped not.

"I didn't know it was a gun."

That was a lie, but he stated it like he was his only answer.

Zimpel went a different way. "What's important is who was asking you."

"Look, I was told to drive deliveries for free for Petrini's. You know, the butcher over on Masonic, and I'd get off."

Petrini had made a name for himself by being the best butcher in San Francisco for the past 20 years and revolutionized the grocery business. "What exactly were you told to do?" Zimpel spoke in a low voice.

"A guy gave me a list of drop offs, and packages marked for each one. I didn't have any choice, or I would have been thrown out of school. I didn't know what was in the packages. I just delivered them."

"Who, son, who asked you?"

"He made my dad mad, that he was asking me to do this. I don't know his name but he said he would fix everything with the DA if I ran the meat delivery for one day for his friend at Petrini's."

"So the guy didn't work at Petrini's?"

The kid shook his head. "I don't think so. He wore a suit. Said it was a favor for a friend."

"Your dad know his name?"

The kid shrugged. "I guess so."

Zimpel made eye contact with Kay. "I think I need to give Mr. Mullin here a ride."

"No way, I'll get in so much trouble."

"You're already in trouble. Planting a gun on an innocent person is wrong."

"I didn't know it was a gun."

"You're a liar." Zimpel stared him down.

Mullin panicked and his arms went out, his head swiveled about looking for an escape. Zimpel grabbed him by the arm. "You want me to cuff you and put you in the car?"

Mullin pulled away. "You can't arrest me."

Zimpel sighed and pulled out his cuffs, spun Mullin around before he struggled away, cuffed him and put him in the back seat of his car.

"I told you what you wanted. You can't do this!"

Zimpel shut the door.

"Thursday?"

"What?" He didn't mean to sound testy but it was late, she had worried him, and he had this kid to deal with now.

"His father—he's the head of Mid-City Development."

Zimpel tilted his head at her.

"The company that was taking Marvin Wright's properties directly instead of going through the Redevelopment Agency."

"That the guy you called on?" Zimpel remembered she had confronted some head of a development company. He half wondered if that hadn't gotten her fired. Or watched by the LCN guy. Or kidnapped?

"Yeah. Small world."

Zimpel wiped his face. "Why are you even near this kid after what happened to you?"

Barb glanced at Kay.

"I didn't put it together until we were here." To Barb she said, "I'll tell you later."

"You go home." He gave both Barb and Kay eye contact. He did not want to be misunderstood. Barb made him uncomfortable. He turned to Kay. "You don't call me in 30 minutes, I'm locking you up myself to get some peace of mind."

Kay laughed. "I'll call you—at the station?"

"Likely. I'll be there with him," he thumbed over at the kid, "doing paperwork."

# CHAPTER 62

Zimpel drove towards Kearny Street, glancing in the rearview at the sullen teenager in his back seat. Doug Mullin stared out the window, not looking cocksure now. "So you want to tell me about the guy who wanted you to toss the gun?"

Mullin looked up at Zimpel catching his eye in the rearview, and then turned back to the window.

"Whoever asked you to do that, they're hiding the real murderer. And so are you."

"Hey. They asked me to do a meat delivery, I did a meat delivery. I don't know about no gun."

Zimpel winced at the tough guy bad grammar. He took the kid in to make his dad come down and get him. If his father was the guy who Kay had confronted, Zimpel wanted a good look at him up close and on his territory. Maybe the shock of seeing his kid in cuffs at a police station would help the dad remember who it was set up the drop and why.

"That what they teach you at that fancy high school?" Zimpel shook his head. This kid had no idea what he had been handed. All the sacrifices Walter and Bernice had made to send their son to SI, and what he went through being there, and here was this kid with all the privilege in the world, wasting it.

He pulled into the station without the kid saying much more than he already had. He gave the kid to a uniform, said he was under arrest for illegal car racing, and to start the paperwork.

"Give me your home number. I'm going to call your dad, tell him where he can find you and his car."

"Ah, you'll wake him up." Mullin kid's eyes were on the floor, but Zimpel saw that he was resigned to whatever hell his father was going to put him through.

"That's the idea."

Zimpel got the number and went to his desk. The phone rang just as he got there.

"Home safe. Can I go to bed now?"

Zimpel smiled. "Good girl. Talk to you tomorrow." He hoped to hell she stayed home and out of harm's way.

"I want to hear about Mullin."

"I'll tell you what I can. Tomorrow. Good night."

He hung up and decided to quickly type up a statement for the kid. The kid was a juvie, but still, it wouldn't hurt to have it. He typed up a decent generic statement then called the kid's dad. Zimpel could tell from his tone that he'd woken up Mr. Mullin, who apparently didn't even realize his son wasn't home.

"You can come down tonight, but you can't get him out until a judge comes in tomorrow."

"The hell I can't. I'll call a judge right now and get him out of bed to bail out my kid."

And he did. The assistant DA on duty for the illegal racing sweep called Zimpel and said the judge had contacted him at home. The kid was being cut loose. Still there was a bit of paperwork to do, and the matter of bail. Within 30 minutes, a bail bondsman showed up with the bail.

"Send him home." Mr. Mullin had called, giving orders again.

"I can't. You'll have to come get him. You have to sign the bail bond."

"He has my car."

"Not right now he doesn't."

Zimpel hung up and went back to the kid.

"It's not going to be pretty for you, especially now we know you did the gun drop."

"I didn't know it was a gun."

"But you did the delivery?"

"I delivered what they gave me."

"And you couldn't tell that it was a gun wrapped in butcher paper?" Zimpel asked.

The kid stared at his shoes and didn't say anything.

"I'm going to send you down to the jail where you can cool your heels."

"No, you can't lock me up?"

"Can and will." Zimpel stood, and finally the kid glanced up at him. "You broke the law, you are charged with a crime, and until a judge releases you, you get to stay with us.

"Now, I can put in a good word with the DA if you help me. If you admit you did the delivery and the gun drop, an innocent person won't remain in jail."

He paused to let that sink in. Zimpel was counting on the kid being tired and a little scared. "The DA would be happy to have that bit of information." That was a lie. The DA didn't know anything about this. Zimpel didn't care. He wanted an affidavit.

Zimpel put two copies of the affidavit in front of the kid, who held up his handcuffed hands. Zimpel took the handcuffs off and gave him a pen. The kid signed it without reading it.

He was underage so maybe it wasn't admissible, but the kid had told him he'd done the drop—in front of Kay and her friend. Whether he admitted knowledge of the gun later or not, Zimpel didn't care, it was in the affidavit. That should be enough to get Leitisha bail, if not completely exonerated. He took the affidavit copies, told the kid to stand up, cuffed him again, and put him in a holding cell alone.

About 40 minutes later, he got a call that Mr. Mullin was at the front. Zimpel went to meet him and brought him to an interview room.

"Can I get you some coffee?"

"I came to pick up my son, Officer. Where is he?"

"I'm an inspector." Zimpel flashed his identification. Mullin merely glanced at it. Zimpel was sure he'd make a note of his name.

Zimpel took him in: expensive haircut, Italian suit, even this late at night he got dressed up to come to the cop shop. Smelled of something expensive. Permeated the room.

"What's my son charged with?"

"Illegal racing on the Great Highway." Zimpel knew the charge was clear when he presented it to the judge. Mullin tried to bully him.

"I called a judge. He granted him a release."

"That'll take a minute. He had to post a bond, and you need to sign that paperwork. Have a seat." Zimpel had already talked to the assistant DA who was processing all these rounded up kids, told him the bail bondsman had been there, and asked him to slow it down.

Mullin senior refused to sit.

Zimpel sat with his pad of paper and pencil in front of him, blank. "Your son made deliveries for Petrini's for a day."

Mullin senior stared at him with big eyes but said nothing.

"In one of those deliveries was a gun."

Mullin glanced up at the two-way mirror.

"Why did you set up your son to do a gun drop?" Zimpel watched Mullin's face carefully. If this is the guy Kay had confronted, he'll have pretty good skills. Still, Zimpel saw the tic by his upper left cheek, the tell he needed. Zimpel got the kid in more trouble with the father by revealing that he had delivered the gun.

He didn't care about this kid who squandered his education and privilege. What mattered was getting Leitisha out of jail. Then he would have to figure out why the gun had been planted, and who had used it to shoot Wright.

"Sure I can't get you anything?"

Mullin had his hands in his overcoat pockets. Zimpel pictured them clenched tight.

"Tell me why your kid was made to do the drop. I'll find out even if I have to talk to everyone at Petrini's."

"You'll do no such thing. Where is my son?"

"Oh, but I will. An innocent woman's been jailed and denied bail because your son planted a gun in her restaurant."

He bit back the rest of what he wanted to say, that it was rich white men like him and the bankers that had redlined San Francisco in the first place, keeping the Negro out of all the neighborhoods but the Fillmore, and now they wanted to take that, too. He let it go. Let Kay argue the politics. He'd stick to policing.

"So I'm going to ask you one more time, who asked your kid to plant the gun and why?"

"I'm here to get my son out of jail, not to respond to your nonsense." Mullin glanced around. "He should be out by now. The bond's been paid."

Mullin treated him like some servant.

"Just sit and wait." Zimpel left and closed the door behind him. He turned to watch the man through the two-way mirror. He wouldn't sit, pacing the room, his hands out now. He cracked his knuckles in nervousness. What would make this man nervous? Zimpel watched him pace another minute or two, and then went to the desk sergeant.

"Let's bring the Mullin kid up and give me the paperwork."

The sergeant handed him a folder of paper.

Zimpel went back into the room. "They are going to bring him up from the jail now."

"You never should have arrested him."

"He shouldn't have been out in the middle of the night illegally racing and endangering people's lives." Zimpel controlled his voice. "And you didn't even know he was out."

He let that criticism sit there. Mullin tried to exhibit confidence, but the tic was going wild now and the hands were moving. That agitation was not caused by his kid being in jail.

The kid slinked into the room with a uniform holding onto his arm.

Zimpel pushed the paperwork towards the father. The kid was a juvenile, so he went into the custody of his parent, who had to sign for the responsibility and the bond.

"I already paid the bond."

"Understood. You are now acknowledging that you're responsible and your kid will show up for the hearing."

"There will be no hearing. I'll get these charges dropped."

"Like you did the last time?" He finally saw some sweat around Mullin's temples.

The father turned to the son. "Where's the car?"

The kid hung back, staying out of his father's aura. "It broke down."

"What do you mean it broke down?" The father's voice hard and quiet. He pulled the papers to him and signed them.

Zimpel let it all play out.

The father stood back up straight, glaring at his kid. "Where is the car?"

"Parked on the Great Highway, by the Beach Chalet parking lot," the kid said in a low voice.

"You left the car there at that dangerous dive?" The comment meant "You're an idiot."

The kid held his cuffed hands up towards Zimpel. "Can we take these off?"

"Sure." Zimpel acted like he was doing them a favor. The father hadn't asked.

Zimpel handed the father his copies of the bond papers but not the affidavit. Not with that attitude. He can find out about that later.

"Here you go."

To the kid, he said, "Maybe you should think about cooperating with the good guys this time and see how your hearing goes?"

Mullin pointed to the door and the kid walked out in front of him, his face blank and resigned. Zimpel watched the back of the two Mullin men leave the station and get into a black limousine. Zimpel wondered if Kay's purse and blood were in its trunk.

Mullin's smell stayed behind.

# CHAPTER 63

The elder Mullin, with or without his fancy lawyers, had put up bail for his kid; even got a judge he knew out of bed. Leitisha, meanwhile, even with a lawyer, wasn't getting anywhere. It was up to Zimpel.

He picked up a manila envelope on his desk with his name in bold letters across the front. There was no postage and he saw the delivery mark on it. Inside was a note from Jeff Giamatti, the reporter he and Kay had spoken with. Maybe someone was answering his prayers after all.

"As promised, here are photographs and ties regarding Mid-City Developers and the Redevelopment Agency. We have a witness who says that for a 'contribution' to the Redevelopment Agency, certain companies had priority in bidding on properties in the Fillmore. Furthermore, the unions supported certain companies, and we saw evidence of kickbacks to the union bosses. We have had the bank accounts subpoenaed in a civil action. I hope you keep your word and call me when the story can be told."

Zimpel smiled. More paper trails to follow up on, and to put in front of Mullin to tie him to payoffs for favored treatment. He needed to connect that and Mullin to the murder.

Giamatti's packet included Redevelopment correspondence with Mid-City and photographs, not only of Mullin with one of the Redevelopment Agency directors but also, to Zimpel's surprise, of receipts for nearly $150,000—a fortune—Mid-City had sent to Redevelopment. Zimpel wondered who had received that money and how it was used.

Lastly, there were five years of Mid-City financials showing that it was cash poor going into the bidding on redevelopment properties, and corporate records indicating what companies were financing Mid-City's redevelopment efforts. Giamatti must have had someone inside taking photos.

Zimpel bet the money originated one step away from local olive oil companies. This evidence pushed them forward. He hoped he could make it admissible.

He returned to the interview room where Frazier brought Madie late in the evening, without identifying her to anyone at the station. They were keeping her cloistered, looking at mug shot books.

Madie had protested being up so late. "I have to work. You can't start me looking at those books now!" Still she took dogged care going over each photograph.

When Zimpel walked in, Madie had a long stare and was shaking. "What's wrong Madie?"

She shook her head, staring at the ground.

"She hasn't talked to me since she came back from the bathroom," said Frazier.

"Madie?" Zimpel spoke softly to her.

She raised her face first to Zimpel, then to Frazier. "That was him," she whispered.

Zimpel barely heard her.

"What? Who was?"

"That man in there. That was the man in the limousine."

"Damn," said Frazier. "Now he's going to go home and sleep in his nice comfortable bed." He turned to Madie. "How did you see him?"

"On the way back from the bathroom, he was there." She shuddered again. "I hope he didn't see me."

"Nah, he won't recognize a little colored girl. To a man like that, one looks the same as the other." Frazier smiled without humor, to put her at ease.

"You're sure Madie? That's was the man that got out and shot Mr. Wright?"

"I don't know if he's the one that shot him. There were two of them."

Zimpel glanced at Frazier. The chauffeur was there, too.

"What happened?"

"I was," she hesitated, staring at the ground, "working Mr. Wright, when I heard a car door slam. I looked up and a man stared down at me, that man. Mr. Wright started yelling. I pushed open the passenger door, and then heard a loud bang and Mr. Wright slumped forward." She hugged herself and started rocking in the chair. "I glanced back, saw the two men and a big limo. I ran as fast as I could, going into alleys, just wanting to get away. I thought they was going to shoot me, too."

Zimpel still wondered why they didn't.

"I will never forget that face, scared me so bad. I see it, I see it in my dreams." She nodded her chin. "Especially now I don't have no drugs to keep it gone."

Frazier nodded at Zimpel, which Zimpel correctly took to wanting to talk outside the room. Madie glanced up suddenly. "What going to happen?"

"Don't worry, Madie, goin' be alright." Frazier gestured towards the door. "Zimpel and I are going to talk—can we get you anything?"

She shook her head and pushed the mug shot books away, still hugging her knees with her other arm, and put her head down, rocking.

"Zimpel, ain't no jury going to take the word of a colored girl over that big shot and his driver."

"Yeah, but now we know." He saw the relief in Frazier's face.

"Black lives don't matter to these men, especially Black girls. That's why they didn't shoot her."

"I always wondered why they didn't shoot her."

Frazier shrugged, "To them, she's just another slave."

Zimpel showed Frazier the affidavit. "I got the statement I wanted tonight. I need to get it to Leitisha's lawyer, or maybe I'll go to the DA."

"You bring it to the DA, ain't going to do too much for your reputation."

"I take it to her lawyer, it'll likely get buried. He doesn't seem to be working too fast."

"Might want to think about that," said Frazier. "No good choice here."

"I'll bring the DA something he can't ignore." Most of all, Zimpel wanted to show the DA that someone inside had framed Leitisha.

"Now, we know. We follow the money. Has to lead to the source of all this."

"Yeah, I may have a lead on the limo." said Frazier. "You got anything else I can use to identify one of them—did Kay say anything in particular about the limo or that night that would help ID the car?"

"She didn't get the plate."

"Nah. Anything else?"

Zimpel recalled that night and felt in his suit jacket pocket. "Kay lost a pearl earring that night along with her shoes and purse. And some blood. Maybe you'll get lucky." He handed the earring to Frazier, who examined it and then put it in his pocket.

Frazier grinned. "Maybe. Too many black limos around."

Zimpel nodded. "I'll call you tomorrow."

"I'll talk to you Monday. Tomorrow's Sunday." He paused. "Can I get something for working today?"

Zimpel shut his eyes, and then opened them again. "I can't get you time and a half."

"I don't beg, Zimpel. I just want to work."

"I'll get you something." Zimpel waited a beat.

Frazier nodded at him. "I'll get Madie back to that lawyer's place now, though. You sure he's ok?"

"He's not into girls."

Frazier shrugged. "She safe enough then I guess." Then he laughed.

"What so funny?"

"You got yourself quite the crew outside the force." Frazier turned and waved Zimpel on, still chuckling to himself.

As he got into his car, Zimpel got a glimpse of something on the passenger side floor. Kay's mangled stockings and a book of poetry. Angry and tired, he resigned to go home and sleep. If Mullin was the guy who'd made trouble for Kay, he'd make trouble for him too. He'd need to watch his own tail.

# CHAPTER 64

## AUGUST 24, 1958 · SUNDAY

Even without overtime, Zimpel was working and making the DA miserable.

"I called you directly because someone in the department or with access to the department is involved, and I don't want this evidence disappearing."

The DA gave a deep sigh. "You don't just want to spoil my golf game today?"

He pictured the DA in golf clothes. "Sorry about your golf game, but at least you're not in jail on trumped up charges." Zimpel didn't give a damn about the DA's golf game. Time to get real. "This stays between us. I don't want anyone else kidnapped or worse." He didn't mention the two young women witnesses, Tildy and Madie. He didn't trust the DA to protect them. Maybe he wouldn't need to.

"Kidnapping? I haven't heard about any kidnapping." Zimpel heard sounds in the background, a chair scraping. He had the DA's attention. "Ok, let's hear it from the beginning. I understood this case was solved, why isn't that it?"

"Depends upon what you mean by 'solved.' If you're a company wanting cheap property from redevelopment, it is. If you're me, the investigator in charge of the case, someone is manipulating the evidence to their advantage."

"Just tell me." Exasperation.

"This was my investigation, yet the patrol cops who got to the scene first made sure to touch everything. The newspaper photo was taken before I got there. These same patrol cops had orders to watch the Blue Moon. For what?"

"Yeah, so what? You need more for your conspiracy. That's just mistakes."

"Maybe. I have evidence that an ABC agent bribed two guys to go into the Blue Moon—owned by your so-called suspect—to cite a violation so he could take away her liquor license to put her out of business. Hence, get the property cheaper without having to pay for the business. I believe the agent got paid off—so he could pay these guys."

"You can prove that?"

He didn't know who paid the ABC agent, but he would. "There's more." He heard the DA cough.

"Someone connected to the DA's office had access to the murder weapon."

"What do you mean?"

Now he had the DA's full attention.

"Someone gave that gun to a developer's kid to plant at the Blue Moon, then tipped the cops to the location. And yeah, I got that evidence." He didn't have it all, but the affidavit helped. Kept Tildy out of it for now.

"Then, they arrested Boone without letting me know because I knew the real facts. I was told to get over it." Zimpel ran his hands through his hair. He wanted a cigarette and felt his pockets.

"She's still in jail without a bond. That's why I'm calling you. It's time to turn her loose. She's in there on manufactured evidence."

"You think someone's inside and manipulating this?"

"I know someone is. It's a matter of time until I finger them." He paused. "So long as it's not you."

"Yeah, nice Zimpel. Screw you. Bring me some evidence and I'll see about cutting loose your 'innocent' suspect."

"Someone knew about the fight at the bar because they had cops watching, and took advantage of the timing. And it's clear someone planted that gun. And the kicker?"

Zimpel lit his cigarette and took a minute to enjoy the smoke.

"We have evidence the LCN is involved. Vito Carelli was stalking a lawyer working for Boone. A cross was burned on her lawn, and then she was kidnapped."

"That's quite a bit of drama—can you prove any of this is connected?

"Yes, connects directly." He'd have it when he needed it. "I have solid evidence that Leitisha Boone was framed, and maybe by someone in your office."

"What makes you think it's my office?" Zimpel heard impatience in his voice but maybe something else.

"Has to be someone who can direct cops to watch a certain bar and get information, who can also forgive a B&E of a cop bar, the San Remo, as a tradeoff for a gun drop, and who has access to the murder weapon. How else would a kid get off on a B&E, only to drop a gun to frame someone?"

Zimpel explained how the kid got arrested for drunken burglary of the cop bar, and then how the charges were dropped because he planted the gun.

"I have an affidavit, signed by the kid." He didn't tell him the kid denied that he knew about the gun.

"You get a parent to co-sign that?"

"The father got a judge in the middle of the night to ok the bail, then picked him up and swept him out of there and wouldn't speak to me."

"Ah, that must be the complaint that is working its way up to me. How one of the cops was reckless for manhandling his son."

Zimpel grunted. "The son who was racing on Ocean Beach in the middle of the night, who was busted breaking into a cop bar while drunk? Yeah, real delicate."

"He's got money, that's what the brass and the mayor understand."

"Yeah, we're seeing that. Someone inside is getting some money, too."

"Send the package over by messenger?" He gave Zimpel the address.

Zimpel didn't want any delay. "I'll drop it by, in case you have any questions. With a release order."

"Question of the hour, do you have another suspect?"

"Working on that." He didn't tell the DA about Mullin. Not yet. He had to figure a way to nail him without Madie.

They came for her again. She heard them unlocking the door. She swallowed, said a prayer under her breath and steeled herself for what was to come.

The door swung open and she stood expecting to be cuffed. Instead, the guard said, "Follow me." She was still scared, but something was different. No shackles, no cuffs. She followed the guard down the corridor, passing the doorway to the now familiar interrogation room. She followed the guard through a locked door and down another corridor until she was standing in front of a barred window.

"Give her whatever she came in with. She's being released. Her lawyer is here." The guard never looked at her.

The man behind the cage, also in a guard's uniform, asked, "Name?"

"Leitisha Boone."

He handed her a paper bag. She saw her dress wadded up inside.

"This way."

No one made eye contact. She felt dirty. And tired.

Zimpel waited for her in the anteroom at the front of the jail.

"You my lawyer?" Leitisha smiled. "Here I am, finally getting out and it's Zimpel waiting for me. Not that fancy lawyer."

"I told them I was your escort to your lawyer."

"My escort?" She laughed. "Does Edelman or Saul know?"

Zimpel shook his head. "I went to the DA, got some evidence. He agreed they couldn't hold you." He waved the order at her. "Got a judge to sign it." Zimpel finally relaxed. He had been truly afraid. "You ok?"

"Other than I look like a tramp's been sleeping in doorways. Get me out of here, and then you can tell me what you found. More than my lawyer found. Saul didn't get his money's worth."

Zimpel kept his opinion of Saul and the lawyer to himself. He took her home to her Victorian on Scott Street, and wondered how long she'd have that before they tore it down, too.

# CHAPTER 65

Zimpel called Frazier at home Monday morning to let him know Leitisha Boone had been released. "My gut tells me get ready, Miss Boone being free will tip them off that we're looking somewhere else. And Madie recognizing Mullin means we got our guy. Now we need to nail him with some evidence, so I'm sticking close to him today to see what he does. I went by Sunday, but he stayed home for the weekend, probably yelling at his kid. Now I want to see if he's going to fix this one, too, and who he calls."

Zimpel heard Frazier breathe, and nearly heard him think.

"We got two colored girls as eyewitnesses, Tildy and Madie. I can't think of anyone a jury would discount less. The case needs evidence that is independent of them." He paused. "DA going to keep his mouth shut or do we have to protect those girls?"

"He understood someone was inside, or he wouldn't have given me the release. Also, I didn't tell him about Tildy and Madie yet."

"Good. That gives us an advantage for a little while. Someone following our every move. The limo that showed up when Wright was killed, the limo that took Kay, and the limo you saw around the Blue Moon, was it the same livery company?"

"I got the license of the limo following Kay." Zimpel appreciated Frazier's methodical process. "Bay Limousine."

"Ok, give that to me, I know a guy over there, he owes me. I still have the earring. I'll see what I can find out about the limousine and its passengers."

"They give you any trouble, we can get a subpoena. Give me a heads up through dispatch and let's meet later this afternoon in North Beach. See what we got. One of us needs to go to Petrini's."

"That better be you. They don't like Black folks in that fancy new plaza."

Zimpel sighed. There were lines neither of them could cross. "What about San Remo's?"

"Yeah, I know someone over there won't throw me out."

Zimpel appreciated Frazier's resources; he had his contacts. "I want to know why the kid wasn't prosecuted. Who decided that?"

"You might have to talk to upstairs to find that out. Bet you dinner at Jimbo's it's about the money. They traded the boy for a favor or money or something. The big boys in this town get what they want."

"Ok, I'll go to Petrini's then follow our target, see what he's up to. Let's check in but be careful what you say on the radio. Someone listening in doesn't want us to find the right guy."

As Zimpel pulled into the block where Mullin lived, he pondered the luxurious homes and the affluent, larger than life corporations, owned by the men who ran San Francisco: the Bechtel, Kaiser, Stanford, Giannini's Bank of America, they were calling the shots. Redevelopment tore down the old Produce Market because they wanted to bring the prosperity that came with new construction. Now they were tearing down the Fillmore.

He wondered if Mr. Mullin had had his car towed yet or if he'd left it to deal with today. In answer to his question, a black limo pulled up to the curb and the driver got out, then straightened and buttoned his jacket before walking to the door. Zimpel made a note of the license plate.

Mr. Mullin was dressed impeccably with the latest Stetson, a low crown and upturned band in the back, at least $20, and a long gray overcoat that equaled Zimpel's rent. The driver closed the door and they headed to the Financial District. Zimpel decided that if Mullin got out at the office, he'd go up to Petrini's on Masonic.

Predictably early to the office. Early to bed, early to rise. He would be at the office for a while. Zimpel headed up to Masonic and Fulton, to Petrini's Plaza Shopping Center.

He felt the moment favored them and he was going to push.

Trucks were loading and unloading around the docking area, which took up two sides of the store. Clerks with dollies hauled goods in to stock shelves.

Zimpel didn't shop here, too far from home, and he didn't buy a lot of groceries. He'd forgotten how large the meat preparation area was, maybe the largest in the city. All the bustle you'd expect from a high-class Italian butcher. The Plaza had been built recently and it was swanky.

Zimpel presented his identification and asked to talk to a manager, who was only too happy to be helpful. He came out wiping his hands and Zimpel wondered what had been on them.

"Pete Yuma, how can I help you?" He held out his hand.

Zimpel shook it. "Did you have a substitute delivery guy the week of August 4th for a route that covers Fillmore Street, around Eddy and Turk?"

Yuma pursed his lips. "That's a very specific request. We have a regular crew that knows that route. They cover for each other, so we don't need substitutes. Service is important to us."

"Is someone in charge of your dispatch of deliveries? I know you deliver all over the city."

"Sure. Come on back. What's this about anyway?"

Zimpel followed him without answering his question and noted that the manager wore a white apron same as everyone else.

"Hey Antonio, do you have your dispatch book for the week of August 4th?"

The man looked startled, his eyes wide. "Uh, sure, I'm sure I do. Let me look." The dispatcher fumbled about a bit. "Should be right here."

Yuma walked over and picked up a green ledger book. "Isn't this it?"

"Oh, yes, Mr. Yuma, it is. Of course."

Zimpel smelled sweat on the guy.

"Are we checking on any particular delivery? Was an order wrong? I check each of them personally."

"You might say that," said Zimpel. The dispatcher got busy flipping through pages in a large, heavy ledger. "Check the order for the Blue Moon the week of August 4th. Who did that delivery?"

The dispatcher wiped his sleeve across his forehead, his face turning red.

"Well?" Mr. Yuma grabbed the book back. "What is this?" He glanced up at the dispatcher. "Pages have been torn out. I don't see the delivery for the Blue Moon. Where are these missing pages?"

Antonio, the dispatcher, shook his head. "I don't know."

Zimpel was sure he was lying. "There has to be a signed receipt?" He had seen a copy of one left behind with Sylvia.

Mr. Yuma shoved the book back to the nervous dispatcher. "We'll speak about this later. This isn't the way we conduct business at Petrini's."

Someone had scrubbed the evidence so nothing showed the regular driver had been paid to look the other way. "Who's the regular driver for that route?" There were other ways to get at this.

Mr. Yuma glared at Antonio, who shrunk back and spoke carefully. "I set up the schedule weekly, I don't remember who was assigned that week."

"How many drivers do you have?" Zimpel had been doing this a long time. Hard to lie, hard to hide real evidence.

Mr. Yuma spoke up. "We have three, with a fourth part-time as needed. I'll get you the names and set up some interviews."

With a sharp glance to Antonio, Mr. Yuma walked back towards the main butcher station and display. "I apologize for that. I've never seen a page missing from our ledger."

"Maybe someone is hiding something?" Obvious to Zimpel, something new to the manager.

"I don't know what's going on, but I'll find out." He went through manila file folders in a drawer in a small side office. "Here's the invoice for that week, delivery was made on Wednesday, August 6." He squinted. "I don't recognize this signature or the scribble that's supposed to the name of the delivery person." He looked up at Zimpel. "What's going on? This isn't about an order. You wouldn't be here for that."

Zimpel shook his head. "No, I wouldn't. I'd like to speak to your drivers."

"Come on."

They walked out to the delivery dock where the trucks waited for their orders. The area smelled of exhaust and cigarettes.

Zimpel lit a cigarette and watched while Mr. Yuma went to talk to one of the drivers, who then walked over to where Zimpel stood. The driver was thin, young, with hair greased back in the way the kids were wearing their hair, Elvis style.

"This officer wants to ask some questions. Please help him out?" Mr. Yuma stepped back. Zimpel didn't correct him to say inspector. The kid was already nervous. His hands were moving, and he swayed a bit from side to side.

"I want to know if you were scheduled to deliver to the route that includes the Blue Moon the week of August 4th."

The driver reflected for a minute. "I don't always know because we sometimes switch off. I can't remember that particular week."

"You a baseball fan, son?"

"Oh, yeah, big Giants' fan. I'm so glad they came to San Francisco."

"Well, the week of August 4, they were in Chicago for two Cubs games, then they went to St. Louis on the 6th and 7th, and beginning on August 8th, they were in LA for three games. Does that help?"

"Yes sir, because I remember someone telling me on the day of that first St. Louis game, that I wasn't needed in the afternoon, and they gave me $5 and told me to take the afternoon off." Zimpel noticed Mr. Yuma's eyebrows go up into his receding hairline.

"So I went over to this new bar I wanted to go to, Lefty O'Douls, you know the baseball player?" Zimpel nodded. "And listened to the radio, they had the game on." Driver shook his head. "They just couldn't beat St. Louis and lost 7-8."

Zimpel nodded. "Who gave you the $5 and told you to take the day off?"

The driver glanced around now, nervous he had to tell. "It was Antonio, he's the dispatcher, and I figured he knew what was what."

The tediousness of this was getting to Zimpel. Each question to each person had to be drawn out.

"Mr. Yuma, who was directing your drivers on August 6th? And why was Mr. Barker here told to leave?"

Mr. Yuma's anger had peaked at this point. "I have no idea what was going on here, but I'm going to get some answers. Officer Zimpel . . ."

"Inspector." Zimpel pulled the rank on him this time and handed him a card. He wanted fast answers. "Can you call me here when you find out?"

Mr. Yuma realized at that moment he was talking to a homicide inspector. His mouth formed an "o" shape. "Yes, sir, I will. It's clear some shenanigans were going on here."

# CHAPTER 66

Zimpel returned to the Financial District to follow Mullin. He dialed up Mr. Mullin's office from a pay phone to make sure he hadn't left.

"Mid-City."

"Is Mr. Mullin in?"

"Let me switch you to his secretary."

In a minute, another woman's voice came on. "Mr. Mullin's office."

"Is Mr. Mullin in?"

"Who's calling please?"

Zimpel rolled it out. "Piscarelli. Antonio," he said mixing up wise guy names to sound urgent.

"Please hold." She came back on the line. "Mr. Piscarelli, he's in a meeting now, told me to get your number and he'll call you right back."

"I'm out and about. I'll call him back. Thank you."

"Sir, if you give me your number . . ."

Zimpel hung up, satisfied that Mullin hadn't left the office yet. He settled in to wait, happy with the information he learned at Petrini's. He was sure the guy paying off the dispatcher was also the arranger for the Mullin kid, and connected to the capital going into Mullin's company.

He spotted the limousine about the time he started thinking about a beer. Instead of heading home to Pacific Heights, the driver took Mullin towards North Beach, ending up at Columbus and Taylor, La Rocca's Corner, where Nick DeJohn had his last drink in 1947, and mafia rubbed elbows with the likes of Joe DiMaggio. But then, that was North Beach. Olive oil shipments mixed with heroin.

The limo parked at the corner and Mullin got out.

It was Monday so La Rocca's was closed, but someone opened the door for Mullin. Zimpel parked at a fire hydrant, glanced inside the bar, then eyed the driver, who waited in the driver's seat. Zimpel wondered if it was the same driver that had driven Mullin when he shot Wright.

Mullin sat with another man at the bar of the closed saloon. Zimpel recognized the other as Jimmy "The Hat" Lanza, underboss to Abati. Well, isn't that coincidental? Runs right to the LCN when his kid gets pinched again. The two men were leaning into each other, Mullin looking a bit exercised, Lanza gesturing "calm down" with his hands.

Zimpel remembered he had a Kodak in the trunk. He pulled it out from under a pile of towels he'd used recently when he changed the oil. Checking it, he advanced the film, and it made the right sound.

He took a couple shots like a tourist outside of La Rocca's. After all, they did bring tours here pointing out it was famous for DeJohn's last drink.

"Hey!"

The chauffeur got out of the limousine. Zimple turned back to the bar, aimed at the window, and got one shot of Jimmy The Hat with Mullin before the chauffeur pulled his arm to get the camera.

"What do you think you're doing? You can't take pictures . . ."

"La Rocca's is famous. I want a photo."

Zimpel pulled away, hitting the chauffeur in the chin with his elbow as if it was an accident. But hard. He didn't want to identify as a cop if he didn't have to. While the man reeled back from the blow, Zimpel made for his car and drove away. Word would get back to Lanza but not until he had these pictures safely developed.

This photo might be enough to get him a subpoena for records, particularly bank records. He drove back to Kearny Street, and once the film was safely in the hands of a technician who would develop it, Zimpel drove back to North Beach to meet Frazier at Frank's to compare notes. And have a beer.

# CHAPTER 67

Frazier parked in front of the limo company's office and walked out to the lot.

"Hey, Monroe, what's happening?"

"Hey Frazier, my man, all good. Fix you up with a limo? I'm in your debt, man." Monroe was polishing a car in the lot.

"Ha, sure I'll take two." The two men laughed. "Seriously, how's it going?"

"I'm working, that's something, right? Kids are good. Can't complain. You?"

"I'm working a case . . ."

"Whoa, I thought you only a beat cop?"

"Working a homicide . . . an important one." Frazier kept his demeanor neutral.

Monroe stopped polishing the limo and stood up, making eye contact with Frazier. "Oh, wow. What's up?"

"Seems the man wanna do some damage is riding around in one of your limos."

"What? Nah, couldn't be one of our guys. You trace the license number?" Frazier stood there not moving.

"Yeah, well, let's go see."

They walked over to the office.

"Which number?"

Frazier handed him the number.

"What's up?" An older, white man at the counter was talking with a driver in a nice suit.

"Hey, Steve, this is my friend William Frazier."

The old white guy behind the counter nodded. "He want a job?"

Monroe laughed. "No, he's a cop."

"He's a cop?"

Frazier was used to the doubts. "Yes, sir." He reached for his ID, but the guy didn't look at it.

"We didn't have any traffic infractions."

"Just double checking some records."

Frazier noted the guy thought he was a traffic cop, and left it. He'd get more information that way.

"Yeah, no one got into accidents, isn't one of ours, I'm sure." He went back to talking to the driver, who said something to Steve that Frazier couldn't hear, and left.

Frazier watched him go.

"Who was that?"

"That's one of the drivers, Robert, he's new. Kind of jittery."

"They always dress that sharp?"

"They're dealing with the mighty and the rich, need to dress the part."

Monroe pulled out a ledger and flipped it open. "This is the job book for that license plate, and we usually have the same driver on the cars because, you know, they can have their stuff, they get picky about how it is, the cleanliness and all. This is Emmet's limo, and he has a regular gig with an older couple that like to go out for lunch."

"Last name?"

"Steen." Monroe nodded at Frazier.

Frazier made a few notes. "The driver was seen in the Fillmore."

Monroe shook his head. "Nah, he wouldn't have been there."

"Why not?"

"He has a regular gig, regular customers. Wouldn't be in the Fillmore."

Frazier understood. He pushed again. "How about downtown, Financial

District around 9 p.m. on August 22nd?"

Monroe flipped a couple pages. "Sometimes we let him take the car for the night. Like I said, he caters mostly to this elderly couple in Pacific Heights, who have early morning doctor appointments."

"Did he have the car on August 22nd. It was a Friday night." Patience was the name of the game.

Monroe checked the book again. "Yeah, looks like he did."

"I need to talk to the guy, can you get me his address?"

"Here, but you didn't get it from me," said Monroe quietly. "He's out in the car now until 5. He's not a bad guy, hope he's not in trouble."

"He may not be, but someone is. Thanks for this. I owe you back."


Frazier drove by the driver's house, and luckily, the limo was in the driveway. He knocked on the door. "Emmet Steen?"

"Yeah?" The guy looked through the peephole in the door, and then opened the door wide enough to look out.

Frazier held out his ID. "That your limousine?"

"You're a cop?"

"You want to look at this again? Maybe call it in?" White guys never liked it when he asked questions.

"What's this about?"

"That limo was identified at being at the scene of a crime."

"Hey, I haven't been in any accidents . . ."

"That your limo?" Frazier started the questions over.

"No, belongs to work, they let me take it home sometimes. I drive this old couple around and they get up early."

"Where was the car on August 22nd around 9 p.m.?" Frazier had a hunch about Kay's kidnapping. He'd go after the murder next.

"I don't know, listen . . ."

"Your work said you had the limo. Where were you that night?" Frazier slightly raised his voice. The guy started to come apart. Sweat broke out along his forehead. Something was wrong. Frazier pushed a little more.

"You need to answer my question."

"I don't have to talk to . . ."

Frazier put his foot in the door. He was getting the "I don't have to talk to you, you're not a real cop." The guy was pissing him off; he was close to some truth. There was a risk, being a good cop but bucking up against racial taboos.

"You need to tell me. Unless you want me to arrest you for kidnapping."

"You can't arrest me for kidnapping! I don't know about any kidnapping."

"Your limo was there. That's why I'm asking you these questions." Frazier pressed him, guessing the truth.

"Listen, it wasn't me. Sometimes I switch limos with a guy."

"What guy?"

Emmet Steen froze, now realizing he didn't want to give someone else up. "Just a guy."

"Don't force me to drag it out of you." Frazier stood tall now, menacing.

"Are you threatening me?" Steen fell back on the color thing again.

"With that," Frazier pointed to the limo, "you have been at the scene of two crimes, kidnapping and murder." Frazier was playing with fire, but he bet that the guy didn't need his employer to know he was moonlighting. "I'm ready to haul you in unless you tell me why I shouldn't?"

The guy broke.

"I have a friend, he works for a rich guy up in Pac Heights pretty exclusively. Sometimes his car goes out and he uses mine, especially when I have it overnight, and slips me a little extra, you know what I mean?"

"Yeah, sure. Name and address?"

The guy squirmed, but Frazier was going to get it. The guy had crossed the line.

Frazier took out a pencil and a notebook.

"Cory Fortnum."

"Got an address?"

"Nah, he calls me and comes here. Hang on." Frazier didn't want to have the guy take off, so he stepped into the doorway of the house.

"Here's his number." He had written it on a scrap of paper.

"Did you switch cars the night of August 22nd—it was a Friday night, if you need reminding."

The guy hesitated a bare couple of seconds, but he knew exactly what night Frazier was talking about.

"Yeah, we switched. He specifically asked me to bring it home so he could use it."

"Any reason you remember it so well?"

The guy was all in now. "He didn't get it back to me on time, and when he did, it was a mess. I was pretty pissed off, as he made me late for my regular gig."

Frazier wondered what was "messed up." "How many times has he used it?"

"I don't know, maybe four or five, maybe a couple more. His goes on the fritz I guess, and it would cost him a lot more to go rent one and he didn't want to tell the rich guy he couldn't maintain the limo I guess. I don't know."

"Who's the rich guy he works for?"

"I don't remember, some big developer. I'm not sure."

"Let's open your trunk?" Frazier asked, pushing the guy.

"What?"

Frazier turned his tone down a bit. Now that Emmet Steen had given him the nugget, they were on the same side. "Humor me, another minute and I'll get out of here."

The guy shrugged, pulled the keys off a table.

Frazier pulled a flashlight out of his car while the guy opened the trunk. He flashed it around inside. It looked pretty clean, although dried blood blended into black interior. Frazier bent over and ran the light along the inside of the back bumper, and reached down and pulled out a pearl clip earring.

"Sometimes you get lucky." He held it up to the guy. "Kidnapping."

The guy's face fell, staring at the trunk. "Oh no, man, I didn't do anything."

Frazier dropped the earring in a little envelope, folded it, and put it in his pocket. He'd found the car that Kay had been in. They were getting warmer now.

"Don't leave town, I'm going need your testimony. Understand?"

The guy nodded, all bravado gone now.

"When you described the limo as messed up, what else did you find?"

"I just remember I had to clean it in a hurry."

"You find any shoes, a purse?"

"Nah, nothing like that."

He did a little homework. Zimpel had given him the license plate of the Mid-City mogul's limo and he ran Fortnum's driver's license. Bingo.

They'd follow up with Fortnum next. He'd talk to Zimpel first. If he was right, he was coming up against a man who wasn't afraid to kill someone. He might want back-up this time.

# CHAPTER 68

Kay pushed a document under Zorn's nose. "When Mid-City's bid was accepted, they were running red. How did they win their bid with those finances?"

She was sure if she followed the money, she'd find involvement by the LCN. With the kid's near admission, the evidence against Leitisha fell away. Who told him to plant the gun and why?

"So tell me again what the bid says?" She finally had Zorn's attention.

"First, their bid offers $150,000 to cover 'expenses' of the city's Redevelopment Agency as an 'enticement' to accept their bid. The terms also state that if the city adopts their plan, Mid-City has the right to purchase a certain block of property in the A-2 redevelopment area, and if Mid-City and the city can't agree on a price, the buyer will have to reimburse the planning funds to Mid-City."

Kay pulled out a map and pointed to certain properties. "This is outrageous. Their newest bid involves at least these four properties, including the Blue Moon, all owned—or used to be owned—by Marvin Wright."

"That's a big chunk of dough to entice the Agency to give them the bid."

"Explain to me why that's a proper payment and not a bribe?"

Zorn smiled at her. "Paying the 'costs' of the public agency. Can't be right." He picked up the papers she had pushed at him. "Where did they get that $150,000? They also have to have the capital to carry out the redevelopment once they get the property."

"How does it happen that a woman builds a business that can be taken from her and then sold to the highest bidder for their own use but she gets nothing? How does that happen?" Kay stood. Her mind was balled up like a fist. She wanted to physically fight someone. The people and their scores of small businesses in the Fillmore area were obviously expendable.

"So let's put our anger aside and think this through." Zorn said.

She wanted to stay mad. To push through all this paper and get to an answer.

"I don't know," Zorn said looking up at the ceiling. "You're the tax and real estate lawyer. Where's the money need to be? In a bank? Are there tax records we can review? Has to be some evidence of the money connections. You looked at their annual report?"

"They had to submit some financials, which I found through your brand new—how do you get these things?—wire service from Dun & Bradstreet. According to their report, Mid-City has been doing poorly: unpaid bills, bad credit, and low balances. But in the financials submitted to Redevelopment," she held up her notes, "they look healthy and flush, with a fat bank account at Bank of America. All of a sudden they have all this cash?"

She put the map down and stood. "I need coffee. I need to figure out who to ask about this money."

Zorn headed for his makeshift kitchen. "I can always use coffee."

Soon he had beans whirling. Where was this last piece of the puzzle?

"Maybe that's the ticket. I need to go ask someone at the bank."

"Why would they talk to you and tell you anything about their customer—it's confidential."

She shrugged. "I'll figure something out." She sipped the coffee and made some notes.

Kay put on a suit, tied up her hair and went into the Bank of America branch in North Beach. This was Giannini's bank, the original name was

Bank of Italy. She was sure there was a connection because this branch was the escrow holder in the bid.

The cavernous building—banks were so grand—felt cold as she waited for the branch manager.

"Yes, how can I help you?" A short man with a trimmed mustache smiled at her as if she were an idiot. It was uncommon for women to do banking business. Kay stood and held out her hand.

"Susan Hardy," she said. "I'm with the Redevelopment Agency."

If the big boys can imitate Redevelopment to cart away a restaurant, she could ask a few questions for information.

His eyebrows went up.

"Yes? What is it you're here for?" He held his hands together, nearly praying. He did not introduce himself.

"We have detected some . . ." she paused, not wanting to be overheard, "irregularities, in a developer's account held by your branch." she fished. "I'm sure it's nothing," She gave him a curt smile. "I've been sent to ask you about it. Just a formality, you see."

"Of course." He tilted his head slightly.

She wasn't sure what she was going to say, but she wanted to trace that money.

"Why don't we step over here," he gestured to a desk away from the main throng of people waiting in line to cash checks or deposit money.

Finally. She was glad he'd gotten the hint.

She took her notes out of her briefcase. At least they were based on Redevelopment docs. She looked around for a chair. She didn't get invited to sit. You'd think he'd suck up a little to the Agency, but the bank manager remained standing. Wanted it kept short.

She put her briefcase between her feet, her heels slightly moving, and reviewed her notes. She regretted not training to be a trial attorney; she'd have this down better.

He stood waiting on her, making the moment awkward.

She nodded, showing him she was working up to it.

"Your bank has recent large deposits in escrow for this account number." She recited the number she'd noted from the redevelopment application. "This was related to purchasing property surrendered in eminent domain by the Agency, yes?"

Zorn had taught her not to ask open-ended questions, and if she didn't know the information, she'd make it up. That way, when they corrected her, she'd have the right information.

"Who is the account holder you are asking about?"

"Mid-City Development."

She watched him get wide-eyed at the mention of Mid-City. "We may not provide confidential information about our account holders without proper papers."

"I understand that, and I can go get a subpoena, but I was hoping for your cooperation, to avoid an audit."

That was a word he clearly didn't like. His face puckered slightly. "May I see some identification, please?"

She feigned looking for her identification while thinking about what to do.

He heard someone call his name, and turned.

Michael Abati was walking toward them. Kay felt a cold shock down her legs.

# CHAPTER 69

Kay sidled to a countertop with deposit slips and pens, and hid behind her briefcase, appearing to search for papers. She intended to back out of the bank, with the manager distracted by the striding Mr. Abati.

"Mr. Abati," said the manager.

Mr. Jewell, we need that money wired today." Abati adjusted his sleeves, his voice low, commanding.

"We were waiting for . . ."

"No waiting. Do it now."

"Of course." The manager glanced around and then led Abati to an office across the room. "Please," he said, gesturing. "Susan Hardy" was forgotten.

Kay relaxed a minute, watching several young men scurry between the manager and what she assumed was the room where the wires were sent. Money was traveling. Something was happening. There was a moment of quiet. Kay looked up.

Jewell and Abati stared at her from across the room and then looked beyond her. She followed their gaze behind her to the main entrance. A man in a brown trench coat and fedora walked towards her. She saw his face and her stomach roiled. The sweet smell in her nose. Her abductor.

Kay scanned the room and headed towards a side door, papers still in her hand. She stuffed them into her briefcase and walked out the door past a black limousine.

She nearly ran to the corner, turned left, and then left again down an alley, and stood in a doorway, to both hide and see. Her heart beat loudly and she held her breath to keep it quiet.

Damn. She didn't see anything either way. She headed towards North Beach.

She wound through outdoor tables of gregarious restaurant customers, bar patrons flowing in and out of clubs, strains of music coming from the Hungry i. She stood in front of City Lights Bookstore, eyeing a doorway to slip into. Glancing over her shoulder, she saw a long brown coat and fedora moving quickly up Columbus.

No time.

She fought her way through the crowd to the bar in Vesuvio's. At the far end of the bar, there was a microphone and a man reading poetry, beatniks pressed up against where he stood, hanging out in the booths, loud and raucous. She hoped she blended in here.

She scanned the crowd and saw a familiar face.

"Jake. Jake Holmes, the neighborhood greeter," she said, squeezing passed a couple making out, and two large men shouting at the poet.

"Hey, it's the lawyer lady. What are you doing here?"

Young people dressed in black packed the room, holding cigarettes, wine, clapping and snapping for the next poet. She recognized Michael McClure, in a suit, looking so serious.

"Yes, how are you?" She kept watch over the door and hunted for another exit.

"Can I get you a drink?" He had to shout it in her ear.

She shook her head. "Is there a rear exit?"

"Yes, Miss, out past the restroom." His face showed concern. "You being chased again?"

"I think still, this seems to be the same folks."

"Bad guys?"

A fedora passed by the front of the bar and she ducked down.

"Come on, Miss . . . what was your name again?"

"Kay."

"Right, come on this way." He grabbed her hand and maneuvered her in front of him and held his arm out to make a way through the crowd. He pulled her into a back room. "He won't find you in here."

Kay leaned up against the wall, willing her heart and breath to be normal.

"Thanks for the rescue . . . again." She eyed him, making sure his hands stayed where they were supposed to.

"Last time we got you to a phone, and you called your cop friend. Where is he tonight?"

She shook her head. He was out working the case but he wasn't sharing.

"So what did you think of the poetry?"

She had sort of half listened. "What I listened to sounded good. Sorry, I was a little distracted."

He nodded. "Ah, you're probably not that into it. The performance and all."

"Oh, no. You'll have to come hear me play piano sometime, if this calms down." She didn't have time to placate him.

"Piano?"

"Yeah, at the Blue Moon." Each action against the Blue Moon was connected—Leitisha's frame up, the Redevelopment grants without process, the attacks on the restaurant and the attacks on her. When she'd gone to Mid-City to confront Mullin, she'd hit a nerve.

Good to be right but better to be alive.

"I need to get out of here. I'm going to go out the back."

"You sure you want to leave now?"

"Yeah, I'm sure. I need to keep moving."

"Wait." He dug through a box and pulled out a black sweatshirt. "Here, put this on over your clothes." He laughed. "We'll get you dressed in black one way or the other."

She pulled it over her jacket and dress. It was large, with "City Lights" across the front. She felt like a fluff, all bulky and out of sorts.

"Height of fashion," she said, descending the short stairway and waving before she snuck out the back.

Kay came out in the alley and spotted Fedora at the corner of Broadway and Columbus, scanning the street. She headed for Frank's, in the alley across from Tosca's. Fedora wouldn't go in there, too Bohemian, and she hoped it would be crowded enough to get lost inside.

# CHAPTER 70

Frazier walked around to the back door of the San Remo Restaurant. The sous chef knew him, even if he pretended not to.

"Whatcho doing here?"

"Chef, man, I need some information."

"I don't want to lose my job. They see me talking to a cop . . ."

"This is a cop restaurant."

"You know what I mean, stay on the job. Not supposed to be lollygaggin' around."

"They'll think I'm getting a free meal off of you." That's what they always said about him, but he had never done it. Just out of principle. He always paid. "You can tell them you said, 'No.'"

"So make it quick." Chef wiped his hands on his apron and kept glancing over his shoulder.

"Heard these two kids broke in a few months ago. Stole some booze, made a mess. You know anything about that?"

"Yeah, that was weird. They broke in, went after the booze. There's no money in here, that goes out every night."

"They broke into a favorite cop restaurant?"

"They were stupid, drunk, high school kids, and easy to spot. Alarm went off and cops showed up before they left. It's the Remo."

"I heard they didn't they get prosecuted?"

Chef shrugged. "Both white, wealthy, figure their parents got them out."

"I heard they had to do someone favors." Frazier dug at it.

"I don't know nothing about any of that and I don't want to." He backed away towards the kitchen. "I gotta get back to it." He went in and shut the door.

A young, Black kid came around the corner headed for the back door to the restaurant, then turned to Frazier. "Heard you talking to Clancy."

"You know anything about the break-in?"

"You a cop?" He said the last word like it hurt him a little.

"Yeah." Frazier kept eye contact with him. If the kid only knew how hard it was.

"I do some dishwashing and chores here, they give me a job. I'm lucky to have that so don't get me in trouble, but I see those boys. They got so much, why they break in here?" Glancing side to side, he lowered his voice. "They was talking with some of the Eye-talians who come by here all the time, and it seemed to me there was some favors being made like you said." The kid slipped in the back door.

Frazier wiped his hand down his face. Italians in the cop bar? That made no sense. He got into the patrol car he had managed to take for today's work. Maybe Zimpel said something.

He didn't have much to show. Two white boys from a prestigious high school get their hands slapped for breaking and entering and stealing liquor. Their daddy knows someone who can get them a deal with the DA. Two Negro boys who attended public school wouldn't get any deal. Here, someone cut an arrangement off the books.

Zimpel would have to ask the DA who got them the deal. DA wouldn't tell Frazier. Although he'd heard that one of the assistant district attorneys was Black, a first for San Francisco.

Zimpel said to meet him in North Beach, and Frazier finally found a place to park off Columbus. He liked North Beach fine. It was full of Italian immigrants mostly, with the Chinese spilling over, and while each ethnic group had its boundaries, he didn't feel so stark here as he did in pure white neighborhoods. He headed for Frank's. Might be all right to have a drink, to think on what they had.

What they found pointed to the untouchable, rich, white guy in Pacific Heights. He had the job, the house, the family, and means, so why risk it all to kill someone. What does it take to make someone that desperate?

Frazier stood at the end of the bar, in the shadows, where he kept his back to the wall and an eye on the door. He ordered a beer and a shot.

# CHAPTER 71

It was Monday afternoon, and Frank's regulars sat at the bar. Long past lunch many lingered for another drink. Kay saw a table open in the back corner of the long bar. She sat outside the sightline from the front door and, just in case, the back hallway led to a door into the alley. If someone came looking for her, they'd have to come inside to see her.

She probably shouldn't have gone to the bank. She wouldn't have run into Abati. Then again, the fact they'd gone after her proved she was right. So subpoena the records from the bank and find money from a questionable source. She'd guarantee there was "funny money" to be found—if the evidence hadn't all been dumped by the time she told Zimpel and he got a subpoena served.

As she thought of him, Zimpel walked into the bar. Was he following her, too? He was scanning the room; he found someone else. She looked over. He was meeting a man who had been standing at the end of the bar.

She caught Zimpel's eye. He gestured to Frazier, and then both men headed towards her table.

"Do you know William Frazier?"

She put her hand out and he shook it."

Frazier didn't let on that he'd met her when she was in her cups at the Silver Dollar. He also didn't like sitting with his back to the door, so he turned the back of his chair to the wall. The lawyer took the deep corner of the table. She must have something on her mind to take that place, and she had on a City Lights sweatshirt over her clothes.

"What's up with the sweatshirt?"

She glanced down and laughed. "Someone handed it to me as I was going out the back at Vesuvio's."

Zimpel sat up straight. "Why were you going out the back at Vesuvio's?"

"I was avoiding a guy in a fedora . . .

Zimpel waited for the rest.

"I had a run in with Abati at the bank, and his guy . . ."

Zimpel closed his eyes slowly.

Frazier watched them. He didn't understand their dynamic and wondered why Zimpel never moved on her. Then, she was pretty bossy and stubborn. Career woman.

"Wait a minute." Zimpel didn't let her finish. "I've rescued you at least four times in the last couple of weeks, and still you confront the one guy I said for sure to stay away from? Are you out of your mind?"

"It wasn't on purpose. I went to the bank and was talking to the manager. Abati walked in just as I was attempting to persuade the manager to give me information about Mid-City."

Zimpel couldn't get more pissed off that she jumped right into the snake pit. Again. "Mid-City."

"Abati didn't notice me right away, so I started moving away, listening in."

"Where were you?"

"At the bank."

"Which bank?" He was going to throttle her. "Just tell me the damn story and leave in the details." He gave her the gimme sign with his hand.

She told him she had gone to Bank of America to see if someone would give her information about the Mid-City account.

"You're a lawyer; you know they won't disclose information about a bank customer."

"I told them I was with Redevelopment. Maybe they would tell me something to reassure me . . ."

"Great, I'm sure there's something illegal about all that."

"You lie all the time, why can't I?"

He would not concede she had a point. She wasn't a sworn law enforcement officer.

"In any case, the bank manager must have said something to Abati. I saw them turn to me and then look at the door. Abati's fedora thug came into the bank clearly after me. In fact, I recognized him. So I left and came here."

"You recognized who?"

"The guy coming at me, he was the face I saw when I got kidnapped."

He saw the realization on her face. "Abati was involved with the kidnapping, that was his guy."

"So the bank manager presumably told Abati about your inquiry into Mid-City, which indicates LCN involvement. I wonder if that's enough, plus the other information we have, to get a subpoena for those bank records."

"See? That was helpful."

"We would have gotten there without your risk."

She ignored his statement, as he knew she would. "Zorn and I have some documents that might help with that subpoena. We've been tracing the money from Mid-City."

"I'll take those." He got in her face. "But do not, I repeat do not, endanger yourself any more for this case. It's not worth you getting snagged off the street again or worse." He saw her face fall a little, but he didn't care. She was not to put herself in danger like that again. He took a long pull on his beer.

# CHAPTER 72

"I did find this." Frazier pulled out the earring. He liked the reaction he got from both of them.

"That's my earring." Kay's hand went to her ear. "Where did you find it?"

Zimpel nodded. "You found the car."

"Yep. And I'm pretty sure your boy, the Mid-City bigshot's chauffeur, was using it. Guy's name is Cory Fortnum. Traced his driver's license, checked out his address. Limo registered to him matches the one you gave me that picks up Mid-City guy."

"Well that's a nice break."

Kay held her hand out and Frazier shook his head. "Evidence. You can have it when we're done."

They left Frank's after sharing what each knew. Zimpel was going to put it all together for a subpoena of the bank records, a search warrant, and an arrest warrant. They had enough for probable cause. Frazier returned the cop car and had his own places to go.

Zimpel wanted to stop by the Blue Moon and see how Leitisha was faring the day after her release. Make sure she talked to a lawyer, to keep her out. In any case, he'd have someone for that murder soon. He knew it.

"You want to come, I'll take you home afterward." He said to Kay. He knew she'd be game. She always was.

He settled in for a beer and to think how to approach Mullin when he saw Saul walk in the door. Zimpel glanced from Leitisha to Kay. This was going to be ugly.

Kay heard a familiar voice and turned, saw Saul.

Leitisha gave him a cold glare that froze all the way across the room. "You didn't do me any favors and you're supposed to be looking out for me?"

"Well, hello to you, too." He walked up to her and gave her a kiss on the cheek before she backed off of him. "I got you one of the best lawyers in San Francisco."

"So what? Didn't help me at all. That man didn't want to represent me, didn't believe me, and didn't listen to anything I had to say."

"Now that's exaggerating Leitisha, he worked hard . . ."

She jumped on him. "He didn't do anything. Zimpel got me out, that's who. That's who went for the evidence that cleared me. That's who was waiting for me at the jail and took me home, not you."

"Leitisha, you need to understand, that this," he gestured, "is all going to be redeveloped. It's time for you to let go . . ."

Leitisha shook her head. "I'm sorry you see it that way. It's you I'm letting go of." She turned away from Saul and walked deliberately into the kitchen.

Kay observed the interaction, her stomach tight.

"You didn't really mean to help her, did you?" She wanted to say a lot more.

Saul 's face flickered with several emotions, and Kay didn't care a lick. "I want what's best for her, I love her." Saul's eyes held genuine sadness, which disgusted Kay. He was thinking only of himself.

"I think this is too much for her to do. If she had time to think about what it meant, and how exposed she was, she would see what I am saying makes sense and she would give it up, especially now."

"You really are a square. I suppose you don't think I should be a lawyer either?" She didn't like the word but it fit him tonight.

"Oh no, that's not what I'm saying at all." No sadness now in his eyes.

"That's exactly what you're saying. Did you leave her in there on purpose, so she'd lose the restaurant?"

"Now you're exaggerating."

She noted his defensive posture. "That seems to be your line when women say things you don't like. Saul, you can't be that stupid or believe that I am." Kay turned back to her drink. She wanted to throw it at him. He had deliberately left Leitisha in jail. Unforgiveable.

# CHAPTER 73

## AUGUST 26, 1958 · TUESDAY

That Kay recognized the thug with Abati as one of her abductors did not give Zimpel any comfort. She was still in danger because they knew she had something on them. She asked too many questions. He had Leitisha out of jail but remained at risk she'd be hauled back in. He needed to take what he had—the limo and the financials—and work fast, get the bad guys to go back into their hole, and arrest Mullin and whoever else ordered the Wright killing.

Mullin's driver had borrowed the Bay Limousine car the night Kay was kidnapped and Frazier had found her earring inside the trunk, lodged on the inside of the bumper. With that, they got lucky. Kay had recognized Abati's driver in the bank as the man she'd seen before she passed out. Just a matter of time before they got a name. And Kay would be a good witness. So what was the relationship between Abati's driver and Mullin's driver?

The next lead came from Kay's visit to the bank. That didn't give him enough for a subpoena, however the work she and Zorn had done, pulling records and piecing together financial information, plus what he'd received from the journalist, did. So he drafted it and got it out, using the district attorney and no one else for help. Because he still hadn't figured out who the inside snitch was.

The Petrini's manager had followed up saying someone from the DA's office had talked to the dispatcher. He played that card to get the DA to stick with him. Had the manager known about it, he never would have said 'yes' to such a strange request—to have a substitute driver.

Zimpel suspected the dispatcher was also paid for the transaction, most likely in cash and not traceable.

Kay had also given him information on all of Wright's properties, some of which led back to Mid-City. The reporter's evidence bolstered this, showing pay offs to Redevelopment from Mid-City for concessions in the A-2. That would explain the lack of process for the Wright properties Mid-City acquired directly so soon after the man's murder. And might explain the murder.

Zimpel finished up that paperwork to get his subpoenas ready for the judge to sign. He'd had it with these arrogant assholes that bought up property and people's lives without consequence. This time, there would be consequences.

Zimpel called the DA. "I got something you're going to want to see. And in exchange, I want a search warrant and at least one arrest warrant."

"This better be good, Zimpel, because getting your girl free spoiled my golf game."

"She's not my girl, she's a business owner and a taxpayer, and yeah, it's good. I'll be over there in 15 minutes." Zimpel hung up. They were supposed to be on the same side, damn it. He didn't understand the headwinds here. Why it was so difficult to get what was right?

Zimpel walked up to the DA's office and a man passed him in the hall. Zimpel recognized him.

"Hey." Zimpel turned around and called out to the guy. "What's your name? I've seen you . . ."

The guy took off. Zimpel took off after him, tucking the envelope for the DA inside his shirt. "What the hell."

The man hit the stairs taking two at a time, pushing other workers out of his way. Zimpel followed. He wished he was in better shape and recalled the pickup game in the Bayview.

This was the guy he'd seen leaving the ABC's man's office. What was he doing in the DA's office? The guy reached the bottom of the interior staircase and yanked open the door to the street and took off. Zimpel was a half-floor behind him and winded.

Zimpel exited the door and saw him turn the corner. The guy glanced over his shoulder, saw Zimpel still coming after him, and headed across Washington Street, making cars honk and skid to a stop. Zimpel said a prayer and went after him, holding up his ID, yelling, "I'm a cop." If that guy can run in oxfords and a suit, so can I.

The guy darted over Sansome and then down Jackson towards the construction on the Embarcadero Freeway. This guy was going to hurt when he went down.

For once, Zimpel wished another cop was around to help, if not a partner. He didn't have a radio. It was him and the runner for now.

Crews laboring on the Embarcadero Freeway watched as the guy ran right into the middle of them. Zimpel gestured and yelled, "Get that guy, I'm a cop." He waved his shield.

Two construction workers stood close together blocking the guy, who frantically tried to get past them. Several more surrounded them. A construction worker got on each side of the guy, took an arm and lifted him up off the ground. "Hey buddy slow down, I think someone wants to talk to you." If Zimpel wasn't so winded, he would have laughed.

Zimpel flashed his shield again. "Homicide inspector" was all he uttered. He pulled his handcuffs out of their sheath and cuffed the guy struggling between the two construction workers.

"I may be in civilian clothes but I carted these bracelets around just for you."

"Thanks, gentlemen," he said to the two construction workers, "I appreciate the back up."

"No problem, inspector, glad to help."

"Do me one more favor. You all have a telephone on site?"

"Yeah, we got one in the office."

"Can you call dispatch?" He gave them the number to call. "Tell them an inspector needs some uniforms to come and get us?"

They went to call while he held onto whoever this guy was that he was done chasing.

"What's your name?" asked Zimpel.

"Hey I didn't do anything. Let me go."

Zimpel noticed that the guy was really a kid, a lot younger than he thought at first. He felt a little better about the chase. "You looked pretty guilty when you saw me and realized who I was. What were you doing in the ABCs office?"

"I want a phone call."

"Let's find out who you are first. You ran from the DA's office. Who are you really working for?"

The guy pulled back on him but Zimpel held firm. "I'll put you smack on the ground."

Shortly a patrol car showed up and Zimpel loaded him in the back and went in with him.

"Take us back to Kearny Street gentlemen, I need to talk to this guy."

Zimpel got the runner booked and in custody. He called the DA.

"I got this guy, do you know who he is?" Zimpel described him. "I guess you need to come back over here now because I'm going to question him. I saw him leaving the ABC agent's office the same day they pulled the bogus bust on the Blue Moon."

"I think that's our 'free' intern. No free lunch. I'll be over there shortly."

# CHAPTER 74

After the intern was booked and put into an interrogation room, Zimpel told one of the uniforms to watch him, then went back to the DA.

"I had no idea." DA shook his head. "You okay?"

"Glad the guy was stupid and ran into a group of construction workers. What's the story with that guy?" Zimpel had identified the runner, Nat Sieman. "He was in your office."

The DA shook his head. "An unpaid intern. I asked while you were going after him. Public policy major at SF State. His dad is some kind of union boss."

"Do you know who placed him in your office? He was acting for the LCN."

"Are you sure?"

"Yeah, I can connect the dots." Thursday bluffed a little, but not at all doubtful.

"He showed up from the mayor's office, part of the "special force" to clean up the city. And to coddle his daddy with the unions."

"So far, we've had a bribed ABC agent, a Petrini's meat route bought out, and a rich developer's kid get away with a B&E on a cop bar. I'm guessing he's behind all those actions."

"What cop bar?"

"San Remo?"

The DA groaned. "If there are leaks in the mayor's office, it won't be the only one."

Zimpel pulled the envelope out from his shirt. "I wasn't going to drop this for anyone to find once I took off after the guy. It's a bit wrinkled, but here. And still confidential."

The DA opened the envelope and started reviewing the report and the evidence. "Isn't the kid who supposedly left the gun behind some developer's kid? And this intern was a union kid? What's with these parents, using their kids in these schemes?"

"Tell me what happened with the developer's kid's arrest. He got away with it because someone in your office let him off the hook."

"This is one that didn't make it to my desk, and I'm going to find out why." He turned back to the report. "In the meantime, I know you want to talk to Sieman, so let's get these subpoenas going."

"Good to know we have at least one of the insiders. If we connect him to the replacement of the Petrini's driver, we're close to finding who had the murder weapon, and planted it."

"Tell me again how the LCN is involved?"

"Besides the amount of money at play? We have a number of connections we can string together like Christmas lights." Time to show his cards. He showed him the photograph of Lanza with Mullin at La Rocca's. "The driver didn't like me taking photographs and chased me out of there." Zimpel laughed. "Like I was a tourist."

"That's Lanza."

"Yeah, and Mullin. The day after we took Mullin's kid in. The kid that planted the murder weapon at the Blue Moon."

"What else?"

"We have Mullin's driver using the limo that was used to kidnap Kay Schiffner. With one of Abati's drivers."

"Who is she, again, and how does that connect?"

Zimpel pointed to the portion of the report. "Here. One of her earrings was found in a limo trunk when Frazier questioned the guy the limo is assigned to. She lost that earring during the kidnapping—the night Mullin's driver had the car. She identified Abati's driver as one of the guys that picked her up."

"Is she mixed in with the LCN?"

Zimpel sighed. "No, she's a lawyer and representing some of the businesses in the Fillmore against redevelopment."

"A lady lawyer? Getting kidnapped by the LCN. That's pretty sloppy, getting her involved."

Zimpel kept his mouth shut. He wasn't going to say how much he'd tried to keep her out of danger.

The DA took his time going through the evidence. "If you have an ID on the man who did the kidnapping, we can get a warrant based on her ID."

Thursday wondered if the earrings would be enough. And the scotch. And if the guy didn't disappear.

"I see some money issues here, soliciting favors and maybe some money laundering. But tell me, how does this tie Mullin to the murder?"

"We have witnesses who saw a black limo pull up to Wright's car."

"There's a lot of black limos in this town."

"We can place Mullin's driver there. Guy's name is Cory Fortnum. I'm guessing he's part of the gang keeping an eye on the money. Maybe he'll talk, before they silence him." With some pressure, let's hope the guy talks rather than take a fall for the big man. "We're going to talk to him. Be easier if we had a warrant to arrest Mullin."

"I'll get you a warrant for the graft so you can do the looking; there's some bad behavior going on with Redevelopment, but you need better evidence for the murder. I released your friend and folks aren't happy. Everyone wants that sewn up."

Zimpel was in the hot seat after convincing the DA to release Leitisha. She'd been arrested for business expediency not the truth, so the truth didn't necessarily protect her.

He picked up Frazier to help him with Mullin. He didn't trust anyone else. Unlikely the DA's "office intern" had acted alone so the sooner he solved this, the safer his witnesses would be, including Kay.

"How's this going to go down?"

Zimpel noted that Frazier wore a suit. Good. A uniform wouldn't have the same effect. "We're going to walk over and talk to the driver. I see him polishing the car."

"We going to arrest Mullin at the same time?"

"Let's talk to the driver first. I want to see if we can move Mullin farther down the line of admitting what he did. And the driver might point a finger, not wanting to take the fall for his boss."

"Works as well as anything. They not going to like a Black cop asking them questions."

"Good," said Zimpel getting out of the car. "They aren't going to like me, either."

# CHAPTER 75

Frazier wanted to see the guy's eyes bug out when he approached with Zimpel. It'll either piss him off or scare the piss out of him. Frazier smiled. Either way.

Zimpel flashed his ID at the driver who was polishing the limo with a clean white cloth in Mullin's three car driveway. "Can we talk to you?"

"About what?" The driver glanced at the ID, then Zimpel's face, and kept polishing, ignoring Frazier.

"This your limo?" Zimpel took a step towards him.

The driver stopped polishing. "Yeah, it's my limo. What about it?"

"May I see the registration?"

"You want to see my registration?"

"Yes," said Zimpel. The guy gave a cold glare and went into the glove box.

On cue, and Frazier counted the seconds, Mullin came out to see what was keeping his driver.

"What's going on here?" His gaze raked Frazier up and down and then set on Zimpel. "You, again. What are you doing here?" He paused. "I complained about you." He was surprised Zimpel was there.

Frazier enjoyed watching Mullin tussle to take control. While Zimpel and Mullin locked eyes, Frazier pulled the registration from Mullin's reluctant driver. Registered to Cory Fortnum. He knew that already. Frazier made a note of the address in his notebook. Sunset neighborhood. Nice place for a home. Did a guy like this have a wife and kids?

"Get off my property." said Mullin in a fight stance. Every atom the white boss.

Frazier asked for the driver's chauffeur's license, bracing for some push back and knowing Zimpel had the arrest warrant to use if he needed it. The driver hesitated, watching Mullin.

Zimpel stepped between Mullin and his driver. "Mr. Mullin, please step back. This limousine may have been involved in a crime."

"Bullshit. Get off." Mullin took another step towards Zimpel. "This isn't authorized."

Frazier kept an eye on Mullin's threatening stance. Are powerful people like Mullin really above the law? He must have someone else inside. Someone besides the intern Zimpel had run down.

"We're having a conversation with your driver." Zimpel still being cool.

"I see what you're doing, and I'm ordering you to get off my property."

"We're not doing that." Zimpel patted his inside pocket. "I have a warrant here."

"Warrant for what? You want to search the limo?"

The driver, still now, watched the exchange. Frazier moved to search his limo. He opened the glove box. The driver focused on Frazier. "Hey, what are you doing?"

Zimpel shook his head. "For your arrest."

"What?" Mullin stopped and his weight slightly shifted. "Based on what?" Arrogance came off Mullin like bad aftershave.

Mullin stepped towards Zimpel, becoming more belligerent. He was a big man in good shape. "You can't do this. I'll have your job."

"You don't want my job," Zimpel said under his breath. "Mr. Mullin, you're interfering with our interrogation of your driver—who was involved in a kidnapping. You stay out of the way or I'll arrest you."

Frazier finished with the glove compartment and ran his hand under the front seats. Fortnum stood watching, his eyes flicking back and forth from Mullin to the car. Frazier pulled out a flask with his handkerchief. "Drinking on the job . . . does your boss know?"

"Hey," the driver swung his hand out and Frazier backed off.

Zimpel wished Frazier wouldn't taunt them, it just made things worse. "This is bullshit." Mullin's face got red. He stood in front of the driver, blocking him from Frazier. "You have no reason to talk to him and you certainly have no basis to arrest me."

"Come on," Mullin said to the driver, and he headed for the house.

"You're under arrest," said Zimpel reaching for his cuffs. He'd had enough.

"This is outrageous. Leave at once or I'll call . . ."

Zimpel headed towards Mullin. "Please turn around."

Mullin raised his voice, still walking. "You should thank me, the changes we're bringing to this city. You people are shortsighted and stupid. Without us, the world's going to hell, to lazy bums like Wright, creating slums, and to immigrants taking American jobs."

Zimpel wondered about the lazy bums stealing Wright's property. He was going to have to take Mullin. He saw Frazier in his peripheral vision quietly position himself to Zimpel's left.

"They're stealing bread off my family's table and communists are setting the government against us. We need to take back our country."

"That's all fine, Mr. Mullin, but we're taking you in." He nodded at Frazier and they both moved towards Mullin.

"You're not serious." Mullin backed towards the house. "What could I have possibly done that would cause you to arrest me, besides the fact you don't like me?"

"Happy to explain when we get you downtown."

Mullin shook his head. "You resent me because you're not smart enough to do what I do. You resent this." He waved his hand at his mansion.

Zimpel grabbed Mullin's arm, fully intent on putting him on the ground if he fought. "Don't touch me." Frazier gripped Mullin's other arm and held tight. "Linda!" Mullin called for his wife, then tried to pull away. Zimpel and Frazier held fast.

"Hang tight or I will take you down right here." Zimpel kept his eyes on

Mullin, mainly his hands. He hoped the driver didn't bolt.

Mullin twisted back towards the house. "Let me make a call." Mullin tried to shake Frazier off.

"You can make your call when you get downtown." Zimpel reached for Mullin's shoulder and pulled his arms back with some force.

"Brad?" Mullin's wife came out of the back. "What's going on?"

Mullin pulled against Zimpel, turning to his wife. Zimpel yanked him back and Mullin lifted his shoulders to get a hand free. Frazier then held Mullin in front while Zimpel forcefully put the cuffs on Mullin with a jerk and glanced up at Frazier, nodding. Frazier backed away slightly.

"Hey." Mullin twisted but Zimpel held fast. "You're going to pay for this. Linda, go in and call Arthur Hale." A man used to giving orders.

"What are you doing?" The wife kept walking down.

Frazier stood in her way.

"Who are you? Get out of my way," she said to Frazier. "Brad?" She nearly pushed Frazier aside.

"I'm a police officer ma'am and you need to stand back." Frazier didn't let her through, but he was careful to hold his arms out, hands closed.

"A police officer?" She took note of his suit, glancing over at Zimpel, and then back at Frazier. "I didn't know a colored man could arrest someone with the stature of my husband."

Frazier stayed in her way, his face neutral.

"Ma'am, please go back into the house."

"They don't have anything. They are trying to intimidate me and they can't do that." Mullin started to move his arms and Zimpel shifted his weight. "I'm a businessman and this city needs us." He jerked at the cuffs. "Now go and call Arthur please. Tell him these cops arrested me for no reason. I want to make sure we sue them, too."

"Arrested?" She put her hand to her mouth and then ran back into the house.

Zimpel got Frazier's attention and quietly said to his ear, "I'll put him in the car. Let's bring in the chauffeur?"

Frazier pulled his cuffs out, and the chauffeur nearly jumped him. Frazier stepped easily out of the way and turned the guy around. "I'll mess up that fine suit, you don't play nice."

"Screw you, asshole. You can't arrest me."

Swearing beat racial slurs any day. Frazier locked his hand on the guy's arm and put on the cuffs.

He put Mullin in Zimpel's car, and picked up the radio. "I'm calling in for a couple black-and-whites." He identified himself on the radio and made the request with the address.

"Who is this again?"

Zimpel took the receiver from Frazier. "Inspector Zimpel. Get me two patrol cars to transport suspects. Now!" He handed it back to Frazier. "Sorry. Assholes," he said under his breath.

Mullin rotated away from Zimpel. "You'll pay for this." Sweat beaded up on his forehead.

Zimpel's gut was taut. He would have loved to pummel this guy. "Not if I get you for murder first."

"Murder?" Mullin sneered at Zimpel. "That's far-fetched."

"We have an eyewitness." He hated Mullin's smug look.

"Who? I'm sure they're lying." Mullin didn't register it yet.

"She's not lying. She saw you pull the trigger."

Mullin smiled. "That little whore? I don't think so."

Mullin's face tic said differently as it started to go. Zimpel smelled Mullin's fear in his sweat as he pushed his head down to get him into the back seat. He had this bastard.

But at a cost. Frazier gave him a cold stare. He had put Madie at risk.

# CHAPTER 76

## AUGUST 28, 1958 · ZIMPEL

"Here's my report. I don't want any talk about slowness or laziness." Frazier was only half joking.

"Thanks, good. You did good work out there, and we have solid evidence."

"Yeah, of graft. All we did with the murder was put a young girl in danger." Frazier was accusatory.

"I wanted Mullin to know we knew. I didn't want him to get away with it. Even if we can't prove it, he'll pay for the other stuff we have him cold on. I'll make sure she's safe."

"Not sure you can do that, but now you got to try."

Zimpel wasn't sure either. Madie was staying at Zorn's for now. "Still, we got him. Mr. Pac Heights." He paused. "That flask helped."

"Yeah, that story about Kay smelling that peaty scotch . . ." Frazier laughed. "She'd make a pretty good cop, if they let women be inspectors."

Zimpel thought so, too, but didn't comment.

"How does someone with all that money and power go so bad?" asked Frazier.

"Think about what you just said. Money and power."

The desk Sergeant came down the hall to Zimpel. "Hey, Zimpel, thought you should know. One of Lanza's boys sprung your chauffeur."

"Shit. We needed to hold that guy. How am I going to tell Mullin he turned if he's out? I bet the guy disappears. Damn."

"What can I tell you? They got a judge, set bail, and he got out."

"And you say it's one of Lanza's guys?"

"Yeah, I recognized him. I know we're wanting to get those guys, but this was all by the book."

Zimpel wiped his hand down his face.

"We need to follow that chauffeur—he's going to disappear if we're not careful."

Frazier nodded. "When did he get cut loose?"

"Just a few minutes ago," said the sergeant.

"Sarge, get Frazier a car?" Zimpel turned to Frazier.

Frazier nodded. "I'll go see what I can see. They won't notice me."

"I need to get this information to the DA. I don't want Mullin getting out and disappearing on me, too."

He had Mullin on the graft based on the journalist's evidence and what Zorn and Kay had put together, and that would all be confirmed by the subpoenaed bank records. It wouldn't be long before Mullin put his weight in with his lawyers to get sprung.

The intern knew not to talk. Coached well. The son of a union leader hip deep into redevelopment. The intern must have gotten the Mullin kid off through his father's contacts, which may or may not lead back to Abati, and orchestrated the drop. And sent down the message from the DA's office for a black-and-white to watch the Blue Moon. Maybe even Leitisha's arrest. Hard to know, the kid wouldn't talk. Probably wise. Zimpel hoped he didn't disappear like the driver.

Zimpel asked the DA to go for a walk and didn't apologize for being paranoid. He didn't trust that there wasn't another LCN person in their network.

He did not want to put the two young women in any more danger. He had kept Tildy from having to identify the Mullin kid in person by having the kid sign the affidavit. Minor or not, he had never denied it. But Madie had been in the Cadillac and had seen Mullin senior and his driver.

He explained the evidence to the DA, and what had happened.

"I'm happy getting him on the graft. I don't want to have to explain to a jury that they should believe a drug addicted, under-age hooker over a respected CEO." He stopped and turned to Zimpel. "And I'm being polite." He started walking again. "They'll eviscerate her if they don't kill her first. Abati will make sure of it."

"I know all that. It doesn't make it any easier to swallow."

The DA nodded. "You did what you said you would do. You got him."

"It's not fair that the murder of a prominent Black man goes unsolved because of politics."

"Zimpel, of all people, you know that life isn't fair. Once in a while, it's just. We got Mullin and he'll do time. We'll get Abati. Maybe not for the murder, but for something. It's only a matter of time."

A jury wouldn't take Madie's word over Mullin's, even if it did convict him of graft or money laundering. Still, it didn't mean the LCN wouldn't "clean up" what was out there. Zimpel was concerned for Madie's safety and wanted her out of harm's way. He wasn't sure what to do here, so he called Kay.

"I'm worried about Madie."

"She's still staying at Zorn's for now, but pretty soon she'll have her own place. She's been working for us. She's good at it, once she learns. Will she have to testify?"

"No, no appearance by her. The DA doesn't think it's worth it, the jury will choose Mullin over her."

"Bloody hell. Sorry, I shouldn't swear but that he gets away. . .

"He's going to jail."

"But not for the murder. She saw him do it."

"No, but would you put Madie in front of a jury knowing her life is danger and the jury wouldn't convict?"

"How is anything going to change—who is calling check on these guys if we don't?

"'We're not Madie, and we can't endanger her, use her, because we want change. Change has to come some other way—not at the expense of another life."

"Well, Zorn and I seem to be making our own waves bringing these lawsuits. Redevelopment will have to change how they use eminent domain, and pay real money, if we win."

"Exactly." These efforts were heroic. Zimpel was glad Kay had decided to stay and fight with Zorn. She was a good advocate.

"Ugh. We know the truth, and yet we can't use that truth to make things right.

"We do the best we can with what we have, and sometimes it doesn't come out all neat and tidy. We got him for something really serious, it'll unravel his life, and his kid will have a hard time paying for college now."

"Did you arrest Abati?"

"We don't have enough evidence for an arrest warrant. It's all the folks around him we've identified—Lanza, his driver . . ."

"You can't arrest him? He had me kidnapped!"

Zimpel took a breath. This was always hard, even with her being a lawyer. "First, Mullin's chauffeur made bail and then disappeared." Frazier had followed him almost immediately but the driver had disappeared. Never showed up at his home or otherwise. They had surveillance on his house but Zimpel presumed him deceased, or if still useful, in Mexico somewhere. He hadn't handled that quite right.

"But it was Abati's driver that I recognized."

"Yeah, but it was the borrowed limo we needed to connect the dots between your earring and Abati. Unfortunately, he's practiced at not having connections."

"So he walks? I don't understand how you can get Mullin for money laundering but not bust the guy that gave him the money."

"You want to be a prosecutor, too, now?" He understood her frustration.

"Explain to me how that makes sense."

"Connecting the companies and the money isn't always that easy, but we're close. We'll feed some of this to the Feds, much as I hate to. They're building a case against Abati and maybe we can deport him, get him out of here."

"So what about Madie?"

Zimpel sighed. He'd gotten off track. She did that to him. "Yes, what about Madie?"

"We can ask her to stay at Zorn's for the short term. She's safe there if she's careful when she goes out. I mean, I said this before, if they really want you . . ."

"I know." Zimpel didn't need to be reminded. "Ok, we'll leave her there for now, but it might be good for her to get out of SF for a while."

"Always the woman that has to disrupt her life and leave."

"Don't start. This is crime."

"Same standards apply."

But not to you, Zimpel smiled. You won't allow it.

# CHAPTER 77

## AUGUST 29, 1958
### FRIDAY

"Michael, this is Walter," Kay gestured at each of them and Zorn reached his hand out and Walter took it, firmly. It was Friday night, the first normal one since Wright's murder. Kay knew it was temporary.

"Pleased to meet you. You're the other young lawyer fighting this . . ." Walter gestured to the outside, "this Negro removal."

Zorn paused a beat, "Yes, sir. Thank you for remembering."

Walter had already poured her a whiskey, which she picked up and saw Zorn following her hand. He nodded at Walter.

Kay was satisfied that the evening, with everyone together, would go fine. She wasn't going to let on that Zorn was gay, a word she hadn't used before she met Michael. She figured Zimpel knew since he had put Madie over at Zorn's.

"And this is Barb," she said. Her friend had just arrived.

"Pleased to meet you and finally be invited." She cast a glance at Kay and then laughed. "Do I get to see you play?"

"What'll you have, Miss?" Walter had already served everyone else. Turned out Zorn would drink gin martinis (with an olive) when he wasn't drinking coffee.

"Oh, a Sloe Gin Fizz, please?"

Barb missed Walter's brief eyebrows-up reaction, but Kay caught it and laughed. Gin was still very popular. She'd stick to whiskey.

She waved at Percy and he gestured her up. She'd play her heart out tonight. The sax player was back, if a bit raggedy. She didn't care if he was raggedy, he was fine enough.

"Come on, y'all, let's get it with some 'Blues for Alice.' Start at the F major seventh . . ." The band broke into Charlie Parker's composition, with its rapid bebop blues chord voicings, complex and juicy. Just what was called for. Kay wondered at a world that embraced Black art but rejected the artists that created it.

The music brought Leitisha out of the kitchen, wiping her hands, and taking a glass of champagne from Walter. They toasted all around. The next fight was to get Leitisha into a new location, and get her a fair price for the Blue Moon. Everything changes. Need to be ready when change comes.

That Leitisha had to be in jail so long, subjected to repeated interrogation with no lawyer present, haunted Kay. People deserved basic rights. So much change needed to happen.

Zimpel gestured at Kay with a beer. "Stay out of trouble for a week, please?" he called to her as she played. "I need a rest."

Zorn laughed. "She's been great to have working alongside me."

Zimpel turned back to the bar. "Good. Keep her in the office. She's a tough woman who needs a lot of rescuing. Not sure what that means."

"It means you need another beer." Walter set one down.

Frazier came in the door and Zimpel caught his eye. "Bad news. The chauffeur is nowhere to be found. He never came back to his house. No airplane tickets, just vapor."

"I was afraid of that. On a vacation, compliments of Abati."

"Maybe a permanent vacation."

"We'll get Mullin on the money, but it rankles."

Frazier nodded.

"Get you something, Will?"

"Nah, that's ok, Walter. I'm going down to the Silver Dollar to see a young lady there." He smiled at Zimpel. "Might as well do it while we can."

Frazier turned to Miss Leitisha. "I wish you well, Leitisha, and know you got a good team here."

"I found a new place outside the A-2. They won't beat me."

Kay wasn't feeling Leitisha's optimism. Especially after working with Zorn. Leitisha was doomed, even if she got outside the redevelopment zone. This city would never let a Black woman own a nightclub and be successful. She was too rich.

And that made her mad. She had had a good job, one that was hard to get as a woman, and lost it defending Leitisha and the Blue Moon. A man would have been able to do both. Kay would make the same choice again. She knew this was what she was supposed to be doing, to balance the injustice.

Those in power, whether legitimate or not, murdered Marvin Wright to get him out of the way, and framed Leitisha to get the property for redevelopment.

Even proving a developer guilty of corruption, never mind murder, wasn't enough to stop the juggernaut of redevelopment from bulldozing the life in the Fillmore. The "deference" the law (and thus a judge) gave to a government agency, if redevelopment—partially financed by the companies that profited from eminent domain and run by racists—was a government agency, was just a funnel through which to send money to the white unions and white developers and away from those who built the value in the Fillmore.

Kay realized she was meant to follow this unconventional path, to fight back however it manifests. She'd push back against the money and racism—that's what was driving her, like the music she wanted to play but wasn't supposed to.

Like how Leitisha wanted to, planned to, and deserved to succeed but wasn't supposed to. Working with Zorn and playing music suited her more than proving she worked as hard as the white guys for half the money. She'd prove a lot more, for herself, and for others.

# ACKNOWLEDGEMENTS

First, many thanks to Bronzeville, my publisher, who provided all the support and leeway I needed to get this book right, so any errors are mine alone. Danny Gardner's insight into his business and the purpose of the work was essential and life affirming, Erin Mitchell's kind and uber knowledgeable guidance was (and is) invaluable, and we're changing the industry for the better. Also, thank you to Jim Gleeson for the fabulous illustration for the cover and Reggie Pulliam for all the design work.

Secondly, deep and profound thanks for preserving the rich history of the Fillmore to Professor Emeritus Lewis Watts and Elizabeth Pepin (KQED) for their now fourth version of Harlem of the West, the definitive history of the Fillmore, replete with original source interviews on the website. Any history misstatements or mistakes are strictly mine.

Thanks to Sal Rosano, former detective for the South San Francisco police department in the late 1950's and early 60's, and later its Police Chief for providing me background and information as to policing at that time. Any errors are mine.

My parents' love of all literature, including my Dad reading to us at the dinner table well into our teens, made me a writer. They also both wrote. Neither lived to see this, but they knew.

Thanks to all my mentors at *Murderati*, so many I can't count but among them, Alex Sokoloff, who wrote years ago: "We're all rooting for you and your book. I have a ton of distractions right now. Do just ONE sentence a night sometimes, if that's all you can do. A book responds to that kind of commitment. I swear." Me, too.

The teachers of the Book Passage Mystery Writers classes—I took it several times and many I remember with fondness as teaching me real skills and spending good time on my work (Hallie Tougher, Kirk Russell, David Corbett, Cara Black and Kelli Stanley come to mind, but there are others).

Naomi Norberg and Naomi Kappel for the excellent final edits.

To Peter Blauner for helping me with the title.

Stephen Jay Schwartz and Susan Shea for reading early copies and giving me useful notes.

Sheldon Siegel for being a good friend, fun to work with on the MWA board, and for giving me my very first blurb as a novelist.

To Danny, Cody, my family, and friends like family, for your constant support.

www.ingramcontent.com/pod-product-compliance
Lightning Source LLC
Chambersburg PA
CBHW072313020726
47501CB00002B/495